C000213669

DANCE OF DEATH

It was like a dance, turn, swing, fire, the only dance he had ever done. Turn, wheel, extend the arm. Boom! Blam! Turn again, gracefully duck, turn, fire, fire again, then go forward. . . .

Gill turned and saw the faintest glimmer of grayness penetrating the profound gloom of the hive. He let go of the depleted plasma rifle and pulled a chemical slugthrower out of a side pouch. Four quick shots blasted a close-packed group of aliens with high explosive. Then Gill turned and ran, with Stan on his shoulder, toward the light.

His feet slid on the hard clay of the tunnel's floor, and then suddenly he was out of the hive and into the sepulchral gray light of planet AR-32. . . .

AL/ENS™

ALIEN HARVEST

OMNIBUS EDITION

ROGUE

Robert Sheckley & Sandy Schofield

(Based on the Twentieth Century Fox motion pictures, the designs of
H.R. Giger, and the graphic novel Aliens Hive by Jerry Prosser, and the
Dark Horse comic Rogue written by Ian Edington, art by Will Simpson)

A DARK HORSE SCIENCE FICTION NOVEL

Aliens™ © 1992 by Twentieth Century Fox Film Corporation
All rights reserved. ™ indicates a trademark of
Twentieth Century Fox Film Corporation

MILLENNIUM

Orion Paperbacks
A Millennium Book
First published in Great Britain in 1996 by
Orion Books Ltd,
Orion House, 5 Upper St Martin's Lane,
London WC2H 9EA

Copyright © 1994 by Twentieth Century Fox Film Corporation

Aliens™, © Twentieth Century Fox Film Corporation
Cover art copyright © 1995 by John Bolton

First published in separate volumes as
Aliens™: Alien Harvest, Millennium paperback 1995
Aliens™: Rogue, Millennium paperback 1996

All rights reserved. No part of this publication may be
reproduced, stored in a retrieval system, or transmitted, in
any form or by any means, electronic, mechanical,
photocopying, recording or otherwise, without the prior
permission of the copyright owner.

A CIP catalogue record for this book
is available from the British Library

ISBN: 1 85798 620 2

Printed and bound in Great Britain by
Clays Ltd, St Ives plc

ALIENS™

ALIEN HARVEST

To my wife, Gail, with all my love.

Captain Hoban's Prologue

I was in the middle of the whole thing with Stan and Julie. I guess almost everybody on Earth knows how it ended. But they don't know how it began. I've been putting together everything I know about it. I figure it started the morning Stan got the summons.

1

That morning Stan had to go downtown to the Colonial Mercantile Building on Vesey Street. The day before there had been a ring at his doorbell. Stan hadn't been doing much when it came. He had several experiments going in his cellar laboratory. The lab took up most of the space in the old frame house on Gramercy Park that he had inherited from his father. Stan hadn't been feeling well lately, and although he tried to tell himself it wasn't anything, some little voice within him kept on intruding, telling him, "This could be very serious. . . ."

He had been avoiding his doctor for a while, but now he called up and made an appointment with Dr. Johnston at the Fifty-ninth Street clinic for the next day. That was when the doorbell rang.

The man standing outside was tall and thin, and dressed in a badly pressed gray business suit.

"Are you Professor Myakovsky?"

3

"I am," Stan replied.

"Are you the Stanley Myakovsky who wrote the book about Ari the ant?"

"Yes, I am," Stan repeated. He was starting to feel a little better. This guy seemed to be someone who had read his book, was probably a fan, maybe even wanted an autograph. "What can I do for you?"

"I got a summons for you," the man said, taking a folded paper out of his pocket and slapping it briskly into Stan's hand. "You are served. Have a nice day, Doctor." He turned and left.

Stan went back inside and looked over the summons. He had no idea what it was about and the document itself didn't enlighten him. It simply said he was to appear in Courtroom B at 311 Vesey Street the following day, or face the consequences.

Have a nice day.

What a laugh.

It had been so long since Stan had had a nice day, he couldn't remember what one looked like.

The next day he left early for Vesey Street. The Broadway trolley was running again, rumbling past the newly restored buildings of midtown. It was a bright day outside, and despite his depression, Stan started to feel just the slightest lift to his spirits.

That lasted until he got to Vesey Street.

Vesey Street was filled with city and federal buildings, some of them quite old, dating from before the time of the aliens, miraculously unburned during the anarchic days when the aliens ruled. Some of the buildings in this area were brand-spanking-new. There had been a lot of rebuilding since those days. Stan would have liked to have been part of the first days after humans reoccupied their own planet. It must have been exhilarating, reoccupying your own country, having a future again on your own planet. Now, of course, it was business as usual.... More or less.

Times were pretty good. America was experiencing

a boom. Business was strong. A lot of people were making a lot of money. Some people, of course, were losing a lot of money. It had to come from somewhere. So it came from people like Stan.

He mounted the stone steps of the Criminal Courts Building. Within, he found a clerk who checked his summons and directed him up a flight of stairs to the correct courtroom.

He walked in. It was a small room with a half-dozen chairs facing a raised desk. The sign on the door had said JUDGE JACOB LESSNER, PRESIDING. Behind the desk sat a small man in black robes. He said, "Dr. Stanley Myakovsky?"

"Yes," Stan replied.

"Come in. I suppose you know what this is about?"

"No, I don't."

Judge Lessner frowned. "Your lawyer really should keep you better informed."

Stan nodded, although he knew very well he hadn't been answering his lawyer's calls over the last few days.

"Well, this is a pretty simple matter." The judge searched among the papers on his desk until he found what he was looking for. "This is a government order seizing your spaceship."

"The *Dolomite*?" Stan asked.

The judge searched his paper until he found it. "Yes, of course, that's the name of your ship. You may no longer go aboard."

"But why?"

"You were sent a notice a month ago advising you of the government's decision to take action against your unpaid bills."

Stan thought the paper must be somewhere among the unopened mail on his desk. He had been too depressed of late to open any of it. Most of the letters had something bad to say: how this investment or that was sliding to hell on him, or how his patents weren't earning as expected. And even more papers about all his back taxes.

He felt a wave of hopelessness engulf him. He tried to struggle out of it. "They are not allowed to do that. My spaceship is one of the few ways I have of conducting business. If they take that, how am I supposed to pay them what they say I owe?"

"That is not my concern," the judge stated flatly. "You should have taken that into consideration when you fell so deeply into arrears. In any event, I am hereby notifying you of the government's decision to take your ship. If you have any difficulty with this, you or your lawyer can file a complaint with the clerk down the hall."

"Thanks a lot," Stan said bitterly, and left the courtroom. A few blocks away he found a park bench to sit on. He needed to collect himself. His heart was beating wildly and he was sweating, though it was a mild day. At least, he thought, maybe my bad news for the day is over. I've had my share.

That was before his doctor's appointment, of course.

Dr. Johnston of the Fifty-ninth Street clinic came to the dressing room just as Stan finished knotting his tie.

"How did my tests work out?" Stan asked.

The doctor looked uncomfortable. "Not so good, I'm afraid."

"But I was here a year ago; you said I was fine!"

"A lot can happen in a year," the doctor said.

Stan wanted to say, *Sure, tell me about it*, but he held back.

"Exactly what is the matter?" he asked.

Dr. Johnston answered, "I might as well give it to you straight, Dr. Myakovsky. You were correct in your surmise about those black marks on your chest and back. They are indeed cancers."

Stan sat down. He needed a moment to think about this. He couldn't believe what he had heard. And yet he had suspected it for months.

Finally he asked, "Is my condition terminal?"

"Yes." The doctor nodded gravely. "In fact, you don't have much time left. A matter of months. I'm sorry, but it's best to give you the news straight. The condition, as I'm sure you know, is incurable. But its progress can be slowed, and we can ease some of the symptoms. I've already made out a prescription for the medicine we prescribe for such cases." He handed Stan a folded slip of paper. "And there is also this."

The doctor held out a small plastic box. Within it, packed in foam rubber, were a dozen ampoules of a bluish liquid.

"This is Xeno-Zip. Have you heard of it?"

Stan nodded. "If memory serves, it is produced from the royal jelly of alien females."

"That is correct," Dr. Johnston said. "I must tell you it's no cure for what you have. But it should relieve the symptoms. The stuff's illegal and I shouldn't be giving you this ... but it could be just what you're looking for."

"Does it have much in the way of side effects?" Stan asked.

The doctor smiled grimly. "It has indeed. That's why it hasn't received government approval yet, though many people still use it. Indeed, it has become the most-sought-after consciousness-altering substance in existence. Although the effect is not invariable, it does give most people an intense feeling of well-being and competence. Others experience levels of their own being not normally perceived. Still others have an orgasm that seems to go on forever."

"At least I'm going to die happy." Stan wasn't smiling as he spoke.

2

It was cold that night. Wind demons seemed to chase up and down the streets of New York, wailing at the high-flying moon like all of the banshees of Howard Phillips Lovecraft.

The block that Stan's house stood upon had once been genteel, a part of Gramercy Park. Now, armed citizens patrolled the streets night and day. Insurrection and disorder were rife all over the city, brought on by the breakdown of law and order since the troubles with the aliens. Some people could remember the coming of the aliens, and the many deaths that had resulted from their macabre practices. Their effect on New York had been to make it seem a much older city than it in fact was, one of those ancient cities like Baghdad or Babylon. Now, after the aliens, the city felt like it had seen unimaginable evil, and was resting, a little exhausted, waiting for the good life to start up again.

After making himself a light dinner from an Insta-Pac protein ration, Stan went to the living room and started a fire in the fireplace. He sat down in a rocking chair and stared morosely into the flames, listening to the wind whistling outside the window and thinking of how little time he had left.

It was strange how, upon hearing that your life had an imminent termination date, you began to think of suicide. Stan had never before understood Schopenhauer's saying that he got through many a long night with thoughts of suicide, but now it made sense. To kill himself might even be a triumph; it would rob the cancer of its victory. No longer would he dance to death's tune. No longer could the pain curl him up and make him beg for relief. He could get out of it, laugh at it all, and, as Hamlet had said, "Make his quietus with a bare bodkin."

From the plate of apples near his chair he picked up a short, keenly edged knife and looked at it like he'd never seen one before. Where in his body should he put it in? Should it be done hara-kiri style? Or was there another manner more appropriate for a Westerner?

And yet, tempting as the thoughts of suicide were, they were mainly interesting when considered in the abstract. He didn't really want to kill himself. He wanted to do something. But he didn't know what it was.

These were long, sad winter thoughts he was thinking, and he was startled out of his reverie when he heard the front door chimes.

Stan looked up in surprise. He wasn't expecting anyone. He was a lonely man as he had been a lonely boy. He had gotten used to his solitary condition early in life, and had learned there was no sense struggling against it. He felt that it was written somewhere that he should be alone. This was his fate. He had no girlfriends—in fact, no real friends at all. No one came to take him to the movies or a concert, or for an evening's drinking. Since his parents' death four years ago in a traffic accident, he had become even less sociable. Sometimes he talked with colleagues at the laboratory, but even among people who should have been his own kind, his macabre and ironic sense of humor kept him apart. Stan lived alone in the house. He had set up a laboratory in the basement, and as far as possible, he did his experiments, wrote his papers, and lived his life at home, in solitude, among familiar things.

It was here that he had written *Cyberantics*, his children's book about a cybernetic ant named Ari, based on an ant he had actually constructed himself. In fact, Ari was in the room with him now, perched on a small box on the mantel. The ant could see Stan as he hesitated a moment at the door.

The chimes rang again. He arose and went to answer the summons. The front door creaked in his hand, almost as if it were reluctant to open. Stan peered out, his nearsighted eyes blinking behind his thick glasses.

A young woman stood under the porch light and the first thing Stan noticed was the sheen of copper on her dark chestnut-red hair. She was tall and slender, and had masses of hair pushed back and tied behind her neck with a white ribbon. She wore a dark belted trench coat, severely cut, but not severe enough to hide the fact that she had a very good figure. Her face was oval and attractive, lightly made up. An old scar, now almost completely faded but visible even in the darkness of the porch, ran from the outside corner of her left eye to the corner of her full lips. It looked like an old dueling scar, such as they had once sported in places like Heidelberg some centuries earlier. Could it really be a dueling scar? Did people still fight duels? Some accident, perhaps. But then why hadn't she had it surgically removed? One thing was certain; the scar seemed to enhance her beauty, just as ancient people believed that scarification increased a woman's charm.

"Dr. Myakovsky?" the woman said. "I am Julie Lish.

I have a matter of considerable importance to discuss with you. May I come in?"

Stan had been staring at her hard, as if she were a lab specimen. Now he came back to himself with a start.

"Oh certainly; please. Come in."

He escorted Julie Lish inside and led her through the gloomy hallway to the well-lighted room where he had been staring into the flames of a dying fire. He picked up a poker now and stirred the fire up, then indicated a pair of matching armchairs just a comfortable distance from the flames. She took one and he seated himself in the other, then quickly got up again.

"May I get you something to drink?"

She smiled at him, amused by his bumbling eagerness. "You don't even know what I've come for."

"It doesn't really matter. . . . I mean, whatever it is, you are a guest in my house. Perhaps I could bring you a fruit drink? I'm afraid I have no alcohol to mix with it. Alcohol has an adverse effect on my can—my condition."

"A glass of fruit juice would be nice," Julie said. "I am well aware that you do not drink, Dr. Myakovsky."

Stan had already begun pouring from a pitcher on a sideboard near the two armchairs. He looked up.

"Well aware? Why?"

"I've made it a point to find out about you," Julie said. "I am always careful to research my future partners."

Stan stared at her, his lips slightly parted, trying to make sense out of all this. Was she laughing at him? Girls were such unfathomable creatures! Although he was fascinated by them, Stan had always kept his distance, conscious that he was not the athletic, glib, casual sort of man that women liked. And here was this beautiful and exotic creature already talking about becoming partners with him?

"Please explain," Stan said, with what he hoped was dignity. "You say you've studied me?"

"Probably better than you've studied yourself,"

Julie stated. "For example, I know about your first date. You were fifteen."

"Do you know what was special about it?" Stan asked.

"I do indeed," Julie replied. "You never showed up for it. You got cold feet at the last moment. And that, Doctor, could be said to characterize all your dealings with the opposite sex."

Stan remembered the incident. He wondered if he had revealed it in some memoir he might have published at the invitation of a computer magazine. How else could she have found out? And what did she want to know that sort of thing for, anyhow?

"I don't get this." Stan looked at her. "What have you come here for? What do you want?"

"Stan," Julie said, "I'll make it short and sweet. I'm a thief. A good one. No, I'm a lot better than just good. I'm one of the best who ever lived. Unfortunately I can't bring you press clippings. Really good thieves don't get written up. You'll just have to take my word for it."

"All right, let's say I accept it," Stan said. "So?"

"I've made a lot of money in some of my enterprises," Julie went on, "but not as much as I'd have liked. Stan, I want to be rich."

Stan laughed without humor. "I suppose a lot of people want that."

"Certainly, but they don't have my qualifications. Or my desire."

Stan acknowledged this. "I take it you have some ideas on how to realize that goal?"

She nodded. "I have thought of a way you and I could make a fortune."

"A fortune," Stan mused. "How much is that in dollars?"

"Don't laugh at me," Julie said. "I don't know exactly how much it would be. But it would come to millions of dollars, perhaps even billions, and we'd neither of us lack for anything ever again."

"Nothing?" Stan asked, looking at her and thinking how pretty she was.

"We'd have it all," she told him. "That's worth something, isn't it?"

She slipped off the severe trench coat. Beneath it she wore a nylon, military-style jumpsuit. The tight-fitting clothes set off her well-shaped bosom and fine shoulders to advantage. Stan thought she looked great. He wondered if Julie was one of the things he'd also have if he made a deal with her. He liked the idea but kept that thought to himself as well. Although he was extremely susceptible to beauty, he had culti-vated a brusque manner around women so they would never think he was coming on to them and then reject him. He had had a lot of rejection in his life, and he wasn't going to have any more if he could avoid it.

"Tell me your idea," he said.

Julie reached into a small purse she carried, took out a package, and handed it to him.

Stan looked at her questioningly.

"Do you know what this is? Open it and find out."

The package was wrapped in thick manila paper and was held together with tape. He tried to pull the paper off, but there was no place for his fingers to take hold. He went to his desk and found the paper knife, and managed to saw through the tape. Then he slit the paper carefully and opened the package. Within was a plastic box. Inside it, padded with foam rubber, was a stoppered test tube.

Stan held it up to the light. It was a heavy viscous liquid, with bluish lights in it. He unstopped the tube and sniffed. The aroma was unmistakable.

"Royal jelly," he said.

She nodded. "Do you know what this stuff is worth?"

"As a matter of fact, I do. It is one of the most val-uable substances in the galaxy."

She nodded. "And the stuff is in even shorter sup-ply now that we've got the aliens on the run. That's part of what makes it so expensive. And it's a monopoly. The big bionational research companies have it all tied up. They've got places out on other planets where they get the stuff from the aliens. It's all a closed transaction."

"Which is all well-known," Stan said. "Tell me something new."

"Suppose I tell you that I know where we can lay our hands on an entire shipload of the stuff. At least a hundred tons. What about that?"

"Who does it belong to?"

"Whoever gets it."

"Who did it used to belong to?"

"A freelance honey-collecting expedition. But it came up lost, and has never been heard of again."

"So what makes you think they struck it rich?"

"Before vanishing, they sent out one signal by sub-space radio. It was intercepted by a certain Bio-Pharm official. He never got around to using it. I guess he was going to take it to the grave with him, but I persuaded him otherwise."

Stan didn't ask her how she had managed this. At that moment her face looked quite sinister. But it was no less beautiful because of that.

"So you know where it is?"

"I know approximately."

Stan studied her for a while and pursed his lips thoughtfully. Then he said, "And you think it's as simple as walking in and taking it?"

"Flying in," she corrected.

"There might be objections to our appropriating this cargo," Stan said.

"So what? It's not illegal. Salvage rights belong to whoever gets them. The stuff's ours if we can get it."

"And we're dead if we don't."

Julie shrugged. "It's a lot of money, so there's going to be a lot of risk. I don't know about you, Stan, but I'm tired of being small-time. Just once I want to go for all the marbles. Don't you feel that way some-times?"

Stan could feel the pains of his condition eating

away at him through the haze of the medication. He knew he was sick as hell.

But he also knew he was still alive.

"I think I'm ready for a big one, too," he said slowly. "But there's still a difficulty. Where there's royal jelly, there'll be aliens. How are we going to get through them?"

"The same way your ant, Ari, got through the enemy ant nest, Stan. That's how."

Stan stared at her. "You know about Ari?"

"Of course. I told you I researched you. And I read *Cyberantics*."

"You think I could make a cybernetic or robotic alien and he could get through an alien ant nest?"

"I know you've been working on such a robot," Julie said. "Why don't we find out if it works?"

She looked at him challengingly, and Stan felt his heart lift. At last something was happening to him, an adventure with a beautiful woman.

"Then there's the question of a ship," he said.

"You have one."

"Had. The government just seized it."

She looked at him levelly. "Let's worry about getting the ship later. What we need even worse is a spaceship pilot who's willing to do something illegal."

"I can think of one man. . . ."

"Who's that?"

"Just someone I know. Julie, you flatter me by coming to me with this partnership offer. But evidently you don't know my full situation."

"I don't? Tell me, then."

"Julie, I used to be quite a wealthy man. One of the youngest millionaires on the Forbes list. I have several key patents in bioengineering, and the plans for my cybernetic ant, Ari, are a standard for the field of medical miniaturiation."

"I know all this, Stan."

"Sure. But did you also know that all that has changed? Did you know the government has put a lien on my assets? It seems that Bio-Pharm, one of the biggest of the international pharmaceutical houses, has filed suit against me for patent infringement. What a laugh. They stole most of their processes from me! But it's not easy to prove, and in the meantime they've got me on the run. I don't own a damned thing anymore—nothing except this house and Ari." He lifted up the cybernetic ant to show to Julie. "I even have to beg my grocer to extend me credit so I can go on eating!"

Julie looked at him without sympathy. "I know all that, Stan. It's tough, isn't it?"

He thought he detected a tone of irony in her voice. "You're damned right it's tough!"

"Granted. But so what?"

He stared at her, uncomprehending. "Did you actually come here to insult me?"

"There's nothing insulting in what I'm saying. I came here to make a deal with you. What I find is you sitting around feeling sorry for yourself. I'm offering you something you can do about it."

"It's not just that I'm broke," Stan said. "There's also ... my condition."

"Tell me about it," Julie said.

Stan shrugged. "There's not much to say. Melanoma. I've got six months. Maybe a little longer if I want to lie in a hospital bed and breath pure oxygen."

"You look like you're moving around pretty good just now," Julie said.

"Oh yeah, sure. But that's just now. This stuff is the only thing that keeps me going." He took out a vial of Xeno-Zip and showed it to her.

"I know all about that stuff," Julie said. "It's my job to keep track of precious substances that come in small packages. And this is the only stuff that does you any good?"

"That's right," Stan said. "It's expensive even for a rich man. For someone whose assets have been seized ... Well, I'll run out soon, and I don't know what happens then."

"Tough," Julie said, with no pity in her voice. "So this stuff won't cure you?"

Stan shook his head. "Some doctors have theorized that if I could obtain absolute unadulterated royal jelly fresh from an alien hive, before any by-products were added, and before it had time to lose any of its potency, it might buy me more time. But it's impossible to get."

"Except by going to the source," Julie said.

"Yes, that's right," Stan repeated slowly. "Except by going to the source. To a place where the Aliens actually produce it."

"That's the sort of place I had in mind for us to go," Julie said. "Like I told you, I know where there's a shipload of the stuff."

He stared at her, his eyebrows raised. Then his head slumped and he looked sad and worn. "No, no. It's quite impossible. Even if you knew of such a place—"

"That's exactly what I do know," Julie said.

"You know a place where an alien queen produces royal jelly?"

She patted the sleek leather pouch that she carried at her side. "I've got the coordinates right in here, Stan. They're a part of my contribution to this venture."

"Where'd you get that information?"

She smiled. She was so lovely when she smiled. "Like I told you, I was good friends with a Bio-Pharm executive. We were a little more than good friends, actually. Well, when he died—he was quite old, you understand—when he died, he decided that that particular secret shouldn't go to the grave with him."

"So what is your idea?" Stan asked. "Do you think we can just go there and get it?"

"That's about what I had in mind," Julie said.

"The Bio-Pharm people might have something to say about it."

"I figured we could sneak in, grab the shipload, and get out before they spotted us."

"You think it would be as easy as that?"

She shook her head. "I never said it would be easy."

"Or within the law."

She shrugged impatiently. "There's nothing illegal about salvage. Why don't you think of it as your counterclaim to their lawsuit?"

"What do you mean?"

"They're suing you for patent infringement. Wrongly, you say. Well, prove you mean it. Go in there and take what is yours—then take them to court the way they're taking you."

Stan thought for a long while, then he began to smile. "You know, I think I'd like that."

"Now you're talking!"

"But wait a minute, there are still a lot of problems. We don't have a ship. My alien robot has never had a field test. And I don't have any money."

"We can do something about all that," Julie said. "But there really isn't much time. Not for you and not for me. If we're going to do this, we'll have to start real soon. And once we begin, there's no turning back."

"I understand," Stan said.

Julie leaned forward and took Stan's face in her cool hands. He felt something like an electric shock pass through him. Looking at her, he thought he'd never seen anyone so beautiful and so brave. Yes, and maybe a little crazy, too, but what did that matter?

"I want you to think about it, Stan," Julie said. "Give me your answer tomorrow night over dinner. If you don't want to do it, fine, no hard feelings. But if you do—listen to me carefully."

"I'm listening," Stan said. In fact, he was barely breathing.

"If you do decide to do it, then no more crap about something being difficult or you being sick or any of that. If you're going to do it, simply decide to do it, and we'll go on from there."

"That sounds pretty good to me," Stan said. "Julie, where'd you learn all this stuff?"

"From my teacher, Shen Hui."

"He must have been a pretty wise old egg."

"It didn't prevent him from dying," Julie said. "But while he lived, he really lived. Till tomorrow, Stan."

"Where are you going?" Stan said in alarm as she stood up.

"I'm sure you've got a spare bedroom here," Julie said. "I'm going to take a shower and change, and then look over your library and lab. Then I want to get some sleep."

"Oh, fine. I was afraid you were leaving."

She shook her head. "Play your cards right and I'll never leave again."

3

Julie had always been unusual. She'd never known her parents. Her earliest memories were of an international orphanage in Shanghai. This was the place from which Shen Hui bought her, when she was still a very little girl. He had been very good to her, treating her like a favored child rather than a slave. But she was still a slave and she knew it, and it rankled. Shen Hui taught her independence of spirit as well as how to be a good thief. It was inevitable that she would try out her need for liberty on him, the one who was holding her.

She was devious about it, just as he had taught her. She put aside money from jobs she did for him. And she studied and learned so she would know all she needed when she was ready to cut loose from him. And then came the question of finding the right time. It seemed to take forever, and the right moment never seemed to come.

At last they traveled together to Europe. Shen Hui had it in mind to relieve some of the largest art galleries on the continent of some of their smaller and most prized possessions: miniature paintings, small sculpture, carved objects. They went to Zurich first.

The first night Julie excused herself in the lobby of the Grand Basle Hotel, went to the ladies' room, and never returned.

She had planned well. From the powder room, with a small fortune and a forged passport secreted on her person, she made her way to the airport, and then to Madrid, Lisbon, and London. She made the trail difficult for Shen Hui to follow. And she prepared something else.

He came after her, as she had known he would. He wasn't going to let her get away that easily. He had invested a lot of money in her, and besides, his feelings were hurt. He had thought she loved him. He had forgotten his own advice—never trust a slave. His love was replaced by hatred, all the more powerful because it was based on his own guilt and ignorance in being duped by the illusion he had created and named Julie.

They met up almost a year later. He came upon her in one of the public squares in Paris, near the Seine. Julie was wearing a black sealskin coat and a chinchilla hat. Shen Hui noted sardonically that it hadn't taken her long to outfit herself. He added that she had been silly to expose herself to him in this way.

"What do you mean?" she'd asked.

"I mean if you had any brains, you wouldn't have let me catch up with you. Do you realize how easily I could kill you? And you could do nothing about it, not even with all the skills I taught you."

"I know that," Julie said. "And I wasn't careless. I chose to let you find me."

"What are you up to?"

"I don't choose to spend my life running," Julie said. "I am extremely grateful to you, Shen Hui. You have taught me respect for the deeper law that underlies appearances. I appeal to that law now. Although you legally own me, your investment has been repaid many times and it is time that I went free. I served you well and you know it. I would like to shake hands and have us part friends."

Shen Hui stared at her. His skin had aged incredibly, with a yellow cast to it like parchment that has been dried too long in the sun. She had never seen him looking so old. Even his thin mustache, which dropped down on either side of his face, seemed lifeless. And his eyes were brown and opaque.

She wasn't sure what he would say. She knew that her life hung in the balance. Old as he was, and apparently unarmed, she had no doubt he could kill her anytime he chose.

"You are my greatest creation," he said at last. "How could I kill you? Who would I have left to hate?"

Her life had really begun at that point. She spent several years on her own, accomplishing unbelievable feats of thievery in Europe and America. She made money easily, and spent it easily. Her life was rich and pleasurable, but she began to sense a loss of purpose, a slackness that was beginning to alarm her. It was a question of motivation. Shen Hui had taught her too well for her to be content with mediocre motives. Why was she doing what she was doing? What was she living for?

The only thing she could think to do with her life was to get rich. It wasn't enough, she knew, but it was a start. After she accomplished that, she'd take the next step.

For the present she was here with Stan, and Stan was as good as hooked, if she had any knowledge of men.

For dinner that night Stan had ordered a special Moroccan feast catered by a North African couple he knew. Although it was short notice, he had told them to go all out, and he served the meal himself using his best china and silverware. There were game birds roasted on spits, half a sheep braised in many exotic spices and served with rough tasty Arab bread, platters of fruits and vegetables, several different wines. The Moroccan couple followed instructions, delivering the feast and then leaving. Stan paid for it with almost the last of the cash he had on hand. One way or another, no matter what decision he made tonight, it was going to be a new life for him tomorrow.

Stan hadn't thought about what he was going to say. He didn't need to. He was suffused with a knowledge that he couldn't articulate yet. That would have to come later. For now it was enough to sit across the table from Julie while the strains of a Monteverdi madrigal tinkled in the background.

Julie had found an old ballroom dress upstairs, one of his grandmother's, neatly folded in a fragrant cedar drawer. It fit perfectly, and she had worn it down to dinner with a set of large pearl earrings that had once belonged to Stan's mother.

Stan, noting her preparations, had taken out the tuxedo he had worn to his recent college reunion. He put in the cat's-eye opal cuff links and the diamond pin in the buttonhole. He felt tall and graceful in this outfit, and a little ironic. It was playacting, of course, and he knew that; but it was also in some strange sense real. And Stan knew that there were many costumes he could have worn that night. He wouldn't have felt out of place in the golden mantle of Alexander the Great. Because just like the famous Macedonian, he was on the verge of new worlds to conquer. He was also up against a sea of trouble and pain, and he suspected he was doomed to die gloriously and young as well.

At dinner that evening Julie was radiant in the antique gown, Stan looking handsome in his tuxedo. He had saved a bottle of wine for a long time, waiting for an occasion like this. The bottle had been handed down to him by his parents—a rare St.-Emilion, the great vintage of thirty-seven years earlier. Stan had taken good care of the bottle, storing it on its side in the temperature-controlled basement, making sure the cork was properly intact. He brought it up now and opened it with care, pouring a little into a fluted glass and tasting it.

"Just on the verge of turning," he said. "But still superb. We've caught the St.-Emilion at its peak, Julie. This is probably the last bottle of this stuff in the world."

She tasted the ruby-red liquid he had poured for her. "It's marvelous, Stan. But what are we celebrating?"

"Need you ask?"

"I think not," she said, "but I would like to hear it anyhow."

"And hear it you shall." Stan smiled. Never had he felt so at peace with himself. He didn't know where this course of action was going to take him, but he was satisfied to follow it.

"We're going to go with your plan, Julie. And we're going to follow it all the way. We both know the risks. We discussed them yesterday. We both know the odds are against us. But no more talk about that. I've decided, and I know that you have, too. We'll start in the morning."

She reached across the snowy tablecloth and held his hand tightly. "Why tomorrow morning?"

"Because that's when my bank opens," Stan said. "I'm ready for whatever we have to do."

"I'm ready, too, Stan."

"Well," he said, half as a joke and half seriously, "I guess we've taken care of everything except what to name our alien."

"What would you suggest?"

"What about Norbert, after the great Norbert Wiener, father of cybernetics, the science that gave it birth?"

"Sounds good to me," Julie said. "I guess that just about covers it, Stan. Except for one thing."

"What's that?"

She leaned close to him. He felt dizzy with her face so close to his. She bent closer. Her lips were partially open. He was fascinated by her teeth, all perfect except one small one to the left, an eyetooth. It was a little crooked.

And then he stopped thinking as she kissed him, and Ari the cybernetic ant stood in his box on the mantel and watched, and the flames of the fire lifted and died away, and Stan watched Ari watching and watched himself kissing Julie, not knowing that Ari was watching, and all this from within his frozen moment in time and all of it stained in the blue light of the royal jelly of memory.

4

Next morning he had a chance to show Julie around his house. She admired the fine old silverware he had inherited from his grandparents, and looked with something approaching awe at the portraits of his ancestors that hung on the great staircase that led to the upper rooms. There were dozens of somber oil paintings in ornate gilt frames, showing stern-faced men—some with side-whiskers and some clean-shaven—and proper-looking ladies in starched black bombazine and stiff Dutch lace. Stan had been lucky that this stuff still remained after the great destruction.

"It's wonderful, Stan," Julie said. "I never knew who my parents were. They sold me before I knew them."

"I've got more than enough relatives," Stan said. "You can have some of mine."

"Can I? I'd like that. I'll take that fat one with the smile for my mother."

"That's Aunt Emilia. You've picked well. She was the best of the bunch."

There were other treasures upstairs. Eiderdowns whose cases were heavy with intricate embroidery; gaudy antique jewelry; massive furniture cut from gigantic tropical trees whose species had become extinct.

"This is such beautiful stuff," Julie said. "I could look at it forever. How do you ever pull yourself away?"

"You know, it's funny," Stan said. "I never liked any of this before. But since you've come here . . . Well, it looks pretty nice to me now."

The next day Stan was pleased when it was the time for action. He felt like his life was just beginning. He was very pleased with this notion, although he also dreaded it, because if his life was beginning, it was also drawing to a close. Which would come first, he wondered, victory or death? Or would they arrive simultaneously?

He refused to think about it. What was important was that he and Julie were in this together. He was no longer alone.

He dressed with special care that morning, humming to himself as he shaved. He selected an Italian silk suit and a colorful Brazilian imported shirt made of a light cotton. He wore his tasseled loafers, even going so far as to buff them up to a high polish. He usually laughed at people who took pains over their dress and appearance, but for this morning, at least, he was one of them. It was a way of reminding himself that he was making a fresh start.

He had been thinking a lot about fate and chance, and how they were influenced by the human will. He had come to the conclusion that what he wanted very badly was going to happen, as long as he willed it hard enough. It seemed to him that he was allied to a universal spirit that determined the course of things.

As long as he wanted what the universal spirit wanted for him, he couldn't go wrong.

Although these were exhilarating thoughts, Stan also had some doubts. He wondered if the fire caused by the Xeno-Zip might be affecting his mind. Was he getting a little ... grandiose? Did he really think he had found a way to cheat death?

Sometimes it seemed obvious to him that death was what was really happening to him. This was the real meaning of the disease rotting out his insides. There were too many details of his everyday life to remind him; the spitting and spewing into basins; the many pills he was continually taking, and their many strange effects.

He knew he was a very sick man. But he thought it represented some ultimate courage in himself that he was refusing to face the facts. He decided that if people really faced the facts, they'd all be licked before they could start.

He was determined to go on. It was not yet time to give up and let go. That would come later, when he found his doom; for Stan sensed a horrible fate awaiting him, one that was presently without a name or a face. Then he shook his head angrily and put those thoughts out of his mind.

He found a fresh daisy from the garden for his buttonhole. It was a bright crisp day outside, a day that seemed filled with infinite promise. He could hear Julie humming from the kitchen. She had come down after her shower and was making breakfast. He went in. She was wearing his long fluffy bathrobe. Her hair was tied up in a Donald Duck towel. Her face sparkled, and she looked very young, ingenuous. It was a nice thing to see, though he knew it was an illusion, and only a temporary one at that.

They had bacon and eggs over easy, toast, coffee. A simple breaking of the fast. And now they were ready to discuss plans.

"The first thing we need," Stan said, "is operating capital. I've got a lot of ideas for how to get this project of ours going. But it's going to take some money. Have you any thoughts on how we could acquire a cash flow?"

"I do," Julie said. "Raising money at short notice is what a thief does best, Stan. And I'm the best thief that ever was. How much do we need?"

Stan made some calculations. "A hundred thousand, anyway."

"And how much money do you have right now?"

"I don't know," Stan said. "A couple hundred, I suppose, maybe a thousand in savings."

"That's not enough, is it?" Julie asked.

"Nowhere near. We need fifty thousand anyway."

"As much as that?" Julie said. "Are you sure we need so much?"

"I'm afraid so," Stan said. "We'll have a lot of expenses to set up what we need in order to get a ship, put Norbert into final working shape, get the equipment we need, and get on with our plan."

"All right, Stan," Julie said. "I think I can be of some use here. Give me what you've got. I'll double it."

"How will you do that?"

"Watch and see."

"Will you use your skills as a thief?"

"Not immediately," Julie said. "There's an intermediate step I need to take."

"Could you be a little clearer?"

"I'm talking about gambling."

"I didn't know you were a gambler as well as a thief," Stan said.

"My real profession is thief, but I'm a gambler also because everyone needs a second line of work. The fact is, I'm lucky at certain games. Like Whorgle. I've been told that I've got latent psychokinetic abilities. I can affect the fall of dice sometimes. But they don't play dice at Callahan's, only card games. Well, Whorgle is a new game that depends on hand-eye coordination. I've got that, and I've also got something else. A certain X-factor that sometimes does the trick."

"Well, I guess you know what you're doing," Stan

said. "Although I've been wanting to see some of this thieving of yours in action."

"Being a good thief costs money, Stan."

"That's a funny thing to say. I thought you were supposed to make money that way."

"That's the result, of course. But when you work in the upper echelon of crime, you don't go in and hold up a candy store. And you don't knock off a bank, either. Those are not what I was trained for. You never asked what kind of thief I was, Stan. Well, I'm telling you now. I'm a high-society jewelry thief. I knock off only the best people. I work at political conventions, movie openings, awards ceremonies, great sports events, things that bring together crowds of people with lots of money. But that requires a setup. Otherwise I'd have to spend too long just trying to dope out how to do it. I buy a ready-made plan from an expert in the field. It comes high. But it's guaranteed to bring me to large amounts of money and jewelry."

"How much does a plan like that cost?"

"If you buy one from an expert like Gibberman, it can cost plenty. I'm going to use your money to win more money so I can pay Gibberman to give me one of his great plans. It may sound like a roundabout way to you, but name me any other profession where you can go from a thousand dollars to around a million in less than three days."

"Sounds interesting," said Stan. "Can I come along?"

"Well, of course you can, at least for some of it, but you have to be real cool. You mustn't even act like you're with me. You see, gambling is hard work. I'm going to have to give it all my attention. Then, assuming I win, there's the next part of the operation, which calls for even more attention."

"Yeah? What's that?"

"That's walking out of the gambling place with your money, Stan."

5

At first Stan didn't want to show his robot alien to Julie. On the one hand, he thought it was the best piece of work he had ever done. But would she realize that? What would her reaction be?

It didn't matter what she thought, of course, Stan told himself logically. Yet all the time he knew it did matter, very much. He realized he wanted Julie to think well of him. He had been alone too long, and he had hidden from everyone, including himself, just how lonely and desperate he had been. It would have been too much to have realized that earlier. But now that Julie had come into his life, he could no longer bear being without her. He wanted to make sure that never happened.

He didn't know what was going to happen. He was scared. But he was also strangely happy. Over the last few days the individual moments of his life felt better

than they had for a long time. Maybe he'd never felt
so good.

He was thinking about this while he showered and
put on clothes fresh from the dry cleaners. He shaved
with special care, and he laughed at himself for doing
all this, but that didn't stop him. He saw Julie over
breakfast. She was looking radiant, her hair sparkling
in the sunshine.

After breakfast, Stan showed her his lab.

After that, it was time to show off his robot alien.

He kept it in a special temperature-controlled room
behind a locked door. The door was to keep people
out, not to keep the robot in, he told Julie. It stood
perfectly immobile, since it was not presently acti-
vated. Its black, heavily muscled body seemed ready
to lunge. Yet Julie did not hesitate when Stan took her
hand and peeled back the robot's lips to show its
gleaming rows of needle-sharp fangs.

"Your pet looks like evil incarnate," Julie said.

"As a matter of fact, he's suprisingly gentle. I hope
I haven't made a mistake in the circuitry. He may need
to be trained to fight."

"I can be of some help there," Julie said.

6

In Jersey City, lying on a rank bed with a filthy mattress, Thomas Hoban stirred uneasily in his sleep. The dreams didn't come so often, but they still came. And always the same . . .

Captain Thomas Hoban was seated in the big command chair, viewscreens above him, clear-steel glass canopy in front. Not that you get to see much in space, not even in the Asteroid Belt. But even the biggest spaceship is small in terms of space for humans, and you get to appreciate even a view of nothingness. It's better than being sealed up in a duralloy cocoon without any vision except for what the TV monitors can offer.

The *Dolomite*—a good ship with an old but reliable atomic drive, but also recently fitted with tachyonic gear for multiparsec jumps—was currently on a local run within the solar system, tooling around doing a job here, a job there, trying to pick up some money

for the owners. Then they got the signal that took
them to Lea II in the asteroids.

Lea was a fueling base, owned by Universal Obsid-
ian but open to all ships. It was a refueling spot. It
even had a kind of café, only a dozen seats and a
menu like you'd expect at a place that hired their
cooks by how little they would steal and cut costs by
never bringing in fresh provisions. Not that fresh
produce comes easy in the asteroids. It costs too
much to make special runs with your iceberg lettuce.

After leaving Lea, Hoban had taken the *Dolomite* to
Position A23 in the asteroids. That was the location
for the Ayngell Works, a refinery on its own slab of
rock, where a robot work crew purified metals and
rare earths mined elsewhere in the asteroids. A23 was
located in one of the densest parts of the cluster. You
had to navigate at slow speeds and with care, but who
didn't know that? And Hoban was a careful man. He
didn't let his second-in-command do the job for him.
Even though Gill was an android and a top pilot and
navigator, Hoban did it himself, and he did it well. In
any event, no one had any complaints about him before he came to A23.

His job on A23 was to take a big metals hopper
into tow and bring it to the Luna Reclamations Facility. Taking it up was no small job. It was a big mother,
too big to fit into the *Dolomite*'s hold. But of course
the asteroid it was perched on had negligible gravity,
so there was no difficulty in pulling the hopper away
from the surface once the magnetic clamps that held
it to its massive base plate were released. Hoban's
crew, by all accounts, were trained men; it should
have been a piece of cake.

The trouble was, they weren't really a trained crew.
There were three Malays aboard who spoke no English and only understood the simplest commands.
That usually worked out all right, but not this time. It
had never been proven, but one of those Malays must
have gotten confused working in the lowest bay.
Somehow he or someone had missed the towline en-

tirely and had locked a fuel-line feeder into the coupling winch. The next thing Hoban knew, the feeding mechanism had been jerked out of the atomic pile, which had shut down automatically, leaving him floating in space without main power.

This wasn't the first time a spacecraft had lost a main engine. Gill estimated six hours to repair it. Meantime the backup accumulators and the steering jets would provide enough propulsion to get back to A23 so they could pick up the five crewmen who had gone down to manhandle the cargo ties into position.

At least that's what should have happened, or so it was claimed in the court inquiry later.

Instead, Hoban had turned the ship toward Luna and got away as fast as he could. He claimed afterward that there was a lot more wrong than just losing an engine. Down on A23, an inexperienced crew member had accidentally pulled the interlocks on the atomic pile that kept A23 running. The damned thing was going critical and there was no time to do anything but run for it. . . .

Leaving the five crewmen on A23 to their fate.

Hoban had had to make a quick decision. He calculated that the pile was going to blow up in three minutes. If he stayed around or moved in closer, the blast would take him with it. Even a class-four duralloy hull wasn't built for that kind of treatment. And anyhow, nonmilitary spacecraft were usually built of lighter-gauge metal than the fighting ships.

It was pandemonium aboard the *Dolomite*. There was a crew of twenty aboard, and five of them were down at A23 with the blast coming up on them in minutes. Half of the remaining crew had wanted the captain to ignore the lapsed-time indicator, ignore the risk, and go back to pick up the men; the other half wanted him to blow off what remained of battery power and get out of there as fast as his jets would take him.

The crew had burst into the control room, hysterical and entirely out of order, and they had begun to come to blows right there while Hoban was trying to con the ship and Gill into attending to the navigation. Letting those men in there had been the captain's first mistake.

Crewmen were not allowed in officer country except by specific invitation. When a crewman trespasses, shipboard code says he should be punished immediately. If Hoban had ordered Gill to seize the first man to come in and put him into the crowded little locker belowdecks that served as jail space, the others might have had second thoughts. Crews obey strong leadership, and Hoban's leadership at this point was decidedly weak.

It was in the middle of that shouting writhing mass of people that Hoban had come to his decision.

"Open the accumulators! Get us out of here, Mr. Gill!"

That had shut everybody up, since the acceleration alarm had gone off and they had to get back to their own part of the ship and strap down while the faux gravity was still in operation. It was Hoban's hesitation that had almost set off the men, but once he'd made up his mind, things were better.

The question was, had he made the right choice? The jury decided there was reason enough to believe that Hoban had panicked, had not thought through his position, had not properly calculated the risk. The jury's report said that he had had more than enough time and could have gone in for the men without undue risk to the ship. It would have been cutting it a little fine, but in the atmosphere of the trial, men didn't think about that. They didn't really ask themselves what they would have done in Hoban's shoes. They just knew that five crewmen were dead, and the company was liable.

But the question was, under which clause of the insurance contract was the company liable? If what had happened was beyond anyone's power to change, that was one thing. But if it was due to pilot error or poor judgment, then the company had less direct liability. Guess which the jury went for?

Spaceship pilots were important men, like star athletes, and most of them had, in addition to solid abilities, good-to-excellent connections. Hoban didn't have any of that. Just top marks in his class throughout the university and Space School after that. He was the corps' token poor boy; proof that anyone could make it in the corps if he was smart and diligent. But when it came right down to it, after the accident, the company didn't want to pay out on the higher figure of the insurance and Hoban didn't have any friend in high places to keep a watch over his interests. Juries had been known to be bribed, and Bio-Pharm had been known to bribe them.

The case had faded quickly from the news. There were lots of other things to get excited about. No one was even interested in doing a vid special on the Hoban case. But if they'd looked into it, they might have been surprised.

7

Callahan's Sporting Club near Delancey Street was an illegal club. The authorities were always closing it down, but Callahan's always managed to open again in a day or two. Many city mayors and police commissioners had sworn to close the place once and for all, but somehow they never got around to it. Too much money changed hands. It was nice to know that some things, like the power of bribery, never changed.

A panel slid open in a reinforced door, and a face looked out. "Whaddyaa want?"

"I want to gamble," Julie said.

"Who do you know?"

"Luigi."

"Then come on in."

After they were inside, Stan whispered to her, "Who's Luigi?"

"I have no idea," Julie said. "In a place like this,

looking like you know someone is worth almost as much as really knowing."

Callahan's was filled with well-dressed, prosperous-looking people, most of them crowded three deep around the horseshoe-shaped bar. The general depression and malaise that seemed to grip so much of America didn't operate here. Here, things were booming. Stan could see people sitting in the adjoining dining room, eating as though there were no food shortages. It looked like they were eating real steaks, too. From beyond the dining room he could hear the excited sounds of people betting. The gaming rooms would be right down there, and that was where Julie led him.

"What game are you going to play?" he asked.

"I'll try Whorgle," she said.

She pushed her way into the circle, and they made way for her. There were a dozen men and three women betting on the action. They waited while she set out her cash. Then the game went on.

Stan found he couldn't figure out how Whorgle was played. There were cards, of course, and a small ivory marker, and something made it spin and jump between the numbers painted on the table. How long it resided in a square seemed to decide who won, but the cards had something to do with it, too. There were also disk-shaped markers with odd symbols on one side. The money, thrown down on the painted stake lines, passed back and forth too quickly for Stan to figure out what was happening. He knew he could work it all out if he just applied his mind, but right now he was feeling light-headed. It had been quite a while since his last shot of Xeno-Zip. The artificial fire that had enlivened his nerves and dulled his senses was fading out of his system. He was beginning to feel very bad. The pain was simply too hard to handle without something to help it like essence of royal jelly.

At last the pain became too much for him. He had to go into a nearby room and lie down on a couch.

After a while he fell into a troubled sleep and dreamed of grinning skulls dancing and bobbing in front of him.

After a while Julie came and woke him. She was smiling.

"How did you do?" Stan asked her.

"Nobody beats me at Whorgle," she said, riffling through a stack of greenbacks. "Let's go home and get some sleep. Then I need to see Gibberman."

8

Gibberman was a small man who wore a tweed cap pulled low on his forehead and crouched behind his Plexiglas-protected desk in his Canal Street pawnbroker's office, looking for all the world like an inflated toad. He wore a jeweler's loupe on a black ribbon around his neck and spoke with some indefinable Eastern European accent.

"Julie! Good to see you, darling."

"I told you I'd come," Julie said. "I'd like you to meet a friend of mine."

"Delighted," said Gibberman. "But no names, please." He shook Stan's hand, then offered Julie a drink from a half-empty bottle of bourbon beside him.

"No, nothing," she said. "Look, I'm going to get right to the point. I need plans for a job, and I need them quickly."

"Everybody's always in a hurry," Gibberman said.

"I've got places to go and things to do," Julie said.

"Rushing around is the curse of this modern age."

"Sure," Julie said. "You got anything for me or not?"

Gibberman smiled. "A good job is going to cost, you know."

"Of course," Julie said. "Here, check this out."

She took an envelope from her purse and put it down on the desk in front of Gibberman. He opened it, looked inside, riffled the bills, then closed the envelope again.

"You got it there, Julie. All you've got, that's the price."

"Fine," Julie said. "Now what do you have?"

"A piece of luck for you," Gibberman said. "Not only have I got a first-class job, probably worth a million or more, but you could do it tonight if you want to move that fast."

"Fast is just what I want," Julie said. "You're sure this is a good one?"

"Of course I'm sure," Gibberman said. "There's an element of risk in all these matters, as you well know. But with your well-known talents, you should have no particular difficulty."

Gibberman twirled around in his chair and pushed a wall painting out of the way. Behind it was a small safe set into the wall. He twirled the combination, blocking Julie and Stan's view with his body. Reaching in, he pulled out half a dozen envelopes, looked through them rapidly, selected one, put the rest back, then closed the safe.

"Here's the job, my dear. Set for New York, and on a street not too far from where we are just now."

"This had better be good," Julie said. "That's every cent we've got in the world."

"You know how reliable I am," Gibberman said. "Together with my accuracy goes my well-known discretion."

9

"What is this?" Stan asked. They had gone back home and had opened the manila envelope that Gibberman had given her. Inside was a map, a floor plan of an apartment, several keys, and a half-dozen pages of notes neatly printed in a tiny handwriting.

"This, my dear, is what any successful thief needs—a plan."

"That's what you got from Gibberman?"

"I've used his plans for several years," Julie said. "He's very thorough."

"So who are you going to rob?" Stan asked.

"A wealthy Saudi oilman named Khalil. He arrived in New York two days ago. He's going to the Metropolitan Opera tomorrow night to watch a special performance of *The Desert Song*. While he's away I'll relieve him of certain items he usually keeps in his apartment."

"Where is this to take place?"

"He's staying at the Plaza."

"Wow," Stan said. "I never thought I'd be doing this."

"You're not," Julie said. "I am. You'll have to wait for me at home. I always work alone."

"But we're partners now. We do everything together." He looked so crestfallen that Julie felt a pang of sorrow for him.

"Stan," she said, "you know that robot you've built? Would you trust me to do micro-soldering on his interior circuits?"

"Of course not," Stan said. "You haven't had the training. . . . Oh, I see what you mean. But it's not really the same thing."

"It's the exact same thing," Julie said.

"I just hate to see you going into this alone."

"Don't worry about me. Nothing ever goes wrong with my plans. And if it does, I can take care of it."

10

The Plaza Hotel had suffered some damage during the recent time of the aliens, but had since regained at least a semblance of its former elegance. Julie went there that evening wearing a stunning red cocktail dress. She looked, if not exactly like a celebrity, then definitely like a celebrity's girlfriend. The doorman opened the door for her, bowing deeply. She entered the big, brilliantly lit lobby. The reception desk was straight ahead. She didn't want to get too close to it yet. She glanced at her watch as if she was expecting to meet somebody. All the time she was taking in the details.

People were very well dressed. This was a place where money was in very good supply.

To one side a small orchestra was playing a quaint song from olden times called "Smoke Gets in Your Eyes." People were coming in and out of the bar with its glowing mahogany paneling and its soft indirect lighting. She would have liked a drink now, but she had an unbreakable rule: no alcohol or any other kind of drug while she was on a job.

She looked around the bar and then the lobby. Her practiced eye picked out the security men, two of them near the potted palms. She could always tell who they were. They just didn't look like the guests, no matter how well they dressed. She counted five of them. They gave her admiring glances but there was nothing suspicious in their looks. So far so good.

The big hotel was in full swing. There were lights everywhere, and elegant people, and the accoutrements of success. You could smell it in the five-dollar cigars and the expensive perfume on the white shoulders of the women; in the aroma of roast beef, the real thing, wafting out from under silver servers as black-coated waiters brought the well-laden plates around; in the very carpet, permeated with expensive preservatives and subtle-smelling oils.

Julie went to the elevators. One was reserved for the penthouse suites. There was a man standing near it, rocking back and forth on his heels as he surveyed the passing crowds. Julie made him for a plainclothes cop, maybe somebody's bodyguard. She walked on past and went through a set of corridors back into the main lobby. She was pretty sure the guy at the penthouse elevator hadn't noticed her. She was also sure a frontal assault on the apartment wasn't the best idea.

Gibberman had taken this possibility into account. Next door to the Plaza was the Hotel Van Dyke. Khalil's apartment was a penthouse in the Plaza. If, for any reason, Julie didn't want to use the elevator, Gibberman had indicated an ingenious alternate way of gaining entry. It involved swinging from an unoccupied top-floor apartment in the Van Dyke, and going in through Khalil's window. A cat-burglar act, but that was one of Julie's specialties. She wished Stan could be here to watch her. But it wouldn't be safe, and it might distract her.

She had no trouble slipping into the Van Dyke with a group of people going to the top-floor restaurant. When they got off at the top floor, Julie got out with them, but instead of entering the restaurant, she ducked into the short flight of service stairs that led to the roof. From there she had a fine view of upper Manhattan, with the dark mass of Central Park directly in front of her and traffic crawling by a long way below on the street. A cutting wind blew her hair around, and she slipped on a knit cap to hold it in place. "Here we go!" she said aloud.

She fixed her ropes and swung over to the roof of the Plaza. From there she tied her rope to a cornice and, taking a deep breath, swung out again into space, bracing herself with one foot so as not to spin. The stars and the street seemed equally distant as she lowered herself to the level of the apartment windows.

They were open, saving her from having to cut through them with a vibrator tool.

She swung in through the billowing white curtains, landed soundlessly inside the darkened apartment, and rolled to her feet. She could see pretty well with the infrared-enhanced goggles she now snapped on. Her feet were set in a defensive pose, but there was no one there. She gave the rope a snap and it came free from the cornice. She wound it around her waist. Now there was no evidence of her means of entry.

She looked around the apartment. It was large, with a drawing room and a separate bedroom. She checked out the kitchen. The refrigerator was filled with a very good brand of champagne, and there were tins of caviar in the pantry. This Khalil seemed to live on the rarest of fare. The question now was where did he keep the jewelry?

She knew that Gibberman had chosen this mark carefully. Ahmed Khalil was renowned as an international playboy. He loved to give expensive gifts to his ladies of the evening. But where did he keep the trinkets? She had already learned from inside sources that he didn't entrust them to hotel safes. He wanted them close at hand for the moment when he chose to reward his current lady.

She moved quickly around the apartment. Although the place was big, it was still only a hotel suite. The stuff has to be here somewhere....

And then, suddenly, the lights came on.

"Good evening, my dear," a deep, resonant voice said.

Julie saw a tall, very thin, dark-faced man leaning negligently against the wall. He was wearing a checked headdress. He had a short beard and luxuriant mustache. His face was narrow, and he had a hawk's nose with a large mole in the left corner. Standing beside him was another man, also an Arab, but large—in fact, huge—with a full head of fuzzy black hair and so much facial hair that his features were all but obscured. Julie, however, had no trouble seeing the knife he held in his right hand.

"What are you doing here?" Julie asked. "You're supposed to be seeing an opera."

Khalil, the tall thin man, smiled. "Your information is reliable, but so was my counterintelligence service. We always keep an eye on Gibberman when we come to New York. He's stung us before. We knew when you visited him to set up the job. Didn't we, Sfat?"

The giant smiled and touched the point of his dagger with the ball of his thumb.

Khalil said, "Gibberman was happy to tell us what he had set up for this evening."

Julie nodded. Talk about luck.

"You mustn't hold it against Gibberman for talking," Khalil said. "When Sfat takes the knife to somebody, secrets are shouted from the rooftops. His skill is better than a surgeon's. With that knife he can lay bare a single nerve, in the arm, for example, and play on it as if it were the string on a violin. It is an unforgettable experience, my dear, and one I'm sure you wouldn't want to miss."

Julie thought of how she had told Stan that nothing ever went wrong. What a laugh! Of course, it was all bad luck. How could she have guessed that Khalil would find out about Gibberman? She had discounted the efficiency of the counterintelligence corps these rich Arabs employed.

"Well, Khalil," Julie said, "looks like I'm foiled and caught in the act. Have your man step away from the door and I'll leave quietly."

Khalil smiled. "I'm afraid it's not going to be so easy, my dear."

"You're going to turn me over to the police?"

"Eventually. If there's enough left of you. First, however, it will be necessary to teach you a lesson. Sfat!"

The big man took a slow step toward her.

Julie said, "I thought it would be like that. Thanks, Khalil."

"For what?"

"For freeing me of any scruples. If I ever had any, you've put them completely out of my mind."

She turned to face Sfat, and took two steps toward him while Khalil folded his arms and waited for the fun to begin, a small smile on his lips.

Sfat lifted his arms, hands formed into blades. He bent his knees, feet pointed outward, and Julie recognized the typical fighting stance of a Saudi karate fighter. It was a technique that had its limitations. Sfat advanced, mincingly for so large a man, and his bearded face was set in a mask of cruelty. As he came within range his left hand darted out, the finger's shaped like a hawk's head.

She was ready for it, had been anticipating it. She ducked under the swooping blow and, with a short, economical kick, connected with Sfat's left kneecap. He had been turning as she kicked, and some of the force of the blow was lost. Nevertheless, it was enough to take his feet out from under him. He fell heavily, and Julie pounced.

But this time he caught her unawares. Sfat's clumsy fall had been feigned, and as she came leaping at him his arms and legs were drawn up cat fashion, and he lashed out, expecting to catch her in the solar plexus. She had seen her danger a moment before his counterstroke, however, and turning in midair, managed to avoid his flailing limbs. Her stiffened elbow caught him in the pit of the stomach, knocking the air out of him, and in the second it took him to recover, she rolled away and regained her feet.

Khalil had been watching all this dumbfounded. Now, belatedly, he stirred into action. He stepped forward, crouching in a classic knife fighter's pose. The weapon he carried in his right hand and low against his body was a *yata*, a traditional Yemeni dagger, about eight inches long, slightly curved, and sharpened to a razor edge. It was made from a Swedish saw blade, and fitted with an elaborate rhino-horn handle. Arabic letters were engraved on the blade. Julie's eyes widened when she saw the weapon.

"You do well to fear the *yata*," Khalik said, advancing, light twinkling off the point like the gaze of a one-eyed basilisk.

"Oh, I wasn't exactly afraid of it," Julie said. "Just surprised to see it. Rhino horn is not legally traded. Is it genuine?"

"Of course," Khalil said, feinting and then making a lightning stab at her. "I always kill with the genuine article."

"I'm sure glad to hear that," Julie said. "That makes that knife extremely valuable!"

The blade darted toward her midsection. Julie spun, and the thing passed harmlessly along her left side. As it passed, her arm snapped down, trapping the weapon. Khalil began a long and elaborate Arabic curse in the guttural dialect of Omdurman, but got out no more than a couple of syllables before Julie's left elbow crashed with piledriver force into the middle of his face.

Blood streaming from his nose and mouth, Khalil stumbled backward, losing his grip on the knife that was still clamped under Julie's left arm.

"I'll just keep this for you," Julie said, slipping the

knife into her belt. "It might reduce its value if we got blood all over it."

A feint to the midsection drew down Khalil's guard. Fingers folded in protectively, Julie snapped a blow. The heel of her hand caught Khalil where the upper lip meets the nose. Four of his front teeth cracked off clean at the gum line.

"You ought to thank me," Julie said. "I've corrected your overbite and haven't even charged you for it."

Khalil fell down screaming. He rolled on the floor clutching his head and whimpering. Bloody foam splattered from his mouth. Julie watched him critically for a moment, then muttered, "That ought to keep you occupied for a while."

She turned to Sfat. He had regained his feet, and although his balance was just the slightest bit off-kilter, he was still formidable. If rage could kill, then Julie would be dead ten times over. He came toward her on the attack. He was about twice the weight of the slender girl and he was containing his fury now as he backed her into an angle of the wall, just to one side of an indifferent copy of Gainsborough's *Blue Boy*. There seemed no way she could get out of this one. Shouting an oath in street Arabic, Sfat launched his attack.

Julie had had long preparation for moments like this. Shen Hui's instructions in self-defense had covered all the basics of unarmed combat. He had not been satisfied with that, however, since he accounted himself no expert in the finer points of self-defense. So he had apprenticed her to Olla Khan, a fat-faced master fighter from Isfahan in central Asia. Khan, beguiled by her beauty, had said, "My arrangement with your master is that you will stay with me and serve me in all particulars until you can beat me at unarmed combat. That might take more than a lifetime, my pet."

In fact it took just five months, and Olla Khan ended up in a hospital for his presumption.

And so, now, with Sfat launching his impetuous

and ill-considered attack, Julie's problem was not how to cope with it, but which of several different methods to choose. She also had to decide to what extent she wished to incapacitate him, and this in turn depended on her estimation of his value to her alive. In the split of a second she decided that this gross hairy-faced man with the bad breath was of no value to her, and indeed could serve her better dead as a message to his master, Khalil, to stop resisting and start cooperating.

She didn't think all that through consciously. Instead, she opposed his charge with a sword hand, fingers stiffened. Sfat crashed into her hand and was stopped abruptly as the fingers took him high between the eyes, shutting down his pineal gland and then going on to break his neck. His eyes rolled up, showing the white, and he crashed to the floor like two hundred pounds of dead mutton.

She turned from him to Khalil. "Ready to go another round?" she asked.

Khalil, his teeth scattered over the floor, had had enough. He mumbled through a bloodstained hand. "Don't hurt me anymore. I'm a dilettante, not a fighter. I'll give you whatever you want."

"That's what I like to hear," Julie said. She took a pillow from a nearby bed and stripped off the pillowcase.

"Fill it with good stuff for me," she said. "Don't put in any worthless crap or I'll have something to say about it."

Khalil, totally unnerved, couldn't even dream of resistance. His collapse was absolute. He opened a compartment concealed in the wall behind the bed and picked several precious bracelets, two handfuls of magnificent unmounted gems in a white chamois bag, and a string of glorious baroque pearls, each the size of a pigeon's egg and no two alike. Soon the pillowcase was bulging. Khalil had other objects he wanted to give her, but she stopped him.

"One bagful is enough. I'm not greedy. Besides, I'd need an extra pair of hands to carry it all."

Khalil recovered sufficiently to say, "If you're finished, then get out!"

"Okay," Julie said. "This is good-bye, then." She moved close to him.

He stared at her. The whites of his eyes went a dirty yellow as she advanced on him. He stumbled away, found himself with his back to a bureau. "What are you going to do?" he asked in a shaking voice.

"Just give you a couple hours' sleep. So I can walk out of here like a lady." She touched a nerve in his neck. He slumped to the floor unconscious.

"Be sure to have a dentist look at those stumps," she said. He couldn't hear her, of course, but she was sure he'd remember anyway.

Julie went to the dressing-room mirror and checked her clothing and makeup. She repaired her lipstick, which had been smeared in the combat, and found an ugly red stain on the shoulder of her red dress.

Luckily, Khalil had a really smart ermine jacket in his closet. It covered the stain nicely. She left by the penthouse elevator. No one stopped her as she walked out, passed through the lobby, and exited the revolving front door onto Central Park South, where she called a taxi.

11

"How did it go tonight?" Stan asked when she got back to the brownstone.

"Not bad," she said, dumping her loot into the bed. "A dream night for a thief. Unfortunately, it's nowhere near enough to buy a spaceship with."

"We don't need to buy one," Stan said. "I've got a plan that ought to work now that we have some money to play around with. The first thing we're going to need is a spaceship driver."

"I'd love to talk about it," Julie said. "But first I need a bath. And I'm famished! Sometimes stealing can be hard work. Oh, by the way, here's a present." She tossed the dagger onto the bed.

Stan picked it up and admired the gleaming narrow blade and the rhino handle. "Where'd you get this?"

"Just a little trinket I picked up during the evening."

12

Over the next two weeks, Julie converted the loot from Khalil's apartment to cash, and Stan lost no time putting it to work. There was information to buy, people to bribe, and round-the-clock work by hired technicians to put Norbert into full working condition.

Two weeks to the day after Julie's theft at the Plaza, she met Stan for lunch at the Tavern on the Green in Central Park. Since it wasn't a workday for her, she permitted herself a cocktail.

Stan was looking pretty well. A shade paler than usual, but still not bad for a man dying of cancer and sustaining himself on heavy doses of the most addicting narcotic substance known to man. His eyes were a little dreamy, but his voice was firm enough as he said, "Julie, we're ready to make our move."

"Today?"

"That's right. Are you ready?"

She gave him an exasperated look. "Of course. You really don't have to ask me that."

"Sorry, I didn't mean anything by it."

Her voice softened. "No, I'm sorry, Stan. I don't mean to snap at you. It's the waiting. It's hard on my nerves."

"Well," Stan said, "it'll soon be over. If this plan works, we'll have ourselves a pilot."

"And if it doesn't work?"

"We could be dead."

"Fair enough. Where are we going?"

"To look up an old friend of mine and make him an offer he can't refuse."

13

Jersey City, even in its best days, had been a city many people found objectionable. It hadn't improved much since the days before the Human–Alien Wars and the human reoccupation. On the day Stan and Julie went there, half of the streets downtown were awash due to a burst water main from a week before, and the city's repair crews still hadn't gotten around to capping it.

Ragged, mean-looking men and women hung around every street corner. They looked like down-and-outers, but there was something sly and dangerous about them, too. There were soup kitchens set up here and there, and the buildings looked old and delapidated. Even the newly built sections of the city were starting to show wear, their poor construction materials already crumbling. Packs of wild dogs slinked in and out of back alleys; nobody had gotten around to getting rid of them yet.

"It's pretty bad," Stan said, like he was apologizing for it.

"Hey, I've seen worse," Julie said. "Not that I want to hang around this place . . ."

At Central Station, Stan found them a motorized pedicab. The driver was a gnarled old brute, dressed nearly in rags, with a shapeless felt hat on which, incongruously, was the glittering bright medallion that let him legally operate a for-hire vehicle.

Stan peered inside the three-wheel pedicab. Some of these drivers had been known to hide accomplices inside, the better to rob the customers, or so it was said. Stan didn't really know what to expect. He hadn't been outside New York City in years.

He gave the driver the address, and the man grunted. "You sure you want to go there, mister?"

"Yes, I'm sure. Why do you ask?"

"You're going to the heart of the old Gaslight District. Where the space derelicts and the chemheads hang out."

"Yes, I know."

"No place for a lady, either."

"Shut your face and get moving," Julie said.

"Long as you know what you're getting into." The pedicab operator started up the hand-cranked washing-machine motor that ran his little vehicle. Stan and Julie settled back.

Once the driver got up to speed, he gave them a dashing ride. He wove in and out of traffic on Jersey City's wide boulevards, the pedicab dodging in and out of the debris that the striking garbage collectors would get around to picking up once they settled their contract with the city. The street was like an obstacle course, filled with boxes, packing cases, mattresses, wrecked vehicles, even the carcass of a horse. There were also plenty of vehicles, driven by kamikaze drivers who were hell-bent on getting somewhere, anywhere, rushing around and dodging in and out of each other's way like rules of the road were no more than memories. There was a dirty gray sky overhead, the sun concealed behind dark-edged clouds. It wasn't anyone's fault that the day was so rotten, but you felt like blaming someone anyhow. Looking around, Stan thought, To paraphrase Robert Browning, anything so ugly had to be evil.

"How do you like it?" the driver asked, turning back to fix Stan with a hard look.

"The city? It looks like it's fallen on hard times."

"Buddy, you can say that again. This has always been a bad-luck city. Gutted during the Alien Wars. That happened to a lot of cities. Gave them a chance to rebuild. Only crappier."

"Well, things are tough all over," Stan said, wishing the driver would turn around and pay attention to the traffic.

The driver acted like he had eyes in the back of his head. Cars came shrieking at him from every direction, and somehow they always missed and he kept right on talking.

"You're from New York, right? I can always tell. You people didn't get the Pulsing Plague like we got it here in Jersey. Turned whole neighborhoods into madhouses filled with raving lunatics before it did them the favor of killing them. But not all of them, worse luck. There are some plague people still alive, you know. They were infected, but it didn't kill them. But it can kill you if they touch you."

"I've been inoculated against plague," Stan said.

"Sure. But what good will an inoculation do you against the new berserkers you get around here? They're mostly people who recovered from the Pulser, but with something missing. It was like some center of control in their heads just vanished. Berserkers can get into a frenzy over the smallest thing, over nothing at all. And then watch out for them because they start killing and don't stop until somebody stops them."

"I'll watch out for them," Stan said, feeling very uncomfortable. What was he getting himself and Julie into?

"You wanta good restaurant?" the driver said sud-

denly. "Try Toy's Oriental Palace over on Ogden. They
got a way with soypro you'd never believe. They use
real spices in their sauces, too."

"Thanks, I'll remember that," Stan said. "Are we
close now?"

"You can smell it, can't you?" the driver said, grinning. "Yep, we're just about there."

The driver slowed down and looked for an opening
in the traffic, found one that was too small, and decided to make it larger. He propelled the little pedicab
into it, suffering no more than a bruised bumper,
ducked into a narrow street off the boulevard, took a
couple of turns, and pulled up to the curb.

Stan and Julie got out. Stan saw they were in an
evil-looking neighborhood, which was just about what
he'd expected. Above him, rising above the buildings,
he saw a landmark: the spire of the Commercial Ser-
vices Landing Field, a local service facility where non-
stellar spaceships took off and landed. There had
been a lot of discussion about it in the newly formed
city council. Too close to the city, some said. It could
be a source of danger. If one of those things goes
down . . . Some people still didn't trust spacecrafts. It
was a point, but the other side had the answer. "It'll
bring jobs into the city. We'll be the closest full-facility
field within a hundred-mile radius of New York. A lot
closer than the Montauk Point facility. The business
will flock to us." And in Jersey City, where business is
king and corruption is its adviser, there was no answer to that.

The spaceport's spire was several miles away, Stan
figured. He was in a neighborhood of small ramshack-
le buildings built against the bulwark of several sky-
scrapers. He was standing in front of Gabrielli's Meat
Market, advertising fresh pork today in addition to the
usual soypro steaks and turkeytofu butterballs, and
the place stank of blood and chemicals. Next to it was
a small newsstand, and what looked like a betting par-

lor beside that. Betting was legal in the state of New Jersey, an important source of revenue. Most of the state legislature didn't approve of gambling, but money was hard to find these days, even with the giant Bio-Pharm plant recently opened in nearby Hoboken and with MBSW—the Mercedes-Benz Spaceship Works—sprawled out in Lodi.

A young woman, perhaps sixteen or seventeen years old, came up to Stan. She was slender and tall, and she wore a new motorcycle jacket.

Ignoring Julie, she said, "Can I help you, mister?"

Stan shook his head. "I'm not interested today, thank you."

She glared at him. "You think I'm selling sex? Forget it, stupid. I can see you got a lady with you. And besides, you don't have enough to buy me."

"What are you offering, then?" Stan said.

"Advice. Guidance."

Stan couldn't help laughing. "Thanks, but we can do without it."

"Can you really? You people from around here?"

"No, as a matter of fact."

"That's pretty clear. You want to walk out of here alive? You'd better buy a pass."

Stan looked around. There seemed to be nothing much happening on the street. It all looked safe enough. Yet something about her tone of voice chilled him, and he said, "Just out of curiosity, what happens if we don't take a pass?"

She shrugged. "What usually happens to people who stray onto other people's turf?"

"But I'm standing in a public street!"

"It's turf all the same. You're in the territory of the Red Kings. I can sell you a pass that'll keep you out of trouble, or you can take your chances."

Julie had been standing by, listening, letting Stan handle it, but she was getting impatient. "For heaven's sake, Stan, give her something and let's get on with it!"

"I guess I'll take two passes," Stan said. "How much are they?"

Her price of ten dollars didn't seem too bad. Stan paid with a twenty and waited for change.

"For the other ten I'll sell you some advice," the woman said.

Stan hesitated, then decided not to argue. "Okay. What's your advice?"

"When you go into the soup kitchen," she said, "don't forget your pail." And then she turned and walked away.

Stan looked at the pass in his hand. It was a playing card, the five of diamonds. Turning it over, he saw a fine looping scrawl in red Magic Marker. He couldn't read it, but it looked just like graffiti.

"Hey, kin I help?" a voice asked.

It was a vagrant in a shapeless graycloth hat who had spoken to them. He looked fat and stupid and evil.

Julie said to him, "Buzz off, buster."

The man looked for an instant as though he was prepared to take umbrage at the remark. Then, warned perhaps by a sixth sense that told him when he was outmatched, he mumbled something and walked on.

"I should be doing the protecting," Stan said.

"Don't get all bent out of shape over it," Julie said. "I can take care of bums and wise guys, but I don't know how to build robots. It all evens out in the end."

"Yeah, I guess it does," Stan said. "Here we are."

They walked up the crumbling steps of a rotting tenement. An odor of roach repellent fought with the smell of crushed roaches. There was not much to choose between them. Dim yellow lightbulbs burned overhead as they climbed to the third floor.

Stan found the right door and knocked. No answer. He knocked again, louder.

Julie said, "Maybe we should have phoned."

"No telephone." Stan hammered on the door. "I

know he's in there. There's a light on under the door. And I can hear the TV."

"Maybe he's shy," Julie said. "I think we can fix that." With one well-placed kick, she shattered the lock. The door swung inward.

Within, there was a dismal-looking apartment that might have been pretty nice along around the time Rome was founded. It was a hideous place of ancient wallpaper and mildew, and the sound of a toilet running. Smell of frying kelp patties from other apartments overlay the basic odors. There was an overflowing garbage pail, with two cardboard cartons of garbage beside it.

For furniture, there was an old wooden kitchen table. Sitting at it in a straight-backed chair was a strongly made, sad-faced, middle-aged man with iron-gray hair.

This man looked up as they came in. He seemed startled by what he saw, yet uncaring, as if it didn't matter what the world threw at him next. There was a small black-and-white TV on the table, and he turned it off.

"Hello, Captain Hoban," Stan said.

Hoban took his time about answering. He seemed to be reorienting himself in the real world, after a long trip to some unimaginable place, perhaps to the time of his trouble in the asteroids.

At last he said, "It *is* you, isn't it? Why, hello, Stan."

"Hi," Stan said. "I want you to meet my friend Julie."

Hoban nodded, then looked around. He seemed aware for the first time of the apartment's appearance.

"Please, sit down, miss. You, too, Stan. I'll get you some tea. . . . No, I'm sorry, there isn't any left. No extra chairs, either. If I'd known you were coming, Stan . . ."

"I know, you would have had lunch catered," Stan said.

"Lunch? I can fry you a kelp patty. . . ."

"No, sorry, just kidding, Captain. We're not staying. We're getting out of here, and so are you."

Hoban looked surprised. "But where are we going?"

"There's got to be a café near here," Stan said. "Someplace we can talk."

Hoban looked around again, grinned sheepishly. "I guess this place isn't too conducive to conversation."

"Especially not a business talk," Stan said. "Have you got a coat? Let's go!"

14

Danziger's was a Ukrainian café on the next block. It had big glass windows, always misty with steam. There were vats of water perpetually at the boil for the pirogis in ersatz flour gravy that were the specialty of the place. Stan, Julie, and Hoban took a small booth in the rear. They drank big mugs of black coffee and talked in low voices.

Stan was concerned about Hoban's condition. It had been a while since he had last seen the captain, back when Hoban had been captain of the *Dolomite* and Stan had bought the ship. Stan had liked the taciturn, serious-minded captain and had kept him in charge.

Hoban was one of the old breed, a straight-shooting captain, always serious and controlled, whose interests were exclusively in intergalactic navigation and exploration, and who could be counted on to follow orders. Stan had bought the *Dolomite* during his flush period, when the royalties were rolling in from his various patents, before his troubles with Bio-Pharm and the government. In those golden days, it had looked like the sky was the limit.

After the asteroid incident, when Hoban had lost his license, Stan had pulled some strings and managed to get him a temporary captain's ticket. They had all been quite close then, Stan and Hoban and Gill, the android, who was second-in-command. But then Stan's problems with Bio-Therm had begun, and the lawsuits had started flocking in like flies to a flayed cow.

A hostile holding company had taken over the *Dolomite*, and their first act had been to dismiss Hoban, who was known for his loyalty to Stan. They accused the captain of various peccadilloes. That was really a laugh, with a man of Hoban's known probity, but mud sticks when you fling enough of it hard enough, and the licensing board had lifted Hoban's temporary ticket pending an investigation.

The captain had taken it hard. He was reduced in the course of one terrible day from a man who commanded his own little empire to a penniless derelict who couldn't find any work better than washing dishes.

Now they sat together in a Ukrainian café, with the late-afternoon sun streaming in through the windows, and Stan said, "I'm going back into space, Captain, and I want you with me."

"It's good of you to say so," Hoban said. "But no employer would have me without a license."

"I still want you," Stan said. "As for your license, we'll claim it's still in force."

"But it won't be," Hoban said.

"You can't be sure of that," Stan said. "Money talks. I think the courts will find for you, if it comes to an actual trial. And I'll get your case reopened after this trip."

"Can you really do that?" Hoban asked. A ray of hope lightened his heavy features for a moment, then his expression darkened again. "But I have no ship, Dr. Myakovsky. Or do you want me to pilot something other than the *Dolomite*?"

"No, we're going on the good old *Dolomite*," Stan said.

"But, Doctor, you no longer own it! And even if you did, I am no longer allowed to pilot it."

"Possession is nine tenths of the law," Stan said. "Once we're aboard and under way, they'll have to argue with us in court. Their lawyers against ours."

"I don't know," Hoban said, slumping down and shaking his head.

"Money talks," Stan pointed out again. "We'll win your case. After this trip, we'll all have it good."

"Yes, sir. Back into space again . . . Excuse me for asking, sir, but do you have any money for this venture?"

"Enough for what we need. And a way to get a lot more."

"Where do you want to go?" Hoban asked.

"Let's get into that later," Stan said. "You don't mind if it's dangerous, do you?"

Hoban smiled sadly and shrugged. "Anything's better than rotting here, with nothing to hope for."

"My sentiments exactly," Stan said. "This is Miss Julie Lish, my partner. You'll be seeing a lot of her on this expedition."

Hoban shook Julie's extended hand. "But wait," he said. "I'm sorry, Stan, you had me dreaming for a moment. I'm afraid it's impossible."

"Why do you say that?" Stan asked.

"For one thing, no crew."

"Okay. And what else?"

"The *Dolomite*'s in geosynchronous orbit above Earth, ready to go on a mining trip in a few days."

"We'll have to act quickly. Who's running the *Dolomite*?"

"Gill, until the replacement captain comes aboard."

"Excellent!"

"I don't think so, Stan. You know Gill. He's programmed to follow the rules. Gill always obeys orders."

"Not to worry," Stan said. "Are you sure the new captain's not aboard yet?"

"Yes, I'm sure."

"Then it's simple. We'll go aboard and take off at once."

"Yes, sir . . . But it won't work, sir. You and I are both proscribed from boarding the *Dolomite*. There are guards. They'll read our retinal prints, turn us back. . . ."

"No," Stan said. "They'll call Gill to make a judgment. He's in charge now."

"But what can Gill do? Androids are very simple-minded, Dr. Myakovsky. They obey orders. Their loyalties are built-in, hardwired."

"Like a dog," Stan suggested.

"Yes, sir. Very much like."

"There's still a chance. Since he was animated, Gill has only worked with you."

"That's right. But it's been a while since we've been together. And anyhow, when they changed his orders, they will have changed his loyalties, too."

"They will have tried," Stan said. "Actually, it isn't quite so simple. Loyalty in an android is formed by long association with a particular human. I think Gill will lean in your favor when it comes to a showdown between following your orders or those of the new owners."

Hoban considered it and shook his head doubtfully. "Android conditioning is not supposed to work that way, sir. And if you're wrong . . . It'll be instant prison for all three of us."

"Let's worry about that when the time comes," Stan said. "Of course it's not dead simple. What is? The thing is, it's a chance for us all. What do you say, Hoban? Are you with us or not?"

Hoban looked up and down, uncertain, frowning. Then he looked at Julie. "Do you know what kind of a chance you're taking here, miss?"

"It's better than sitting around listening to yourself breathe," Julie said.

"This venture of yours, Doctor—I suspect it's not entirely legal."

"That's correct," Stan said. "It's illegal and it's dangerous. But it's a chance to rehabilitate yourself. What do you say?"

Hoban's mouth quirked. His face twisted in an agony of indecision. Then he suddenly drove his fist down on the table, causing the coffee mugs to jump.

"I'll do it, Dr. Myakovsky. Anything's better than this!"

The three shook hands. Stan said, "Let's get moving. There's no time to waste."

"There's just one problem," Hoban said.

"What's that?" Stan asked.

"We don't have a crew."

Stan's shoulders slumped and he sat down again.

Julie asked, "How do you usually get a crew?"

"There's no time to get them on the open market," Hoban said, "and we'd have a hard time getting people for a dangerous mission. In circumstances like this, we requisition them from the government."

"What does the government have to do with it?" Julie wanted to know.

"They allow convicts to put in for hazardous duty in space, in return for reduced time on their sentences."

Stan said, "But this time it wouldn't work. The government won't release any of the cons to me now that I've been barred from my own ship."

"Of course they will," Julie said. "Government is slow, Stan, and one part of it never knows what some other part of itself is doing. Just go in and ask the way you usually do. You're a legitimate owner, you've hired crews before. They have to serve you."

"But what if they do know my ship has been seized?"

"First of all, so what? People have property seized every day. It doesn't put them out of business. They have a suit against you, but you're still innocent until proven guilty. And besides, the people who actually give you prisoners, the guards and clerks, what do you think they know about that? They don't know and don't care. They do what they have to do."

"I don't know," Stan said. "I'll be too nervous."

"It will work."

"Maybe. But I don't feel confident about this."

"Stan, if you want to succeed in what you and I are getting into, you're going to have to learn how to fake self-confidence. Have you ever acted in a play?"

"Sure, in college. I was pretty good."

"Well, that's what you're going to do now. Act the part of Dr. Myakovsky, brilliant young scientist and upcoming entrepreneur."

"Acting a part," Stan mused. "What a novel idea! But I believe I could do that."

Julie nodded. "I knew right away you had it in you to play the Big Con. Stan, if you weren't already a scientist, I think you could make a great thief."

It was the nicest compliment Stan had ever been paid.

"And as for you, Captain Hoban . . ." Julie continued.

"Yes, miss?" Hoban said.

"You're going to have to get that hangdog look off of your face. You're a spaceship captain again, not a washed-up drunk who did something wrong once in his life and is making himself pay for it the rest of his life."

"I'll try to remember that," Hoban said.

15

orning came early to the federal penitentiary at Goose Lake, New York. Almost two thirds of the great gray concrete structure was underground, buried under one of the Catskills. What showed above was a windowless dome, gray as a ghost in sunlight, unrelievedly ugly despite the rows of quick-growing trees that had been planted around its perimeter in an attempt to dress it up. A ten-foot-high electrified fence surrounded the facility, but it was pretty much window dressing. No convict had gotten as far as the fence yet. The prison had its ways of keeping the prisoners docile.

Within the windowless pile, artificial light shone night and day. It was part of standard policy to keep the prisoners disoriented, and therefore less aggressive. Inside, there were the usual sections of prison cells, with catwalks outside them where the guards walked. There were workshops, food and laundry facilities, and a separate room where the inmates did state-approved work and earned a dollar or so a day for it.

It was free time now. All the men not doing solitary were walking around the grounds, exercising, talking.

A loud voice came from the prison loudspeaker. "All men whose names are on the Alpha Volunteer List, report to the auditorium on the second level."

The Alpha Volunteer List contained the names of those prisoners with space experience who were willing to volunteer for a hazardous assignment in return for a reduction of their sentences. It had been a while since the call went out for crew. The prisoners were well aware of the good things this early release could do for them. And anyway, it was easier to escape from a spaceship than from a federal prison.

It was not easy getting on the Alpha List, because only a limited number were permitted even to apply. You had to bribe a guard to have any chance at all. And you were likely to have problems with other prisoners who wanted to take your place.

Red Badger had been waiting for this chance a long time. Now he got up, smoothed down his unruly red hair, checked his shoes, and started for the auditorium.

He was stopped by an inmate named Big Ed.

"Where do you think you're going?" Big Ed asked.

"I'm on the list," Badger said.

"You got it wrong," Big Ed said. "That last place is mine."

"No," Red insisted, "it's mine."

"Sure. But you're going to give it to me, aren't you?"

"No way," said Red Badger. "Now, if you'll just let me get past . . ."

Big Ed stood in the middle of the corridor, blocking Badger's way. "Do like I say," he threatened, "or else."

Red Badger knew he was being challenged, knew that Big Ed had been waiting for this moment a long time, yet he also knew that Big Ed had picked him figuring he was the easiest guy on the Alpha List to intimidate. Badger already knew what he was going to do about it.

He was known as Red Badger because of his shock of coarse red hair. He had the light, easily sunburned skin that went with red hair, and narrow blue-green eyes that blinked at you from behind sandy eyelashes. He was a big man, heavy in the chest. He wore his leather waistcoat open to show his chest with its grizzled mass of hair. He had large square teeth and a nasty smile.

Badger was an alumnus of many prisons. He had gotten his nickname at Raiford Prison in Florida, and as an act of defiance had taken it for his own. Badger was doing time for armed robbery and assault. He had a criminal record that went back a long way. Quick with his fists, he was also quick with his tongue and was always looking for a chance to cause trouble. "Trouble is my real middle name," he liked to say. "Let me show you how I spell it." And then he'd punctuate his remark for you with his fists. Like the badger, his namesake, he was most dangerous when cornered.

The fight was to be held according to the accepted prison rules: just the two of them, having it out in one of the washrooms. Whoever was still standing after it was over would go to the auditorium. The two combatants went there silently.

Both men knew it did no good to be brawling in the corridors. There were stingray projectors with motion-indicator finders mounted in all the corridors, turning steadily and scanning in all directions. The stingers weren't fatal, but they hurt like hell and could be counted upon to whip recalcitrant prisoners into line. There were no projectors mounted in the washrooms.

Although it was never talked about, the prisoners figured the authorities wanted to leave them places where they could have things out for themselves, establishing who was top dog and who was underdog. Several of them, noticing where Badger and Ed were going, followed along to watch the fun. It had been known for some time that Big Ed was going to try to take Red's place on the Alpha List.

Big Ed was a seven-foot freak from Opalatchee, Florida. A bodybuilder, he looked like a model for Hercules, all gleaming muscle as he stripped off his shirt. Red Badger, on the other hand, was a solid man, but his musculature was well padded with fat. He looked slow, not formidable.

Stripping off his shirt, he stood in the middle of the shower space, looking fat and sleepy, his hands loose and open at his sides, waiting for Ed to make the first move.

"You sure you want this?" Big Ed asked, moving forward slowly, hands raised like an old-fashioned bare-knuckle fighter. "Ain't going to be much left of you when I get through." He looked at the spectators and laughed. "I'm gonna skin me a badger today, boys."

The men laughed dutifully. Big Ed suddenly lunged forward, and Badger responded.

People said later they'd never seen a big fat man like Badger move so fast. One moment he was standing right there, practically under Big Ed's fists. But when Big Ed attacked, Badger was already out of the way, dancing back. He easily eluded a roundhouse right, and, taking his time, delivered a blow to Big Ed's neck, catching him at a nerve junction on the right side.

Big Ed bellowed and moved back. His right arm was dangling awkwardly at his side. He strained to lift it, but could get no sensation into it. He wasn't hurt; not really. It was just that his right arm wouldn't lift.

"Where'd you learn that stunt?" he demanded.

Badger smiled but didn't answer. What good would

it do to tell Big Ed that his most recent cell mate, Tommy Tashimoto, had taught him the fine art of nerve strikes—getting him to practice for hours, hitting over and over again from all angles until he could strike half a dozen targets unerringly where the nerve bundles were near the surface or rode over bone.

Red Badger hadn't been one for formal education. But when he got a chance to learn how to incapacitate a larger, stronger opponent, all the doggedness of his character came out, and he had worked until he knew what he was doing.

Now he circled around Big Ed's right, hitting him quick hard blows to the face and ribs, coming in over the dangling and useless right arm. Big Ed tried to launch himself at Badger. If he could just get his hands on him, even one-handed, he'd tear the smaller man apart. But Red had a strategy to offset that. He hit again and again at the nerve junction in Ed's neck, and soon the numbness was replaced by a galloping pain that traveled up and down Ed's shoulder, from his face to his groin, filling him with an agony so painful as to be exquisite.

At least Badger thought it was exquisite, because he saw he had his man where he wanted him, helpless but still on his feet. A hunk of meat to which he could mete out punishment.

Badger hit and hit, using the heel and sides of his hands. He knew he had this fight won; he just had to guard now against injuring himself. It wouldn't do to be incapacitated for this spaceship call. Big Ed turned and twisted and floundered, but he couldn't defend himself. A shrewd kick on the elbow brought down his left arm. He stood there, his face a mask of blood, while Badger hammered away at him like a man driving nails into a tough piece of wood. He hit and he hit, and Big Ed groaned with pain but wouldn't go down.

"Hell, I got no more time to waste on this," Badger said. He stepped back and, measuring his man carefully, delivered a kick with his steel-capped work shoe right to the point of Big Ed's jaw. The men watching

the fight winced as Big Ed's front teeth came flying
out like a spray of broken china, and Ed himself
crashed face-first to the floor. Badger turned on a tap
and cleaned himself quickly but thoroughly. It
wouldn't do to be all sweaty for his interview. He
checked himself in the big mirror before he left the
washroom to make sure he didn't have any of Big
Ed's face hanging on his clothes.

16

"Hi, I'm Stan Myakovsky," Stan said. "These are my associates. I telephoned ahead. I need a spaceship crew for a hazardous mission."

If the guard at the front window of the entry gate was impressed, she didn't show it. She was a squarely built woman with short bristly hair. She put down her biker magazine and said, "What company you with?"

"Sonnegard Acceptance Corporation," Stan said, and showed his credentials.

Back before his troubles began, Stan had taken over the *Dolomite* by buying the controlling shares in Sonnegard, a spaceship holding company. The company was the real owner of the ship, not Stan, who had never bothered to have the ship reregistered in his own name. In fact, he had decided not to; that way, if the ship got into any trouble, he wouldn't be liable.

"You'll find my name on the list," Stan said. He was hoping that the government hadn't gotten around to proscribing his company and red-flagging it on the computer. It was unlikely. As Julie had pointed out, it took government forever to bring their records up to date. The inefficiency wasn't strictly government's fault. There was neither the time nor the personnel available to record all the crimes, arrests, and dispositions that were taking place around the clock in an America more lawless than it had ever been in all its lawless history. Sonnegard Acceptance Corporation would probably be a legal entity for months to come.

The guard punched the name up on her computer. "Yeah, you're on the list. Go on through." She buzzed open the heavy metal door leading to the prison.

"So far, so good," Julie said.

Stan, accompanied by Julie and Hoban, went through into a long, brightly lit corridor.

"Oh, I didn't expect much trouble getting in," Stan said. "It's the getting out that concerns me."

"You worry too much," she said. "Doesn't he, Captain Hoban?"

"He's worrying about the wrong things," Hoban said. "What he should be thinking about is what if one of those men recognizes me?"

"You're not exactly a cover girl," Julie said. "I don't think you need to worry."

Their footsteps echoed hollowly as they went down the long corridor, following the flashing arrows that took visitors to the recruitment center.

There was a door at the end of the corridor. It buzzed open for them.

Within was a large office, plenty of plain metal desks and chairs, and a guard seated at a bigger desk in front of a computer.

"Come on in, Dr. Myakovsky," the guard said. "I've got all the volunteers in a holding tank just behind this room. There are twenty of them. That is as you requested, is it not?"

"It's fine," Stan said. "I'd like you to meet Miss Lish,

my associate, and Thomas Hoban, my captain. He'll be doing the actual selection in my name."

"As you know," the guard said, "we have already made the preselection for you, giving you the top-twenty men on our Alpha List. You may reject any of them, and you do not have to give a reason. If you're ready, I'll have the people sent in."

Stan nodded. The guard pressed a button. A panel slid up smoothly in the steel wall. There was a sound of moving feet, and then the prisoners came marching out in single file. Following the guard's commands, they formed a line across the room, stopped, and turned to face Stan and his party.

Captain Hoban walked up to the men. He paced up and down the line, peering into their faces. He came to one, hesitated, stopped, and stared.

Red Badger stared back.

Hoban said, "Do I know you? Have we ever met?"

"I don't think so, sir," Red Badger said. "But of course I've got a lousy memory."

Hoban kept on staring at him. Badger said, "I'm a good spaceman, sir. I just want a chance to rehabilitate myself."

Hoban pursed his lips, frowned, then turned away.

"Anything wrong, Mr. Hoban?" Stan asked.

"No, everything is fine," Hoban said.

"Do the men look all right to you?"

"Yes, they look fine."

Stan could see that something was bothering Hoban, but now was obviously not the time to ask him about it. Maybe, he thought, the captain was just nervous.

Stan turned to the guard. "I'll accept this lot. I'm posting money to send them out to their ship."

"Okay with me," the guard said. "What ship is that?"

"The *Dolomite*," Stan said, and waited.

The guard bent over the computer. "How do you spell it?" she asked, and Stan knew everything was going to be all right.

17

They were transporting the prisoners to Facility 12, where they would take the shuttle to the *Dolomite*, their new ship.

Hoban was thinking, Damn it, I know I've seen that man before. He knew who I was, I'm sure of it. So why did I pick him? Because I could tell from his look, if I didn't take him, he was going to tell everyone who I was. It's not just my imagination, I knew what that bastard was going to do. I should never have gotten myself into this in the first place....

Unexpectedly, Hoban found himself regretting his decision to go in with Stan. Some people might have thought it was crazy, but people just didn't understand. He was grateful for this chance to redeem himself, get back on top, prove himself a winner. But another side of his character knew himself for a loser and just wanted a soft place to lie down. Funny to think of Jersey City as a soft place, but it was. Some-

how he always got fed, always had a roof over his
head. And best of all, nobody expected anything of
him. He could relax, take a drink or two, take a lot of
drinks. . . . He knew that wasn't how he ought to feel.
It was like there were a couple of Hobans, and at
least one of them was working actively to undermine
him. He tried to remind himself that good things lay
ahead: he'd soon be piloting his own ship again. You
couldn't do better than that. But somehow, it didn't
have quite the savor it ought to. And Captain Thomas
Hoban became aware that he faced a greater danger
than whatever Stan was getting them into. You can
guard against murder, but how do you guard against
your own thoughts of suicide?

18

There was one way to get aboard a spaceship without having to produce a pass or wait for a computer check. You could go aboard as part of a tour party. It was Julie's idea. They waited a few hours to give the authorities enough time to deliver the prisoners to the *Dolomite*. Then they came to the Staten Island launch site.

All ships picked up extra income by letting sightseeing parties aboard while they were in port, lifting them up to the ship's orbit in a chemical launching craft. Touring the spaceships was a popular entertainment, as in a bygone year people had gone into New York Harbor to visit battleships when the fleet was in. Spaceships were still novel enough that people paid just to walk aboard one.

With the passengers aboard, the little craft lifted lightly and soon was high above Jersey City. Julie looked through a viewport and saw the earth below looking like a swirly blue-white basketball. Passengers ate hot dogs and talked with each other until the lander arrived at the *Dolomite*'s geosynchronous orbit and locked onto one of the ship's entry ports.

Hoban, with Stan and Julie, came aboard the *Dolomite* with a group of eight other people, just a few of the hundreds who came up here every day from the Staten Island Spaceport. Accompanying them was a guide. He was giving his standard spiel about thruster jets and diosynchronous interruptor-type impellers and standard warp capacities.

"Right this way, folks," the tour guide was saying. He was a large man with pale blond hair, and wore a white vest with lavender polka dots under a crimson blazer. "Right this way you'll find the refreshment stand and, just beyond it, the souvenir booth. They carry official ship's souvenirs. Folks, these items are not sold in stores in the city. You can only get them here. There's a hall of diorama views of approaches to various planets. There's even a snack bar featuring delicacies from this world and many others. Right this way—"

The guide broke off his spiel when he noticed something unusual happening.

"Excuse me, you people there!"

He was talking to three people, two men and a woman, who had moved in the opposite direction from the crowd and now were about to open a door marked NO ADMITTANCE EXCEPT TO AUTHORIZED PERSONNEL in five different languages.

"Did you mean us?" one of the men said. He was short and plump and wore glasses. The woman beside him was a handsome creature, slim and with magnificent chestnut-red hair. She was beautiful even with the livid scar that ran down one cheek. The other man, somewhat older than the first two, looked dazed.

"Yes, you," the guide said. "Can't you read the sign on the door?"

"Of course we can," Stan replied. "It doesn't pertain to us."

"You're not trying to tell me you're ship's crew?"

"Certainly not," Stan said. "I'm the new owner."

"Impossible! I would have been told."

"I'm telling you right now. We're going aboard." Stan pushed at the door. The guide moved to stop him, then stopped abruptly when he felt a hand on his shoulder. The young woman had seized him, and she had a grip of steel.

"Madame, unhand me!" the guide said, trying to make a joke out of it, because people from the tour were staring. He tried to shake free, but Julie's fingers didn't budge.

"I'll be happy to let you go," she said. "Just don't interfere with the new owner."

"I have no proof that he's the new owner!" the guide said.

Julie shrugged. "What difference does it make to you, anyhow, who runs the ship? You've got your concession. You're selling your tickets and your hot dogs. You're doing all right."

The guide considered. He didn't want any trouble. Life was hard enough, why stir up trouble with people who were probably nutcases? The woman with the strong hands was right, what difference did it make to him?

"Do whatever you want," he said, stepping back as Julie released his shoulder.

Stan pushed open the door that led into the *Dolomite* proper. As it opened, an alarm went off deep inside the ship. The lights in the corridor behind the door began to flash. There was a sound of heavy running feet, and then two men in brown security-guard uniforms came hurrying up with carbines at port arms.

"What's going on?" one of the guards asked. "Halt, you people! No one is allowed here."

"We're authorized personnel," Stan said. "I'm the

new owner and these are my associates. Kindly escort
us to your commanding officer."

"Back off at once or I'll fire," the guard said. "This
weapon is set for immediate paralysis. The company
is not responsible for any broken limbs or other inju-
ries suffered while resisting authorized orders."

Julie said, "I warn you not to fire that thing." Her
body tensed. She seemed ready to throw herself at
the guards.

There was a moment of impasse. The guards
weren't sure what to do. The situation wasn't quite serious enough to warrant firing. Not yet. On the other
hand, what were they supposed to do? They knew
they could get into a lot of trouble if they didn't handle this right.

A tall man in officer's uniform came from a doorway inside the ship. "What is going on here?" he
asked.

The senior guard said, "These people are trying to
break in, Mr. Gill."

Gill had a long, dark, mournful face. His features
were small. His typical expression, in common with
those of many androids, was impassive and a little
melancholy. He stared at the new arrivals unbeliev-
ingly. At last he said, "Captain Hoban? Dr. Myakovsky?"

"And I am Julie Lish," Julie said, holding out her
hand.

Gill hesitated, then shook Julie's hand.

One of the guards asked, "Do you know these people, sir?"

"Yes," Gill said. "Stand back and let me handle
this."

The guards saluted and moved back against a wall.

"What is going on, Captain?" Gill asked.

Hoban looked unsure of himself, but his voice was
firm enough as he answered, "Mr. Gill, I have decided
to take command of the *Dolomite* again."

"But, sir," Gill protested, "a duly appointed court

stripped you of this command and gave it to me to hold until the new captain arrives."

"They had no right to relieve me of command," Hoban said.

"Are you sure of that, sir?"

"Of course I'm sure, and I am taking over the ship again pending a formal hearing."

"Perhaps you have that right, sir. I wouldn't know. But meantime there is a legal decision against you, and to the best of my knowledge that has not been rescinded."

Hoban looked confused. Stan put in, "We are going to appeal that ruling. A higher court can be counted on to reverse the decision."

"I sincerely hope so, sir. But in the meantime—"

"In the meantime," Hoban interrupted, showing a firmness that Stan had not been sure he possessed, "things return to where they were before. I will retain command of this ship until the higher court rules."

"Unfortunately, sir, I am bound by the lower court's decree."

"Your first loyalty," Hoban said, "is to me."

Gill looked doubtful. "That is not how my orders read, sir."

"Hang your orders!" Hoban cried. "I am giving you a direct command."

Gill looked puzzled, worried. "My orders are to fire on you or anyone else who tries to board this ship."

"I don't believe you'll do that, Gill." Hoban started to walk toward the entry leading to the interior of the ship.

"Guards!" Gill called sharply. "Switch to killing mode."

There was a double click as the guards switched their pulse rifles to killing mode.

Hoban smiled with a confidence he didn't feel and walked toward the entry.

Gill cried, "Stop!"

Stan and Julie fell into step beside Hoban, who continued to advance.

Gill stared at them. There was something like despair on his face. He said, "I must do what I must."

"And what is that, Gill?" Stan asked him.

Gill said, "Guards!"

The guards snapped to attention.

"Meet your new commander."

The guards saluted Hoban, who returned the salute.

"Now turn off your weapons"—another double click—"and attend to the incoming crew. They should be arriving any minute. Then you are dismissed."

"Yes, sir!" Both guards saluted, turned on their heels, and marched off.

"Welcome aboard, Commander," Gill said.

"Thank you, Gill," Hoban said. "I knew I could count on your loyalty."

"It's my conditioning that turned things your way, sir," Gill said. "I could not fire on you, nor ask the guards to do so. After our many tours of duty together, you and I have developed too many bonds. But I still think what you are doing is illegal."

"I know you feel that way," Hoban said. "You may leave when the guards return to Earth, and no hard feelings." He held out his hand.

Gill looked at it for a moment, then shook it. "If you don't mind, sir, I'd like to come along."

"But why, if you think this is illegal?"

"I don't care if it's illegal or not," Gill said. "I was just stating a fact. Since I couldn't fire on you, my conditioning in favor of government authority is canceled. I'm your man again, Captain, if you'll have me."

"It's likely to be dangerous," Hoban said.

"That is a matter of indifference to me."

"Then I'll be pleased to have you, Mr. Gill." Captain Hoban smiled.

"If you two are finished waltzing," Julie said sarcastically, "do you think we could get on with it?"

* * *

They accompanied Gill into the ship and to the control room.

Julie said to Gill, "How did you know what decision to make?"

"I didn't know," Gill muttered. "Androids don't have to make decisions. We just follow our conditioning."

"Lucky androids," Julie said.

"Gill, we're having some baggage lifted up from the space station," Stan put in. "With it there will be a large packing case. Please see that it is handled gently."

"Yes, sir."

"When they arrive, get the crew bundled down in hypersleep. And get all the tourists off this ship. I want us ready to depart an hour after the crew is aboard and bedded down."

Gill looked at Captain Hoban.

The captain nodded. "Accept his orders as if they were mine."

The volunteers for the voyage of the *Dolomite* marched in single file under the watchful eyes of armed guards. They left the olive-drab prison lander and marched into the short connecting tube that led into the ship proper. As soon as they were aboard, they all burst into a cheer. The guards gave them hard looks, but put away their weapons and returned to the lander, accompanied by the two guards from the *Dolomite*. Their job was to see that the prisoners got aboard the ship; once aboard, they were no longer prisoners, though not quite free men, either. The arrangement was that they'd report to the proper authorities after returning from their voyage, and show their good-conduct papers signed by the captain, and receive either a commutation of sentence or a complete amnesty. In practice, many of them never bothered to return, and their names went on a wanted list, to which the authorities gave only minor attention.

There were always plenty of new criminals to deal with; no one had any time for the older ones.

They followed the signs that had been set up to guide them to their quarter. But Walter Glint, a short, dark-haired barrel-chested man from Natchez who was Badger's closest friend aboard, noticed that Red Badger wasn't even bothering to look where he was going.

"Hey, Red! You been on this ship before?"

"You bet I have," Red Badger said. "I know her layout like the back of my hand."

"How come you never said anything about it when that Hoban guy asked if you'd met before?"

Badger shrugged. "If he didn't remember, I wasn't going to remind him. It was a pretty bad time for him. I'll tell you about it later."

They went into the crew's quarters. There was plenty of room. The *Dolomite* normally carried a crew of thirty-five, but Hoban had pared it down to the bare minimum after consulting with Stan. There was no trouble finding berths. Badger and Glint claimed their own corner, and were joined by their best friends from the federal facility. One of these, Connie Mindanao, was a diminutive woman, brown-skinned and black-haired and fierce looking, her features showing evidence of her mixed ancestry. She was the unlikely combination of a Moro from the Philippines and a Mohawk from New York's Iroquois Confederation. The only thing the two peoples had had in common was a history of head-hunting. Of the other two, one was a big black man from California named Andy Groggins, and the second was a taciturn Laotian hill woman who didn't say much but whose actions were direct and sudden, and apt to be lethal; her name was Min Dwin.

There were others who were friendly with Badger, and some who downright hated him. They sorted out their sleeping arrangements accordingly.

Badger was used to being the center of attention.

A voice came over the loudspeaker. "All crew! Put

away your gear and strip for hypersleep. Everybody must be on his acceleration couch in five minutes."

Badger called out, "What's our destination?"

His voice was picked up by a wall monitor. "There'll be a full briefing immediately upon your awakening," the loudspeaker voice replied.

"How long we going to sleep this time?" Badger asked.

"That information will be fed into the hypersleep machinery. No more questions, people! Get ready."

Connie Mindanao said, "What are they trying to pull on us? I don't know if I'm going to stand still for this." She looked at Badger. "What do you think, Red?"

"Relax," Badger told her. "Nothing much we can do about it just now. The ship's sealed, and anyhow, the guards are still outside. We've got no chance of making a run for it."

They all settled down onto their hypersleep couches. The lights dimmed.

19

The *Dolomite* left its geosynchronous orbit and proceeded slowly to jump point: a position in space well enough beyond Earth's orbit to permit subspace operation without peril to others. From there Hoban radioed for permission to disembark, and shortly thereafter received an okay from the Coast Guard monitoring station at L6.

Stan and his party strapped down. Hoban looked them over and asked, "All ready, Dr. Myakovsky?"

"Ready," Stan said.

"All right," Hoban said. "Mr. Gill—get us out of here!"

Gill's hands moved across the switches. The lights dimmed in response to the sudden power surge as the tachyonic converters whirled into action, compressing time and space, tighter, tighter, until—

—the *Dolomite* suddenly vanished from normal space.

The voyage had begun.

20

Julie was used to the dark. It was friendly and warm, and she felt safe in it. Only in the dark had she found security and safety, shielded away from men's eyes and their motives. The dark was the place where she had trained, so many years ago, when she had learned those matters of stealth and suddenness that were her protection and her trademark. It was then that she learned to make the darkness her own.

And so it had been for all her young life. But it was different now. This darkness that surrounded her now felt sinister, evil. Maybe that was because she knew something lurked within it, something that was trying to get her.

She stopped for a moment in midstep, trying to get her bearings. Her hearing extended itself through the darkness, searching. As her eyes became accustomed to the gloom she made out vast shapes on either side of her. They were machines, made of dark, glistening metal, and they towered above her. Spots of white light from some unknown source winked off metallic surfaces, and reflected from coils and condensers. They didn't even look like objects. They were like the ghosts of objects because their shapes were indistinct, ambiguous, swathed in a darkness that had gradation and depth, and was textured with the layers of silence.

A voice crackled in the tiny radio bug implanted in her ear.

"Julie? Do you see him yet?" It was Stan Myakovsky, calling from the *Dolomite*'s central control room. He wasn't far away, as distances go, but he could have been in another galaxy for all the good he could do her now.

"Not yet," she answered. "But I know he's in here somewhere."

"Be careful, huh?" Stan said. "I still think we should have delayed this run. I'm still not entirely satisfied with Norbert's control system."

Now was a hell of a time to tell her that. She decided to ignore it. Stan sounded agitated. Was he getting cold feet? Or was he just having an ordinary attack of nerves?

She snapped on a tiny flashlight. Ahead of her, picked up in the thin beam, she could see more profound glooms, silent caves of blackness where awful things might lurk. Some of these horrors were caused by the power of her imagination, but she was afraid that some were not.

It was not imagination that told her something in this great dark place was tracking her. She knew it was there. But where was it? She strained her senses to the utmost, trying to pick up some clue. Nothing. But she could tell it was out there. She had a sense of presence, almost like a sixth sense. It was what a successful thief needed above all else, and Julie was an extremely successful thief.

She thought back now on her years of training with

Shen Hui, the old Chinese master criminal. She first met him when she was a little girl, the youngest one in the Shanghai slave market that morning. She remembered peering at the crowd that had come to attend the auction, trying to catch a final glimpse of her mother. But she had already left, unwilling to watch her only daughter being sold on the open market. The men started bidding, men from different countries. Then one old man had outbid the rest, and had paid the auctioneer in taels of gold. That was Shen Hui.

He brought her to his house and raised her like his own flesh and blood. Shen Hui was a master thief, a master of the zen of thievery. He had taught her to develop her latent senses so that she could register things without literally seeing or hearing them. That ability came to her rescue now.

Yes, it was not just imagination. There was something near, and it was situated right over ... there!

She whirled as a great looming thing detached itself from the deep knot of shadows near a gigantic machine that lay shrouded in its own dust. She found it fascinating, the way the shadows moved and grew, like something not human, the way they resolved into one, and that shadow suddenly turned solid and launched itself at her with an explosive hiss.

"Julie! Watch out!" Stan's voice rang in her ears. He had picked up the sudden movement. But late. Stan was always late. What good could his warning do for her now? He never seemed to realize it. Not that she had expected anything more. She was responsible for herself. And Julie was already in motion as the thing came at her.

Her long legs, clad in skintight black plastic, pumped smoothly as she sprinted down the central aisle of the *Dolomite*'s great central cargo hold. The creature, three times her height, colored an unremitting black, with jaws filled with long closely packed fanglike teeth, came after her. Feeling herself being overtaken, Julie dodged and swerved around the faintly delineated center line of the hold. This one narrow strip had been set for twenty percent less of the faux gravity that so much resembled the real thing. Running on the light-gravity strip made her feel as though she had wings, so rapidly did she move, dodging fixed objects as they came up to smear her, vaulting over smaller obstacles, always moving, the sound of her own blood pounding in her ears.

The creature came running after her, and a ray of light from a globe in the ceiling picked it up for a moment. It appeared to be a full-size alien, with the typical backward-sloping cranium of its kind.

The thing was as startling as an apparition from hell. Its claws, with their doubled fingers, reached for her. Julie turned and fled down the narrow confines of the hold.

The area she ran in widened, and the creature managed to gain a few steps on her.

Stan, watching the action on a monitor in the control room, yelped in alarm as the creature loomed over her. He asked himself why he had ever agreed to let Julie take this training run. Thinking about it now, he could see that it had been an unnecessary risk. If anything went wrong, it could jeopardize the whole operation.

And aside from that, if Julie got hurt ... But he couldn't let himself think about that.

Julie and the alien dodged around enormous packing cases, cubes of plastic ten feet on a side. There were a dozen or so of them, and they were scattered randomly on the floor, part of the clutter that accumulates in any spaceship. Julie ran her fingers over the edge of a box. With a quick look aided by her flashlight, she had fixed its location. A memory of the placement of the other boxes was burned into her short-term memory. In her mind she could see the zigzag path she would have to follow to get to the next bulkhead. After that, a sally port served as a midpoint connection to the next part of the ship's hold.

She ran full out, counting off step by step. Crossing a crowded room in darkness with speed and silence is

one of a thief's most useful accomplishments. Julie
continued across the hold, her senses on red alert,
trying once again to locate the creature that was
stalking her. Norbert was good, he was very quiet, she
had to give him that. He had learned how to muffle
his body movements, and even to quiet the sounds
of his body functions. Good as he was, she still was
aware of him, but it was an awareness that flickered
in and out of existence.

After the midpoint sally exit, she came to the platform that blocked the way to the farthest exit. It was
a prestressed antimagnetic steel plate approximately
twenty feet wide by two hundred feet long, and five
inches deep. She climbed up onto it. It was drilled
with many large, irregularly spaced holes ranging in
diameter from two to five feet, where components
would be fitted later. Running the length of the plate
left you vulnerable to stepping into a hole and breaking a leg, or falling through an unshielded ventilator
shaft to the deck below.

She had to slow down to make it across. Julie went
down the length of the platform at a half-speed sprint,
unable visually to detect the openings in the darkness,
relying on memory. Norbert came loping along steadily after her. She noticed that he, too, must have mem-
orized the locations of the holes, because he was
moving confidently and quickly. She forced herself to
go a little faster, even though it increased her chances
of a fall.

She reached the far end and hopped off. Norbert
had gained several steps on her. She hoped to make it
up in the next stage.

Just ahead were the spare firing tubes, big cylin-
ders of cold-rolled steel, eighteen of them, each a
hundred and eighty feet long. Moving by touch, Julie
located a pipe with an aperture that would just permit
her to squeeze in. Norbert, with his greater size,
wouldn't be able to follow, would be forced to walk
on top of the slippery pipes, thus giving Julie a brief

breathing spell. A good escape could be composed of moments like these.

That, at least, was how it was supposed to work. Norbert stopped and looked at the pipe, started to go around it, then came back and managed somehow to collapse his shoulders and crawl into the pipe after her. She could hear the tortured metal-to-metal squealing as he pushed himself through the pipe.

Then she realized that not only was he in the pipe behind her, he was gaining, collapsing himself down to half his usual size and scuttling along like a giant malevolent insect. A sudden sense of claustrophobia came over Julie as she imagined Norbert's big clawed hand closing over her foot.

She forced herself to remain calm. "You won't go any faster in a panic," she reminded herself. One of the first lessons Shen Hui had taught her was to be extra cool in the face of a crisis, to force herself to slow down just when her senses were shrieking at her to speed up. This lesson stood her in good stead now. Suddenly the darkness came to an end and she was out of the pipe and running, a fraction of a second ahead of the alien.

She dodged instinctively as Norbert's arm reached out for her. In a moment's inattention, she slammed into a precariously balanced cart containing machine parts and ball bearings. Metal objects flew in all directions and clattered against the sides of the hold. Julie came down on a bearing in midstride and both her feet shot out from under her. Catlike, she turned in midair, throwing up a protective forearm before she went crashing to the floor on her face.

As she sprawled Norbert loomed above her, arms spread wide, jaws open in a terrifying grimace. Through his open jaws the little inner jaws came flickering out, more malevolent than a crazed pit viper.

Norbert lunged at her, and she was momentarily unable to do anything to protect herself. He was almost on her. . . .

She had an instant to wonder what he was pro-

grammed to do if he caught her . . . or did he make up
that part as he went along?

And then Norbert slipped on the bearings and lost
his balance.

His taloned feet raked the metal floor as he tried to
gain purchase. He crashed to the deck with a bone-
shattering sound.

For a moment Norbert sprawled there. His resem-
blance to a giant insect was now apparent as his arms
and legs twitched and vibrated, trying to find something to hold. Then he righted himself and was up
again and towering over her.

Unable to do anything, Stan had to watch. His fin-
gernails were already ragged, for he had been chew-
ing at bloody cuticles while monitoring Julie's
progress. He leaned forward, intent.

Julie, at the last possible moment, slipped through
the alien's claws and disappeared through the hori-
zontally closing metal slabs at the end of the hold.
The creature yowled in rage as the door shut in his
face and Julie shot the lock.

Immediately Norbert began wrenching at the door,
then, having no luck with the lock, turned his attention
to the hinges.

Julie meanwhile was streaking through the clut-
tered compartment, sprinting at full stride and manag-
ing somehow to avoid the clutter of machines and
packing cases that turned the place into an obstacle
course filled with cutting edges.

Stan was able to track her progress on his monitor
against a schematic of the ship's hold.

He watched a tiny silver dot, representing Julie,
dodge around objects ahead of a longer blue-black
streak that represented her pursuer.

"Come on, Julie," Stan muttered to himself. "You
don't have to run it this close! Pull the plug! Bail out!"

But Julie kept running. She seemed to be going for
some kind of a record. Never had she been so graceful, so light on her feet. She had reached the far end
of the compartment. The egress port was dogged

down tight. Norbert was less than five feet behind her now. He reached for her with taloned claws, ending in dagger-sharp tips. Julie stood her ground, and Stan couldn't help but admire the game quality of her courage. Then she ducked down and scuttled between the creature's legs, catching it by surprise, and escaping with nothing more than a shallow scratch on her right shoulder.

She was up to her full speed in two bounds, and for a moment she thought she had gained on it. But Norbert had learned something, too. He ignored her dodging run and came galloping up alongside her. His mouth, impossibly crowded with needle-tipped teeth, snarled and opened wide. From his jaw, and protruding through his mouth, came the hateful small replica of these jaws, composed of a small rectangular body part like a tongue, which ended in a mouth filled with white sharp teeth.

This was it. There was no place to go.

The creature moved in for the kill.

"Julie!" Stan screamed. "For God's sake!"

At that final moment Julie screamed at the creature, "Cancel predation functions!"

Norbert froze in midmovement. His feeding tube withdrew into his mouth. His jaws closed.

Julie then said, "Return to standard program."

She turned away from the creature, who stood frozen in position, and walked through the connecting passageway to Stan, who was still in the control room, sitting numbly in the big command chair near the computer.

21

In the control room, where he had been watching her progress on a TV monitor, Stan heaved a sigh of relief. He knew Julie would join him soon, after she had showered and changed. He just had time to check the condition of the men in hypersleep, and then he and Julie would be able to go over their plans.

He walked through a dilating door, down a short corridor, and into the long gray egg-shaped room that was devoted to hypersleep. The lights were low, leaving the place in an eternal twilight. The only sound Stan heard was the occasional short click of a circuit breaker.

The men lay in rows in what looked like large coffins with glass tops. Pipes and electrical lines connected all of the coffins and ran to power boxes on the walls. All this maze of equipment was run through instruments that measured output and indicated sudden anomalous changes, checking for heart rate, respiration, and for the electrical brain activity. Every hour, samples were taken of the sleepers' blood and stomach contents. Trace chemicals could set up strange chain reactions. It was necessary to keep the crew's internal environments very stable. Other meters on the wall showed dream activity; it was important for the crew members to dream as they slept. Dreaming too long suppressed can lead to psychosis.

For now, all was well. The men lay in their gray coffins. Most had their hands at their sides, some had crossed them on their chests. In one or two cases, the fingers pulled at each other. This was not abnormal. Events were occurring on deep levels of the brain that the dials and gauges couldn't read.

It was to be a journey of almost two weeks' duration. Not a long one, as space trips go. The men could have stayed awake throughout without harm. But it was policy on most ships to put the crew into hypersleep for anything longer than a week. For one thing, it saved on food and water—critical things on a spaceship. For another, it kept the men out of mischief. There was little to do on the outward leg of a deep-space voyage. The ship shuttled noiselessly through space, and time seemed to flow like invisible treacle.

Stan was pleased that there was no crew to contend with at the moment. He was somewhat less pleased that Captain Hoban had elected to take the hypersleep with his men. Stan would have enjoyed conversations with Hoban on the long outward journey.

"I'd like it, too," Hoban had said. "But frankly, I need the sleep. I'm badly in need of reintegration."

Hoban had come under severe pressure after being relieved of his ship's command. The charge that he had been drunk while on duty, though untrue, had been tough to fight. Even with all the recording instruments that were continuously running on the ship, it was unclear exactly how drunk he had been, or if indeed he had been drunk at all. There were matters of individual alcohol tolerance to consider. Even witnesses, the ship's officers, had been of two minds about what had really happened and to what extent Hoban bore responsibility.

If all this was upsetting to the investigating authorities, it was even more so to Hoban. He didn't know exactly himself what had happened in that fateful hour when the accident had occurred. His own defense mechanisms blocked his memory, preventing him from seeing a truth that might be damaging to him.

Hoban knew that, and so he couldn't help but wonder what his defenses were trying to block.

The hypersleep was known to enhance psychic integration. It gave you a chance to drop out of the world of actions and judgments, into a timeless place beyond questions of morality. Hoban had welcomed that.

Now Stan looked forward to resuscitating Hoban. It was a little limiting for him, having only Julie and Gill to talk to. Julie was a darling, of course, and he was absolutely mad about her. At the same time he couldn't help but recognize her limitations.

Although abundantly educated in the school of hard knocks, she had little formal training in the sciences. Worse, she had little interest in the arts and humanities. She tended to assume that material things were always the most desirable ones. This was an error in Stan's judgment, for how do you price a sunset or a mountain at dawn? How much for the song of the swallow? Still, he realized that he himself was no doubt guilty of the typical human error of overvaluing what he liked and undervaluing what others liked.

Talking with Gill was also limiting. Gill had formidable training in the sciences and knew a great deal about history and philosophy. This didn't give him judgment and compassion, however. For Gill, the proposition that the unexamined life was not worth living had no more relevance than $e=mc^2$. He wasn't equipped to examine the emotional dimension, though Stan thought he saw signs of promise.

After showering and changing, Julie fluffed her hair and rejoined Stan in the main control room. "How'd I do, Stan?" she asked.

Stan pulled himself together. In a voice that strove to be casual he said, "Quite well, Julie. You shaved fifteen seconds off yesterday's time. Keep on like this and you'll soon break your old mark of three minutes in the hold with Norbert."

"Norbert's getting too good," Julie said. "He's learning faster than I am. I'm sure he's smarter than the real thing."

The real thing, in this case, was the aliens Norbert so resembled, and who had caused such strange and deadly events on Earth.

Despite his appearance, however, Norbert was not an alien. He was a perfectly simulated robot model of an alien, equipped with a number of computer-driven programs, among which was the predator mode that Julie had been testing out. At the moment Norbert was in the control room with them, showing no sign of his former ferocity.

"How are you, Norbert?" Stan asked.

"I am fine, Doctor, as always."

"That was quite a little run you gave Julie. Did you think you were going to catch her this time?"

"I do not anticipate such things," Norbert replied.

"What would you have done if you had caught her?"

"What my programming told me to do," Norbert said.

"You would have killed her?"

"I cannot anticipate. I would have done what I had to do. Without feeling, I might add. But let me further add, if remorse were possible for a creature like myself, I would have felt it. Is there an analogue of remorse that does not involve feeling?"

"You have a complicated way of expressing yourself," Stan said.

Norbert nodded. "These matters require considerable thought and recalculation. And when they are expressed in words, they sometimes come out differently from what was intended."

"I've noticed that myself," Stan said.

Just at that moment a large brown dog came racing into the hold from a corridor. Stan had named him Mac. No one was quite sure how he had gotten aboard, but no one had gotten around to putting him off and now he was taking the voyage with them.

Mac ran to Norbert's feet and released a blue rubber ball he was holding in his jaws. The ball bounced three times and came to a rest at the monster's instep.

Stan and Julie watched to see what Norbert would do. The robot alien bent down and his long black arm, which somehow resembled an ant's chitinous appendage, brushed past the dog and picked up the ball. The monster's arm came back, then forward, and he threw the ball through the open door into the corridor. Barking furiously, the dog went chasing after it.

"All right, Norbert," Myakovsky said, "you've had your fun. Go to the laboratory. I'll want to scan some of your response codes. And get Mac to shut up. The crew is still in hypersleep."

"Yes, Dr. Myakovsky," Norbert said, and walked quietly out of the room.

22

Adoor slid open and Captain Hoban walked through. He had a dazed look in his eyes, and Stan knew he could not have been awake for long.

"You're early out of the hypersleep, Captain."

"Yes, sir. I had my dial set to get me up before the crew so I could pull myself together and have a talk with you."

"I suppose it is time we had that," Stan said. "I want to thank you again for throwing in your lot with me. I don't know where this will end up, but I'm glad to be on this adventure with you."

"Yes, sir. Could you tell me what it is exactly we are going to tell the crew?"

Julie, seated nearby, said, "Yes, Stan, I'd like to know myself."

Stan nodded. "We'll give a slightly altered version of what's going on."

"Are we on course, then?" Hoban asked.

"Yes. I fed the coordinates for AR-32 into the navigational computer."

"AR-32? I think I've heard of the place," Hoban said. "Wasn't there some trouble there a while back?"

"There was."

"Then why are we going there, sir?"

"We're pretty sure there's an alien super-hive on that planet, which apparently won't support anything else. A Bio-Pharm ship has been in orbit around AR-32, and my information is that they have been illegally harvesting royal jelly."

"Yes, sir. I understand. But what does that have to do with us?"

"I have a right to my share in that matter," Stan said. "Julie and I are going to relieve them of some of their plunder. Royal jelly is like pirate's gold, Hoban. It belongs to whoever takes it."

"Yes, sir. I don't have much trouble with that concept, though Gill might. But what bothers me, sir, is, does that mean we'll have to kill bugs?"

"It could come to that," Stan said, "though it is not the primary intention of our expedition."

"And might it not involve killing Bio-Pharm people, if we have to?"

Stan stared at him. "Yes, it could come to that. I don't expect them to be too happy about our taking what they have come to regard as their own, but frankly, I don't much care what they feel. No one gives up pirate's gold easily. If they insist on making a fight of it . . . Well, we'll take care of ourselves."

Hoban nodded, though he didn't look happy. "I suppose that follows, sir. But I wish you had told me all this beforehand."

"Would you not have come?" Stan said. "Would you seriously have preferred to stay down-and-out in that crummy boardinghouse I found you in?"

"No, I don't wish to be back there," Hoban said. "I'm just considering the situation."

"Then think about this," Stan said. "This situation

could make you rich. Julie and I intend to share our profits with you and the crew. They'll get a small percentage for the dangers they'll run. It won't be much out of our shares, but it'll be more money than they ever saw before."

"Sounds good, sir," Hoban said. But he was still worried. What good was it to be rich if you were also dead?

The time was nearing to wake the crew from hypersleep. The flight was almost at an end. Their destination, the planet AR-32, was coming up on the screens, a glowing dot in the dark sky. Julie knew this would be her last time alone with Stan for a long time.

There was a lot to do, a lot of last-minute details to attend to, and she didn't know when she and Stan would get some quiet time alone. Maybe not until they had finished the expedition—or to call it by its true name, their raid. And that could take time. And if everything didn't go just right . . .

Julie shook her head irritably. There was no sense thinking about failure. Hadn't Shen Hui instilled that much in her?

23

When Julie came into the control room, Stan was still seated in the big, padded command chair. He had taken an ampoule of royal jelly from a dozen that were nested in the padded box on the nearby worktable. He was holding the ampoule up to one of the arc lights, twirling it between his fingers and admiring its bluish glow in the light.

As usual, Julie was both attracted and repelled by the liquid and what it could do to Stan. Yet she had been hoping they could spend this evening together, doing things together instead of thinking about them. Sometimes she thought Stan allowed himself to have real experiences only for the pleasure of reliving them later, as he was able to do with the royal jelly.

Why did he love that stuff so much? She knew it eased the pain of his disease. But it was more than just a remedy: he was using it as a drug. And Julie didn't approve of taking drugs.

She hadn't tried the stuff herself. A well-trained thief allows nothing to dull her senses. Shen Hui and life itself had taught her this lesson. And yet, much as she missed him when he launched himself into the unknown regions that the drug brought him to, a part of her went with him, because she knew how Stan felt about her.

Returning the ampoule to its case, Stan asked, "What did you think about Norbert's performance?"

"He's ready," she said. "You've done an amazing thing, Stan. Created a robot alien good enough to fool the real ones."

"Except for the pheromones," Stan pointed out.

"You've taken care of that, too. With the short-range zeta fields you've developed, plus the pheromone-altering qualities of the royal jelly, the aliens will think Norbert is one of them."

Stan nodded. "Just like it was with Ari." Stan was referring to how his cybernetic ant, Ari, had been programmed to enter the colony of a similar-looking ant species, where the other ants accepted him as the real thing.

"How close are we now, Stan?" Julie asked.

Stan punched up the computer screen in front of him. Numbers flowed across it, and lines weaved in and out and then held firm.

"We're nearing the vicinity of AR-32," Stan told her. "It's time to get the crew out of hypersleep."

"The adventure begins," Julie said softly.

"That's right." Stan took out the ampoule of royal jelly again. "We need a lot more of this stuff, and AR-32 has it for us. It's funny how a single substance can be both more valuable than diamonds and more necessary for life than water. More necessary for my life, anyhow."

He swirled the little glass tube and watched the liquid flow. Then he looked at Julie.

"You look very lovely tonight."

She smiled back mockingly. "Pretty as a shot glass, as they'd say in the Old West."

"No, I really mean it," Stan said. "You know how I feel about you, don't you?"

"Maybe I do," Julie said. "But it's not because you ever talk about it."

"I've always been shy," Stan said. Abruptly he swallowed the ampoule. "I'm going to go lie down now, Julie. Let's talk more later."

Without waiting for her answer, Stan shambled off to his small office just to the right of the main-control-room entrance. Within it a folding cot was built into the wall. He lay down on it now, without bothering to take off his glasses.

With Xeno-Zip there was no habituation. Each time was like the first. It always amazed him just how quickly the stuff took effect. It was like no other drug he had ever tried, neither medicinal nor recreational, and Stan had tried them all. Alien royal jelly was neither a stimulant nor a soporific, though it had effects similar to both. Primarily it was a way of gaining instant access to all parts of your own brain, a royal road to your own dreams and memories. With royal jelly you could zoom in on your past like a skilled photographer zooming in on a detail, readjusting focus to bring up those images that had faded out. You could freeze the frame on what seemed like reality. You could see what you wanted to see, as often as you liked, and then step outside the frame and watch yourself in the act of seeing. Nor was that all it did. Royal jelly was a painkiller, too, relieving the throb of the cancer that was shattering his life.

The vial dropped from his fingers. It fell to the floor, taking no more than a fraction of a second to shatter on the deck. And in that microsecond, Stan watched it all happen again.

24

irst came the rush. It seemed to move along his arteries, and Stan pictured himself, a tiny man in a canoe adrift on the great red waters of his bloodstream. The vision exploded into a thousand fragments, and in each fragment the scene was repeated. The fragments of his vision came together, like millions of diamond particles striving to become a diamond, and then exploded outward again like firework displays arcing in all directions. He could hear a sound that was accompanying this, and he couldn't tell what it was at first, a deep-throated roar that could have come from no human source. At first he thought it was the gods singing, great choruses of ancient gods wearing strange headdresses, some with the heads of ducks and turtles, some jaguars, some foxes. And near them, suspended in shining space, were other choirs of women-gods, full-breasted Brunhildes and slen-

der Naiads, and their song was full of sorrow and
promise.

   As the ampoule fell to the floor, Stan was already
dozing fitfully. Tiny muscles in his eyelids jerked and
twitched: REM sleep, but of a previously unheard-of
intensity. Dream sleep, but with awareness. Blue-
green lights played across his face. It was a broad
face, with the beginning of a double chin. Light
glinted off his glasses and threw a shadow on his
small chin. He looked far younger than his twenty-
eight years; like a schoolboy again, coming back to
the big old house where he had lived with his parents
before the devastation wrought by the aliens. Again
he saw his stern father, the scholar, always with an
ironic little Greek or Latin phrase on his lips; and his
mother, with her high forehead, flinty gray eyes, and
hastily pinned-up mass of dark blond hair.
   Then he seemed to be walking down a long corridor. On either side, standing in niches like statues,
were replicas of his parents at every age and in every
mood. Stan could, in his imagination, freeze the
frame, stop his parents in midtrack, and walk around
them, inspecting them from every angle, and then
start the tape of memory running again. All this while
the ampoule was in midair.
   The ampoule was still falling from his hand, and he
could segue instantly from where he was to another
memory, himself after class in high school, walking
along beside the little brook that ran behind his home,
thinking about everything under the sun except his
homework assignments. Stan looked down on the
work given him by his teachers. He thought it was beneath his intellectual level, unworthy of his efforts. So
disdainful was he of school that his parents feared he
would not graduate. But he did graduate—there he
was at his own graduation, wearing an English
schoolboy's suit his parents had bought him while

they were attending a seminar in London. He had always hated that suit; he had looked damned silly next to the casual attire of the other boys.

There were many scenes like that, ready for him to step into, but Stan wasn't in the mood for childhood memories. There were other things he wanted to look at. Other times. Other people, places, things.

And so he moved, the ampoule still falling, moved as a spiritual presence, down the spiraling, faintly glowing corridors of the years. And now he was a man, in his twenties, already a well-known scientist, and he was in the doctor's office, buttoning his shirt, listening dumbly as Dr. Johnston said, "I might as well give it to you straight, Dr. Myakovsky. You were correct in your surmise about those black marks on your chest and back. They are indeed cancers."

"Is my condition terminal?"

"Yes." The doctor nodded gravely. "In fact, you don't have much time left. The condition, as I'm sure you know, is incurable. But its progress can be slowed, and we can ease some of the symptoms. You already have the medicine we prescribe for such cases. And there is also this."

The doctor held out a small plastic box. Within it, packed in foam rubber, were a dozen ampoules of a bluish liquid.

"This is royal jelly. Have you heard of it?"

Stan nodded. "If memory serves, it is produced by the aliens."

"That is correct," Dr. Johnston said. "I must tell you it's no cure. But it should relieve the symptoms. It could be just what you're looking for."

"Does it have much in the way of side effects?"

The doctor smiled grimly. "It has indeed. That's why it hasn't received government approval yet, though many people use it. Indeed, it has become the most-sought-after consciousness-altering substance in existence. It gives some an intense feeling of well-being and competence. Others experience levels of their own being not normally perceived. Still others have an orgasm that seems to go on forever."

"At least I'm going to die happy," Stan said.

But of course there were also the bad side effects. Some people had been known to go berserk on the drug, or to undergo personality changes so great that their own families didn't recognize them. Could that be happening in his case?

And then he forgot his concern as the images swept him up again. There was so much to look at! So many memories, all nicely staged and lighted, waiting for him, the sole audience, to put them into motion. It was like owning all of the theaters in the world, and in each of them a different movie was playing, and each movie starred himself, Stan Myakovsky, in all the scenes of his life. He glided past them, a ghostly presence in his own memories.

25

Red Badger was one of
the first crewmen revived from hypersleep. He
stretched and yawned, then carefully unplugged the
leads that connected him to the central sleep inducer.
He looked around. The rest of the crew was starting
to revive. Cheerful music was playing over the PA system. There were sounds of coughing and spitting as
men cleared their throats for the first time in almost
a month.

Coffee was available at a little table. Crew were always given coffee mixed with a new amphetamine
upon first awakening. It was needed to help them
throw off the effects of hypersleep.

Badger sipped at a black sweetened cup of coffee
and felt his head clear.

"You okay, Red?" It was Walter Glint, his sidekick.

"Yeah, I'm fine."

"Min?"

The Laotian hill woman grunted her assent.

"Connie?"

"I'm great, Badger," Connie Mindanao said. "You figure this might be a bonus run?"

"For extra-hazardous duty? They haven't said yet."

"I hope so."

"Why?"

"I've got a ranch house in Bangio I'm trying to pay off."

"There just might be easier ways," Badger said. He looked around. "That's funny."

"What's that, Red?"

"They usually post the ship's destination in the crew quarters. But look for yourself—the board's empty."

"Yeah, that *is* funny," Glint said. "But there's a notice there."

Badger said, "I can see it, dummy. General assembly in twenty minutes. The captain and the owner's gonna talk to us."

Glint said, "You've been on these ships longer than I have. That's not the way they usually do it, is it, Red?"

"Nope." Badger scratched his jaw. "I'll bet they're up to something. This might be interesting, Glint."

The loudspeaker said, "All crew! Assemble at once in the main theater."

Stan and Julie walked out onto the raised stage. The crewmen looked up attentively when he rapped a pointer on the lectern to get their attention.

"Our destination is not far away now," Stan said. "It is a small O-type star named AR-32 in the standard catalog. Around it revolves a single planet, with several good-sized moons to keep it company. These moons create violent and unpredictable weather currents on the planet, which has been named Vista. Captain Hoban, do you know anything about this planet?"

Hoban had been sitting to one side of the stage. He

cleared his throat now and said, "I have heard of the place, sir. They used to call it the Festerhole, back when there were still a lot of pirates and privateers operating in the space lanes. There was once a jelly-gathering operation there involving one of the bionationals. That was some years ago. To the best of my knowledge it has been deserted since."

Stan thought, Good old honest Hoban telling the crew more than they need to know! Still, they'd have to find out sometime what this mission really involved.

The crew stirred and looked at each other. This talk of the Festerhole was making them uneasy. What was this assignment, anyhow? What was it the powers wanted them to do this time? No one had spoken about a bug-hunting expedition. That called for extra pay!

There was a rising murmur of protest from the crew. The greatest menace of recent times were the aliens, those big black monsters who had been pushed off Earth with difficulty, and elsewhere continued to show their murderous abilities in the face of everything Earth had been able to throw against them.

Badger rose to his feet and said, "Sir, this wouldn't by any chance be a bug-hunting expedition, would it?"

"Not exactly," Stan said.

"Then what exactly is it . . . sir?"

Stan ignored the red-haired crewman's insolent tone. "This is basically a salvage operation," he said. "We'll be taking a load of royal jelly off a wrecked freighter."

"Yes, sir," Badger said. "And aren't the bugs going to have something to say about that?"

"Our information is that there are no bugs on the wreck. We'll go in fast, take what we need, and be out of there again. There's also the possibility we'll find an abandoned hive on the planet. The jelly in that could be worth millions."

Walter Glint said, "Nothing was said about bugs when we volunteered, sir."

"Of course not," Stan said. "My information is secret. If I told you back on Earth, half the freelance salvagers from Earth and the colonies would be there now."

"Bugs can be dangerous," Glint said.

"Not when you take precautions," Stan quickly put in. "You were warned that this was hazardous duty. You're not getting time off your sentences for sitting around in some holiday spot. And remember, there's bonus pay in this for all of you. It could come to quite a lot, if the salvage is as rich as I think it is."

"How much?" Badger asked.

"That's impossible to calculate before we have it," Stan said. "Don't worry, there is a standard formula for crew shares. I intend to double it."

The men cheered. Even Badger smiled and sat down. This was interesting, he thought. He wondered what would come next.

26

Stan rapped for attention. But before he could get started again, a door opened and a man came in. He moved rapidly and with a strange grace, a cross between a glide and a lope. His face was expressionless. Although all of his individual features were human, the total result was not human at all. The crew knew at once, even before the introduction, that this man was a synthetic. Captain Hoban's introduction clinched the matter.

"People, this is Gill, an artificial man from the Valparaiso People Factory. He's the second-in-command."

"Sorry to be late, Dr. Myakovsky," Gill said. "I just finished the energy readings."

"No problem, Mr. Gill. Take a seat."

Gill sat down by himself in the back of the room.

Gill was a solitary. In recent years the People Factory in Valparaiso, Chile, where many of the better synthetics were produced, had been doing an im-

proved job on skin colors and texturing. Gone was
that old look of damp putty that had once character-
ized synthetic people and had provided a basis for so
many jokes by bad comedians. Now the only reliable
visual gauge for detection of an android was the
speed of their comprehension responses. That and a
certain mechanical jerkiness to their movements,
since the final stage of fairing the input levels and
ranges of the synthetics' operating systems was a
slow, expensive process, and many employers didn't
care if a synthetic's hand trembled as long as he didn't
drop the test tube or light stylus—or whatever.

Despite their artificial origins, synthetic men were
full-fledged members of human society, with voting
rights and a sexual program.

Stan was about to go on. But just at that moment,
from an outer corridor, Mac the dog came trotting
into the room. He had a bright blue rubber ball in his
mouth, and he looked around expectantly.

Someone in the crew laughed. "Fetch it here, boy!"

And then something else came into the room behind the dog.

It came loping in on all fours, and at first glance it
looked like a beetle the size of a rhinoceros. It was
colored a shiny, unrelieved black. Its skull was very
long and curved back over its shoulders. It was
toothed like a fiend and taloned like the devil itself. It
was Norbert. And he looked like he had just come
from hell.

There was silence for one long straining moment.

And then pandemonium broke loose.

The crew scrambled to their feet and started running for the exits. Their work boots clattered on the
metal deck as they surged toward the exit door, trying
to push each other out of the way.

Stan grabbed the microphone and shouted, "Just
stay where you are! Do not make any aggressive
movements! Norbert will not harm you, but he is programmed to resist aggression. Just stay calm!"

It was not a calm-making situation. Yet even now

catastrophe could have been averted. The crew was quieting down, coming out of its panic, starting to make jokes. Norbert was just standing there, making no sign that he was going to attack anyone. And then he was bending, slowly picking up the dog's rubber ball, throwing it back to him.

It could have ended right there. But there was always a wise guy around, someone who had to push things a little too far.

This time it was a crewman known as Steroid Johnny, an overmuscled hunk in a skimpy T-shirt, tight jeans, and lineman's boots, who carried an unlicensed pressor rod in his boot and liked to cause trouble.

Steroid Johnny saw his chance now. "Come on, Harris," he said to a lean, grinning blond man lounging beside him. "Let's take this sucker down. Shouldn't be no aliens here anyhow."

The two men advanced on the motionless robot alien. Steroid Johnny winked at Harris, who went slinking around to the right, picking up a crowbar from a toolbox as he went. The robot's head swiveled, keeping both men under surveillance. Johnny feinted to his left, then went straight in at Norbert. Five feet away he stopped and turned on his pressor beam. He directed it at Norbert's back-sloping head.

Norbert was pushed back hard—for a moment.

Then the big robot shrugged his way around the pressor beam, ducked under it, and was moving toward Johnny. Johnny backed up and tried to get the pressor beam into a blocking position, but Norbert moved faster, lunged forward, his jaws opened, the inner jaws shooting out of his mouth. The pressor beam fell to the deck. Johnny tried to get out of the way, but Norbert already had one big hooked claw clamped on his left shoulder.

Johnny screamed as he was lifted straight into the air by the skin of his shoulder. He hung there in Norbert's grip, screaming, struggling to break free. Norbert's inner jaws, impelled with all the energy of his powerful crysteel-mesh throat muscles, drove through Johnny's chest, splitting him like a side of beef. Norbert dropped the red dripping thing to the deck and turned, ready for the next one.

Harris, seeing the way things were going as he ran to attack Norbert, tried to pull up in midstride. Too late. Norbert swung around like a grotesque yet graceful ballet dancer and struck out with one of his taloned feet. The blow landed high on Harris's sternum. Norbert's talons made an audible hissing sound as they cut through the air, driven by the force of his heavy shoulder muscles. The talons ripped Harris apart from the left shoulder blade to his right hipbone. Harris opened his mouth to scream, but no sounds came out. His lungs had been punctured in the blow. He made an ugly squishing sound as he fell to the deck.

The rest of the crew took this in and froze in position. They had never seen anything move as fast as Norbert, when he was aroused.

Norbert halted, looking around. He seemed about to attack again. Just in time, Stan shouted out the shutdown order: "Priority override! Code Myrmidon!"

Norbert froze in position, awaiting further orders.

It was a moment of balanced possibilities. The crew seemed on the verge of panic, ready to run out of the control room screaming.

Captain Hoban gulped hard and felt nausea at the back of his throat, but he knew he had to control the men. He got hold of himself and said coldly, "Two of you there, get pails and mops and clean up that mess. See what comes of not following orders? This didn't have to happen. Now get a move on. . . ."

There was an awkward, sullen moment, and then the crew obeyed. And the ship *Dolomite* hurtled on toward its rendezvous with AR-32.

27

Subdued, the crew returned to their quarters. The men seemed dazed, unsure of what to think. All of them except Min Dwin, the Laotian hill woman. She went directly to her bunk and pulled out her spacebag. From it she took out a long object in a flat leather sheath. She pulled it free. It was a machete, sharpened to a razor edge.

Badger said, "What are you up to, Min?"

"Those bastards killed Johnny," Min said. "I'm going to get me some officer meat."

"With that? They'll cut you down before you get within ten feet of them."

"Maybe I can pick up a gun. One of those that fires the softslugs. I'd like to see that weird doctor with the glasses take one in the gut." She started toward the passageway leading back to the main ship's stations.

"Hold on a minute, Min," Badger said.

She stopped and turned. "Yeah, what is it?"

"Johnny was your man, huh?"

"Yeah. It was a recent thing. Now it's over. What about it?"

"Come over here and sit down," Badger said.

Reluctantly she complied, sitting on a locker with the machete balanced on her knees.

"Min, I understand you're plenty pissed off. I am, too. I wasn't all that fond of Steroid Johnny, or his friend Harris, but I wouldn't have wanted what happened to them."

"Right. So?"

"So this. It was Johnny's own fault, Min."

"It would never have happened if that professor guy hadn't brought that thing along."

"Sure. That thing he calls Norbert is obviously dangerous. But so what? We work around dangerous stuff all the time. That's what we volunteered for."

"I know. But Johnny—"

"Johnny disobeyed a direct order. He thought he knew better. I hate to say it, Min, but him and Harris got what they deserved."

"I never thought I'd hear you saying this, Red," Min said. "Who's side you on, anyhow? You suddenly turned into a company man?"

"I'm just telling it like it is," Badger said. "It's like somebody told Johnny not to stick his hand into a buzz saw, and he went and did it anyway. Who would you kill then?"

Min twisted her fingers together in an agony of indecision. "I don't know, Red. It doesn't seem right just to leave it."

"You're right about that," Badger said. "But now's not the time to do anything about it. You go walking out of here with that machete, they'll put you down fast and ask questions later."

"Aren't we going to do anything?"

"Sure we are. But not now."

"When, then?"

"Look," Badger said, "don't push it with me. I know you're sad over Johnny. You'll get over it soon and find someone else. As for what we're going to do, we're going to wait and see how things develop. When we make a move—if we do—they won't be expecting it. Is that fair enough?"

"Yeah," Min said. "I guess it is. You got any drugs on you, Red?"

"Walter here takes care of my supply. What have you got, Glint?"

Glint had a first-rate stock of assorted chemicals. He was the crew's supplier and he always had plenty to sell.

"Try this one," he said, taking a pillbox out of his spacebag and shaking out two into his hand. "This'll make you forget Johnny ever existed. If you like them, I'll make you a good price for a hundred. But these two are on the house."

"Thanks, Walter," she said.

"Hey, what are friends for?" said Walter Glint.

28

Gill sat at the control board, his fingers playing sensitively over the buttons. A telltale above his head gave a readout on orbit and showed a digital display of gravity vectors. Another telltale showed electromagnetic activity. AR-32, the planet itself, had come up rapidly and now filled most of another larger screen.

The planet was colored a dusty yellow and gray, with occasional black and purple markings indicating barren mountain ranges. Large livid splotches showed dead seabeds. A faint shadow darkened the upper right hand corner of the screen; it was cast by Ingo, second largest moon of AR-32, made of nearly seventy-percent telluric iron.

While Gill set up the orbiting procedure, Captain Hoban slid into a control chair beside him and ran up a readout on electrical and solar phenomena on the planet's surface. His sad face creased into a puzzled frown.

"I'm getting some strange signals," he told Stan.

"Where are they coming from?"

"That's what's strange. I can't get a fix. They keep on shifting."

"Can you derive any information as to their production?" Stan asked.

"Beg pardon, sir?"

"Is someone making these signals, or are they natural phenomena?"

"At this stage I can't tell," Hoban said. "We have no definite data on any other ships in the area."

"There's a lot of solar debris around, though," Stan said. "No telling yet what it might be."

Gill punched up another set of numbers. "The weather down there on the surface is even worse than you expected, Dr. Myakovsky."

Julie came into the control room. She had already changed into a plasteel landing outfit. The cobalt-blue plastic form-fitting clothing with its orange flashes looked stunning on her. Stan's heart was in his mouth as he watched her.

"Are we ready to go down?" Julie asked.

Captain Hoban said, "I wouldn't recommend it, Miss Lish. The surface phenomena are worse than we were led to believe. Perhaps if we give the weather time to settle down a little ..."

Julie shook her head impatiently. "There's no time for that. If our worst peril is from the weather, Captain, we're doing very well indeed!"

"I suppose that's true," Hoban said. He turned to Gill. "Are you ready to accompany the party, Gill?"

"I am, of course, ready," the synthetic man said. "I have taken the liberty of asking for volunteers for this. There are five of them, and they are waiting for your orders."

He stood up from the control panel. He was tall, and even with his mismatched features, he was good-looking. If he had been a true man, you would have said there was something haunted about his expression. Since he was only a synthetic, you had to figure there'd been something amiss with his facial mold.

"Captain Hoban," said Stan, "can you show us our target in more detail?"

Hoban nodded and fine-tuned the controls. AR-32's surface sprang up into high magnification. Fractal-mapped shapes blew up in size and complexity. Hoban adjusted the magnification again. A tiny dot on the landscape grew quickly, until, at extreme magnification, it turned into a low dark earthen dome that rose up from the flat plain, showing up well against the rugged landscape.

"That's the hive," Hoban said. "Not easy to miss it. It's the biggest thing in this part of the planet."

"Looks pretty quiet," Stan mused.

"We're still a long way from the surface," Gill reminded him. "Things could change by the time we get there."

"True enough," Stan said. "But what the hell, this is what we've come for. Julie? Are you ready?"

"Ready, Stan," Julie said. "It's going to be a walk in the park."

Stan wished he shared her confidence.

"Why are you going to the surface?" Hoban asked. "I thought we were coming to look for an orbiting wreck."

"All in good time," Stan said. "Right now we've got the hive below us and no sign of life around it. If we can get a load of royal jelly from there, we can take care of the freighter later."

"Right on," Julie said. "Let's go for all the marbles."

Stan felt encouraged by the beautiful thief's cheerfulness and determination. Maybe this thing was going to go all right, after all.

29

The number-one lander was in its own bay, stacked parallel to the backup lander, just behind the big hold where Julie had made her last training run with Norbert. Now Norbert walked behind Stan and Julie, holding Mac the dog in his arms. There was something doglike about the robot's posture; in a sense he was a mechanical watchdog, ferocious when challenged, utterly loyal to his master, Stan. Behind Norbert, and keeping their distance, were the five volunteers for the landing party. They had been promised a sufficient bonus for this undertaking, enough for avarice to overcome common sense. But, of course, if they'd had common sense, they wouldn't have been in space on the *Dolomite* in the first place.

Captain Hoban, who was already at the number-one lander waiting for them, initiated the hatch-opening procedure. The lander, nestled in its bay, was almost a hundred feet long. It contained a miniature laboratory and was fully equipped with the telemetry needed for the mission.

Norbert was proceeding to the hatch when Mac the dog came streaking out of the corridor, the rubber ball in his jaws. He raced into the lander just ahead of Norbert.

"We'd better get that dog out of there," Hoban said.

"Let him stay," said Stan. "He may be of some use accompanying Norbert once we're on the surface."

"Just as you wish, sir," Hoban said. "I wish I were going with you."

"I wish you were, too," said Stan. "But we need you here on the *Dolomite*. If anything goes wrong, we're absolutely dependent on you for backup."

"Don't worry, Stan, nothing's going to go wrong," Julie said. Her smile was brilliant. "Don't you agree, Gill?"

"Optimism has not been factored into me," Gill said. "I am constructed to understand situations, not to have feelings about them."

"You're missing the best part," Julie said. "Having feelings about stuff is what it's all about."

"I've often wondered about that," Gill said.

"Maybe someday you'll find out. Are we ready?"

"After you," Stan said.

She made a mocking little salute and stepped into the lander. The others followed. Captain Hoban waited until he heard Stan report on the voice channel that the lander was well sealed and all systems were on-line. Then he returned to the control room and initiated the takeoff procedure.

The lander fell away from the *Dolomite*'s hull and dropped toward the swirling surface of AR-32. Stan adjusted his restraining harness and called out, "Everybody secure?"

The five volunteers from the crew were strapped down in the forward cabin. They were carrying weapons that had been issued to them by Gill: pulse rifles and vibrators. All had been given suppressors. These state-of-the-art electronic machines, about a meter long and weighing less than a pound, were clipped to their belts. The suppressors emitted a complex waveform that confused an alien's vision, rendering the wearer invisible.

Julie and Gill were lying on deceleration couches in the main cabin behind Stan. Norbert was crouched all the way in the rear, holding a stanchion in one clawed hand and cuddling Mac with the other. There was no seat aboard the lander large enough to hold the big robot alien. But his strength was such that it was likelier the stanchion would move than his grip be torn loose.

Then Captain Hoban's face appeared on the screen. "Dr. Myakovsky, are you ready for release?"

"Ready, Captain," Stan said. "Open up and turn us loose."

There was a powerful humming noise from the *Dolomite*'s interior motors, a noise that could be felt inside the lander as vibration. The *Dolomite*'s bay doors slid open revealing the star-studded sky as seen from AR-32's upper atmosphere. There was a click as the doors locked in the open position. Then a bright green telltale on Stan's control board came to life.

"You've got control, Stan."

Stan felt his stomach turn over as the lander pulled away from the *Dolomite*. G-forces twisted at his gut. Sudden sharp flashes of pain went through his chest. A haze of pinkish red enclosed his vision, with blackness beginning to form on the edges.

"Stan!" Julie called out. "We're coming down pretty fast."

Gill said, "Hull ionization is beginning to be a factor."

Stan got himself under control. His fingers danced on the controls. "Okay, I've got it. Gill, give me a landing vector."

They were deep into AR-32's atmosphere. Long, thin, ragged yellow clouds, twisting and turning into fantastic shapes, whipped past the Perspex viewing

window. There was a rattle of hailstones striking the
hull as they passed through a temperature inversion
layer in the atmosphere.

The image of Captain Hoban jumped in and out of
focus on the screen. But his voice was steady as he
said, "Dr. Myakovsky, this planet has a heavy radia-
tion belt. Better kick on through it at best speed."

"What do you think I'm doing?" Stan gritted. "Sight-
seeing?"

"Are you all right, Doctor?" Hoban asked. "You
don't look so good."

"I feel great," Stan said through gritted teeth. Black
dots were swimming behind his eyes as he fought to
hang on to consciousness. His chest burned with a familiar agony. He could feel the straps of the restraining harness tug at his shoulders as he cut down
power and started to bring up the ship's nose. The atmosphere lightened and darkened as they went
through more cloud layers. On the computer screen,
the flight path for their landing came in glowing am-
ber.

Gill said, "We're on the final approach now. Good
going, Stan."

Stan forced himself to concentrate, though he
was none too sure he could remain conscious. The
g-forces eased as he pulled the lander into position
for its landing run.

There was more visibility near the ground. In the
tawny yellow light Stan could see house-sized boulders strewn across a tilted plain. They were fast approaching an old riverbed, wide and level, and that
seemed a good place to make the final landing.

Stan adjusted the trim tabs and began the landing
procedure. The lander put her nose up and steadied.
Wind gusts shook the ship just as it touched down.
There was a crunch as they smacked the ground, then
a bad moment as the lander soared into the air again.
Then it came down again, hard, and this time it stayed
down.

When the lander had come completely to a stop, Julie looked around and said, "Welcome to AR-32, everyone. It may not look like much, but this planet is going to make us rich."

"Or dead," Stan muttered, but to himself.

30

Back on the *Dolomite*, Captain Hoban watched the lander spin away on the viewscreen. He felt hollow, useless. There was nothing for him to do at the moment. Gloomy thoughts began to invade his mind.

Captain Hoban had continued to think about suicide. This didn't surprise him. He only found it strange that he hadn't thought of it before, during all the bad days of the trial.

He shook his head. Back then, something had buoyed his spirits, some belief that he was going to come out of this all right. And then his opportunity had seemed to arrive when Stan visited him in Jersey City and made his offer, and here he was in space again. But he had a bad feeling about it. His thoughts were full of foreboding images, and the men torn apart by Norbert hadn't helped his mood any. He suspected there would be a lot more deaths ahead, maybe even his own. Maybe he wouldn't have to commit suicide after all.

On the other hand, he could do it now. Gill could handle the ship all right. Stan and Julie didn't really need him. . . .

Somewhere in his mind, Hoban knew this was a crazy line of thinking. He was a valuable person with reasons for living. He had nothing to be ashamed of. And yet the shame was there, constantly bubbling up from the depths of his mind, a seemingly automatic process that he couldn't shut off.

It obsessed him that he had been dismissed from his own ship. He still burned with shame when he remembered how the authorities had revoked his license. It was all so terrible, and so unfair. Probably there was no hope of real reinstatement. He had let Stan talk him into joining this crazy venture without thinking it through. When he got back to Earth—if he got back—the authorities would be merciless with him. Maybe he'd gone far enough.

He was preoccupied with his thoughts, and so was not pleased when he heard a crisp knock at the door of his stateroom. Now that the lander was away, he'd been hoping for a few minutes alone so he could get caught up on writing the ship's log.

"Who is it?" he asked.

"Crewman Badger, sir."

Hoban sighed. He still didn't know why he hadn't rejected Badger at the prison, when he had the chance. He had finally remembered where he'd seen him. Badger had been one of the crew of the *Dolomite* when he'd had his accident in the asteroids, one of the men who had witnessed his disgrace.

Damn, damn, damn.

He didn't like Badger, thought he was sly and untrustworthy. But he had to admit, the man hadn't given him any trouble before. He did know Badger's type. Hoban had looked over the comment sheets on the crew, sheets compiled by other captains on other flights. The word on Badger was that he was cunning, insubordinate, and a troublemaker. There was no specific charge against him on the evaluation sheets, but the implication was clear enough. "Come in, Crewman Badger. What do you want?"

"I have the latest report on the debris in this area of space, sir."

"Why didn't you just put it on the computer, as usual?"

"I thought you'd want to see this one before it was opened for general access, sir."

"Why? Is there something unusual about it?"

"I'd say so, sir. Our new radar overlays show there's more than just space junk out there in orbit, Captain. I'm pretty sure there's a wreck in orbit near us."

"A wreck? Are you sure?"

"Can't be absolutely sure at this range, sir," Badger said. "But the pictures show smooth metal surfaces that must have been machined. It looks to me like a Q-class freighter, sir. Or the remains of one."

Hoban took the radar printouts from Badger's hand and carried them over to his desk. He studied them under infrared light, then, using a grease pencil, outlined an area.

"You mean this bit right here?"

"That's it, sir."

Hoban studied the readouts more closely. He had to admit that Badger had a good eye for this sort of thing. It appeared to be a ship's remains, floating out there in an orbit around AR-32, along with a lot of other stuff, mostly stellar debris.

This, he decided, might be the wreck that Stan Myakovsky had been looking for. Hoban decided to find out and have the information for Stan when he returned.

"We're going to have to check it out," he said. "Badger, I want you to take one man, suit up, and go to the wreck's location. See if you can find its flight indicator."

"Yes, sir!" said Badger.

"And don't go talking about this with the rest of the crew. That wreck has probably been there a very long time. No need for them to get excited too soon."

"Right, sir. No reason to alarm the crew over something like this."

Hoban nodded, but he didn't like agreeing with Badger. It seemed more natural that he should be on the opposite side of anything Badger felt. But he decided that perhaps he was being unfair. All that anyone had against Badger were rumors, and the man's unfortunate personality. No charge against him had ever stuck. And his decision to bring the wreck immediately to Hoban's attention had been quite correct.

Badger went back to the crew quarters. His sidekick Glint was drinking a cup of coffee at one of the wardroom tables. He looked up quizzically when Badger came in.

"Come on," Badger told him. "We got a job to do."

Glint swallowed the rest of his coffee and stood up. "What sort of a job?"

"There's a wreck out there. It's going to take spacesuits."

"Yeah? What's up, Red?"

"I'll tell you about it as we go," Badger said.

31

Stan had brought down the lander within viewing distance of the humped-up mound that was the alien hive, which he was able to inspect closely through the viewscreen magnifier. Gill and Julie stood behind him as he manipulated the views.

The hive was not only the largest nonnatural feature on this planet; it was also larger than any natural feature Stan had yet seen there. Even the mountains were no more than a few hundred meters in height. The hive, standing over a thousand meters above the windswept plain, was huge, imposing, with a dark majesty. The winds scoured it, grinding it down, and there was constant activity from the aliens, who stood out as little black dots at this distance, building the hive up again like ants repairing an anthill.

Aliens, so soon! But, he reminded himself, he had been expecting them . . . hadn't he?

"I hope you're taking note, Ari," Stan said, holding the cybernetic ant on his fingertip so it could get a good view.

"I don't know if Ari is," Julie said, "but I sure am. I didn't know the hive would be so big. And I didn't know we'd run into aliens so soon."

"We've got the suppressors," Stan reminded her.

"Sure," Julie said. "But are they reliable? It's pretty new technology." She sighed and looked out across the plain again. "That's one big hive."

"This one could probably be classified a super-hive," said Gill. "It's far bigger than any other recorded in the literature on the aliens."

"Why do you suppose?" Stan asked.

"This is only a conjecture, of course, but it seems to me the odds against survival on this planet are so great that the aliens had to concentrate their forces, keep one big hive going rather than a lot of smaller ones."

"Saves us from having to make a lot of choices about which hive we plunder," Julie said. "Let's get to it, shall we?"

Gill shook his head. "I advise you to wait until the storm activity on the surface has abated somewhat."

Outside, through the Plexiglas, they could see the raging gale that was the usual weather on this planet. The wind had whipped itself into new heights of frenzy. Sand and small stones were blown across the plain like exploding shrapnel. Larger rocks, swept from the low crags in the distance, tumbled across the plain like steamrollers gone berserk. Lightning forked and crashed in vivid streamers of electric blue.

Beneath the lander, the ground shook and heaved in a nausea-inducing motion. Stan thought: Volcanic activity, just what we need. But he wasn't really worried. He had taken an ampoule of Xeno-Zip before leaving the *Dolomite*. He felt strong and confident, and the pain was gone.

There was a burst of high-pitched static from the speaker, and then Captain Hoban's voice came on.

"Dr. Myakovsky? Are you reading me?"

"Loud and clear, Captain," said Stan. "What do you have to report?"

"We spotted some debris in orbit near us," Hoban said. "Upon further inspection, I have found the wreck of a space freighter, just as you predicted. It's broken into several pieces, but there's a main section that could even contain human life. I doubt that'll be the case, however. This wreck looks like it's been there a long time."

"Do you have any identification on it yet?" Stan asked.

"I've sent two men over to check it out," Hoban said. "With a little luck we'll pick up a flight recorder and find out what happened."

"Contact me as soon as you have it," Stan said. "That could be very important information."

"I'm well aware of that, sir. I'll let you know first thing. Sir, ship's telemetry and remote survey equipment tells me you've put down the lander on potentially unstable ground."

"Everything around here is unstable," Stan said. "Except for the rock outcropping the hive stands on. You wouldn't want me to put down right beside the hive, would you, Captain?"

"Of course not, sir. I was just pointing out : . ."

"I know, I know," Stan snapped. He took a deep breath and tried to get control of himself. He was getting weird flashes now from the drug. It seemed to be taking him on an elevator ride; one second his mood was up, the next minute down. And too soon, the pain was coming back. Take it easy, he told himself.

Still, his breath sobbed in his throat as he said, "I'm going to sign off now, Captain. We have to wait until the storm calms down before we can carry out the next step. I will use that time to get a little rest."

"Yes, sir. Over and out."

Captain Hoban's face faded from the screen. Stan closed his eyes for a moment, then opened them again. Julie and Gill were both standing nearby, watching him. Stan felt a sudden shame at his own weakness, and at the pain that was mounting in intensity throughout his throat and chest. At a moment like this the only thing he could think of was the next ampoule of Xeno-Zip, nested in its padded box with the few others he had brought along.

He shook his head irritably. It was too early for another ampoule. He hadn't planned to take one just yet, he didn't know what it would do to him, but the pains were getting very bad, perhaps even affecting his judgment.

"I'll see you both later," Stan said. Even before they turned to leave the control room, Stan's fingers were at the table drawer where he kept the box of royal jelly ampoules.

32

Julie and Gill returned to the aftercabin. They were alone except for Norbert, who stood silently against the curving wall like a futuristic basilisk, with Mac the dog asleep in his arms.

"Well, Gill," Julie said, "what do you think of all this?"

Gill looked up from his inspection of the armament they had brought. His expression was mild, quizzical. "To what, specifically, do you refer?"

"Stan and his mad trip for royal jelly. This planet. Me."

Gill took his time before answering. "I do not ask myself that sort of question, Miss Lish. And if I did . . ."

"Yes?"

"If I did, my conclusions would have no value. I am not like you humans. I am a synthetic."

"How do you differ from real people?"

Gill looked disturbed, but managed to smile. "No soul, for one thing. Or so they say."

"And for another?"

"No feelings."

"None at all, Gill? Yet you look like a man."

"Appearances can be deceiving."

"Don't you even find me attractive?" Julie asked.

Again there was a long pause. Then Gill said, "There is an old saying of your people. 'Let sleeping dogs lie.' I would advise that here."

"Why is that?"

"Because synthetic people with feelings are something the human race wants no part of."

"That must be some other race," Julie said. "Maybe I'm not part of it. I wouldn't mind it at all if you had feelings. You could tell me about yours and I'd tell you about mine."

"Our feelings would be nothing alike," Gill said.

"Are you so sure?" Julie said. "Sometimes I've felt that I've been set up to follow some program written by someone else. 'The Beautiful Thief,' this one is called. I sometimes wish I could just rewrite my programming. Do you ever wish that?"

"Yes," Gill said. "I know what you mean." Then he shook his head irritably. "Excuse me, Miss Lish, but I must go finish checking out these weapons. Dr. Myakovsky is going to need us at any time."

"Do what you have to do," Julie said. She walked away, and Gill watched her go.

33

Starlight glittered on his space armor as Red Badger left the *Dolomite*'s air lock and soared weightlessly toward the freighter wreck. Behind him came his backup man, Glint, illuminating the wreck with a powerful duolite beam.

Badger gestured, though their destination was plain enough: the gray mass of the wreck, lying in several distinct parts, blocking the stars.

Getting there was simple: both men, on a signal from Badger, opened squirt cans that propelled them across the intervening space.

Badger said into his helmet radio, "You reading me okay, Glint?"

"Loud and clear," Glint said.

They landed on the hulk's largest section with a clank of magnetic boots. Badger's power wrench opened the airtight door that led into the ship.

A lot of the freighter's metal covering had been

peeled back by strong explosions. It was no trouble at all, once they were past the external armor, to slip in between two structural girders and make their way to the interior.

The searchlight picked out the bodies of men, trapped in the sudden inrushing vacuum when the ship's side had been pierced. Exploded bodies lay across girders and floated unsupported in the zero gravity.

Badger and Glint moved slowly, clumsy in their airtight space armor, their searchlights throwing brilliant swords of light through the gloom. A corpse, hanging over a loop of high-pressure hose, seemed to reach out and touch Badger's helmet, lightly, as if just saying hello. . . .

The redheaded spaceman laughed and pushed the thing aside. The body floated slowly across the shattered compartment, its arms held out loosely in front of it like a swimmer doing the dead man's float.

They reached the flight deck. Here there were more bodies, some terribly mangled by the pieces of flying machinery that had taken on the power of exploding shrapnel as the ship had come apart, others looking strangely peaceful, as if they'd never known what hit them. Death had had a busy few moments here before the eternal silence of space had entombed them all.

"Here's the control section," Glint said over the little space-helmet radio that connected the two men.

"Good enough," said Badger. "Let's find what we came for and get the hell out of here."

They floated past an operations console that looked as good as new. The ship's name was still stenciled on the bulkhead, and the paint looked almost new.

"Valparaiso Queen," Glint spelled out. "She won't be going Earthside no more."

"Tough luck for her," Badger said, his tone flat and unemotional. "Here's what we're looking for."

Under the command console was a panel with

three fingertip-sized indentations. Badger pressed them in counterclockwise order, starting at twelve o'clock. The panel slid away. Badger directed Glint to shine the searchlight inside. Using wire cutters from the tool kit strapped to his waist, Badger cut the leads inside and withdrew a small heavy box made of a metalized plastic substance.

"This is what we came for. Now let's get out of here."

34

Back aboard the *Dolomite*, Badger and Glint passed through the air lock and removed their suits. Glint started walking toward the elevator that led to the ship's command territory. He stopped when he saw that Badger was not following him.

"What's up, Red? Aren't we going to give this to the captain?"

"Of course we are," Badger said. "But not just yet." He led the way down a passageway to a door marked WORKSHOP D—AUTHORIZED PERSONNEL ONLY. Glint followed him.

"What're you doin'?" Glint asked. "You going to fix that gizmo?"

Badger stopped and looked scornful. "You really are some kind of a moron. No, I'm not going to fix the gizmo. Why do you think I volunteered us for this job?"

"I was wondering about that," Glint said.

"I want to get a look at what's on this flight recorder before I give it to the captain. Fat chance Hoban would ever tell us."

Glint looked admiringly at his partner, then hurried to catch up as Badger pressed the stud that operated the door to Workshop D.

35

The lander was too small to have separate staterooms. There was a cubbyhole in the rear with a deceleration couch that pulled down from the wall. Stan had lain down there. When Julie came in he was asleep, his glasses still on, his round face momentarily untroubled. Julie bent over to shake him, then hesitated. Stan looked so peaceful there. His large face was calm, and quiet handsome. She noticed what long eyelashes he had, and what delicate skin, fine-pored like a young boy's.

The most recent ingestion of Xeno-Zip had taken Stan's spirit far away, into the limitless perspectives that were the psychic environment of the drug. He was traveling through a place of pure light and color, and he smiled at the friendly shapes around him.

Julie stared at him almost in awe. She knew that Stan was moving down the visionary trail in some impossible dreamtime, walking down a hall of memory

filled with all the images of everything that had ever
been or would be. And these images were melting like
wax in the warmth of the soul's embrace. Stan was a
sorcerer forcing time itself to stand still and be ac-
countable to the moment. He had found eternity in an
instant, and he was balancing it on a needlepoint.

He was in his own time now, a time that had no duration and no limit. He was in a place she could never
get to. But, she wondered, out here in the world of
solid objects and fiery forces, how much time did he
have left? How much time was at Julie's disposal, for
that matter? Could Stan see their time lines in that
strange place where he was?

"Stan," she whispered to him, "what are you dreaming about? Am I in the dream with you? Are we
happy?"

Stan mumbled something but she couldn't catch
the words. She reached out and touched him on the
shoulder. His eyes snapped open, as if he had been
waiting for this signal. She watched his face tense as
pain returned to his consciousness. Then he had himself under control and said, "Julie . . . What is it?"

"Captain Hoban wants to speak to you again. He's
pulled a flight recorder from that wreck."

"Okay, fine." Stan sat up, then got somewhat unsteadily to his feet. Julie's slender, hard arm was
around him, supporting him, her warm fragrant hair
was at his shoulder, and he breathed her fragrance
gratefully.

"Thanks," he said.

"Hey, don't mention it. We're a team, aren't we?"

He looked at her. Her eyes were enormous, brilliant, with dark pools at the center. He felt himself
melting into them. A wave of emotion came over him.

"Julie . . ."

"Yes, Stan, what is it?"

"If you're doing this for my sake . . . please don't
stop."

36

The voices on the flight recorder were very clear.

"What ship is that?"

"This is the Valparaiso Queen, *Captain Kuhn commanding, thirty-seven days out of Santiago de Chile. To whom am I speaking?"*

"This is Potter of the Bio-Pharm ship Lancet. *Do you realize you are trespassing?"*

"I think you exaggerate, Captain. There's no trace of your claim in the recent issues of StarSwap."

"We haven't chosen to go public with it just yet. But there are electronic warnings posted at the beginning of the quadrant. Surely you intercepted those warnings?"

"Oh, those!" Captain Kuhn laughed. *"An electronic warning hardly constitutes a legal claim! No, Captain Potter, unless you publish your intent with the*

151

federal Department of Interplanetary Claims, it can't be said to exist. I have as much right here as you."

Potter's voice was low, and hoarse with menace. "Captain Kuhn, I am a man of little patience. You have already used up my entire store. You have about one second to go into retrofire and get your ship out of there."

Kuhn replied, "I do not take kindly to peremptory orders, Captain, especially from one who has no legal right to give them. I will leave this vicinity in my own time, when I'm good and ready. And you may be sure I will file a complaint with InterBureau over your attitude."

"You will have more to complain about than an attitude, Captain Kuhn, but I doubt you will ever file that report."

"Do not try to intimidate me!"

"The time for words is past. The torpedo that puts paid to your pretensions is now coming toward you at a speed well below that of light, but fast enough, I think you'll find."

"Torpedo? How dare you, sir! Number two! Full power to the screens! Take evasive action!"

And then Badger had to turn down the volume as the recorded sound of the explosion shook the walls of Workshop D.

37

"What's the latest on the storm?" Stan asked.

Gill looked up, his long melancholy face half in a green glow from the ready lights on his control panel. On the screen above him, data waves danced in long wavering lines, the numbers changing with a rapidity that would defy the computational abilities of any but a synthetic man with a math coprocessor built into his positronic brain. Gill was such a man, and his computational abilities were enhanced by the rock-steadiness of his mind, which was not subject to the neurotic claims of love, duty, family, or country. Yet he was not completely emotionless. It had been found that intelligence of the highest order presupposes and is built upon certain fundamental emotional bases, of which the desire to survive and continue is the most fundamental of all. The designers of artificial men would have liked to have stopped there. But the un-

153

certain nature of the materials they were using—in which minute differences in atomic structures eventually spelled big differences in output, as well as the inherent instability of colloidal structures—made this impossible. Gill was standard within his design parameters, but those parameters expressed only one part of him.

"The storm is abating," Gill said. "There's been a twenty-percent diminution in the last half hour. Given the conditions here, I think that's about the best we're going to get. In fact, it's apt to get a lot worse before it gets better."

"Then let's get on with it," Stan said. He turned to Norbert, the big robot alien, who still crouched patiently in a corner of the lander. Mac the dog, growing impatient, whined to be put down, and Norbert obliged. The dog investigated the corners of the little lander and, finding nothing of interest, returned to curl up at Norbert's taloned feet.

"You ready, Norbert?"

"Of course, Dr. Myakovsky. Being robotic, I am always ready."

"And Mac?"

"He is a dog, and so he is always ready, too."

Stan laughed, and remarked to Julie, "I wish now I'd had more time to talk with Norbert. His horrible appearance belies his keen intelligence."

"You are responsible for my appearance, Dr. Myakovsky," Norbert said.

"I think you're beautiful," Stan said. "Don't you think so, Julie?"

"I think you're both pretty cute," she said.

38

In the forward cabin of the lander, the five volunteer crew members were sitting as comfortably as they were able in the cramped confines. Morrison, big and blond, an Iowa farmboy, had unwrapped an energy bar and was nibbling at it. Beside him, Skysky, fat and balding with a walrus mustache, decided to eat an energy bar of his own and fumbled it out of his pocket. Eka Nu, a flat-faced Burmese with skin a shade lighter than burned umber, was mumbling over the wooden beads of his Buddhist rosary. Styson, his long face as mournful as ever, was playing his harmonica, monotonously repeating one phrase over and over. And Larrimer, a city boy from New York's south Bronx, was doing nothing at all except licking his dry lips and brushing his long lank hair out of his eyes.

They had been excited when they volunteered. It was a chance for some action, after the confines of the ship. They'd heard stories about the aliens, of course, but none of them had seen one. They hadn't even been born at the time of the alien occupation of Earth. Aliens now seemed an exotic menace, a weird kind of big bug that would fall easily to their guns.

Morrison was fiddling with his carbine. He decided to insert a new feed ramp. He stripped the receiver and replaced the ramp, then snapped the connector into place. The ramp toggled through a diagnostic code and then clicked into place. He shoved a magazine into the carbine, touched the bolt control, and cycled a round into the firing chamber. The magazine's counter showed an even one hundred antipersonnel rounds ready to go.

"Hey, farm boy," Skysky said, "you planning to shoot something?"

"If I get the chance," Morrison said, "I'm going to bag me one of them aliens and bring home his horns."

Eka Nu looked up from his rosary. "Aliens no got horns."

"Well, whatever they got, I want to bring a piece of it home. A piece of skull maybe. Wouldn't that look good mounted over the mantel?"

Styson said, "You better just hope one of them critters doesn't nail your hide up over the mantel."

"What're you talking about?" Morrison asked. "Them creatures ain't civilized. They ain't got mantels."

Just then Stan's voice came over the loudspeaker. "You men! Get ready to embark into a pod. Check your weapons."

"Okay," Morrison said, getting to his feet. "Time we had ourselves a little hunting."

The men were all on their feet, checking their weapons and talking excitedly. They were clumsy, some of them seeing modern weaponry for the first time. Morrison—who was their natural leader due to his size and self-confidence, though he was of the same rank as the rest of them—had to show Styson how to release the safeties. He was beginning to wonder if the guys would be all right, but he figured as long as they knew which end to point and what to pull, they'd be fine. What creature could stand up against military caseless ammunition?

39

The number-one lander had three escape pods. These were used for close-up maneuvering, in order not to jeopardize the lander itself by piloting it around poorly mapped ground features. This standard-model pod was shaped like an enormous truck tire. Its circular form allowed for the miles of complex wiring that took up most of its interior and allowed it to ride the planet's electromagnetic currents with some success.

Norbert fitted himself in, and Mac nestled up to his chest.

"Comfortable?" Stan asked, peering in.

"The question has no relevance for me," Norbert replied. "When your body is electronically operated, one posture is as good as another. But Mac is fine, Dr. Myakovsky."

"Glad to hear it," Stan said. "Good luck, Norbert. I'll be sending down the five crew volunteers in a separate pod. This moment brings us to the whole point of this operation—getting you and Mac and the men to the surface of AR-32 near the alien hive. Have you got all the stuff you'll need? Did you remember to check the charge in the inhibitors?"

"Of course, Dr. Myakovsky. They should give me enough time to do what I have to do."

"Okay," Stan said. "Good-bye, Mac. You're a nice little dog. I hope I see you again one of these days."

"Not likely, Doctor," said Norbert.

Suddenly Stan was furious.

"Just get the hell out of here!" he said, slamming the pod's hatch shut. "I don't need your comments. Did you hear that, Julie?"

"Take it easy, Stan," Julie said. "Norbert didn't mean anything. He only states facts. Anyway, what's the big deal?"

Norbert's voice came over the radio. "I am ready for the descent, Dr. Myakovsky."

Stan turned to Gill. "Cut the pod loose. And then get the volunteers into their own pod."

Gill, seated at the control panel, turned a switch. The pod came loose from the landing platform with a soft explosive sigh of power. It ejected straight into the air, dipped for a moment, then its electromagnetic receptors came up to full and the pod darted across the stormy landscape of AR-32 toward the distant hive.

40

Badger and Glint left the
workshop and entered crew country from the corridor into the crew's commissary. A wave of sound and
smell hit them. The sound was of fifteen men and
women, mostly young, celebrating their arrival at
AR-32 with song and booze, hamburgers and pizza
(these latter accounting for the smell), and a level of
noise that had to be heard to be believed.

Celebrating landfall was an old custom among
ship's crews. Columbus's men had celebrated in the
same way, their arrival in the New World offering
them a good excuse for a spree. That's what the arrival at AR-32 meant to the crew of the *Dolomite*, too:
a chance to cut loose and tie one on in the secure sur-
roundings of the commissariat, where officers were
not permitted and where scanning procedures were
prohibited by the strong Spacemen's Union.

Here the men could say what they wanted, and

there were no ship's officers nearby or at the end of an electronic listening device ready to take their names and report them for summary discipline. The union wouldn't allow it, and Red Badger had counted on that when he made his entry.

Long Meg, a wiper third class from Sacramento back on Earth, slapped Badger on the back and pushed a bulb of beer into his face. "Where you been, Red? Not like you to miss a spree!"

"I been out to the wreck," Red said.

"What wreck? They didn't tell us about no wreck."

"No, they didn't," Red said. "That's very like them, isn't it?"

Meg pushed her face close to Badger's. "None of your bullshit. What wreck are you talking about?"

Badger grinned at her easily. "That's what the captain sent me and Glint here to investigate. It showed up on the radar and he sent me to get the flight recorder."

"Oh. Is that all?" Meg asked. "I guess the captain will tell us what was on it all in good time."

"I don't think so," Badger said. "If we knew what was on that recorder, it might change our minds about a few things."

"Come out with it, Red! What are you talking about?"

"Suppose that flight recorder showed a freighter just like ours, poking around here just like we are, then being blasted to hell by someone who didn't want them here? What about that, huh?"

"That would be serious," Meg admitted, and several other crewmen nodded agreement. "Are you saying that's what it said?"

"I'm not saying nothing," Badger said. "You can decide for yourselves."

"You took the flight indicator?"

"I listened to it in the workshop. And now I'm going to play it for you. Once you've heard it, you can come to your own conclusions."

"I hope you know what you're doing, Red," Meg said. "I'm sure the captain is expecting you to give that to him immediately."

"Don't worry," Badger said. "The message on it is pretty short."

41

The pod, with Norbert and Mac aboard, was dancing around like a leaf in a storm. Norbert had lost contact with the other pod containing the five volunteers. Wind force threw his pod up into the air, and crosscurrents spun it like a top. Mac howled, and Norbert just clung tight.

"Hang on, boy!" Norbert called. Mac, cradled in his arms, was whimpering, his eyes rolling, in a paroxysm of fear.

Norbert had brought along some extra equipment in case of distress to the dog. The trouble was getting to it. Norbert was practically compressed into the space of the pod, and his size made him take up more room than an Earthman. The little ship was swinging around violently, but Norbert did not suffer from vertigo. He managed to reverse one of his wrist joints and grabbed a large piece of felt he had brought along. He managed to wrap this around Mac, cushion-

ing him. The dog gave a little yelp as the cloth came
around him, but he seemed to appreciate it. His spas-
tic movement became calmer, and he began to adjust
to the violent movements.

The pod, descending on automatic, danced and
veered in the wind. Norbert was tempted to manually
override the pod's controls and see if he could ease
out the movements. But he decided against it. The
pod's autopilot had been designed with a program
that softened out its jerks and slides. He couldn't
hope to do better. He concentrated instead upon pro-
viding a firm platform for Mac and keeping the felt
wrapped around the shivering beast without smothering him. Norbert himself didn't breathe, and he had to
remind himself that all other creatures did.

The ground was coming up fast now to meet them.
Wind shear, this close to the ground, added another
factor to the dangerous uncertainties of the descent.
(The pod's own pulsar beams had to slow them and
absorb the shock as the ground rushed up to meet
them.) Then they were bouncing across it, and finally,
spinning, they came to a halt.

Then Dr. Myakovsky's voice: "Norbert, are you all
right?"

"Perfectly all right, Doctor. And so is Mac."

"Was the landing very difficult?"

Norbert had something new in his vocabulary,
learned from Julie, and he hastened to use it now. "A
piece of cake, Doctor. A walk in the park."

"Hurry up and get the job done," Stan said. "We
want to get rich and get out of here."

42

After Badger played the recorder for the crew, there was an utter silence for a brief moment. Spaceship crews, with their volatile mix of people from all walks of life, tend to have low boiling points. The crew of the *Dolomite* was no exception, particularly since it included a high percentage of criminals.

"What the hell does it mean?" Meg asked.

"It means that a ship like ours was fired upon and destroyed. If they did it to them, then why not to us?"

"Wait a minute!" one of the crew said. "They aren't allowed to do that!"

"What does it matter what they're allowed?" Badger said. "People with power do what they please."

The crew began quarreling among themselves. Badger waited for them to sort it out. He was pretty sure what conclusion they'd come to. And if, by a remote chance, they didn't, he'd steer them toward it.

He knew that cons were always open to the charge that they were being exploited, a supposition that had proven true too many times in the past. The crew had listened to the flight recorder from the *Valparaiso Queen* and, aided by Badger's comments, came to their own conclusions.

It was obvious that there was danger out there. Danger that Captain Hoban would soon know about. Danger that impinged directly on the lives of the crew. So what would Hoban do about it?

After a while the first babble of talk died down, and Walter Glint said to Badger, "Captain Hoban will see this soon. What do you think he's going to do about it?"

"I'll tell you what he'll do," Badger said. "Nothing, that's what he'll do! Hoban is paid by the crazy doctor. The one who's always zonked out on fire. The one who's got the robot alien that killed two of our ship-mates. Hoban will do what the crazy doctor tells him to do, because he's gettin' paid plenty to take the risks. But what risks are you being paid to take? Tell me that, huh?"

It was easy to get a spaceship crew angry, less so to drive them to action. Excited and desperate though they were, it still required work to goad them into taking the law into their own hands. But they were half-way there, Red thought.

Badger was starting a rebellion, but he didn't know quite what he would do next. The quirks of his own mind had perplexed him since childhood. Although he was starting this revolt, paradoxically he felt a strong sympathy for Captain Hoban. At one time he had thought he was going to help him. After all, Hoban had gotten him out of prison. But that was before he saw the tapes, before he realized the extent of the danger they were running, before he decided to do what he could to prevent it.

It's necessary to get them moving, Badger thought. Before there are more deaths.

43

"Dr. Myakovsky? This is Captain Hoban. Do you read me?"

"The atmospherics are difficult, Captain, but I am able to understand you. Please note that just a few minutes ago we launched the pods containing Norbert and Mac and the volunteers. We have them now in distant visual range."

"Excellent, Doctor. I'm glad that part of the operation is going according to plan."

With his sharpened senses, Stan caught the note of uncertainty in his captain's voice. "Is something the matter, Captain?"

"I'm afraid it is, sir. It concerns the flight recorder that we salvaged from the wreck I reported to you about. Before saying any more, let me play it for you, sir."

"Okay, go ahead," Stan said.

44

Stan, Julie, and Gill listened in attentive silence as the tape ran. They heard the exchange between Kuhn of the *Valparaiso Queen* and Potter of the *Lancet*. Although they knew the tape was going to reveal some kind of trouble, they were unprepared for the explosion of the *Valparaiso Queen* as she received the *Lancet*'s torpedo amidships.

"Let me just make sure I've got this straight," Stan said, when the tape ended. "The recorder shows that *Lancet* blew up *Valparaiso Queen*?"

"There seems no doubt about that, sir," Hoban said.

"Well, so what?" Stan said.

"There seems good reason to believe that *Lancet* is still in the vicinity."

"And you think we are in danger?"

"Given Potter's record of violence, it is entirely possible, sir. Even likely."

"Let me point out, Captain, that we are not a defenseless freighter. We have the normal armament against piracy. If *Lancet* should attempt anything against us . . ."

"I will point that out, sir."

"To whom?"

"The representative from the crew. They are sending him to ask what I intend doing about this situation."

"Are you telling me that you played the tape for the crew?" Stan asked.

"No, sir. They took the liberty of listening to it before turning it over to me."

"Well, damn their presumption." Stan turned to Gill. "Have you ever heard anything like it?"

"Unfortunately, yes," Gill said. "The annals of space exploration are full of accounts of insubordinate crews."

Stan said to Hoban, "You must point out to them that *Lancet*'s action was illegal and exceptional. Our situation is not more hazardous because an overzealous captain performed an illegal deed. Nevertheless, I think that in view of the men's feelings we propose a special bonus to them."

"I agree, Doctor," Hoban said. "I was going to make the suggestion myself."

"Do what you can with them, Captain. We'll talk again later." Stan signed off.

"What do you think is going to happen?" Julie asked.

Gill said, "Obviously there's trouble. But I'm sure Captain Hoban can handle it."

"I hope so," Stan said. "We have a few problems of our own to take care of down here."

He turned back to the screen. The others looked now, too. They were viewing the landscape of AR-32 through Norbert's visual receptors. Norbert's head was turning, checking out the landscape as he walked forward. Ahead of him, Mac suddenly started barking and ran toward a little hill. They heard Norbert say, "Come back, Mac. Wait for me!"

Then the view began to shake as Norbert broke
into a run. For a moment they could see nothing but
jagged brown-and-yellow lines. Norbert was watching
the uneven ground, struggling to keep his balance.
Then he went over a little rise. There was a sudden
red-yellow explosion and his screen went into a wild
array of colors and test patterns.

"Just what we needed," Julie said. "Stan, can you
clear up that view?"

"I'm working on it." Stan turned the controls. "Gill,
you got any ideas?"

"Let me just try this," Gill said. His hand probed the
front controls on the computer. "I think that's getting
it, sir. The view is beginning to come back. . . ."

The confrontation on board ship flared up suddenly. One moment Captain Hoban was talking with
the crewmen and apparently getting somewhere, then
the whole thing blew up.

Badger had rapped at the door to the control room.
"Sir. Permission to speak to you about a grievance."

"Now is not a very convenient time, Mr. Badger."

"No, sir. But the union laws state that grievances of
a serious nature are to be settled on the spot."

"And who determines whether they're serious?"

"A duly authorized shop steward, sir. Me."

"All right," Hoban said. "Come in. Let's get this over
with quickly."

Badger entered the control room followed by Glint
and four other members of the crew. They looked ill
at ease in the officers' area, with its soft lighting and
flickering wall scanners. The helmsman stood alone
in a little fenced-off enclosure to one side, scanning
the ship. Two engine-room officers were also present.
None of the officers was wearing sidearms. In the inquiry that later followed, Captain Hoban was faulted
for this omission.

"What seems to be the problem?" Hoban asked.

"As you know, we took the liberty of viewing the

ship's log that I brought back from the rest. You've seen it, sir?"

"Of course," Hoban said.

"What did you think, sir?"

"They caught *Valparaiso Queen* napping. They won't find us so easy."

"Yes, sir. But what has that got to do with us? We're not soldiers, sir."

"We are going about our peaceful and lawful business," Hoban said, hoping it was true. "We aren't out looking for trouble. But if it comes, they'll find us ready. That is a perfectly normal situation in space, Mr. Badger."

"Sure, a crew has to be ready for trouble. But it doesn't have to go out of its way to find it."

"We don't have to run from it, either," Hoban said. "But it is an unusual situation and additional compensation would not be out of order. I will make an announcement shortly, granting the crew extra hazard pay."

"That's not good enough," Badger said. "We want some assurances now that this Potter isn't going to blow us out of space."

Hoban knew it was time to be firm. "I don't care what you want, Mr. Badger. You're a troublemaker. This situation will be resolved and we will let you know what our disposition of it is."

"That is not good enough, Captain."

"Well, it's just going to have to be good enough! You are all dismissed."

One of the engineers tugged at Captain Hoban's sleeve, trying to get his attention. Hoban turned, and saw that Glint had sneaked over to the weapons locker and helped himself to some of its contents. He had pulled out a Gauss needler. This weapon, with its big side magazine of steel slivers, had not been allotted in the standard issue, where favor was given to primitive slug throwers and the newer beam weapons. Glint may just have been fascinated by the handgun's deadly lines, and by the bulbous housing that contained the magnetic impulse equipment.

"What do you think you are doing?" Hoban shouted. "Put that down!"

One of the engineers reached for the weapon. Glint fired, perhaps by reflex. Steel splinters drove through the engineer's left shoulder. There was a moment of shocked silence. And then all hell broke loose.

The second engineer was diving for the weapons locker even as the first was going down. The first thing his hand encountered was a Wilton tangler. He swung it at Glint and pressed the release stud.

Glint managed to duck out of the way. The tangler bolt, with its rapidly expanding core of sticky plastic, soared over his head like a gray bat and wrapped itself around one of the crewmen behind him.

The man screamed and tried to tear the stuff away from himself. The tangler held him tight and began to contract.

He fell, still inextricably caught in the mess.

Suddenly it seemed that everybody in the control room had picked up a weapon. Threads of light from beam throwers glanced off metallic surfaces and glowed against the Perspex windows. Solid projectile loads ricocheted off the ship's walls, darting around like angry hornets. Explosions rocked the control room, sending up dense, greasy clouds of acrid smoke.

The second engineering officer had the presence of mind to bar the entry port, thus stopping any reinforcements coming from crew country.

Hoban ducked down behind a spare-parts case bolted to the floor. The crewmen found shelter in various parts of the control room. The officers were dug in at various locations. Most of them had managed to pick up arms.

For a while there was a strenuous exchange of small-arms fire, its intensity in that confined space enormous. Hoban thought it was like being inside a snare drum that some madman was attempting to play.

45

"It's gettin' too close for comfort!" Badger cried as his refuge in a corner of the room was zapped with blue-white flame.

"You can say that again," Glint said. "We better get out of here!"

"I'm thinking about it," Badger said. "We might need to regroup, reorganize. . . ."

Machine-gun bullets stitched across the ship's walls above their heads, showering them with fragments of metal. There was more noise as a concussion grenade, thrown by Hoban, landed just outside of effective range.

"Okay," Badger said. "Time we got out of here."

The normal egress port was barred, but an elevator to other areas stood with its doors open. Badger and Glint and the remaining crewmen beat a hasty retreat, and managed to shut the doors and get the elevator moving.

Captain Hoban, wounded in the arm by a beam weapon, refused medical attention and led the pursuit.

Most of the crew had not joined the rebellion. Those who had been wavering now decided they'd had enough.

Only Badger and Glint and their close friends, Connie Mindanao, Andy Groggins, and Min Dwin, were irrevocably committed.

All together now, they moved down one of the corridors, maintaining a rolling fire to keep the pursuing officers at a distance.

Glint was saying, "Where we going, Red? What we going to do now?"

"Shaddap," Badger said. "I've got it all doped out." He led them through the now deserted commissary and out to the rear hold. "Where we goin'?" Glint asked.

Badger didn't answer.

"There's no place to go!" Glint said.

"Don't worry, I know what I'm doing," Badger said. "We're going to get out of here."

"Out of here?" Glint looked puzzled.

"Off this ship," Badger said. "We'll take one of the escape pods and leave this death ship behind. We'll go down to AR-32."

"Yeah, okay," Glint said. Then he thought of something. "But where'll we go after that, Red? There's no civilization down there!"

"We'll then make contact with *Lancet*."

Glint turned it over in his mind. *Lancet*? Dimly he remembered that that was the name of the Bio-Pharm ship that had nuked the other ship, the *Valparaiso* something. The one they had gotten the flight recorder from.

"Red, are you sure we want to do that? Those people are killers!"

"Of course I'm sure. We're on their side now. They'll give us good money for turning our information over to them. They're going to be very interested to hear about Captain Hoban and the doctor and what they're up to. We'll be heroes."

"I don't know," Glint said.

"Trust me," Badger said. "Anyhow, what else can you do?"

"I guess you're right," Glint said. You could tell from his voice that it was a load off his mind, letting Badger make the decisions for both of them.

The others in the party weren't interested in asking questions. They wanted to be led, to be told what to do, and that was what Badger liked to do, lead people. It made him feel strong and good, until something went wrong, which, unfortunately, it did all too often. But not this time. This time he knew what he was doing.

"Come on," Badger said. "We've got to get the spare lander."

Andy Groggins said, "They're apt to be waiting for us there, Red."

"If they are," Badger said, "then so much the worse for them."

46

Stan sat in the lander and watched through Norbert's viewing screen as the robot's view of AR-32 swayed precipitously and began to slide off the screen. The lander was still vibrating after its bobsled descent through AR-32's turbulent atmosphere. Stan felt battered and bruised: sitting at the controls trying to steer all that liveliness and power to a safe landing was like going fifteen rounds with the Jolly Green Giant. Stan still wasn't sure which had won.

He fine-tuned the knobs on the viewing screen, trying to focus on the images Norbert was sending back from the surface of AR-32. The picture lurched with each of the robot's footsteps, and jumped in and out of focus.

Stan hated out-of-sync pictures like that. They seemed to trigger some long-dormant primeval receptor in his brain stem. He found the oscillations of the picture upsetting his own psychic balance.

He tried consciously to steady himself. He didn't want to go freaking out now, but the way that picture jumped was going to do it to him yet, and they'd have to scrape him off the wall.

Then the picture stabilized and the focus locked in. Stan was looking at a pile of wind-polished boulders in various shades of orange and pink. When Norbert raised his head, Stan could see ahead of him a narrow valley of stone and gravel. The swirling clouds of dust made visibility difficult after about fifty feet.

"Look at this place," Stan remarked to Julie. "We haven't seen a green thing since we got here. I wouldn't be surprised to learn that this place has no natural vegetation. None on the surface, anyhow."

"If plants won't grow here," Julie remarked, "how are the aliens able to sustain themselves?"

"I said there was no vegetation on the surface," Stan said. "Belowground it could be a very different story. There's an ant species that practices underground gardening. The aliens might have followed the same course of evolution."

"This isn't their home world, is it?" Julie asked.

"I doubt it very much. It's extremely unlikely that they evolved here. No one knows the location of their original home planet."

"So how'd they get here?"

"I have no idea. But however they did, they must have brought their culture with them. And their nasty habits."

Norbert's picture began to bounce again.

"He's going uphill," Stan said. "Have you spotted Mac yet?"

"He ran on ahead," Julie said. "He's out of the picture now."

Gill said, "There's something in the viewer's top right quadrant."

Stan studied it. "Yes, there is. Norbert, magnify that quadrant."

Norbert did so. The object sharpened, resolving from a black dot to a blocky shape of lines and angles.

Gill said, "It looks like a cow skeleton, Doctor."

Norbert walked over to it. Up close, it did turn out to be a cow skeleton, though the head was missing. Norbert panned the remains. Mac had found it, too, and had pulled loose a thighbone. The animal's rib cage had been exploded outward under great pressure from something inside.

"What could have done that?" Julie asked.

"Probably a chestburner," Stan said, alluding to the young of the alien species.

"I doubt that cow creature came here naturally," Gill put in.

"Of course it didn't," Stan agreed. "If those bones could speak, I think we'd find that cow and a lot of her sisters were brought to this planet from Earth."

"As hosts for the alien young?" Julie asked.

"No doubt. That's what Neo-Pharm was up to back in those days. And as T-bone steaks for the crew of the *Lancet*."

"Speaking of *Lancet*," Julie said, "I wonder when we're going to run into them?"

"Soon enough, no doubt," Stan said. He studied the image Norbert was sending. "Hello, what's that? Another cow skeleton?"

"Lower left quadrant, Norbert," Julie said, spotting it.

Norbert turned obediently and walked over. Within twenty yards he came across the body of an alien.

It lay facedown in the gravel, its long black form alternately concealed and revealed by the windows of dust that blew incessantly across the valley floor.

At Stan's instruction, Norbert viewed it through an infrared scanner, and then an ultraviolet, to make sure the body wasn't booby-trapped.

It appeared to be free of danger. He approached and bent over it, with Mac—hair bristling and teeth barred—coming along at his heels.

"What can you see?" Stan asked.

"It is an alien," Norbert replied. "There is no doubt of that. It is perfectly motionless, but not dead. There is no sign of life, but also no sign of damage or decay. It looks almost as if it could be asleep. I'm switching to ultrasonic scanner to conduct a survey of the internal organs."

After a short delay Norbert reported again. "It's internal organs are functioning, but at a very slow rate. It's like it's asleep or unconscious. There are several more tests I could try—"

Whatever Norbert had in mind, it didn't happen, because Mac chose that moment to sense movement on the other side of a nearby hill and ran there, barking. Norbert got up and followed.

When he reached the crest of the hill and looked over, the first thing he noticed was the small, fat-bellied little spaceship, resting on its supports, nose pointed skyward, ready for takeoff.

The second thing he noticed was the aliens, a dozen or so of them, lying motionless on the ground, just like the one he had left.

And the third thing he noticed were the humans, three of them, bending over the unconscious aliens.

47

For the men from Potter's ship, the *Lancet*, it had begun as a normal day's harvesting operation. This three-man work crew had been down on the surface of AR-32 for half of their five-hour shift.

After relieving the previous crew, their first task had been to inspect the suppressor gun. It was mounted on top of the spaceship, where it could be powered by the ship's batteries.

It was a jury-rigged contraption, thrown together by a clever engineer from Potter's ship, a man with a knack for coming up with useful inventions on the spur of the moment.

Suppressors were a new technology in the continuing war against the aliens. They had resulted so far in small modules worn on a man's person. But Potter's engineer had taken the suppressor principle one step farther. He had theorized that the aliens would be susceptible to a stunning effect from certain vibratory impulses if they were narrow-band broadcast at sufficient intensity. He based this hunch on his study of alien anatomy. It seemed to him that the aliens had developed a great sensitivity to electrical cycling pulses. These could excite or stupefy them, depending on the velocity and amplitude of the waves broadcast. He experimented with electromagnetic bombardment.

Now, from its mount on top of the spaceship, his cannon turned like a radar dish, blasting electronic impulses that kept the aliens stupefied while the crew of the *Lancet* milked them of their royal jelly.

It was not difficult duty, as Des Thomas had remarked to Skippy Holmes, with whom he was working. "I mean, if you forget they're aliens, it's much the same as taking honey from bees."

"Big bees," Skippy said.

"Yeah, very big bees, but it's the same thing. Hey, Slotz!" Thomas called to the third man of their crew, who was on top of the spaceship, working with the bracing that held the suppressor in place. No matter how well you put those things up, the incessant wind eventually worried them loose.

"What is it?" Slotz said, pausing with power wrench in hand.

"You almost finished up there?"

"I need some more bracing material. A flying rock tore some of the support away."

"We'll radio it to the ship. The next shift can bring the stuff out. We're nearly out of here."

Slotz turned back to his work. Holmes and Thomas took up positions around the recumbent alien. Together they heaved the big creature over on his side. Arnold took up the scraper, working quickly around a leg joint. He packed the sticky, light blue residue into a canvas bag. From here, it would be transferred to a glass container within the potbellied little harvester ship. As Des Thomas finished milking his alien he heard a barking sound and looked up. He was amazed to see a large brownish-red dog running over the top of the hill. Given the circumstances, he couldn't have been more amazed if it had been an elephant or a whale.

"Come here, boy," he called. "I wonder where your—"

It was at that instant that Norbert came striding over the crest of the hill and down into the harvesting area.

There was a brief tableau: three human crewmen frozen like dummies, Norbert striding forward like a fury from the deepest hell, and Mac, all innocence, barking and capering along like he was on an outing.

Holmes came unfrozen first. "One of them's come awake!" he shouted. "Get that sucker!"

Slotz got off the top of the spaceship rapidly. The three men dived for their weapons. These were always kept handy because, although no alien had woken up suddenly like this before, no one really trusted the new suppressor technology—especially when you took into account how goofy looking its inventor was.

Holmes got his hands on the carbine he had propped against a rock outcropping. He slipped off the safety, aimed hastily, and pulled the trigger. A stream of caseless forty-caliber slugs streaked toward Norbert, who was no longer there to receive them.

The threat toward him instantly pushed Norbert into predator mode. You could almost hear the new program click into place.

Softslugs bouncing off his carapace, Norbert slid under the fusillade of projectiles from Des's Gauss needler. A fragmentation grenade bounced off his chest and exploded as it was bouncing away. Norbert was showered with white-hot fragments of metal, but they didn't have the force to penetrate his metallized hide.

Although he wasn't hurt, Norbert was not pleased. Skippy Holmes was the closest, and the crewman just had time to scream as Norbert hooked his face at the temples with two curved talons and tore it off in one economical move.

It was a moment of gratuitous horror, though Norbert didn't view it that way. Just doin' my job, sir.

Skippy buried the raw meat of his face in his hands and fell to the ground, gurgling, blood bubbling from his shattered skin. He didn't suffer for long; Norbert's spurred foot hooked out the man's stomach and a good selection of his internal organs.

Seeing this, Chuck Slotz gagged and took to his heels, sprinting toward the harvester's open entry port, closely followed by Des.

Norbert came racing after them, and almost made the entry port. It closed in his face, and Norbert slammed into it with a force that shook the harvester on its six slender legs and caused the radarlike suppressor apparatus on its roof to topple over and fall to the ground in a crackle of sparks.

Slowly, very slowly at first, the aliens lying on the ground began to stir.

48

Gill gasped as the scene of carnage was played over Norbert's visual receptors and relayed to the screen aboard the *Dolomite*'s lander.

Norbert, standing in front of the harvester's sealed door, was saying, "I am awaiting further orders, Dr. Myakovsky."

"Yes," Stan said. "Just stand by for a moment." He turned to Gill. "What's the matter? Why are you looking that way?"

"I—I wasn't prepared for the violence, Doctor. I had no idea Norbert was programmed to kill."

"How could you have thought otherwise? What do you think we're out here for? A sight-seeing trip? Gill, we're all programmed to kill."

"Yes, Dr. Myakovsky. If you say so."

"You, too, are programmed to kill, are you not?"

"In defense of human lives, yes, I suppose I am. It

is just that I didn't know we were going to exercise that option so . . . lightly."

"We're here to get rich," Stan said. "Whatever it takes. Right, Julie?"

"That's right, Stan," Julie said, then turned to the artificial man. "You'll share in the money we get, too. Even an artificial man can use money, right?"

"All sentient beings need money," Gill said dryly.

"That's right," Julie said. "Anyhow, we're in it now, and it's us or them. You know what Potter will do if he finds us? The same thing he did to the *Valparaiso Queen.*"

Gill nodded but didn't answer.

"Think about it, Gill," Stan said. "Don't get humanitarian on us too soon." He paused, then added, "If it's really against your principles, perhaps you'd like to wait in the back bay until this phase of the operation is over? I wouldn't want you to do anything foolish."

"Do not worry about me, sir," Gill said. "I have no sentiment about matters of killing. Sentiment was not programmed into me. I was surprised, that is all, but now I understand. I am ready to do whatever is necessary to protect you and Miss Julie."

"Glad to hear it." Stan wiped his forehead. He looked like he himself was having a little trouble getting used to killing. Only Julie showed no signs of upset.

Gill hesitated. "Sir, we have no visual contact with the crew volunteers."

"Damn it!" Stan said. "Does everything have to go wrong at the same time? Norbert! Can you get into the harvester?"

"The door is locked, Doctor," Norbert said.

"I doubt it's a very advanced locking mechanism. Give me a close-up of the lock."

Norbert leaned forward, focused on the locking mechanism and switched to the X-ray mode.

Stan studied the picture for a moment. "It looks like pretty standard stuff. Tell you what, just rip off the keypad and you'll be able to turn the handle manually."

"Yes, sir."

"Better hurry up about it. It would be best to prevent those guys from getting in touch with Potter."

49

Inside the harvester, Slotz and Thomas fell over each other getting to the radio. Thomas got there first and flipped the transmission switch

"Lancet? Come in, *Lancet!"*

Slotz, standing just behind Thomas, heard a banging sound on the entry port and made sure he had his carbine.

"Hurry up, Thomas! I don't know if the door will hold him!"

"I'm trying," Thomas said. "But I've come up with nothing so far."

"The antenna!" Slotz said. "It came down with the suppressor gun when the alien slammed into the ship."

"That's just great," Thomas said. "So we can't transmit. And it's two hours before the next shift comes down."

"Maybe we can hold out." Slotz found a fresh magazine in his pocket, ejected the spent one from his carbine, and snapped the new one into place.

The hammering suddenly stopped. The men heard a sound of metal ripping.

"He's tearing off the lock cover!" Slotz cried.

"Nobody can do that," Thomas said.

"Trust me," Slotz muttered. "He's doing it."

There was silence for a moment. Then a clicking sound.

"He's through the cover! He's working the unlocking mechanism!" Slotz shouted.

"Whaddaya want me to do about it?" Thomas said. Into the radio's dead transmitter he shouted, "Mayday, Mayday!"

Then the door slammed open with great force and Norbert was coming in, a towering black fury. Slotz tried to level the carbine, managed to get off one round that glanced off Norbert's shoulder and ricocheted around the cabin like an angry bee. Then Norbert was on him. The robot alien caught the back of Slotz's head, leaned forward, mouth open, second jaws extending through his slavering mouth. Slotz, eyes wide and wild, tried to pull himself out of the way, but there was no budging Norbert's grip. The second jaws shot out like a piston and smashed through Slotz's open mouth and continued through, snapping the man's spine like a dry stick.

Seeing what had happened, Thomas scrambled away from the radio. He had a pulse rifle in his hand and he triggered it. A tongue of brilliant light licked out against Norbert's chest. It had no apparent effect on the robot, but at that close range the heat was reflected back into Thomas's face. He shrieked as his hair caught fire. And then Norbert was on him, two taloned hands on his shoulders, hind legs raking the man's middle with razor-sharp claws. Simultaneously fried and eviscerated, Thomas fell to the floor, dead before he landed.

In the ensuing silence, Mac came trotting into the

harvester, looked around, seemed unimpressed by the blood and gore that coated the walls, and trotted up to Norbert.

The robot alien patted him once on the head, then said, "That's all for now, Mac. I have to report."

The interior of the harvester was a shambles. There were bits and pieces of crewmen scattered all over the struts and inner bracing members. Bright arterial blood lay in puddles on the metal floor. Blood lapped at the corners of the room, and the self-cleaning units were clogged with it.

Mac sniffed around, whimpered, then barked excitedly. He was getting a lot of mixed signals. Finally he decided something was wrong, but he'd have to let somebody else figure it out. He found a corner and lay down with his muzzle on his paws. Norbert came along behind him, stopped, and surveyed the damage he had caused.

Stan, back on the lander, was following visually. His voice was low. He was coaching Norbert.

"You're doing fine, Norbert. We want to check out the whole ship for possible damage. You're really quite violent once you get started, aren't you?"

"Not intentionally, Doctor."

Julie leaned over Stan's shoulder. "What's that in the background, Stan?"

"I'm not sure. . . . Norbert, make a hundred-and-eighty-degree turn and do a slow pan. That's it. Now freeze. And magnify. Okay, freeze it right there. And correct the color. Good!"

Julie said, "Plastic storage units. Each of them would hold—what? Five liters?"

"More like seven," said Gill.

"There are hundreds of them stacked there," Stan said. "More on the other side of the hold."

"Are they royal jelly?" Julie asked. "Can we be absolutely sure of that?"

Stan replied, "There really seems no doubt. What

else would they be filled with? Cloverleaf honey? The harvester is packed with the stuff. They must have been just about ready to take off back to *Lancet*."

"Good thing we got here when we did." Julie laughed. "They've done our work for us, Stan. We're rich!"

Stan grinned. "We'd better not start trying to spend it just yet. Norbert, have you completed your assessment of the damage yet?"

"Yes, Dr. Myakovsky."

"Any problems?"

"I'm afraid that in the fight this unit here was destroyed." Norbert indicated the interior suppressor gear, which was strewn around the cabin, most of it broken into fragments of crystal and plastic.

"Ah well," Stan said, "Can't make an omelette without breaking eggs, as some famous man once remarked. Do you know who said that, Gill?"

"I'm afraid I don't," Gill said.

"And here I thought you knew everything. Well, well . . ." Unexpectedly he began to giggle.

"Stan," Julie said, "what's the matter?"

Stan pulled himself together. "Whom the gods would destroy they first make mad. I don't suppose you know who said that, either. Well, never mind. Of all the stuff you could have destroyed, Norbert, I'm afraid you picked the worst. I think that's the interior equipment for the ultrasonic suppressor."

"Are you certain?" Julie asked. "How can we know for sure?"

"There ought to be a serial number here somewhere." Stan examined the bits of twisted metal. "Yes, as I thought. Now we need to go to the next step."

"Is that difficult?" Julie asked.

"Easy enough . . . Norbert, give me a picture through one of the portholes."

Outside, Stan could see a yellowish-brown haze with dark shapes moving through it. Half the aliens were up, the others were reviving swiftly. They moved sluggishly at first, then with increasing vigor, toward the harvester.

"Clear up the focus," Stan snapped.

"Sorry, Doctor . . ." With the focus cleared, Stan could see the distinct dark alien shapes milling around outside the ship.

"Okay," Stan said. "The suppressor is kaput and the aliens are awake. That's okay. Basically, our job is over. We've got the harvester. It was a little messy, but we got it. We need only pilot it up to the *Dolomite* and get out of here. Norbert, check the controls."

The robot alien moved to the control panel. After a moment he said, "I'm afraid we've got trouble, Doctor."

Stan could see for himself through Norbert's visual receptors. The battle inside the harvester had wrecked some of the controls.

"Oh, Stan," Julie said, "can Norbert fly that thing out of there?"

"Sure, if conditions were right," Stan said. "But I'm afraid it's not going to be as easy as that. The controls are all screwed up."

"Can't he fix them?"

Stan shook his head. "Sure, given time, but we don't have much of that. First we're going to have to get into communication with the *Dolomite* again. Gill, have you had any luck in raising Captain Hoban?"

"I haven't gotten him yet, sir," Gill said. "Something serious seems to have happened to the *Dolomite*."

"That's just great," Stan said. "I wish he'd call."

"He will," Gill affirmed. "I know Captain Hoban. He would make contacting us his first priority."

"Well, it gives us a little time. A chance to do something I've long wanted to do."

Julie looked at him. "Stan, what are you talking about?"

"I want to take a look inside that hive." He looked hard at Gill, as if daring him to challenge him. Gill felt momentarily uncomfortable and glanced at Julie, who gave an almost imperceptible shrug. Gill reminded himself that it was difficult to assess the situation and impossible to pass judgment on humans.

"Just as you say, sir," Gill said at last.

"Norbert, are you standing by?" Stan demanded.

"I am, Dr. Myakovsky."

"Okay. I take it all your systems are functioning properly?"

"All my readings are in the green," Norbert reported.

"Is your suppressor working properly?"

Norbert checked. "It is, sir."

"And Mac's?"

Norbert bent over the dog. "It is functioning correctly."

"Then turn it off and open the harvester port."

"Sir?"

"Norbert, are you having synapse failure? Didn't you hear me?"

"It is such an unusual order, Doctor, that I wanted to be certain I understood it correctly. When I turn off Mac's collar, that will render him visible to the aliens."

"That's exactly what I had in mind," Stan said. "We're going to make the aliens a little present of Mac."

"Give him to the aliens?"

"That's right. You aren't going soft on me, are you, Norbert?"

"No, sir. But is it necessary?"

"Of course it is. They'll probably take Mac directly to the queen. They give the queen all the best stuff first, don't they?"

"I think so, sir. So it is reported in the literature."

"That's right," Stan said, with a laugh. "For a moment I forgot you weren't one yourself."

Gill and Julie looked at each other. Gill frowned slightly and looked away. Julie pursed her lips. She didn't much like what was happening. But what the hell, it was no business of hers.

Stan explained. "Mac will represent food to them. A tasty little morsel fit for a king. Only in this case it's a queen. That's who they'll take Mac to. And you, my dear robotic friend, will follow them. Protected by your own suppressor, they won't even see you. Without suspecting a thing, they'll lead you through the labyrinth to the royal birthing chamber. Through your eyes I'll get the first pictures ever taken of the queen of this hive. I'll be doing a unique service to science. That's worth any number of little dogs like Mac. He's just a common mutt. But you, Norbert, are unique."

Stan turned to face Julie and Gill. Light glinted off his glasses. His face was drawn. His voice, high and strained, rose as he asked, "Does anyone here have any objections?"

Gill looked away and didn't answer. Julie looked faintly annoyed as she said, "Give them Mac or a kennelful of mutts, it makes no difference to me. But would you mind telling me, just to satisfy my own curiosity, why are you doing this?"

"It's the only way I can be sure of getting Norbert into the hive quickly without him having to spend God knows how long looking for a way in. The outside of the nest is sealed against the weather, as you might have noticed. Did you check that out? The aliens must have a whole system of tunnels for getting in or out. There must be a hundred miles of tunnel in something that big. This way I'll have Norbert lay down an electronic path."

Gill said, "What purpose will that serve, Doctor?"

"Two at least," Stan said. "First, with Norbert videotaping as he goes, we'll provide science with an invaluable record of life inside an alien hive. And second, we can come back here whenever we like to collect more jelly."

"Now you're talking, Stan," Julie said. "I knew you weren't just antidog."

"Of course not. As a matter of fact, I'll have Norbert try to rescue Mac when they've reached the queen's chamber."

"That might not be possible," Gill said.

Stan shrugged. "Let's get going. Norbert, do it!"

50

"**N**ope," Morrison said. "I can't get a reading."

"Let me try," said Larrimer. He fiddled with the controls. But it showed no trace of the first pod, the one with Norbert and Mac aboard.

Almost as soon as the five volunteers from the crew had entered the second pod, they lost visual contact with the first, and found themselves flying blind into a whirling sandstorm. Overhead, purple-black ranks of clouds had formed, and soon their visibility was further cut by heavy, driving rain. After the rain let up, the ground below steamed, and a thick mist arose from the land.

Definitely not flying weather. But the pod was equipped with autopilot and a landing program. Their direction finder was slaved to the first pod's beacon. All they had to do was sit tight and the pod would take them to Norbert.

In theory.

In practice, the autopilot was unable to compensate for the driving wind, a wind that roared loudly enough to be heard inside the pod. The autopilot's little computer had all it could do to keep them from piling up on the ground below. It brought them down safely, then the comedy of errors began.

First Larrimer, who had been entrusted with the radio, found out that it would not transmit or receive. Not enough power, maybe, or maybe interference from the electrical storm overhead. Maybe it had even taken one bang too many during their hectic descent.

"Well," Morrison said, "they can probably find us even if we can't find them."

"Are you sure of that?" Skysky rubbed his bald head nervously.

"Sure I'm sure." Morrison spoke with a confidence he didn't feel. "They'd want to retrieve the pod, anyhow. Those things cost money."

Eka Nu looked up. "No," he said. "Pods are considered expendable. So are crew, sometimes."

Not a cheering thought.

"Anyhow," Morrison said, "all we have to do is find Norbert. The professor is not about to abandon his favorite toy."

That cheered them up a little. Morrison brought out an electron detector and tried to tune it to the trail Norbert was supposed to leave. The little machine buzzed steadily, but showed no sign of a direction. Morrison turned it in every direction. It still didn't indicate anything.

"Maybe the hull shielding is stopping the signal," Morrison said. "We've got to go outside anyway, so maybe it'll be better there."

"Go outside in this?" Larrimer asked, jerking his thumb at the mist that rolled in a slow wave across the plain.

"We can't stay here," Morrison said. "If they did try to find us, they wouldn't stand a chance. Our only hope is to find Norbert and await pickup with him and the dog."

"Great," Styson exclaimed. "What about if we run into aliens?"

"We've got our weapons," Morrison said, "and we have suppressors. What more could you ask for?"

The others grumbled, but it was obvious that they had to make a move. First Morrison told them to check their weapons, and there was a clatter of metal on metal as they shoved magazines into their carbines and set the plasma burners on standby.

"Ready?" Morrison asked. "Okay, here we go."

He cracked the hatch. It opened smoothly, and they stepped out one by one onto the plain.

The first thing they discovered was that they couldn't see worth shit. It wasn't quite as bad as that, actually. About three feet visibility, Styson estimated.

Cautiously they stepped out of the pod and tested out the land. It was solid underfoot. Moving only a few feet away from the pod, they formed a circle around the electron detector and tried to get a reading. The thing buzzed, and the needle swooped erratically, but there was no definite and unambiguous signal. At last Morrison decided to follow the biggest needle deflection and hope for the best.

"It's this way," he stated. He didn't know where he was going, but he knew they had to go somewhere. He was beginning to think this volunteering hadn't been such a good idea. The bonus had sounded good, but you don't get to spend it if you're dead.

In single file, staying close to each other, the volunteers moved across the plain. All five men had weapons at the alert. The mist billowed around them like white waves in a sea of clouds, sometimes covering them completely, which was like walking through a sort of impalpable white cotton candy. Sometimes the mist would begin to dissipate, and then the men could see each other's heads and shoulders, rising ghostlike out of the whiteness, with wisps of mist clinging to them. But then the mist rose again and buried them.

Morrison, in the lead, was following a compass course he had set after taking his best guess as to what the electron detector was indicating. It didn't occur to him that it might not mean anything at all. That would be too unfair.

Styson, bringing up the rear, kept on turning around and trying to look behind him. He was sure something big and terrible was going to materialize out of the mist and snap him up. It was a crazy, kid's sort of thinking—he knew that—but he couldn't control his fear. His hands tightened on his carbine. He wished he was holding his harmonica. That always gave him confidence. But it was in his pocket, because he needed both hands to hold his carbine. Now his fingers tightened on the weapon, and he checked to make sure all safeties were off. He missed his harmonica, but he knew it was a lot more important to hold on to the weapon. Stood to reason . . .

And then the mists closed down again and the men lost all visibility. Styson staggered along, carbine held out in front of him like a blindman's cane, trying to peer into the numbingly white world in which he found himself. What a rotten job this had turned into!

And then he bumped into something.

Styson stumbled, then regained his balance. Larrimer had been next in line. He called out, "Larrimer, is that you?"

There was no answer. Whoever was ahead of him was just becoming visible, a dark shadow in the pale glimmer of the surrounding mist.

"Whoever it is, try to keep the pace up," Styson said. "We need to get out of here. . . . Who is that, anyway?"

He reached out and poked what he thought was Larrimer on what he thought was Larrimer's shoulder. There was a movement, and the shape ahead of him turned. The mists started to dissipate, and Styson saw something too tall to be Larrimer or any other man, something so tall that he had to crane his neck back to see it.

No mistaking what it was now. It was an alien, and there was something about its quick, questing movements that decided Styson that this was not Norbert. This was the real thing.

He tried to get his carbine up, but the sling had somehow gotten tangled around his left arm. And the massive creature was too close to him, anyhow. He closed his eyes and made a quick, fervent prayer.

Moments later he opened his eyes. The alien had walked right past him, brushing against him as it did so. It continued to move away, still looking around as if seeking something.

"Hey, fellas!" Styson called out. "We got company!"

The men ahead of him were aware of this. They had spotted aliens before Styson did, but had kept quiet in order not to alert the creatures. Aliens were primarily visual hunters, but no one knew to what extent they could also use their hearing. This didn't seem the time to find out. Now, as Styson caught up with them, they shushed him into silence.

Morrison continued to lead. The mist thinned, and soon they could see black shapes moving through white cotton. Aliens, moving in the same general direction the men were going, walking singly or in small groups. They passed the men and paid no apparent attention to them. One went by within a foot of Morrison and never turned its head. Morrison was starting to feel a modest confidence. . . . And then it happened.

The mist closed down again. The men fumbled their way forward, fighting to keep their balance, and then there was a loud gurgling sound followed by silence.

"What was that?" Morrison asked.

"Damned if I know," Larrimer replied.

"Is anyone missing? Call out your names, but not too loud."

Three men responded to Morrison's request, but the fourth, Skysky, did not answer.

Morrison risked shouting. "Skysky? Are you there, Skysky?"

Nothing.

"Watch yourselves, boys," Morrison said. "I think we got trouble."

It made no sense, Morrison thought, but it seemed like an alien must have grabbed Skysky, broken his neck before he could do any more than gurgle, and taken his body away.

The suppressors were supposed to hide them from the aliens.

But Skysky was definitely gone.

So, one of two things. Either Skysky's suppressor had failed, or he had walked right into an alien, and that close, it had been able to figure out what Skysky was.

A six-foot breeding organism.

Don't think about that.

"You gotta really watch hard," Morrison said, as if the men needed to be told. "Skysky must have gotten careless. The mist is lifting again. Maybe we can find someplace to hide."

The mist dissipated swiftly. The men could see about fifty yards on all sides of them. The visibility continued to improve, and Morrison told them to fan out. The men complied and, following Morrison's lead, continued to move steadily toward something that looked like a brown breast on the horizon.

They were passing groups of aliens, but now were able to keep a better distance. The aliens continued to ignore them.

Until one alien stopped ignoring them.

It stopped in midstride, swiveled, turning its huge head slowly, and then locked in on something. It turned toward it and began to run.

When Styson looked to his left, he saw an alien coming straight for him—not for anyone else in the group, but him. He threw up his rifle and fired. The caseless round broke through the alien's shoulder, almost severing the arm at the shoulder joint. It just seemed to make the creature angrier than it already was. Aliens start out angry and build from there.

Ignoring the arm dangling from its side, it grabbed Styson around the waist with its good arm. Styson screamed and tried to get the carbine into line. The alien opened its jaws. The secondary jaws looked out for a moment, then rammed into Styson's face.

Styson had tried to duck at the last instant, so the secondary jaw caught him in the left eye rather than the mouth. The tooth-lined mouth punched through to Styson's brain, and when it withdrew, it took a fair amount of gray matter along with it.

And then the alien turned away from Styson and revolved its head again.

The other four men had frozen into position, not daring to move while the alien was prowling around Styson, unable to shoot without hitting their comrade.

It turned out that shooting wasn't necessary. Not at that moment, anyhow. The alien turned and loped away, rejoining the group it had left earlier.

Morrison got the men moving again.

51

Their breathing space was short. Aliens continued to stream past the three crewmen. But now, some of those closest to the humans were slowing down, turning their heads this way and that. Morrison prayed that they had stiff necks or something. But no such luck. Two of the aliens turned away from the stream and started toward the group. After a moment a third one joined them.

"Shit!" Morrison said. There was no doubt where that bunch were going. Straight at him. He started firing when they were still thirty yards off, then pushed the selector and fired a grenade. In fact, he fired off all his grenades, something he hadn't meant to do, but he wasn't used to these weapons, which were military style. The grenades went lobbing in the air, and most of them came down behind the aliens. Morrison's last one hit an alien in the chest and, a moment later, exploded in its face. The alien was thrown backward by

the force of the explosion. He picked himself up, but
his face, such as it was, was ruined. His mouth was
gaping open, and through his jaws protruded the
smaller secondary jaws. They hung limp at the end of
their muscular tube. The tube appeared to have been
bitten through. The alien was not out of it yet, though.
Shaking its head, it moved again toward Morrison,
limping but still deadly.

Morrison didn't have time for that one yet. The two
closer ones were coming up fast. He took the one to
his left, blasting caseless projectiles into its chest. He
could hear firing near him. It was Eka Nu, who had
moved up to join him. Farther away, Larrimer tried to
join them, but a long black arm came out of nowhere
and caught him in midstride. He jerked around like a
trout on a hook as the alien brought him close to his
face. Then it released the facehugger, and Larrimer
fell to the ground, moaning and twitching. The alien
hoisted him to his shoulder. Larrimer knew he was
going to have the worst death he could have imagined, hanging just barely alive from a wall in the hive
while a newborn grew within him, getting ready to eat
its way out.

Morrison and Eka Nu had their hands full with the
two aliens, who were coming at them at a full charge.
Morrison saw his projectiles slam into the alien, and
still it kept coming. He fired until the magazine was
empty. He fired the last rounds with his eyes closed.
When he opened them, the alien was dead at his feet.
Eka Nu hadn't been so lucky, however. The alien on
his side had kept on coming on all fours, had grabbed
Eka Nu around the shoulders, hugged the crewman to
him, then turned him. The two stared face-to-face for
a moment, then the facehugger hit and Eka Nu knew
no more.

Morrison found himself alone. He was panting, exhausted, trembling. The guys were all gone. He looked
around. He didn't see any aliens. Maybe they had left.
Maybe he could still find . . .

Then something moved on the ground. It was the

alien he had winged. He was still coming, crawling.
And behind him, half a dozen others were starting
over.

Yes, Morrison thought, I guess you could say the
suppressors had failed. No other explanation.

I did the best I could, he thought as he turned the
carbine so its muzzle faced him. He preferred a slug
in the mouth to a facehugger.

The harvester's entry lock gave way under repeated
blows from the outside. The door flew open. Big-
bodied, ghastly, and weird, three aliens crowded into
it, their eager, evil faces turning at all angles on short
powerful necks, checking out the place, alert for danger. They ignored Norbert, protected by his suppressor. The dead crewmen from the harvester required
no attention.

Stan, watching from the lander, said, "All right,
Norbert. Do it now."

Norbert lifted Mac, removed his collar into which a
suppressor was built, and handed him to one of the
aliens. The alien showed no surprise, quietly accepted
Mac from Norbert's arms.

Handling the dog carefully, the alien turned, left the
ship, and joined the others outside. Then, as if in response to an inaudible signal, they all started marching across the plain. Stan, Gill, and Julie watched on
their screen as Norbert fell into line behind the group
of aliens carrying Mac. Watching from the lander
through Norbert's vision sensors was uncannily like
being within the robot alien himself, feeling his body
sway and move as it negotiated the uneven ground.
Stan had to adjust the audio because the wind out
there on AR-32's plain had risen swiftly after the mist
dissipated and now was shrieking like a banshee,
pushing and pulling against the line of aliens, slowing
but not stopping them as sand was alternately pushed
into mounds in front of them and then suddenly
scoured away.

They were moving toward the hive, which was now
and then revealed as Norbert changed the angle of his
vision from the ground immediately in front of him to
the hazy horizon line. The hive was still quite a long
way away, perhaps a hundred yards, when the aliens
stopped and began looking around.

Stan leaned close to the screen and stared but he
couldn't tell what they were looking for: a specially
coded pheromone signal, perhaps, because they
fanned out and continued searching, their heads turning back and forth like hounds following a scent.

At last one of them found something. A silent signal seemed to pass between him and the others, and
they all moved together to a piece of ground that
looked no different to Stan's eyes than any other.
Rooting in the soil, the leading alien dislodged a large
flat piece of stone, revealing a shallow tunnel leading
into the earth.

The tunnel sloped downward for perhaps twenty
feet, then leveled out. It had been made with some
care. The light, friable soil was held in by flat rocks,
some of which were highly phosphorescent.

"Look at how the roof is shored up," Stan remarked
to Gill.

"That's more technical skill than we ever gave the
aliens credit for."

"It is possible, sir," said Gill, "that their tunnel-
building abilities are genetic, as is the case with the
ants you have studied."

"Yes," Stan said. "Can you see what they're doing,
Ari?" He lifted the cybernetic ant on his fingertip and
moved his hand toward the screen. "These are like big
cousins of yours, aren't they?"

Ari raised his head, but it was impossible to tell
whether or not he was thinking anything.

Down in the tunnel, Norbert was reporting that the
passageway was widening as they moved closer to the
hive. Soon other branchings appeared as the aliens
moved; as if by instinct, making their way through the
increasingly complex maze without hesitation.

"Norbert, you've been laying down an electronic trail, haven't you?" Stan asked.

"Yes, Doctor. Ever since we were on the outside of this tunnel. But I'm not completely sure the job is getting done."

"I hope it is. It could come in handy. Don't you think so, Julie?"

"Sure, Stan," Julie concurred. "But I don't understand why you're sending Norbert in there. We've already got what we came for."

"You mean the harvester full of royal jelly? Yes, that was the purpose of our mission, and we have accomplished it. But we still have some time on our hands until Captain Hoban gets back into communication. So why not choose this moment for the advancement of science? It will profit all of mankind to know what the inside of a hive really looks like."

"That's true enough, Stan," Julie said. "I didn't know you cared that much about science, though."

"Julie, there's a lot I care for that I don't put into words. You ought to know that."

"I guess I do, Stan. You're not really interested in getting rich from this mission, are you?"

"Not as interested as you, my dear. But that is because I may not have much *tiempo para gastarlo*, as the Spanish say. But doing this is better than staying home trying to argue the doctors into giving me a better prognosis. At least here I can be with you, and I can't tell you how much that means to me."

Stan coughed, self-conscious for a moment, then glanced again at the screen. "Norbert is getting deeper into the hive and we still haven't heard from Captain Hoban. I think this might be a good moment for me to take a brief nap." Without further ado, he got up and went to the cot in the lander's rearmost living area.

Julie and Gill watched for a while in silence as Norbert, on the screen, continued to penetrate deeper into the hive. At last Julie said, "What did it mean, that thing he said in Spanish?"

"Tiempo para gastarlo," said Gill. "It means 'time to enjoy it.' "

Julie shook her head. "Stan's got a lot of knowledge."

"Yes," Gill said. "But perhaps not much time."

There were four crew members with Red Badger as he set up his next plan. Walter Glint was there, of course, and Connie Mindanao, limping from a beamer scorch in the side, and Andy Groggins and Min Dwin, both unwounded. That was a pretty good force to match against the five or six loyal men Captain Hoban probably had available.

That was the good news. On the bad side, they had been forced back to a rear area of the ship. It would be difficult to mount an attack through the corridors, with Hoban and his officers now armed and ready for them. And probably the rest of the crew would come in on Hoban's side, now that the first attempt at a takeover had failed. Things might have been different if Hoban hadn't responded so quickly. Badger, who had thought the captain to be a burned-out case, had to reevaluate the situation now.

Red was annoyed that his first plan hadn't succeeded. His people hadn't moved fast enough, and Hoban had been unexpectedly decisive. Now the best move was to get off the *Dolomite* and plan to contact Potter on the *Lancet.* Trouble was, getting off the ship wasn't going to be quite as simple as he'd like it to be.

There was just one lander left, the backup, now that Myakovsky and his people had gone to the surface of AR-32. It was sure to be guarded. Captain Hoban would have radioed the crew guarding the rear facilities, putting them on the alert. How many were there? Two or three, including the sergeant of the guards? Badger knew they'd have to get around or through them somehow.

"When we reach the storage bay, no firing until I

say so," Badger told the others. "I've got a little plan that just might work."

"Whatever you say, Red," said Glint.

Badger led them down the gleaming aluminum corridor, over deep-piled carpeting that seemed to soak up sound, past flickering lighting fixtures. The ever-present hum of the ship's machinery sounded in the walls like somnolent wasps. The only thing that told of the recent action was a faint smell of propellant and burned insulation in the otherwise antiseptic air; that and the labored sound of Connie Mindanao's breathing as she waited for the antipain shot to take effect.

At last they reached the transverse corridor that led to the pod bay. A faint hum warned Badger that all was not well here. He looked carefully and noted the violet-edged nimbus that extended from the walls.

"They've turned on the beam restraints," Badger said.

Glint came up from the rear and examined the situation. "They sure did, Red, but they don't have them on full."

Badger looked again. "You're right, Walt. They must not be running full power through the ship's net. Probably because of the damage we caused in the control room. Those beams should be visible to a distance of six inches from the side of the wall."

Min Dwin looked the situation over and reported, "Their circle of interdiction will extend beyond their visible range."

"Sure it will," Badger said. "But there'll still be a hole we can get through."

The entrance to the corridor was like a tall O. The violet flame burned on all sides of it, surrounding it entirely, but leaving the middle of the hole open.

"We'll have to dive through," Glint said. "Make sure not to touch the sides or the bottom."

"Shouldn't be too difficult," Badger said.

"Maybe not for you," Connie Mindanao said. "But

I've been wounded. How am I going to take a good jump through?"

A cruel little light glittered in Red Badger's eyes. "We'll take care of it for you, won't we, Glint? Grab her other arm."

Although she protested, the two big crewmen grabbed Connie. They swung her back and forth and, on the command from Badger, threw her headfirst through the corridor. Connie gave a shriek of protest as her foot trailed in the violet glow, but landed safe on the far side.

"Now the rest of us," Badger said. "The lander is just around the next bend. We're almost there!"

52

"Do you ever get sick of us so-called real people?" Julie asked suddenly.

Gill looked up, startled. He had been intent on the screen, watching as Norbert followed the group of aliens through the tunnels. Gill wanted to be ready to report to Dr. Myakovsky when the doctor awoke from his nap. But Julie's question seemed worthy of serious thought and he gave it, though not taking his eyes off the screen that showed Norbert's progress.

"I'm afraid," Gill said at last, "that I do not understand the question. It implies a precondition: that there is something in human behavior that I might get sick of. To what are you referring, Julie?"

"Wow!" Julie laughed. "I didn't expect to get that much out of you. But it isn't an answer."

"I am asking you to define your question, Miss Lish."

"You know very well what I mean," Julie said.

Gill found himself caught up and bewildered by the complexities of human thinking. It seemed to him that Julie was saying one thing and meaning another. The technical semanticists who had programmed his response bank had not given sufficient attention to the problem of ambiguity. Perhaps they couldn't solve it.

Gill and Julie looked at each other for a few moments in silence. Then Gill spoke. "You are referring, perhaps, to the fact that human actions are not always logical in terms of advantage? That they sometimes appear to be downright self-defeating?"

"Okay, that's one way of saying it," Julie said. "What do you think of that?"

Again Gill paused before answering. "I can only believe that illogic is essential to being human, since it is the one thing we synthetics are not capable of."

"You can't go against logic and programming, is that it?"

"It is, Miss Lish."

Julie didn't answer at once. Presently she reached out and took Gill's hand. Startled, the synthetic man let it go limp. Julie held it like she had never seen a hand before. She studied it, turning it slowly this way and that.

"What an amazing piece of construction this is." She marveled. "How perfectly the skin has been rendered and textured. It's hard to believe that anything as cunning as this could belong to someone not human."

"Yet so it is," Gill said.

"Is it? Or are you just being modest? A very human trait, I assure you."

"I don't know," Gill muttered. "One thing I do know is, Dr. Myakovsky loves you very much."

"Yes," Julie said, "I think he does. It's why he's here, isn't it?"

"I believe it is, Miss Lish."

"But why then am I here?"

"I do not know," Gill said. He hesitated. "It is a difficult way to get rich."

"Do you know of any easy ways?" Julie asked. "Do you know any better ways to pass your time on Earth than doing what I'm doing now?"

Gill shook his head. "I know nothing about these things."

Julie frowned and let his hand drop. "I like you, Gill, though you're very naive about some things. Look, Norbert seems to have reached the queen's chamber."

"You're right," Gill said. "I'll go wake up Dr. Myakovsky."

"I appear to be in an anteroom deep in the middle of the hive," Norbert reported. "I can see the queen's chamber just beyond. These surfaces and angles resemble nothing in my memory bank, Doctor. They seem to have been constructed according to a completely alien system. But that would stand to reason, wouldn't it?"

"You're doing fine," Stan said over the radio. "I just woke up and I'm pleased to see your progress. None of the aliens has sensed yet that you're not one of them?"

"No, Doctor. Though their examinations grow more stringent the deeper we go into the hive."

"I think we have them foxed," Stan said, sounding very pleased with himself. "This anteroom you're in appears to be an interesting place. Can you fix the focus? I can't make out what's on the walls."

"They are large containers," Norbert said. "They appear to be made from a waxy substance similar in molecular makeup to royal jelly. They appear to be filling those containers with jelly."

"Might they be storing water?" Stan asked.

"I don't believe so," Norbert said. "The containers seem to be holding liquids of slightly different colors and densities. The aliens grow quite excited when they go near these containers. They have to be urged by what I take to be the guards to move on. I think that these containers hold royal jelly deposited by certain especially potent queens or queen types. These may be more efficacious than the common run of the jelly, and be prized by the queen accordingly."

"With your equipment," Stan asked, "can you ascertain which is the purest?"

"There's no difficulty in that, Doctor."

"Then draw me off a sample. This sounds like the pure royal jelly I need."

After a moment Norbert said, "It is done."

"Good," Stan returned. "We'll meet up soon. Bring the sample with you. What are they doing with Mac?"

"The alien holding him has brought him into the queen's chamber. He is offering him to the queen."

"That is the queen ahead? The image is not distinct."

"There is a diffracting vapor in this room, Doctor. It is difficult to make out anything clearly. Take it easy, Mac!"

Stan said, "Why did you speak to the dog?"

"To get him to be quiet, sir. We don't want to mar matters as he is presented to the queen. She is receiving him now. Although I am not expert in alien physiognomy, I'd say she finds pleasure in the gift. She's holding him up to her olfactory receptors—"

"You should have killed him first," Julie interrupted.

"I was not instructed to do so," Norbert said. "No matter. He is beyond pain now. Doctor, one of the guards is coming over to me. It is to be another inspection."

"Well, you've passed them before."

"Yes, sir. But there are three guards interested in me this time. It must be because I came so close to the queen. Or maybe it was when I took the sample. I am stepping up my production of pheromones."

"Good idea," said Stan. "Is it helping any?"

"It doesn't seem to be doing much good. They are making odd head movements. I do not know what it means."

"What the hell has gone wrong?" Stan asked urgently. "What are they doing now?"

"They seem suspicious. They have seized me. What do you want me to do, Doctor?"

"Damn it," Stan spat. "I should have gotten you out of there before this! Norbert! Break free and get out!"

"Yes, sir," Norbert said. The big robot whirled, tearing himself free from the aliens' hooked claws. Then, dropping to all fours, he began scuttling down the corridor.

A reverse sensor in the back of Norbert's head clicked on and showed the view: the long winding tunnel curving behind, the three aliens scurrying on all fours after him.

Norbert was running full out. Stan had never seen him go so fast before. A thrill of pride went through him as he witnessed his creation in action. With speed like that, surely . . .

Stan could tell from the jarring movement of his sensor lens when the alien guard landed on Norbert's back. Stan winced as though the blow had landed on him. How could the guard be that fast? he wondered.

To Norbert he said, "Fight him off! Get out of there!"

"I'm trying, Dr. Myakovsky. But there are three of them—"

Abruptly the screen went blank.

Stan cried, "Norbert! Can you hear me? Come in!"

"Nothing," Gill said. He touched a dial, shook his head. "He's off the air."

"He's dead!" Julie cried.

"I didn't want this to happen," Stan screamed. "Not Norbert! Not Norbert!"

Julie said urgently, "Stan, get a hold of yourself."

Stan shuddered and let out a deep breath. He seemed calmer. "Can you get Captain Hoban?" he asked.

"Not yet, sir," Gill said.

Julie had stepped out of the control area for a moment. Now she was back, and her hair was flowing around her head like a network of electrical sparks had gotten into it.

"Stan," she said. "I just checked the short-range weather forecaster in the rear cabin. It's going haywire!"

"Just what we need," Stan groaned.

53

"**T**here's the Bay port, just ahead," Andy Groggins said. He had run ahead of Badger and the rest of the party. He had a slug-thrower with telescopic wire stuck under his arm. Strapped to his waist was a Geiss needle. He'd tied a bit of cloth around his forehead to keep sweat out of his eyes.

"We'll just ease our way in it," Red Badger said. His synthide shirt was torn, revealing his hairy freckled chest and prominent paunch. His small eyes gleamed as he pressed forward. He had a Krag beamer under his arm, its selector pointing to rapid intermittent.

The corridor widened at this point. There were separate passageways leading to "stores" in one direction and to "power" in the other.

As they came out into the wide opened area between corridors, a voice called out, "Freeze, you!"

Badger stood motionless. The others, coming along

behind him, managed to slink into the shadows. But Red Badger felt very exposed. He didn't let his apprehension show, however.

He took two casual steps forward and said, "It's all right, the captain sent us."

"He didn't tell me nothin' about that," the voice said.

Badger had it located now. It was coming from a paint locker on the far side of the corridor. The guard who was stationed here must have taken refuge when the trouble began elsewhere in the ship. But where was his partner?

"I don't blame you for being cautious," Badger said. "But I'm telling you it's all right. We're here to relieve you."

As he talked he peered ahead, trying to figure out how long it would take him to blast through the paint locker and kill the man inside. Too long, he decided. The guard could get him in a single well-placed burst first.

"Stop right there and drop your weapons," the guard called out.

"You're making a mistake," Badger said, and kept on coming. "Captain Hoban told us to secure this area as quickly as possible. Damn it, man, this is serious!"

"Stop right now, or—"

At that moment there was a double burst of slugthrower fire as Glint and Connie opened up almost simultaneously from opposite sides of the corridor. They held down their fire while the paint locker rattled up and down and bounced against the corridor wall, finally letting up only after blowing the door off the hinges and seeing the single guard inside fall out onto the deck.

"Let's go," Badger said, leading the way to the pod. "We're getting out of here."

54

"It's Badger and his men," one of the engineers remarked, reading the terse information that flowed to the TV screen from all parts of the ship. "He's killed the guard."

"Damn it!" Captain Hoban said. "Can you see what they're doing now?"

"They've just entered the pod."

"Seal the ports!" Hoban ordered.

"Too late. They've already opened them."

"Close them again!"

The engineer punched buttons then shook his head. "They've locked them into place. They're blasting off."

Hoban watched on the screen as a schematic came up, showing the *Dolomite*'s landing pod lifting out of its bay and maneuvering away from the ship's side.

"I can still pull them back with the short-range

tractors," the engineer said, his fingers poised on the controls.

Captain Hoban hesitated. At this range, he knew that the tractors would pull the pod apart. Badger and the others wouldn't stand a chance. He didn't want to go that far. There would be a court of inquiry over this. He needed to keep his record clean.

"Book their departure in the ship's log," he ordered.

"I don't know that they'll make it," the engineering officer said. "The weather's really bad out there."

Hoban looked and saw that an entire weather front had moved in while they were dealing with Badger. Long ragged clouds covered the planet's surface, clouds that were whipped and torn apart by the wind's violent action. Lightning flashed, huge jagged blue-violet bolts, several miles long, lancing out of the black-bellied clouds into the naked land below. Although the *Dolomite* was well above it, Hoban gave an involuntary shudder at the size of the storm.

"Try Dr. Myakovsky again," he ordered. "We have to warn him."

"I'm trying, sir," the officer said. "But no luck so far."

55

"**I**'m getting something," Gill reported.

"Thank God," said Julie.

"Is it Hoban?" Stan asked.

"Yes, I think it is."

Stan swung around in his big command chair and took the microphone from Gill's hand. "Hoban? What's going on there?"

"Sorry for the delay in transmission, sir," Hoban said, his voice echoing eerily around the lander's cabin. "We've had a revolt onboard. It's in hand now, but a group of crewmen have seized a pod and are on their way to the surface."

"Nothing much they can do to us," Stan said. "Listen, Captain, something really important has happened here. We've lost Norbert."

"Your robot alien? I'm sorry to hear it, sir, though I was never that fond of him."

"At least he died doing what he was built to do," Stan said.

"What about the dog?" Hoban asked.

"Yes, the dog's gone, too," Stan said brusquely. "Why is everyone so upset about the dog? The dog's not important. We've got troubles of our own."

There was no reaction to that. Stan cleared his throat and wondered how soon he could take another ampoule. Then he brought his attention back to present matters.

"Captain Hoban, we've found what we were looking for. The beekeepers have done our job for us. Norbert took over a Bio-Pharm harvester ship. It's packed full of royal jelly. We're rich, Captain."

"Yes, sir. If we can just get out of here now. Can you get up to our orbit?"

"Negative," Stan said. "We're still in the lander, which is barely maneuverable in this weather. Taking shelter in the harvester is our best bet, but it's going to take some doing to get there."

"Yes, sir," Hoban said. "I copy."

"Secondly, preliminary visual inspection shows the flight controls of the harvester were badly damaged in the fighting. I doubt it'll fly, but it'll provide more refuge than the lander. You'll have to come down to us."

"Yes, sir," Hoban said, without enthusiasm. "What about the volunteers?"

"We've lost touch with them," Stan answered. "As soon as we get ourselves out of here, they'll be our first order of business."

Hoban didn't like it, but it didn't seem the time or place to voice a disagreement.

"It ought to be simple enough," Stan said. "What you need to do, as soon as the weather stabilizes a little, is send the backup lander down here to pick us up. Our situation here is none too stable."

"We can't send the backup lander," Hoban said. "I told you, sir, Badger and his men took it. Can you maneuver at all in your lander, Dr. Myakovsky?"

"I don't know," Stan said. "They weren't made for

that sort of thing. And the weather down here is getting pretty severe."

"It's a major storm," Captain Hoban told him. "The worst of it is heading your way."

"Damn!" Stan spat. "You can't maneuver the *Dolomite* to pick us up, can you?"

"Not in this weather. None of us would stand a chance."

"All right." Stan paused. "Just a minute, let me think."

It was then that the storm front burst in all its fury upon the lander and the unprotected splinter of land it rested upon. Despite its weight, the lander was rocked to its foundations. The earth beneath it rippled and swayed. Lights went out and were replaced by the dull red glow of emergency lighting. Julie screamed as another motion of the storm shot her legs out from under her. Gill caught her before she was slammed into a support.

"Into the pod!" Stan shouted, referring to the small escape vehicle that the lander carried. "Gill, get in there and get power up."

Gill paused for a moment, looking at the five-point steel door separating them from the lander's rear compartment. "Maybe I should stay and try to help the crew?"

"They don't have a chance," Stan said. "We need your help to keep us alive! Now move!"

The three of them, Stan, Gill, and Julie, struggled back to the pod and, during a brief lull, got in. Stan slammed home the hatch and Julie dogged it into place. Gill waited until they were all strapped in, then blew open the lander's exit doors. The storm swept in.

Gill took the pod out under full acceleration. There was a moment of intoxicating freedom as the pod pulled away from the ship, then the full fury of the storm caught the little craft.

Stan just had time to secure himself into a command chair by magnetic clamps, then the pod was launched into the air like a rocket from a launcher. As it turned, Stan could see the land beneath the lander collapse, throwing the vehicle into a deep pit that suddenly yawned beneath it.

Glancing around, he saw that Julie was secured on a deceleration couch. A moment later the internal lighting went out.

The storm blazed at the pod's windows. There were long, stunning lines of force, outlined by a driving rain, lashing in at them. The pods spun around, its automatic stabilizers working hard to keep it on an even keel. The ground came up sickeningly below them, and the pod's jets blazed, avoiding the collision. They were airborne, and the sky through which they tore was colored ocher and purple. It was a world without stability, a place where titanic forces battled as though it were the beginning of time.

"Can't you get her down, Gill?" Stan called out above the deafening clatter.

"I'm trying, Doctor," Gill said, busy over the controls.

"You can do it, Gill!" Julie cried.

"We hope," Stan said.

Gill's long fingers played across the controls. The pod seemed to flutter and skitter like a crazed bat in the luridly lit space between the harsh ground below and the beetling thunderheads above. The little craft spun like a leaf driven by a storm. Julie had to shut her eyes tightly to control the vertigo and nausea that racked her as the pod trembled and shook and rattled like a riveting machine gone berserk.

For Stan the pain was almost unbearable as his tortured lungs strove to replace the air that the violent motions of the storm were driving out of him. He had never known such pain. And yet, paradoxically, he was also experiencing a moment of great exhilaration, a feeling of himself as a conquistador of the new age, persevering through pain and hardship as a new world and new opportunities came into sight.

Yes, he thought, it has all been worth it. The pain

reminds me that I'm alive. This is the way to go. But I do wish it would stop!

And then, abruptly, they entered a space of quiet air and Gill was able to maneuver the controls. Suddenly the pod dropped thirty feet and hovered for a moment on its jets, bare inches above the ground. Then, with an almost grudging sigh—as though the insensate machine had enjoyed its experience of being airborne in the midst of fury—it settled to the ground.

Gill set the clamping system that secured the ship to the bedrock it had settled upon.

He said, "Last stop, Grand Central Station. All passengers prepare to detrain."

Stan unbuckled himself shakily. "Why, Gill, I didn't know you had a sense of humor."

"I don't," Gill said. "My words were for the purpose of helping you and the others keep your spirits up."

"Commendable," Stan said. He closed his eyes for a moment, enjoying the blessed relief of relative silence and no motion. Then he asked, "Everyone okay? Then let's take stock."

56

Red Badger and his people sat together on the semicircular couches that almost filled the main section of the pod. Red had remembered to bring aboard a carton of emergency rations, each in a self-heating aluminoplex container. He passed these around now. Walter Glint had a half-full canteen of raisin wine he'd brewed himself in the ship's locker room, before the hypersleep procedure, using copper tubing he'd liberated from the heat circulation system. He passed around the brew, and Min Dwin came up with some narcosmoke cigarettes. In a little while they were quite a cheerful bunch. If only they'd been able to raise some dance music! It was one hell of a party shaping up.

Badger liked to party as well as anyone. But the unfamiliar duties of command distracted him from really letting go. He turned to the little all-wave radio receiver tucked away in one of the pod's storage compartments. He needed to keep his people content, because he was counting on them to see him safely through this.

Although he wouldn't let on to the others, Badger was more than a little disturbed by how things had gone so far. He had counted on seizing the *Dolomite* in his first attempt, when surprise had been in his favor. Back then, taking the initiative had seemed the thing to do.

That was not how matters had worked out, however. Now they were alone, isolated on a savage planet that favored no life except alien. Badger had been thinking furiously, trying to find a way to wrest victory from the jaws of defeat.

Then he thought he had it.

He set the sweep alarm on the radio to wide scanning and began searching the radio waves. It required no master radio operator to find a signal in a place as barren of radio activity as this one. Red locked onto the signal and began transmitting.

57

Adams, the *Lancet*'s radio operator was a tall gangling youth with red hair and a prominent Adam's apple. He came into the main control room without knocking, because Captain Potter had posted standing orders that messages of urgency were to be transmitted at once and without the usual protocol that prevailed on the interstellar ships.

"Yes, what is it, Adams?" Potter snapped. The captain was tall and strongly constructed. His features were handsome and coarse, from the big knife of a nose to the heavy tufted eyebrows that gave his face a sinister character. He wore a midnight-blue uniform with gold flash marks on the sleeves, showing his years of service in the Interspace Mariners' Association. His voice was low-pitched, harsh, and resonant, the sort of voice you paid attention to the first time you heard it.

"Radio signal, sir," Adams said.

"Is it from the people on the harvester?"

"No, sir. We still haven't been able to establish contact with them. Their radio doesn't respond. I don't think it looks good, sir."

"Nobody gives a damn what you think," Potter said, his voice dropping to a sawmill rasp. "Who's the message from?"

"A man who calls himself Red Badger," Adams said. "He says he's a crewman from the *Dolomite*."

"*Dolomite?* Never heard of it. What location did they give?"

"They're descending to the surface of AR-32, sir."

Potter stared at the crewman, eyes narrowed, dark brows creased. "That's quite impossible," he said at last. "This planet is our exclusive preserve."

Adams was about to reply, but perceived just in time that Potter was talking aloud to himself.

"I'll speak to him," Potter said. "Put it through for me."

Adams went to the console and made the necessary adjustments. Badger's voice came through on the loudspeaker.

"Captain Potter? Sir, this is Crewman Badger from the ship *Dolomite*. Sir, a situation has arisen which I would like to acquaint you with."

"Go ahead," Potter said, and listened carefully as Badger told about the revolt he had led on the *Dolomite*.

"We didn't think it was fair, sir, Captain Hoban taking us into an area that was under the exclusive control of Bio-Pharm. The men asked me to speak for them. I talked with Captain Hoban, sir, in fair and reasonable terms, asking him to get a ruling from Bio-Pharm before taking us into this area. Can't say more reasonable than that, can I, sir? But Captain Hoban didn't see it that way. He ordered me and my men put into irons and held to face criminal charges back on Earth. We didn't agree, there was a fight, and me and some of the men came down to the planet."

"You're on the surface of AR-32 now?" Potter asked.

"Yes, sir. And we're not the only ones. There's a Dr. Myakovsky down here, too, in his own pod, sir. He's come to this place to steal your royal jelly. He and Hoban are criminals, and they want to put us on charges!"

"That's very interesting," Potter said. "Do you happen to have their exact location?"

"I'm afraid not, sir, since me and my mates had to leave ship in a hurry, so to speak. But I'll bet anything they're heading for the hive, where they sent that robot of theirs."

"What robot are you referring to?"

"The one they call Norbert. Looks just like an alien, sir, only it's not a real one. There's a law against that, isn't there? The damned thing already killed some of my shipmates."

"There's a law against it, all right," Potter muttered. "My law, if no other!"

"Beg pardon, sir?"

"Never mind. What is this robot supposed to do?"

"Collect royal jelly, sir. And leave an electronic trail showing Myakovsky where to go."

"Damn it!" Potter sputtered. "They could get what they came for and be out of here before we could stop them."

"No, sir," Badger said. "I've heard them talking to Captain Hoban on the radio. They plan to get through the hive by following an electronic signal that their robot is to lay down for them. But if me and my mates was to wipe out that electronic trail . . ."

"I like the idea of that," Potter said slowly. "Can you do it? You would be rendering me a valuable service."

"Indeed we can, sir. We're hoping it'll be taken into consideration when you pick us up. You are going to rescue us, aren't you, sir?"

"You can count on it," Potter said. "There could be a reward in this for you. Does that sound good, Mr. Badger? Get in there and wipe out that trail. Then

come to coordinates 546Y by 23X. We'll rendezvous
with you there. You men will be rewarded for your
good work."

"Thank you, sir! You'll be hearing from us soon."

The transmission ended. Potter turned to Adams.
"Well, what are you standing around for? Get back to
the radio room! And not a word of this to the crew, or
I'll have your hide!"

"Yes, sir!" Adams saluted smartly and backed out of
the room.

Potter waited until he was gone, then looked
around the control room. The only ones present were
his chief engineering officer, Ollins, and the helmsman, Driscoll.

"Driscoll," Potter snapped.

"Sir?"

"You've heard nothing of this."

"No, sir!"

"You can take a break now, mister. Ollins and I will
finish out your watch."

"Yes, sir. Thank you, sir." Driscoll saluted and left
the control room.

Lieutenant Ollins was a grizzled old veteran of
many space flights who had served with Potter before. In fact, the two men came from the same town
in Tennessee. Ollins relaxed when Driscoll was away
from the control room. Potter afforded him great priv-
ileges when none of the men were around. When they
were, it was spit and polish and punctilio all the way,
because that was the sort of man Potter was.

"Well, Tom," Potter said. "Seems we've got a bit of
a situation on our hands."

"Seems so, sir," Ollins said. "But unless I miss my
guess . . ."

"Yes? Go ahead, Tom."

"Unless I miss my guess, sir, you've thought up an
interesting way to take care of it."

Potter permitted himself a smile. "I don't know if
I'd say 'interesting,' Mr. Ollins. But 'thorough' . . . Yes,
I think you'll find my way very thorough."

58

Rain hammered against the pod's hatch like shot from a battery of shotguns. The pod quivered and shook as the storm shrieked and swore to itself, its voice falling to a whisper then rising to a banshee wail. Stan and the others were suited up in all-weather outfits that would give them some protection against the elements, though not much against the aliens. It was time to go.

"Okay," Stan said. "Julie, you feel up to this?"

"I'm perfectly ready for a stroll," Julie said airily. "It's just about sunset, isn't it?"

"Yes," Gill said. "I've checked out the hive on remote sensing. The activity is reaching a peak."

"A perfect time for us to drop in," Julie said.

Stan felt a warm glow go through him when he looked at her. She was young, beautiful, and very brave. They were in about as difficult a situation as he could imagine, but she wasn't giving in a bit to it.

He turned to Gill. "What weapons do we have?"

Gill opened a locker and showed what he had brought. "Five chemical slugthrowers with fifty slug clips. These are somewhat old-fashioned weapons, but they are reliable. And their fifty-caliber slugs pack a wallop. I brought three Gauss needlers. They're recoilless, and their steel slivers ought to have a good effect against the aliens. I was only able to bring one Gyroc, and a bandolier of point seventy-five-caliber spin-stabilized rockets. Two high-impulse laser rifles, both fully charged, and that completes the arsenal, except for half a dozen concussion grenades. I would have liked a greater selection, but that was all that was available at the moment."

"You have done admirably," Stan said. "That's quite an array."

"And, of course, I also have the light tracker, a heavy-duty communicator. As well as the suppressors to get us past the aliens undetected."

"Very important, that last," Stan said. "What range do the inhibitors have?"

"They'll dampen at close to one-hundred-percent strength for approximately three meters in all directions."

"And how long will they last?"

"That's the bad part," Gill said. "They may be good for half an hour at full strength, but it could be less."

"Well, we'll just have to move quickly and hope we have some luck. Julie, have you reached Captain Hoban yet?"

"Just getting him now." Julie spoke into her wrist enunciator. "Can you hear me, Hoban?"

"Loud and clear," Hoban's voice came back to them. "I was beginning to worry. What happened to you people?"

"Nothing good," Julie said. "But we're on AR-32 and we're still alive and in one piece. Three pieces, I should say."

"What are your plans?" Hoban asked.

Julie turned to Stan. He said, "We have to get out

of the pod, Captain. The storm is shaking it to pieces. What news do you have about your mutiny?"

"The mutineers grabbed our backup lander and took off for AR-32. It'll be a miracle if they weren't destroyed on their way down."

"A miracle for us if they were," Stan said. "Captain, we have our suppressors and there's only one thing we can try that'll bring this off. We're going to go through the hive, following Norbert's trail. That'll get us out of the storm, which will destroy us otherwise. We should be able to follow Norbert's trail to the far side, where the harvester is. We'll board that and come up to you. You, meanwhile, will take geosynchronous orbit at the harvester's coordinates. I'm transmitting those coordinates digitally. Please acknowledge."

Stan's fingers flew over the computer's keys. Soon he heard Captain Hoban's acknowledgment. "I've got it, Dr. Myakovsky."

"Good. What do you think of the plan, Captain?"

"It seems to me the best, given the circumstances. Does Gill concur?"

The android nodded. "There's really nothing else to do," he added in a quiet voice.

"It's perfect," Julie said. "What have we got to lose but our lives?"

"Signing off, then, Captain," Stan said. "See you in an hour or so, I hope."

He turned to Gill. "Have you any objections?"

"As I said, Doctor, given the circumstances, there's nothing else to do."

"But you wouldn't have gotten us into this fix in the first place. Is that it?"

"I didn't say that, sir."

"You didn't have to." Stan looked out the port at the lurid sunset that had just begun flaming behind the upthrust bulk of the hive. He reached into an inner pocket and brought out a small aluminum case, like a cigar case only slightly larger. Opening it, he extracted an ampoule of royal jelly.

"Well," he said, "time for a little ride down the street of dreams, eh?" He looked at Gill and Julie, who were watching him. "I need it," he said defensively. "It's the pain. . . ." Abruptly he pulled himself together. He returned the ampoule to the case and put the case back in his pocket.

"No, I'll do it straight," Stan said. "That ought to be ever so much more amusing. Ready, then? Gill, crack the port!"

Gil undogged the hatch. It took his and Julie's combined strength to push it all the way open against the wind pressure. And then it was done, and the three of them staggered out into the raging storm.

59

There was no easy way to hold a conversation as Stan, Julie, and Gill made their painful march across the wind-whipped plain toward the great rounded mound of the hive. Behind it the sunset flared, sending streamers and columns of radiance around the basalt-blue solid-looking clouds that seemed to march across the plain like giants.

Julie looked at the sunset in awe. She did not consider herself a nature lover, yet this kindling of shapes and colors that seemed too intense to be natural almost brought tears to her eyes. The display touched off a memory.

She was a little girl in the high, carven house of Shen Hui. It was one of his holiday houses in Shan Lin Province, and there was a pool in the garden in which golden carp moved back and forth, and a wind chime in a nearby temple sent forth a sad melody that seemed to speak of ancient days and old-fashioned manners.

It was only then that Julie thought of her mother, whom she had never known, but who visited her almost nightly in dreams whose memory she lost upon awakening.

They walked for a long time, bent into the driving wind, and came at last to the base of the hive. Looking up at the great, pitted, gray-brown surfaces covered with branchlike vines, Stan saw that it resembled some exotic plant. It was pockmarked with puckered holes, many of which were large enough to admit a man. Stan wondered if the hive might not be an organism in its own right, symbiotically connected to the aliens, coexisting with its own weird life-forms.

It was an interesting fancy, but Stan thought it was more logical to assume that the aliens had constructed the hive, following instinctual instructions laid down in their DNA aeons past.

Still, it pleased his fancy to imagine that the hive and the aliens were two different types of living matter. What a startling possibility! He could see the headlines now, heralding his discovery. . . .

He smiled wryly and reminded himself that his only job now was to stay alive, to keep on going until he could find the pure and unadulterated royal jelly that might extend his life—if there was any truth to his conjectures.

He and Julie walked around the hive until they found an opening. It loomed ahead of them, a dark and ragged hole that plunged into the depths of the hive.

"Are you ready for this?" Stan asked.

Gill didn't answer. Julie said, "If that's where you want to go, I'll go with you."

There seemed no way into
the hive. They found what looked like a pathway that
spiraled up its side.

They climbed up the long, narrow ramp that looked
to be part roadway, part vine. It went up the side of
the hive in long sloping curves, and there were rough-
barked vinelike things along the side that served as
handholds, and other things that looked like snapped-
off tree limbs and might have provided footholds for
taloned feet.

Using these as handholds, they half hiked, half
climbed, up the side of the hive. The storm was still
buffeting them, its wind gusts swirling in from all directions. The slanted rain made the footing slick and
unsafe. When Julie was able to spare a glance to the
side, she saw the great plain of AR-32 spread out below, all bathed in strange red-and-violet sunset colors,
cut through here and there with deep, black fissures.

She was leading the way, with Stan in the middle and Gill bringing up the rear. Stan was short of breath already, and Julie, listening to him labor as he walked, decided it didn't augur well for the future.

She was worried about Stan, but he had gotten them into this situation. She just hoped he was well enough and sane enough to get them out of it.

Then they reached an opening camouflaged against the side of the hive by a dense growth of vines. They pushed inside and found a broad roadway that curved inward and upward.

The spiraling roadway terminated in a wide opening that seemed to lead deeper into the hive. Julie was less than ten feet away from the opening when something within it, a darkness against the darkness, stirred and moved.

She whispered, "Oh, shit," and froze.

Stan noticed that she had stopped and also halted.

Gill stopped, too, peering upward, trying to make out what was the matter.

As Julie waited, barely breathing, an ugly dark head with a long backward-sloping cranium poked out of the hole above her. Its fangs were clearly visible, gleaming white, impossibly sharp and packed together, dripping with green matter.

Then the alien's muscular body came out slowly, foot by foot, and its claws grasped the spiraling track on which Julie and the others were standing. The alien began to descend, moving directly into their path.

"I think it can't see me," Julie said, praying that it was true. The indicator on her suppressor showed less than half an hour left in the batteries.

Well, she thought, half an hour is a long time. But then she wondered, What if the gauge is simply stuck at the half-hour mark?

The alien came right up to her, so close she could smell the acrid tang of its hide.

Julie moved to the far edge of the narrow pathway.

Taking a grip on one of the vines at the side, she leaned far over, giving the creature room to pass.

Its ferocious blind-looking face passed within inches of her, its hard black flank brushed her side, and then it was past, descending toward the ground.

Stan and Gill, below her, moved to give it room.

Julie slipped into the opening at the top of the hive, the others following close behind. The passageway widened out to a tube about ten feet in diameter. It curved downward and to the left, and soon there was only a ghostly memory of light for them to see their way by.

About twenty feet down, the tunnel widened into a cave. It was difficult to make out its dimensions in that shadow-infested place, perhaps fifty yards long by twenty wide, but it could have been twice that, the remaining dimensions lost in the gloom.

There were things growing between the floor of the cave and its low ceiling. Then they moved into a wider area, where they could stand upright.

Stan and his party paused here to redistribute their loads, make a final check of their weapons, take a drink of water, and have a last conference before plunging deeper into the hive.

Stan was disturbed that Norbert had been unable to lay down an electronic trail. But he was too tired to worry about it much.

He lay down on the uneven ground. He needed a moment to catch his breath. It was tough going, there was no doubt about that. His chest burned incessantly. It had been a long time since he'd had a dose of royal jelly. The case with the ampoules was still in his pocket; it felt comforting there. He wanted one now, badly. Anything to get out of this incessant pain, which seemed to radiate out from his chest and course down his arms and legs, following the pathways of his arteries and veins.

He pulled out an ampoule and hastily swallowed its contents. And then he had to scramble to his feet as he heard sounds from somewhere in the tunnel.

They had to depend on searchlights now to find their way, for the last of the natural light was cut off as they rounded another turn.

And came face-to-face with another alien.

It was moving toward them on all fours, its ugly head questing right and left, seeming to be sniffing the stale, earth-flavored air. It was clear that it had picked up a scent or cue, but apparently it couldn't tell where it was coming from. The creature slid past them like liquid black iron, and they moved on in silence.

There was a sort of grim interminability about that nightmare journey into the hive. Julie felt that time itself was standing still as they proceeded into the silence of that awesome construction. She felt she was on a dream descent into depths that corresponded in some way that she didn't understand to the depths of her own being.

Abruptly she came back to attention. Her searchlight picked out incomprehensible shapes as she moved ahead. There seemed to be huge things with tall stooped shoulders and folded wings towering above them. There were oval things scattered here and there, like ostrich eggs, only with a strange cross-hatched texture of fine lines. There were plants with wide, white faces, and they turned toward the searchlight beam as if it reminded them of something they had once known a very long time ago.

Stan said, "This is some weird place, huh, Gill?"

Gill shrugged. "I suppose this hive has been in existence for a long time. Centuries, maybe. It stands to reason that a lot of different life-forms would have tried to establish themselves here. It's one of the few places on this planet that's out of the wind."

"I wish I could get a videotape of this," Stan said.

"You planning to do a TV special?" Julie asked.

"It would be a first. What's that up ahead?"

By the light of Stan's searchlight, he saw that the floor of the cave abruptly declined and became a large hole. Stan approached it cautiously and played his light along it. The sides sloped down sharply for about five feet, revealing that the interior of the hole was filled with a mixture of substances. Stan's flashlight picked out bones and body parts, vegetables in advanced stages of rot or desiccation, bits of wood and rock, and other kinds of debris he couldn't make out.

"What is it, Stan?" Julie asked.

"It appears to be a midden. A garbage dump."

"Ugh!" Julie said.

"No, it's really very interesting," Stan said. "A midden can tell you all about the life of the hive. Look at all that stuff! Isn't that a cow carcass down there? And what's that over there . . . ?"

He focused the searchlight beam and looked again.

"It looks like a dog collar," he said at last.

The three of them were silent for a moment. The memory of Mac the dog hung in the air like something evil, something they would have preferred to forget.

"I suppose this is where they threw Mac when the queen was through with him," Stan said. "That's certainly his collar with the suppressor attached. We can use that for ourselves."

He leaned over the pit to pick up the collar. Suddenly the ground crumbled beneath him. Stan scrambled for footing, fell backward, his arms windmilling wildly. Julie lunged for him and almost managed to grab his ankle, but lost her grip as Stan pitched over the edge with a bloodcurdling yell.

For Stan, that moment of falling into the aliens' garbage pit was so intensely terrifying as to be almost pleasurable. In the split second a million things flashed in front of his eyes like high-speed movie images. Some residue of the royal jelly in his veins kicked in, and he had a moment of pure illusion.

He dreamed in that instant that he was on a mountaintop, and on all sides of him were birds and beasts, waiting to hear what he had to tell them. Mac was there in his dream, sitting up on his hind paws begging, his tongue lolling out. Stan himself seemed to be wearing a robe made out of a luminous golden material, and he was not entirely surprised to find a golden halo circling his brow, casting a mellow light of its own. He was about to address all of the birds and beasts, tell them it was all right, when he struck the bottom of the pit with a resounding jar.

"Stan!" Julie cried. "Can you hear me?"

Gill came up beside her. "Is he alive?"

"I don't know yet. Stan!"

Stan stirred, then fell back.

"Stan! Call out if you can hear me," Julie cried.

Stan didn't answer, but something else did. Something that spoke in a sibilant hiss, with many overtones. It was not a single voice. It was many voices. The hissing voices were like the tumultuous waves of an acid sea. Julie tried to direct her light. Gill was beside her, his hand on her shoulder. Suddenly his grip tightened.

"What is it?" she said, and then she saw it, too.

There were passageways into the lower part of the midden. From them, heads peered; the characteristic heads of aliens. This was apparently a shortcut into a lower level of the hive. The aliens must have heard the noise Stan made while he was falling.

The aliens had come out to investigate. It was like before when they had met the alien coming into the hive. Only this time something had changed. It took Julie a moment to figure out what it was. Then she shuddered in horror.

"Gill, my God!" she said. "The suppressor must have quit. They can see him!"

61

When Stan recovered consciousness, he had one delicious moment of thinking he was ten years old and had just awakened from a particularly terrifying dream. How grateful he was to find himself in his own bed! There, just across from him, was his computer, a good one, which his parents had bought for his last birthday. His floppy-eared toy puppy was there, though of course he was too old to play with it. Still, Mr. Muggs watched while Stan did his experiments.

Now Stan stretched luxuriously and tried to think how he'd spend his day. There were some spiderwebs down near the brook that he wanted to investigate. . . .

His outstretched fingers touched something wet and sticky. He recoiled, turned his head, looked. It was Mac, dead. He had pushed his fingers into the sticky wound in Mac's throat. What he had thought was his computer was actually the skeleton of a cow. And there were aliens glaring at him, seeing him, and starting toward him. . . .

"Gill!" Julie screamed. "Start shooting! But for God's sake don't hit Stan!"

Julie was firing as she spoke. She had unslung the plasma rifle she had been carrying by its strap over her shoulder. Red-orange flame lanced out from its muzzle, painting the garbage pit in lurid colors and huge dancing shadows.

The concentrated fury of the plasma blast danced around the aliens, who had begun advancing on Stan from a passageway that led into the midden. Red, acetylenelike cutting flames poked and probed at them, lancing through their bodies, stabbing into arms and legs. Gill was firing simultaneously, caseless carbine rounds that blew the aliens off their feet, sending them halfway up the pit, to tumble back again in a welter of severed arms and heads.

The plasma fire and the caseless rounds wove a dance of death around Stan's recumbent body. The fire approached him and then, almost delicately, backed away again.

Julie ran around the circumference of the pit, firing to keep the aliens from coming up on Stan from behind. Gill held his position, blasting a way clear for Stan, who finally stumbled to his feet and made his way to the side of the pit. He tried feebly to climb back out.

"Can you hold them, Gill?" Julie asked.

"I think so," Gill muttered.

Julie slung her plasma rifle and reached out for Stan's hand. Their fingers touched and clasped. No sooner did Julie have a good grip than she heaved, putting into it every ounce of strength in her slender body. Stan seemed to fly into the air, landing on the edge of the pit.

While he tried to catch his breath, Gill finished off the last of the aliens, scattering arms and legs everywhere. Then he turned to help Stan. Stan tried to get

to his feet, then slumped again to the ground. Before
anyone could grab him, he slid again into the pit.

"Oh, no!" Julie said. "Hold my ankle, Gill, I'll get
him."

They tried, but couldn't reach. Stan appeared to be
on the edge of unconsciousness. His eyelids fluttered
briefly behind his thick glasses, which miraculously
had not been knocked off. His fingers clawed at the
debris-strewn surface. From behind him, there was
another hissing sound. An alien suddenly appeared,
two others behind it.

"Kill it!" Julie cried.

"I can't!" Gill said. "Stan's in the way!"

"He's in my way, too!" Julie began to run around
the side of the pit, trying to get a clear shot.

The leading alien looked somehow different to her
from the others. But at first she couldn't determine
how. Then Gill threw a phosphorus flare and she saw
that the alien had half his shoulder chewed off. There
was also damage to his midsection and head.

But what she wasn't prepared for was the look of
those wounds. Instead of flesh and blood, there appeared to be cable and metal fittings in the wound,
and small humming servos.

For a moment she couldn't process this information. Then she understood.

"Norbert!"

62

Since they pulled him out of the midden, Stan had drifted into a different place. He seemed to be in a spaceless space and a timeless time. It was a world filled with little blue-and-pink clouds. There were stars in the background, and pools of water. He was not surprised to see Norbert standing in front of him. Nothing could be strange to Stan any longer. He had passed beyond weirdness, into a place where all effects were the same, all part of the great symphony of death, whose opening notes he could hear as though coming to him from a great distance, but getting louder, louder.

This couldn't have been an illusion because it answered him.

Norbert said, "Yes, I am here, Dr. Myakovsky. I am functioning at only twenty-seven percent of capacity."

Stan blinked and his vision cleared. He was in the

alien garbage midden, lying on his back on mounds of refuge. In front of him, bending over, was Norbert.

"It must have been quite a fight," Stan said, surveying the robot.

"I would say so, Doctor. I killed three of them in a running battle through the hive. Unfortunately, they did damage to me that I fear will prove terminal."

"Are you afraid?" Stan asked.

"Not in the personal sense, Doctor. By fear, I meant regret that I will no longer be able to serve you as you designed me."

"Can't you turn on your self-repair circuits?" Stan asked.

"I tried that, Doctor. They are down. And you did not equip me with self-repair units for the self-repair units."

"In the future we'll have infinite backups for all systems," Stan said. "Including human ones, I hope. Including mine."

"Are you all right, Doctor?"

"I've definitely had better days," Stan said. "My self-repair circuits aren't working right, either." He felt something in his hand and held it up. "Look here! Mac's collar! I've got it!"

"That's fine, Doctor," Norbert said. "I have something, too."

"What is it?" Stan asked.

"This." Norbert reached into the gaping wound in his shoulder and drew out a gooey mass the color of honey.

"What is it?" Stan asked.

"Royal jelly from the queen's birthing chamber," Norbert said. "I was unable to provide a proper container. I'm afraid it's gotten some oil on it, and some blood."

"Doesn't matter," Stan said. He reached out and took the mass. It had a waxy consistency. He put it in his mouth, made himself chew and swallow it. He experienced no immediate effect.

"Great work!" Stan said.

Behind him he heard big objects move and slide around as something came from the interior of the hive.

"Better get going, Doctor," Norbert said. "They're coming. I'll cover your retreat as well as I can."

"I don't see how," Stan grumbled.

"I improvised a weapon. I hope it will suffice."

Stan pulled himself onto his hands and knees and worked his way toward the edge of the pit. Behind him he could hear sizzling energy beams as Norbert and the others fought off the aliens. Norbert was buying him time.

Stan tried to pull himself up the side of the pit, but the crumbling structure gave way under him and he fell to the bottom again. Pain washed over him in great uncontrollable waves, and in each one he thought he might drown, only to come back again and again, each time more feebly, to the surface of consciousness.

He felt Julie's hand in his, and then Gill's hand. He was lifted into the air. Below him he heard Norbert's battle still raging, and the shrill screaming sounds that the aliens made as they died in the violet-edged bolts that Norbert's impromptu weapon cast. But the aliens kept on coming, and as Julie and Gill pulled Stan out of the pit and beat a hasty retreat down a tunnel, they heard the sounds of Norbert being pulled down and torn apart.

63

Glint asked, "Is this the place?"

Badger checked the crude map he had drawn following Potter's instructions. Yes, there were the two fan-shaped rocks, and over there was the fissure cut like a curly S.

"We're at the spot all right."

"Okay," Glint said. "But where is he? Where's the rescue pod?"

They were standing on a wide flat rock shelf. It stood practically under the shadow of the hive. The wind had died down for a moment. They could look out over the nearly featureless landscape. Toward the west there was a line of lime-green haze, possibly sent up by some natural circumstance. So much about a place like AR-32 was simply incomprehensible.

Yet, even on Earth, despite his thousands of years of occupation, despite his long acquaintance with bird, fish, and fowl, things could still surprise man as well. Strange animals turned up every year. Mysteries abounded. Even the status of ghosts was still uncertain. No one had ascertained for sure whether or not the Yeti or the Jersey Devil really existed. Were there such things as werewolves and vampires?

But on AR-32, the anomalous and the unexpected happened all the time.

You tended to think of such things on a planet like AR-32. Mankind had known of the place for less than ten years. No genuinely scientific expedition had ever visited it. Only commercial vessels called, and for the sole purpose of stealing (though they called it collecting) the aliens' jelly. The men who went on such expeditions were as hard-bitten a lot as conquistadores of old Spain. Like them, they cared little for what lay below them or what it might mean in the scheme of things.

It was not unusual that Badger and his men, who were as much of the conquistador type as the crewmen on the *Lancet*, were surprised but not absolutely astonished when a creature raised its head from behind a rock and looked at them.

"What in hell is that?" Meg asked.

Badger and the others turned. The creature was sitting there looking at them. It had a large head somewhat the size and shape of a hogshead. Eight little skinny legs came down from its sides, terminating in blunt claws. Something about the creature was reminiscent of a pig, right down to the way it snuffled and oinked at the crewmen. It had a small curly tail. It was colored pink, and it had a black saddle marking in the middle of its back.

"What do you suppose that thing is?" Glint asked.

Badger said, "It's some critter indigenous to this planet, I think. Boys, I'll bet we're the first ones ever to look at this thing."

"G'wan!" Meg said. "One of the *Lancet* people might have seen it first."

"No way to prove that," Badger said. "But this thing

could be rare, and never take to hanging around the
places where humans live and work. Like the bobcat
and the wolverine on Earth. If there's animals like
that on Earth, why not here?"

"Here, fella," Meg called. "Why'ncha come over
here?"

The piglike thing lifted its little triangular ears and
stared at them with bulbous blue eyes. It lifted a fore-
paw and pawed the ground. Then it trotted over to
Meg.

"Hey, ain't that nice?" said Meg. She reached over
and scratched the creature above its ears. It made a
high-pitched grunting sound that had about it a tone
of approval. No mistaking that sound for a cry of
pain.

The others crowded around. "Cute, ain't it?" said
Glint, who had raised hogs in Arkansas.

Meg said, "I wonder why it came to us?"

"Can't tell about alien life-forms," Badger said. "I
wonder if we should take this fellow along with us.
Back on Earth sell him to a circus, make a lot of
money off'n him. I wonder what he eats?"

"I'm sure he'd tell us if he could," Meg said,
scratching the creature's back. "Where do you come
from, fellow?"

The creature cocked its head at them as if it were
trying to understand. It seemed to be listening to
something. Or for something. It was hard to tell
which.

Badger listened, too. And after a few moments he
heard a high-pitched buzzing sound, like locusts, only
heavier somehow, meaner. As he listened the sound
changed. It turned into a heavy thumping, as if a thousand bass drums were advancing up the ridge. Then
Badger realized that the two noises were going on simultaneously. He wondered what it could be, and suddenly he didn't want to know.

"Lock and load!" he shouted to the men. "I don't
like the sound of this!"

The creatures came over the top of the little hill, a

couple dozen of them, though of course that was only the first wave. They were different from the creatures they had seen before. They were the size of large dogs, and their heads were big and shaped like raptor birds. They had no feathers, however, just two tails apiece, and those tails appeared to be barbed. Their mouths were filled with long sharp teeth—that seemed to be a rule here on this planet—and they were making a buzzing sound as they came.

Behind them came another group of creatures, a little smaller than the others, about the size and general shape of woodchucks, and colored a lime green with bluish features. They all had mustaches, like walruses. They made a booming sound as they walked, but Badger couldn't see how they produced it.

They came on, all of them, and they didn't look friendly.

"Hit 'em with it!" Red shouted, and he and his three buddies began to pour in fire. They had the caseless carbines going so fast that the firing mechanisms began to grow hot, but they ignored the pain and kept on firing.

One thing was plain from the first: these creatures were hard to hit. They weren't coming on fast, but their dodging and swerving made them difficult targets. Nevertheless, Red scored a hit, and had the satisfaction of seeing one of the woodchuck blow up like an overinflated beach ball.

Meg scored, and then Glint, who shouted in triumph.

Then one of the raptor-headed creatures got under the line of his fire and grabbed his foot. It bit, twisted.

Glint's foot came off at the ankle. He stared at the stump, too surprised to feel pain yet, and tried to take a step away. But he toppled over and they were on him, a dozen of them, biting and tearing. One long-necked creature buried his head in Glint's belly. Glint screamed and tried to tear it away, but the bird-thing was stronger. It got its head deep inside Glint's belly, and then pulled the rest of itself in. Lying on the ground, Glint went into convulsions.

Badger dropped his empty carbine and picked up a plasma rifle. He turned it to full fire and sprayed the area. He caught Meg, out on the periphery, with his blast and saw her wither and collapse before he could turn it off her.

"Damn it, sorry, Meg!" he shouted. It was just the sort of unfortunate thing that happens sometimes in combat.

Meanwhile, Min Dwin, firing from the hip, was seized from behind by an alien. It caught her by her long hair, and she turned, still firing, and put four rounds into the creature's head, had the satisfaction of seeing it blow apart. But it still held her hair in its dying claw, and from its ruined head a gout of acid sprayed, catching her full in the face.

"My eyes!" she screamed, and fell to the ground, clawing at her face. She writhed for a moment, then lay still. The acid had penetrated to her brain.

Andy Groggins tried to turn his carbine to face an alien that had just come up on his side. His feet were yanked from under him. An alien had him by the ankles, another seized his arms. They tugged in opposite directions, and Andy triggered off his entire magazine, spraying the area and nearly catching Badger, who had to dive to escape the blasts. Then Andy roared as his left leg was ripped off at the hip.

The alien who had been pulling his feet fell backward. The other caught its balance and came at him. Badger triggered off a burst and blew the creature away. Groggins was dead before the carbine's reverberations died away.

Looking around, Badger saw that he was alone. The others were dead. The original beast, the barrel-shaped thing, was nearby, sitting on its haunches and watching expectantly.

"Damn you, you Judas goat!" Badger said, and blew it away with a short burst.

The area was a shambles of blood and gore. All

Badger's people were dead, and he expected to go next, but the attack had ended. There were no aliens in sight now except dead ones, and no other creatures, either.

Badger stood there, sobbing with fatigue and anguish, and saw a shadow appear as if from nowhere. He looked up.

There it was, Potter's ship, the *Lancet*, and he had a chance to get out of this. "Drop a line! Pick me up!"

They were down level with him, and he saw four of the crew watching him from one of the big glassite windows. He screamed at them, and finally they opened a hatch and threw out a rope ladder. Badger scrambled up with his remaining strength and collapsed inside the ship.

"Did you get all that on tape?" Potter asked.

"Yes, sir," the second-in-command said.

"The scientists will be interested in these creatures," Potter commented.

"Yes, sir," the second-in-command said. "But the killing of all those men was a little gruesome, wasn't it?"

"Oh, edit that part out," Potter scoffed. "And mark it in the log that we didn't reach the surface in time to save the rest of the mutineers." He turned to go, then stroked his chin. "Not that one ever really wants to rescue mutineers. They set a bad example for the rest of the crew. But don't put that in."

"Yes, sir." The second-in-command saluted and began to walk off. "We did pull one of them out."

"Take him to the medics," Potter said. "We'll get his story later."

"Yes, sir." The second saluted and left the control room.

"And now, Dr. Myakovsky," Potter said to himself, "it is time to deal with you."

64

Stan and his group went through a maze of pathways. They found no sign of Norbert's electronic trail. No sign of Norbert, either. He had dropped behind, after making a gallant stand against the aliens. Stan had last seen him submerged under a writhing mound of black alien bodies.

Stan's breathing was laboring, he could hardly drag himself along. When was the royal jelly going to kick in? Julie and Gill helped him all they could, but they needed to keep their hands free to use their weapons. Because now more and more aliens were appearing, coming out of different turnings in the tunnels. They came in ones and twos, no mass attack yet, but it was probably only a matter of time.

It was clear that the suppressors were no longer doing their job. Stan, Julie, and Gill had to be constantly on the alert, because the creatures were attacking silently, suddenly springing out of the shadows.

Julie was leading the way. Her searchlight beam probed ahead into the profound darkness. She thought she had never seen such darkness before. Even the darkness she saw when she closed her eyes was not as deep as this. This was the darkness of evil, the darkness that cloaked a place where unspeakable creatures performed horrifying rituals. This was the darkness of childhood terrors. This was the darkness out of which monsters swarmed, the place where they tortured little children, and ate them, and then spit them up to make them live again so they could kill them anew.

Glancing back, Julie saw Gill falling back to help Stan, fighting half turned around to keep the aliens from running up their backs. He showed no expression when the searchlight beams occasionally illuminated his long, serious face. The android did his work methodically, but then he wasn't really human, it was all the same to him, he had no feelings, not really. He'd act just the same if he were on an assembly line screwing down machine parts. He's lucky, Julie thought, because it's not all the same to me, no matter how hard I try to make it so.

And Stan? In a way he was lucky, too. Too exhausted to care any longer, and in too much pain, to judge from his twisted features and the sweat that dripped from his face. She felt so sorry for him, and yet, in a way, she envied him. He was too far gone to feel the terror that engulfed her mind and turned her legs to jelly.

Gill plodded along, an efficient machine doing what it was supposed to do. His peripheral vision was enormously extended, and when he caught movement at the outer edges, he wheeled and fired in a single economical movement. When a group of three or more aliens came at him, he switched to the small thermite bombs he carried in a pouch on his left side, setting

the proximity fuse with his thumb just before he let
them go.

It was like a dance—turn, swing, fire—the only
dance he had ever done. Turn, wheel, extend the arm.
Boom! Blam! Turn again, gracefully duck, turn, fire,
fire again, then go forward. . . .

He heard Stan gasp and slip. Gill scooped him up
and put him back on his feet. "Can you go on?"

"Yes. Thanks . . ." Stan was saving his breath.

Gill was worried about the doctor. That dose of
pure royal jelly hadn't seemed to help any. He knew
how much Stan had been expecting to find some sort
of divine elixir that would cure his cancer. Gill had no
particular hope that this would happen. It was illogi-
cal. The royal jelly was not a cure; it served merely to
diminish the pain. Why should a pure strain do more
than the other, adulterated strains?

He knew that humans liked to entertain farfetched
notions. All of the humans, in a way, were like those
Spanish conquistadores he had learned about during
his hypnopaedic learning sessions, those men in armor who had painfully trekked across the American
plains, searching for the Seven Cities of Cibola, imag-
inary places that had never existed outside the
dreams of mythographers.

Stan's belief in a cure for his disease was like that.
It was forlorn, even silly. No android would be capable of such folly. Yet Gill didn't think that made him
better than Stan. Quite the contrary, it made him sub-
human, because he could not participate in the delu-
sions, both the pathetic and the sublime, that made
the human race what it was.

The aliens were massing behind them. Gill had to
slow down more and more to flight rearguard actions.

Julie pressed on ahead, hoping that the turns she
took were leading them toward the outside of the hive
rather than deeper into it.

Gill switched the plasma rifle to automatic fire and
laid down a sheet of flame as half a dozen aliens

came crawling out of a pit and, rearing to their feet, loped toward him.

Stan stumbled and fell, and lay still. Gill scooped him up and draped him over one shoulder, leaving one arm free to aim and fire the heavy plasma rifle.

By now the aliens were coming from side turnings as well as from behind. The little party wasn't surrounded yet, but it looked imminent. Gill threw his last thermite grenade, shifted Stan higher onto his shoulder, and noted that the charge in the plasma rifle was almost depleted. He turned, ready to fight to the end.

Then Julie cried, "There's light ahead! We're almost out of it!"

Gill turned and saw the faintest glimmer of grayness penetrating the profound gloom of the hive. He let go of the depleted plasma rifle and pulled a chemical slugthrower out of a side pouch. Four quick shots blasted a close-packed group of aliens with high explosives. Then Gill turned and ran, with Stan on his shoulder, toward the light.

His feet slid on the hard-packed clay of the tunnel's floor, and then suddenly he was out of the hive and into the sepulchral gray light of AR-32.

Behind him he heard Julie say, "Get out of the way, Gill."

He managed to stagger a few steps farther. This gave Julie a chance to reset her plasma gun to full heat. She held it steadily, hosing the entrance to the hive through which they had come.

It took Gill a moment to understand what she was doing. Then he put Stan down, rummaged in his pouch, and found a plasma-rifle refill. He reloaded and swept the spot where Julie was beaming.

The beams glittered and coruscated on the hive face. The aliens were forced back, deeper into the cave, to wait until the noise and heat died down.

But Julie had something else in mind. She kept on firing until, with a sudden thunderous roar, the cave mouth collapsed. A cloud of dust and smoke arose, and then it was quiet.

Julie turned off her weapon, as did Gill.

"That'll do it for a little while," she said.

"Until they find another exit from the hive," Stan said.

"Well, it's better than nothing. Now, where in hell are we?"

Stan pointed. "You've done a great job, Julie. Look down there."

Julie looked, and saw, less than a hundred yards away, the squat hull of the harvester.

"Now we're getting somewhere!" she said. "We just have to get aboard."

"Yes," said Gill. "But there's a difficulty." He pointed again.

It took Julie a moment to see it. But then she saw the small black dots moving at the base of the hive. She could finally make them out: aliens! They had found another exit from the hive sooner than she expected. And they were blocking the way to the harvester.

She asked, "What now, Stan?" But Stan was unconscious again.

Julie and Gill looked at each other, then glanced up as a shadow crossed them.

It was a ship. For one moment Julie's hopes flared. But then she took in the ship's markings and design, and a great despondency came over her. That was not the *Dolomite*. That was the *Lancet*, commanded by Potter, the Bio-Pharm man. It hovered in the air, and nothing about it stirred. It seemed obvious to Julie that Potter was going to let them die here, watching and maybe videotaping their final agonies.

Stan revived and sat up. "The harvester, did you say?"

"It's right down there." Julie pointed.

Stan looked and nodded. He struggled to his feet. "We've got to get there. From there, something may be possible."

"There are quite a few aliens in the way," Gill pointed out.

"So I see," Stan said. "Have you ever heard of the old American Indian stunt of running the gauntlet?"

"I don't believe so," Gill said.

"You're about to learn history in a very practical way," Stan announced. "Load what's left of the ammo and we'll be on our way."

Despite the mortal danger of their position, Julie could have kissed him at that moment.

65

tan gave the signal and they were off, trotting down the rocky path that led from the edge of the hive to the plain. Fifty yards away, more or less, was the harvester. In the sky above them, the *Lancet* hovered, silent, watching.

And then the aliens came.

They came singly and in pairs, and then in threes. They seemed to crawl out from under rocks and to appear out of holes. They came in silent ferocity, fangs bared, talons extended, forming a rough line between the hive and the harvester. Stan and the others ran through the line, blasting as they went. They had all shifted now to rapid-fire weapons. Never did Julie display better hand-eye coordination. She managed to move at full stride, at the same time keeping a look on all sides of her and releasing sizzling bolts of energy at anything that moved. The rocks turned white-hot under the glancing energy beams. The aliens surged forward, and died. Julie and Gill were doing fine. . . .

And then Stan collapsed.

He had been doing very well, for a man in his condition. But his illness and general debilitation were not to be denied forever. Pain coursed through his chest like a sea of fire. He gritted his teeth and tried to continue, but now everything was turning dark before his eyes. He couldn't see where he was going. His feet stumbled on the rocky surface, a pebble turned under his foot. He felt himself falling, and a black pit seemed to yawn in front of him. He threw his arms wide as he fell, but before he hit, Gill scooped him up.

"Don't stop for me!" Stan said.

"Order denied," Gill said, setting him on his shoulder and running again.

They cut their way through the ranks of the aliens. Flesh, blood, and bile spilled in all directions. It was like a free-for-all in a slaughterhouse. Julie hadn't imagined there was that much gore in the whole world. Scattered parts of aliens lay everywhere, arms and legs, long ugly tails, heads with the teeth still snapping. And still they came on. Julie thought that every alien on the planet must be here, or on its way.

She was firing two weapons now, cutting a path for herself through a growing mound of living matter—the locked bodies of aliens, still trying to get at them. Gill, running along hard on Julie's heels, with Stan bouncing up and down on his shoulder, was cutting wide swaths in the clustered aliens. Julie saw her left-hand weapon flare and die. Firing right-handed, she snatched a vibraknife from her waist pouch to set it on high. The blade had to make physical contact to do any harm, but it had come to that now with the aliens pressing ever closer. It seemed to her that this was the end; aliens pressed in and she had no idea where she was. And then Gill was shouting, "The harvester, Julie!"

They were there. Gill raced up the landing platform and dumped Stan inside through the entry port. Then he turned, feet braced, firing a bazooka-style weapon that gave out great gouts of green flame. Julie ducked into the harvester under his arm.

She saw Stan, lying on the floor, unconscious again. Something big and black and many-toothed was bending over him. It was an alien, damn it! The harvester was filled with the creatures—two, no three of them. She cut them down. "Gill!" she screamed. "Get inside so we can close the door!"

Gill cut and slashed and backed through the door. Julie cut down an alien and now there was one left. It stood in the doorway, towering over her, and just at that instant her gun began to fail.

She must have screamed, because Gill slung a handgun across the harvester to her. She caught it, aimed, and triggered it in one rapid moment. The alien was in her face, but she had no choice: at extreme close range she blasted him.

The alien's throat exploded. One wildly waving claw came completely off. His forelimb, severed at the wrist, waved wildly in the air. The milky white acidic substance that was the blood of the alien spewed forth in a stream.

Some of the acid hit Julie. She screamed and went down, and it seemed to her that she could hear Gill yelling something, too, and then she didn't know anything anymore.

66

Stan returned to consciousness angry that the dose of pure royal jelly hadn't done anything for him. Luckily he still had some of the older product left. He'd take some of that soon.

He was not really surprised that the pure royal jelly hadn't helped him. He had always suspected that it was too good to be true, the idea that some other form of the jelly would cure him in some miraculous way. It just doesn't work like that, he told himself.

His mind raced back to earlier days. He thought of all the work he had done, all his accomplishments. He'd had a lot of chances in the poker game that was his life. Could he have played his cards some other way? He didn't really think so. And it was strange, but he knew that for some strange reason there was no place he'd rather be than here, right here, at the end of a glorious venture, with Julie and Gill, his friends.

Gill was at the other side of the harvester, looking after Julie. There really wasn't much he could do for her. Just see that she was comfortable. Most of the acid had missed her, but some drops had fallen along the side of her neck and penetrated deep under the skin. Her face was ashen, her breathing labored. Her vital signs were diminishing.

Gill found himself struggling with new emotions, things he had never felt before. He realized that there was a comfort in being a synthetic man. The trouble with android status was that nothing ever felt very good. There was no joy, no exultation. But the advantage was that nothing ever felt very bad, either.

Strange, though. Now he was filled with unaccustomed emotions: pity for Julie, and something else, some tender feeling that he couldn't quite identify, couldn't quite find a name for. He touched the vein on the side of her neck. It pulsed, but not strongly. He reached over to make Julie more comfortable and only became aware then that his left arm was missing a hand and half its forearm. He had been too busy to notice when the hand went off-line. It was that advantage, again, of being a synthetic: you felt no pain. Now, looking back, he could reconstruct how it happened. The harvester's hatch had been closing, and he had just managed to get inside. But not quite all of him had made it. One hand had still been outside as the alien's big claw closed over his wrist. Stan had pulled, and the alien had pulled back.

There had been a deadly tug-of-war, with the alien pulling one way and Gill the other, sawing his arm back and forth along the door frame. None of the others had been in a position or condition to help. Stan had been out cold, and Julie, staggered by her acid bath, was out of action, too.

Gill and the alien had fought their deadly game. Gill hadn't been exactly sure what happened next. Presumably the door edge had severed some of the cables that controlled his arm movements. Or the combined pulls of Stan and the alien had pulled

the skin welds on his arm apart. Suddenly, and with
an audible pop, his arm had let go several inches
below the elbow. Cracks had appeared in the tough
synthetic skin, and had immediately widened. Fine-
control cables had come under tension, pulled taut
until they sang, and then snapped.

Cables and wires had coiled around Gill's wrist,
then pulled free when Gill pulled what was left of his
arm the rest of the way inside the ship and the hatch
slammed shut. It had been a good sound, that sound
of the hatch closing. After that, Gill had been too busy
looking after Julie and ascertaining Stan's condition to
pay much attention to his own condition. He looked
to himself now.

He could see that there was no way of fixing himself. He could have tried a jury-rig if he'd had spare
cables with him. But in the close confines of the pod
he hadn't brought along the repair and spare parts kit
that every synthetic tried to keep with him at all
times. And even if he'd had the cables, he was still
lacking several transistors and capacitors. Reluctantly
he took the arm off-line. He had no motion in it at all.
From the shoulder down, it was as dead as a hundred-
year-old Ford.

"Gave you a little trouble, did they?" Stan's voice
came from over his shoulder.

Stan had revived, calling on reserves he never
knew he had. He had even gotten to his feet. He was
filled with a strange knowledge; that he was both a
dead man and a living one. The two sides of himself
were warring now, each trying to establish domi-
nance. Stan thought he knew who was going to win.

Somewhat unsteadily he crossed the harvester and
gazed at Gill's wound.

"Pulled it right off, did they?"

"Yes, sir. Or perhaps I did."

"Comes to the same thing," Stan said. "Doesn't give
you any pain, does it?"

"No, Doctor, none at all. I register the loss of my

arm solely as an analogue of loss, not as the real thing."

"It's abstract for you, is that it?"

"I suppose you could say that, sir." And yet, Gill knew it wasn't quite true. No human could really imagine what it was like to be a synthetic. And to be a synthetic suffering loss—that was really beyond their scope. Except, he thought, maybe Julie could understand it.

67

"Well, Gill," Stan said, "I think it'll be best if you look after Julie for the time being. I have some work to do on the radio."

"I don't think much can be done for her, sir. Not without regular medical facilities."

"No, I suppose not," Stan said. "Maybe there's not much that can be done for any of us. Still, we must avail ourselves of every twist and turn. That's what it's like being a human, Gill. You avail yourself of every little opportunity. You assume you're not dead until you can no longer move. I hope you're taking note of all this."

"Indeed I am, Doctor," Gill said. "Is there anything I can do for you?"

"I'm afraid not," Stan said. "Unless you happened to bring along a replacement body. No? I didn't think so. But the royal jelly is finally starting to take effect. I'm all washed up, Gill, but I'm feeling a lot better."

"Glad to hear it, sir."

"Thanks. We'll talk more later, Gill."

Stan turned to the radio. Gill watched him, and he was disturbed. It seemed to him that Dr. Myakovsky was in some sort of shock. He was hardly registering his grief at Julie's condition. Was it a callousness about him that Gill had missed? Gill thought it was something else. He had noticed that humans from time to time went into a condition they called shock. It was when something terrible happened, either to them or to someone close to them. It was how humans shut down when they experienced overload. But synthetics could never shut down.

68

As Stan turned to the radio it suddenly burst into life. An unfamiliar voice said, "Hello? Is there someone aboard the harvester?"

Stan sat down at the instrument panel. "Yes, there is someone here."

"I thought as much. This is Potter, captain of the Bio-Pharm ship *Lancet*. You are trespassing on Neo-Pharm territory. Identify yourself at once!"

"I am Dr. Stanley Myakovsky," Stan said. "There are only three of us here—myself, a woman, and an android. We are all that is left of a survey expedition sent to inspect the hive on AR-32."

"I knew you were here, Doctor," Potter said. "That says it all, I think."

"Maybe you don't know everything, Captain," Stan said. "Our ship was damaged during the recent storm. We require help badly."

"I understand," Potter said. "I am sending men to

pick you up. Be prepared to leave the harvester. That is all for now."

Stan put down the microphone and turned to Gill. "He says he's sending help. I suppose you can guess what kind of help Potter is going to offer."

Gill didn't answer. He was watching through one of the view panels as the *Lancet*'s primaries flared briefly and the great ship dropped slowly and majestically down through the sky in a shining glitter of landing jets. The big ship settled effortlessly on AR-32's plain. Soon after the landing, there was a sparkle of bright lines along the ground, and then something almost transparent that looked like the ghost of a wall erected itself around the *Lancet*.

"I see you have your force field up," Stan said. "A wise precaution, I can assure you."

"We're able to throw some protection around your ship, too," Potter said. "My men are coming now."

A bay door in the *Lancet*'s side cracked open, then let down to the ground, forming a landing ramp. Stan watched a dozen men come running down the ramp. Carrying bulky weapons, they were masked and shielded, and wearing full space armor.

"You waste no time, do you, Captain?" Stan said.

"You're damned right," Potter said. "The sooner I get you people out of the harvester the better."

"One way or another," Stan said mildly.

"What was that?"

"Oh, nothing," Stan muttered. "But it looks to me like your men are running into a little difficulty."

69

The armed men were moving across the corridors between the force fields that lay between Potter's ship and the harvester. The force fields shimmered faintly in the pelting rain. Low, flat lighting, grim and without shadows, illuminated the scene, and this was aided by the search beam from the *Lancet*, which flooded different areas with its sulfurous, yellow light. The men moved at a brisk trot, helmet shields up so they could communicate better.

Their troubles began slowly and built fast. The first man to scream was hardly noticed, so rapidly were the others moving. But then the squad leader became aware that something was amiss.

His name was Blake and he was from Los Angeles. He was used to skulking around smoking ruins and walking down ruined streets. So he wasn't entirely surprised when he saw one of the men throw his arms in the air as something long and black snaked

out from seemingly nowhere and grabbed him around
the neck. But what had it been? Blake wasn't sure. He
stared, gaped. Another man screamed, and was
dragged away shrieking. Then Blake realized that
somehow the aliens had gotten into the uninterdicted
corridors between the force fields, and were grabbing
soldiers as they crossed from one field to another.

Seeing this, Blake shouted some orders. His little
squadron was already cut in half. He ordered the remaining soldiers to fight back-to-back. They were
closer to the harvester than to the *Lancet*, so he ordered them to continue.

You could see that the men didn't want to go. What
had begun as a nice little bug fight had turned into a
slaughter of humans. It wasn't fair! But there was no
one to complain to.

They fought, their weapons flashing and flaming,
and they caught a group of aliens as they were preparing to charge, caught them dead on and blew them to
hell and back. The air rained black body parts. The
acid from the aliens' wounds sprayed far and wide,
and the ground sizzled beneath them. Luckily the soldiers were in acid-proof armor, or the acid would
have made short work of them.

The sun came out as the slaughter continued, and
the men seemed to be holding their own. Then the
aliens got around the other side of the force field, and
the soldiers were caught between two attacking alien
groups.

They continued fighting, falling one after another. The lucky ones were dead when they hit the
ground. Some of the others, wounded but not yet
dead, weren't so lucky. Aliens draped them over their
shoulders and retreated to the hive. These soldiers
would make fine hosts, just what the queen needed.

Seeing this, Blake fought hard to keep his compo-
sure. It was unnerving, seeing friend after friend
pulled apart, torn to bits, or dragged away unconscious to be glued to the wall of the hive with some-

thing small and deadly growing inside him, after the facehugger had done its work.

Blake turned back. It was all happening too fast. When he looked around, he saw the last of his men collapse, scream, and get dragged off. Blake saw his chance and sprinted to the harvester. He got there before the aliens, but just barely. He pounded at the door. "Let me in! Please, please, let me in!"

Stan's mild-mannered face peered back at him through the viewport. His lips moved. Blake couldn't hear the words, but Stan was saying, "Sorry, I can't open the door. I don't have the strength to close it again."

Blake pounded again, and then the aliens were on him. A claw came around his shoulder and grabbed his face at the forehead. It pulled, tearing the skin right off. Blake felt his nose pull away, felt his lips leave his mouth, felt all this, and then another claw had seized him by the neck, it was pulling out the tendons of his neck! And then Blake felt no more.

70

Potter was shouting, his voice grating on the speaker. "Damn you! What have you done to my men?"

"Not a thing, Captain," Myakovsky said. "They brought it on themselves. Nothing I could do for them. Can you get us out of here, Captain?"

"It seems scarcely worth my time," Potter grumbled. "I ought to nuke all of you."

"But then you'd lose the contents of the harvester," Stan said.

"True enough. But I could always come back for it after things have cooled down."

"I have a better plan," Stan said. "Something that will be of use to us all."

"Hurry up and tell me what it is," Potter said. "I don't like leaving my ship down here."

"It's too complicated to explain over radio," Stan said. "But I think you will like it. Listen, I have an android here who has been damaged in recent fighting. I could send him over to you. He'd explain the whole thing."

"I don't know if I should even bother." Potter was obviously thinking aloud.

"I think you'll be interested in my scheme," Stan continued. "And after all, it won't take very long."

"All right," Potter said. "Send him over. This better be good."

"It'll be very good," Stan affirmed.

"How are you going to get him through the aliens? If my own men couldn't make it, how do you expect your android to get here?"

"Modern technology is a wonderful thing," Stan said evasively. "He'll be right over, Captain. Signing off."

71

"Julie," Gill said. "Can you hear me?"

Julie's eyelids fluttered. Pain contorted her face. She gave a long shudder and then looked around. "Oh my God, is this where I am? I was having such a nice dream, Gill. There's this lake I know of. I went there just once when I was a little girl. I remember fields of spring flowers, a little lake. There was a rowboat. I was drifting in the rowboat, and there were willows hanging down over the boat. Oh, Gill, it was so pretty!"

"I'm sure it was," Gill said.

"Have you ever had a dream like that?" Julie asked.

"No, I have not," Gill replied. "I do not dream."

"Well, you can have half of mine," Julie said sleepily. "It wasn't really a little lake, I don't need it all. . . . Where's Stan?"

"He's right over there," Gill said. "He's trying to save you."

Julie grimaced. "I'm afraid he's cut it a little too fine this time. Poor Stan. He has such great ideas. But I'm glad I came, anyhow. He's not long for this world, you know."

"I know," Gill said.

"It's too bad. He's such a brilliant man. But they've done nothing but crowd him. He hasn't had a chance. Except this one. And I think this wasn't much of a chance."

"I suppose not," Gill said.

She looked at him. "Your arm! What happened?"

"Ran into a little trouble," Gill said.

"You're using understatement, just like a human."

"I suppose it rubs off," Gill said. "A lot of things do. I feel . . ."

"Yes?"

"I feel like I understand a lot more about humans now," Gill said. "It's . . . interesting, isn't it?"

"I suppose it is," Julie said. "Are you all right, Gill? You've got a very strange expression on your face."

"I'm fine," Gill muttered. "It's just that . . . well, even an android can run out of time."

Suddenly Stan's voice came from across the cabin. "Gill? What are you doing?"

"Just looking after Julie, sir."

"That's good. But she needs to rest now. Come over here. I have some instructions for you."

"Yes, Dr. Myakovsky." He turned to Julie. "Julie . . ."

"What is it, Gill?"

"Try not to forget me." Gill stood up and crossed the room.

Stan Myakovsky was huddled up in the control chair. He appeared to be experiencing no pain for the moment. But he had changed. Gill noticed that the doctor seemed to have shrunk inside his own skin, to be falling in on himself.

"Now pay attention," Stan said. "Forget about Julie for a moment. I have work for you to do."

"Yes, sir."

"You are going over to the *Lancet* to parlay with Captain Potter."

"To what end, sir?"

"Ah, yes," Stan said. "Negotiations usually have a point, don't they? Ours will be different. There's no point at all."

"But what do you want me to accomplish, sir?"

"Oh, that I can easily tell you," Stan said. "I want Potter to take his ship away from here. I will retain the harvester. I will find some way to make rendez-vous with Captain Hoban, and we will go back home with our ill-gotten gains. How does that sound to you?"

"Wonderful, sir. But I'm afraid—"

"Yes, I am, too," Stan said. "The captain is not going to like it at all. That's why I have something else in mind. Come over here to the workbench, Gill. I have a modification I must make in you."

Gill hesitated. "A modification, sir?"

"You heard me. What is the matter with you?"

"I wouldn't want to change my thinking on certain issues."

Stan looked at Gill then glanced over at Julie, who was resting with eyes closed. "I think I understand. You've undergone quite a little course in humaniza-tion, have you not?"

"I don't know what to call it. But I've never experi-enced anything like it."

"I won't change any of those qualities you call emotional, Gill. They are rare and special, I agree with you on that, and sometimes they are a long time com-ing to men—and to androids, never. Or just about never. No, it's your command structure I need to mod-ify. And something I need to wire into you. It will make it easier for you to do what you will have to do, unless things go a lot better than I imagine they will."

"I wish you'd explain a little more," Gill said, letting

Stan take him by his remaining hand and lead him over to the workbench.

Stan checked out his instruments. "Better not to explain too much," he said, fitting magnifying lenses over his glasses. I'll know what to do when the time comes. And so will you."

72

There were heavy ground mists when Gill left the harvester and started his trek to the *Lancet*. The ship loomed eerily in the mounting mists. Gill walked between the force fields. There were aliens out there, and he walked past them. The aliens were searching, but they didn't seem to know what they were looking for.

Gill knew that he had a certain amount of natural immunity, since androids did not smell like men. But to be on the safe side he had taken the last suppressor. Gill touched it on his wrist for luck. He wasn't superstitious, but he knew that men were, and of late he had been seeking to emulate them in every way.

The suppressor was working. It had been Mac's, but that was quite a while ago and now Mac was a bundle of wet fur on a garbage heap in an alien hive.

Gill knew he had to keep his mind on business. Usually, this was no problem for an android. Artificial men weren't bothered by random thoughts, stray insights, weasel realizations that came to them like thieves in the night. Not usually. But this time was different.

Gill found that his attention was divided. Part of him was observing the terrain he passed over, noting the presence and position of the aliens, watching as he drew nearer to the *Lancet*. But with another part of his mind he was thinking of Julie, seeing her as she had been just a day ago, vibrant and laughing, filled with life. He had felt something special for her then.

What was it? Was it what the humans called love? How could he find out? No human had been able to explain love to him. Even Stan grew embarrassed and turned away when Gill had asked him to explain the concept and give it a quantifiable value.

Humans were so strange, so filled with odd compunctions that covertly ruled their behavior. And now he had the most understanding of them he would ever have. It all came from stray thoughts, he told himself, and he worked hard to banish Julie's image from his mind as he approached the entry port of the *Lancet*.

73

Two of Potter's crew, heavily armed, were waiting for him in the entryway.

"I don't know how the hell you got through," one of them said.

"I've got a pass," Gill told them. They just stared at him. Gill decided that his first attempt at that key human quality, humor, hadn't been a success. But he reminded himself that he was new at it. Perhaps he would get better as he went along.

The two guards looked through the port visor. They could see the aliens, slowly drifting toward the ship, forming up against the almost invisible walls of the force field. They didn't do anything. Just stood there, their heads facing the ship, and it was as though some great power of attraction held them there. They were surrounding the force field that protected the harvester, too, more and more of them, and the sight of them was singularly uncanny and disquieting.

"We better tell the captain about this," one of the guards said. To Gill he said, "Come on, you. Raise your arms. We're going to search you."

Gill did as he was told. "I carry no weapons," he told them.

"Sure. But we'll just check you anyhow. What happened to your arm?"

"I lost it at the movies," Gill said. Again, the guards did not laugh. They just stared at him like he was crazy. Gill wondered what he was doing wrong. This humor thing was going to take some studying.

74

"Julie, can you hear me?"

Julie had been lying on the deck of the harvester near one of the heaters. Stan had found a blanket in one of the back bays and wrapped it around her. She looked better than she had since the accident.

"Stan?" she said. "I'm very cold."

"Let me see if I can find another blanket," Stan said. "I already have these heaters going full blast."

He stood up to go, but Julie reached out and grabbed his arm. "No, don't leave me, Stan. We're in a lot of trouble, aren't we?"

"To one way of thinking, yes, we are. But to another, we're in no trouble at all. We're together, and we're going to stay that way. Here, Julie, I have something for you. For us both, actually."

He reached into his jacket pocket and brought out the little case containing the Xeno-Zip ampoules.

There were six of them. He uncapped one and lifted
Julie's head so she could drink. When she took down
the first ampoule, he matched her with one, then un-
corked another.

"We aren't supposed to take more than one, are
we?"

"I've got a special dispensation," Stan said. "Don't
worry, it'll do us no harm."

Julie swallowed the contents of a second ampoule.
She shuddered, then laughed. "You were right, Stan. I
feel a lot better."

"Me, too," Stan said, sitting down on the deck beside her and holding her close to share the warmth.
"This is nice, isn't it?"

"It's very nice, Stan," Julie said. "We never found
much time for this before, did we?"

"Unfortunately not. Sometimes it takes a long time
to realize what a good thing is."

"As long as it happens sometime," Julie said.

"Don't worry, Julie. We're going to get out of this."

"I'm sure we are," Julie told him. "One way or the
other." She could feel the pain leaving her body. How
miraculous the Xeno-Zip was! What a pleasure it was
to be free of pain.

She knew it had to be the same way for Stan. For
the moment they were both young and strong and
were going to live forever. This could only last a little
while. But perhaps, she thought, it'll be long enough.

The radio kicked into life. "Dr. Myakovsky! Are you
there?" It was Captain Hoban from the *Dolomite*.

"I have to issue a few last-minute instructions,"
Stan said to Julie. "Excuse me, my dear, I'll be back as
soon as I can."

75

On the *Dolomite*, Hoban had been working hard to keep the location of his ship a secret. He had no doubt what Potter would do if he knew there was another ship in the area, and where it was situated. He had no intention of sharing the fate of the *Valparaiso Queen*, the wreck that silently circled the planet. He hadn't known quite what to do. But then Stan's message had come to him, and he had no choice but to make contact.

"Sir," Hoban said, "I need to tell you, by radioing me, you have compromised this ship's position. You shouldn't have done that, sir."

"Now, now," Stan said. "I have a plan whereby Potter and his crew will be neutralized. There will be nothing to prevent you from making rendezvous with us at these coordinates as soon as possible."

"I understand, sir," Hoban said. "But there is a

problem. From your present location, it is going to take me at least twenty minutes to get to you."

"As long as that?" Stan exclaimed. From where he sat, he could see through one of the viewports as the aliens massed in front of the force field, not trying to get through it—that would have been impossible—but coming together in ever-growing numbers, those behind pushing away those in front. They were crowded as close to each other as they could get, and some of them were mounting on the back of others, and others were climbing on top of those.

Stan saw at once what was going to happen. They were going to keep on piling themselves up until they were able to topple over the rim of the force field, which was only about twelve feet high. Then they'd come for him and Julie.

He didn't want to think about it, so he took refuge in analysis.

This swarming behavior was probably some sort of instinctual mechanism for getting them over barriers that were otherwise impassable. It was really very interesting. Ari had to see this.

Stan took out the cybernetic ant, poised him on a fingertip, and lifted his hand so Ari could see through the viewport.

"See what's happening, Ari? Are you taking it all in? Future generations are going to be very interested in what we have done today."

The little creature gave no sign that he was listening, yet he showed a certain alertness.

Stan continued, "You've been a good companion, Ari. Silent and uncomplaining. Who could ask for anything more? I only wish Norbert were here, too. You'll have to tell them how it was with us, Ari. If you get out of this, that is."

Ari, as usual, was silent.

"Stan!" Julie called.

"I'll be right over," Stan answered. He broke the connection with Hoban and changed frequencies. In a moment the sullen face of Captain Potter appeared on the viewscreen.

"About time you called, Myakovsky. I don't have much patience."

"Not much more is required," said Stan.

"I will listen now to your offer."

"Yes, Captain. What I suggest is that you forget all about this matter and take your ship some distance from here. While you are gone I will take this harvester ship and get away. You needn't worry about losing the royal jelly aboard. There's plenty of it down here for you. You can easily milk yourself another harvester load."

"That's great," Potter said. "And just why should I do that?"

"Because I have a legal claim to this stuff which is every bit as good as Bio-Pharm's claim. And because I want you to."

"I think you've flipped out."

"You're not going to do it? No harm in asking, was there?"

"You're wasting my time," Potter spat. "There's no deal, Myakovsky. I don't need to negotiate with you. I'm taking what I want."

"Right," Stan said. "Gill?"

Gill's face appeared in the viewscreen. "Yes, Doctor?"

"Activate Subroutine Diogenes," Stan said. "Signing off, Captain Potter."

"That doctor of yours is really crazy," Potter said to Gill. "He must think he still swings some weight. You can just forget any order he gave you. Things are going to be a little different now."

"Yes, they are," said Gill. The time was finally at hand.

He put his remaining hand to his mouth and popped in one finger. With a single wrench, he tore the finger off.

"What are you doing?" Potter said. "Stop that!"

"Subroutine Diogenes is beginning," Gill said, tearing off a second finger. "You know the old story about the rich man's house?"

"What are you talking about?"

Off came another finger. "In the rich man's house," Gill said, "a guest has a problem if he wants to spit." Off came the fourth finger.

"You're crazy," Potter said. "Stop or I'll shoot."

"In the rich man's house," Gill said, "there's no place to spit but in his face." The fifth and last finger came off. There was a frozen moment in the control room of the *Lancet*. Then Gill blew up. Literally.

The explosion of the artificial man enclosed the *Lancet* in a rosy glow shot through with yellow diamonds.

76

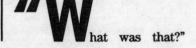

"**W**hat was that?" Julie asked.

"Just somebody knocking at the door," Stan said.

It came again: a heavy booming sound. Stan noted that the aliens had gotten over the top of the force field, scrambling up on each other's shoulders and toppling over. Now they were pounding and tearing at the entry port to the harvester. Stan could hear the metal start to buckle under their blows.

"It's very loud," Julie said dreamily.

"I think our friends are becoming agitated," Stan said. "It won't be long now."

"Is there any more of that royal jelly left?" Julie asked.

"Let me just see.... Yes, my dear, we have another two ampoules. Here, let me uncork that and hold it for you.... That's better, eh?"

"Much better," Julie smiled as Stan swallowed his ampoule.

The radio squawked into life. "Doctor! What in hell is going on! Potter's ship . . ."

It was Hoban. Stan said, his voice very low, "It was nice, eh, Captain?"

"What did you say, Doctor?"

"Gill made a satisfactory explosion, didn't he?" Stan said. "Gill did his part very well. How close are you, Captain?"

"Another five minutes."

"I'm afraid I don't have that long," Stan said. "I hope I won't be alive to see the last act. Hoban, it's been a pleasure knowing you. I hope you have no trouble clearing your name on Earth and going on with your brilliant career. Tell them on Earth . . ."

"Yes, Doctor?"

"Oh, tell them anything," Stan said, suddenly testy. "Over and out." He shut off the radio, then turned to Julie. "Good-bye, sweetheart."

"See you again soon," Julie said.

They kissed. And they were still kissing when the entry port shattered and the aliens came into the harvester.

77

Stan thought that was all. But it wasn't, not quite. There was a long blank stretch. He was vaguely aware that Julie was dead. All the others were dead, too, of course. Ari? He didn't know what had happened to Ari. And as for himself, he was surprised to find he was looking down on a corridor floor. He realized that the aliens had suspended him to the wall. He was in no pain. The royal jelly was still working. But something was growing inside him. He could feel it.

He was about to give birth. And die.

Now Stan summoned up all his courage and all his remaining strength. He opened his mouth and yelled. It was a long, hard, satisfactory yell. He could feel his body vibrating as he yelled. And a poem came to his mind. . . .

I would have mourned the loss of my life
If I had not been already dead.

And then he felt the chestburster come crashing through his chest, its expressionless face already questing for food. And then there was only darkness, and it was warm, like Julie's kiss.

When Captain Hoban finally brought the *Dolomite* down to AR-32's surface, he found the remnants of Potter's crew. Julie was still alive, and Badger was missing, but everyone else was dead. Along with Julie, only Ari, the cybernetic ant, was left.

Once he was back in the ship, Hoban wasted no time trying to read the ant's memory files. But they were locked with an unbreakable molecular combination. Only Stan knew the combination, and Stan had forgotten to unlock the files to permit the final details of his story to be known.

Hoban's Afterword

That was the end of it, all except for cleaning up what was left. When Gill blew himself up, he disabled the *Lancet*'s control system. It took several days for Potter and his remaining men—those who hadn't been killed in the blast—to repair it. It gave me the time to bring the *Dolomite* down to the harvester, where Stan and Julie had made their last stand.

We had a brisk firefight with the two aliens we found inside. But we managed to put them down without further loss of human life. They were carrying containers of royal jelly. All the rest of the aliens were gone.

We didn't know at first where they had disappeared to, or why.

It took us a while to figure it out. First we had to get Julie in the ship and into emergency medical. We did that, and she finally came through it all right. She was nearly well when we got back to Earth. I don't know what she's doing now; we lost touch.

I did see Badger again. He came to visit me one day shortly after I bought my new house on the Pacific Palisades. I had been reinstated, and I was doing well again as a spaceship captain. I owe it all to Stan. It wouldn't have happened if he hadn't stolen that ship, which brought the whole thing to the attention of the authorities and resulted in the reopening of my old case. This time a jury found for me, and against Bio-Pharm.

Badger arrived when I was between flights. He just wanted to say hello. We talked a while. Potter had brought him back to Earth in the *Lancet*, after he'd fixed the damage Gill caused.

"He didn't like me," Badger said cheerfully, "but he couldn't very well kick me out. I was the one who'd tipped him off to you and the doctor."

"And got Stan killed," I pointed out.

"He did his best to get me killed," Badger said.

"That was not intentional."

"No? Well, neither was my blowing the whistle on you to Potter. I was just trying to save my own life."

I didn't know what to say to that.

Badger was curious about one thing. When we'd gone back to get Stan and Julie, why had we only found two aliens, instead of the hordes that had been swarming over the harvester? And why hadn't they gotten to Julie?

"That bothers me, too," I said. "No one will ever really know. But I've got a theory."

"I'd like to hear it," Badger said.

"I figure there'd be communication of some sort between the aliens and their queen. I think she sent them an order that overrode everything else they were doing."

"Why do you think that?"

"You know all that royal jelly that Potter's men had

packed into the harvester? It was gone, all of it. I think the queen told them the first thing to do was to recover all the stolen royal jelly and bring it back to the hive. Then they could go back and finish off whatever humans were left. But we had come and gone by then. I can never prove it, but that's what I think happened."

Badger stared at me, taking it in.

I began to laugh. Badger said, "What's so funny?"

"It's not really funny," I said. "But it is ironic. That the royal jelly that was ultimately responsible for Stan's death should also be responsible for saving Julie's life."

ABOUT THE AUTHOR

ROBERT SHECKLEY is the author of over fifty books in science fiction, fantasy, and mystery. His novel *Immorality, Inc.* was recently made into the movie *Freejack*. The cult classic *The Tenth Victim* was made from his original short story. Mr. Sheckley is a New Yorker currently residing in Portland, Oregon, with his wife and children.

ALIENS™

ROGUE

For Steve Perry
one of the finest writers of them all.

1

The dreams faded like mist on an early fall morning. Real dreams, the kind you can feel, taste, and know you're there. She tried to hold the image of her two children, smiling, laughing. A park, green grass, swings, and happiness. Drake and Cass happy, swinging, up and down, up and down. She wanted to pull the feelings close, hold them against her chest like she would her children. Warm sunshine, the smell of freshly mowed grass, the sound of laughter, all mixed in the comforting feeling of home and family.

Real dreams. Real memories.

But dreams and memories nonetheless.

The harder she tried to grasp the dream, the

thinner, the more distant it became. She reached out for ten-year-old Drake, but his face lit up in playful laughter as he kept swinging and she couldn't seem to catch him. She watched him swing until finally all the pleasant feelings were gone.

The trees, the green grass, the park, were gone.

Drake, his smile, his happiness, were gone.

Cass was gone, replaced by the cold of the sleep chamber and the oily, metallic smell of the transport ship.

Captain Joyce Palmer groaned and fingered the open button for her chamber. The hiss of escaping gas clouded the air for a moment with a blue frozen mist. She forced herself to sit up and swing her legs over the edge. Around her the machines of the transport vessel *Caliban* did their silent work. Slowly she looked around, afraid of what she might see after seven months. The control panels above each of the cold-sleep chambers all showed green and the auxiliary flight board at the front of the room was the same. Everything seemed normal and running, and she let the dread ease away much like the dream had done.

She looked down at her bare legs and for just a moment she felt dizzy. She gripped the edge of the chamber with both hands and it passed quickly, just as it did every time she came out of the damn ice boxes. She hated cold sleep.

She pulled in as large a breath as her lungs would allow and then shivered. The cold had invaded every part of her body and she hated it. She fought to bring back just a little of the feeling of the warm sunshine and the smell of the grass in the park. But the dream stayed just outside her grasp and finally she gave up, taking another deep breath and letting the shaking cold overwhelm her for a moment.

Finally, as the shivering passed, she glanced up again at an auxiliary flight board that showed the status of the ship and its location. She studied it for a moment. All lights green. It appeared they were dropping out of Einsteinian Space right on schedule. No problems, at least that she could see.

She took one more deep breath as beside her Deegan, her copilot, raised the lid on his sleep chamber. Beyond Deegan was the chamber in which their only passenger, Mr. Cray, still slept. The lights on his chamber were also still green and showing progress in the wake-up cycle.

"You all right, boss?" Deegan said without sitting up, his voice hoarse and thick, like he sounded after a hard night of drinking.

She just nodded and rubbed her face.

Unlike her own thin and trim body, Deegan was more of a jellyfish out of water. While she watched her weight and worked out daily, he ate too much, drank too much, and never exercised. He had white, pasty skin and the cold sleep every trip really got to him. She told him that if he kept himself in better shape, it wouldn't be so bad, but he never listened.

She slowly stood, the metal deck ice-cold under her bare feet. She quickly slipped on her sandals and then stretched, loosening sore muscles in her shoulders and back. She wore only brief bikini underwear and a light tank top. Goose bumps formed on her brown skin as she fought to loosen the muscles and shake the chill from the cold

sleep. Even though she was in the best condition
she could maintain, it would still take her hours,
even after a long hot shower and a half hour of
exercise to fully get beyond the chill. That was
her pattern after cold sleep. It never seemed to
vary so she might as well get it started.

She glanced again at the flight board. They
were six hours out from Charon Base. Just the
thought of that name gave her chills. She hated it
there almost more than she hated cold sleep. She
sighed. "Last trip," she promised herself under her
breath. She had more than enough time to take an
extra hot shower after exercising. She had the
feeling she was going to need it.

She gathered up her brown cloth slacks, brown
vest, and the Harley-Davidson baseball cap that
held her long black hair out of her face. Then she
moved over and looked down through the cover
of the sleep chamber at Mr. Cray. He was on his
back, clad only in his boxer shorts. He looked to
be in good shape, with strong chest and arm muscles and a trim waist. His head lolled slightly to
one side and his mouth was partially open. Her
guess was that in normal sleep he snored. She
caught herself hoping she would get the chance to
find out.

"Deegan," she said, patting the lid of Cray's
chamber. "Make sure our guest gets up. We don't
want him asleep for the big meeting with Professor Kleist." With a final glance at his solid chest
and the bulge in his boxer shorts, she headed toward her cabin and her wonderfully warm
shower.

Behind her she heard Deegan moan, "Yes,

boss." Then there was an even louder moan as he sat up.

On Charon Base, in a small wood and metal-lined corridor carved out of solid rock years earlier by prisoners, five Marines in full battle armor gathered. Helmets locked on, faceplates up, automatic Kramer rifles slung over shoulders. Taser Web rifles in their hands, they looked like they were ready to go into a war.

And that's exactly what they were preparing to do.

The corridor dead-ended into a metal, airlock-style door. The white plates of the battle armor contrasted sharply with the brown carpet on the floor and the gray steel of the airlock. The corridor had a slight smell of sweat and fear as it did before any mission.

Sergeant Green, not the tallest of the five Marines, but by far the largest and most powerful in shoulder width and the huge size of his arms, waited until all were silent before he gave them their mission. "We're after an adult warrior, alive and intact. I know that stinks, but that's the drill."

He made a point of looking around at the three men and Boone, the only woman left on his squad. No one answered and he smiled to himself. They didn't like this shit any more than he did, but they would follow their orders and that was what he needed at the moment. He was following his orders, and they needed to follow theirs if they planned on getting out of this alive.

He went on. "Taser Webs only. Kramers slung unless on my order. Is that understood?"

6

Private McPhillips said, "Yes, sir," softly, and no one else moved.

"Dillon, the Sound Cannon ready?"

"Warming up, sir. Just hope the thing works this time."

"Don't we all," Sergeant Green said. This was another stupid mission, but when the Professor said do something, they did it. That was their assignment no matter how bad or wrong it was. Or how many lives it cost them.

"Let's do it. McPhillips, take the point. The rest of you keep it tight."

McPhillips turned and punched the open cycle on the airlock doors that divided the human areas of Charon Base from the alien hive. Thick, hot air blasted the Marines as McPhillips quickly checked both sides of the passage ahead and then slowly moved forward, checking above the door and the ceiling down the rock corridor.

Charon Base was not much more than a large hunk of solid rock orbiting a class-three yellow star in an elliptical orbit. Originally it had been a government prison camp, used to hold the most dangerous criminals from Earth. The prisoners' jobs were to dig more tunnels, expand the base continuously with useless tunnel after useless tunnel. The rock was honeycombed with tunnels fifteen, sometimes twenty levels deep. Most of the prisoners had died doing their "make-work" job.

After the alien invasion of Earth and its recapture, the government didn't have the money or the desire to ship prisoners out this far, so Z.C.T. Corporation bought Charon Base and started the top-secret Project Chimera.

A section of the old tunnels were then sealed

off from the rest of the base and five captured aliens and one queen were let loose to form the beginnings of a hive.

Another small section near the surface was upgraded to the highest human living standards and top scientists from around the inhabited planets were hired and brought in, along with a platoon of government Marines to help deal with the bugs and safeguard the government interest.

The rest of the tunnels were left, forgotten for the most part.

Professor John Kleist was put in charge of finding as many ways as possible to make a profit from the aliens. From the acid blood to the royal jelly. Everything. But Professor Kleist had taken the project beyond even the corporation's fondest dreams. And that progress had come at a high price, paid mostly by the lives of the Marines.

Sergeant Green kicked in his suit's air filters as the thick, rotting alien smell filled the air. Someone once described an alien hive's odor as ten thousand rotten eggs frying in rancid grease. Green had done a hundred missions into hives in the war since he had heard that description. Without fail every time that smell hit him he thought of that image. And then thought it wasn't a strong enough description. Not by far. Thank God for body armor and the filters.

The five white-armor-covered Marines moved forward slowly as the corridor widened beyond the human section and became a large rock tunnel after about twenty meters. It felt to Green like an old train tunnel, only with higher ceilings.

McPhillips, at point, stepped gingerly around puddles of alien slime, picking a path one careful step at a time. The acid slime coated the walls and dripped from the ceiling forming odd pockets of blackness. The Marines' lanterns couldn't penetrate those pockets. It was those pockets that were so dangerous. Aliens slept in those holes and could appear and strike without notice at lightning speed.

"Stay alert," Green said, his voice suddenly sounding hollow in his headset, even to his own ears.

McPhillips, with the shorter Dillon right behind him, continued to pick a careful path through the mess. The new battle armor was good, but it wasn't perfect. Enough of the acid and it could be eaten right through to the skin.

Green glanced back at Choi and Boone as the airlock slid closed behind them. There was a reason Boone was the last surviving woman in his platoon. She was as tough as nails and damn near as fast as a bug on reaction time. She and the redheaded, skinny Choi were inseparable, both being from New York, both being about the same age. The men kidded them about making love like rabbits, but it never seemed to get to them. They just went right ahead and did it, at all times of the day or night.

"Watch the walls," he said to Boone, nodding his head to the right at some extra deep pockets of alien slime. "Choi, keep an eye on those side corridors. We don't want one of the bastards getting in behind us."

"You got it, sir," Choi said.

Green took a deep breath and let it out slowly. His stomach was twisting up, but so far everything was standard.

Another thirty slow, careful meters into the hive. Nothing but them moving. "I don't want to go much farther into this," Green said. Behind him the gray doors of the airlock seemed an impossible distance away. In front of him McPhillips stopped but didn't turn around. "Dillon, any traces on the scanner?"

"Blank as Choi's brain," Dillon said. "Nothing at all—"

The scream filled Green's headset. Oh, God. No! He had heard screams like that far too often over the years.

Instinctively he dropped and spun, his rifle off his shoulder, up and aimed.

"Boone! Cut it loose!" Choi's cry echoed with Boone's scream as the huge alien warrior dragged her up the wall toward its hole in the ceiling.

Like the well-trained Marine that she was, Boone knew some tricks of her own. Kicking out with her boots at the alien's head and arms, she twisted in the alien's sharp claws.

Right, then left, always moving.

Twisting, trying to get an arm free from the alien's grasp to get a shot at the bug's arm or head, anything to get it to drop her.

As if in the worst slow motion of a nightmare gone bad, Green watched in sick fascination, not daring to fire until he had a clear shot at the head or knees of the bug.

Choi looked like he almost might have an open shot at the bug's legs in a second.

Boone twisted to aim her Taser Web at the bug's head.

She almost made it.

But before she or Choi or anyone could get a

shot off, the worst happened. Huge, saliva-filled outer jaws snapped open and the second alien jaws from deep in its throat shot through Boone's armored helmet like it was so much tissue.

Her final scream echoed and then died like someone had cut off the power on a stereo.

Pieces of her helmet, face, and brains exploded over the corridor, raining down on everyone, covering Choi in his lover's blood. Her body twitched in the alien's grasp, still fighting, even though her head was gone.

The alien's smaller jaws retreated into its throat, pulling along the dome of Boone's brains and face.

"No!" Choi screamed. Like all of them he had his rifle unholstered, working for a shot at the alien that wouldn't leave Boone covered in acid blood.

But now that didn't matter and before Green could even react, Choi fired. His shot hit the bug head-on in the body with a full charge.

The bug exploded like a kid's firecracker, raining acid down the walls and onto the corridor. Boone's body dropped to the stone floor, one hand and arm of the alien still attached around her waist. She bounced once among the remains of the bug's body and came to rest on her side, her back to the corridor, her hair filling the hole in the back of her helmet.

Green reached Choi a second too late to stop him. "Hold your fire, God damn it!" He slapped Choi's gun aside.

"Boone . . ." Choi said, and started toward her acid-soaked remains.

Green held his arm. "She's gone and now you

might have killed us all." Green held on as Choi fought to pull away and go to Boone.

"Sarge!" Dillon shouted. "I got signals! Readings coming in all over. From three sides—"

There was a high-pitched, panicked sound to Dillon's voice and McPhillips said, "Shit!" loud enough to echo in Green's head gear.

"Damn it!" Green shook Choi hard, snapping him around and away from the sight of Boone's body. "We just gave them all a wake-up call, and now they're coming down for breakfast. Get your ass ready to fight."

He glanced quickly around at McPhillips and Dillon, then shouted, "Combat spacing front and rear. Hustle! Dillon, the Sound Cannon?"

"Prepared and ready, sir. Max. frequency, wide field focus."

"Let's hope the damn thing works this time," Green said under his breath. Louder he said, "Taser Webs, stand by."

It seemed like only a second before the corridor, the walls around them, the tunnels to the sides of them, came alive with wave after wave of ugly, mad bugs. Every one of them five to six times their size. Green could hear the rustling of their movements even through his armor's shell. He'd always heard the old saying that if the aliens' rustlings and clickings were loud enough to penetrate armor, you were as good as dead because there were so many of them.

This time seemed like it wasn't going to be an exception to the rule. Green couldn't remember seeing so many bugs in one fight. Straight on, without the Sound Cannon, the four of them would never stand a chance.

"Dillon, fire!"

The long metal Sound Cannon looked more like an old bazooka from the Earth wars than anything else. It seemed to jump slightly in Dillon's hand, but there was no sound. No explosion from its end. And for what seemed like an eternity, nothing happened.

Green watched as Dillon focused on the dial on the top of the weapon, nodding, ignoring the certain death around him.

The gun seemed to be aimed at nothing in particular. Around them the air in the tight rock chamber seemed to be shimmering, as if waves of heat were coming off hot pavement. The alien saliva formations wavered in Green's eyes, but he knew it was nothing more than the surface effects of the Sound Cannon. It was working. He almost wanted to scream with joy.

Every bug in the corridor froze, saliva dripping from wide mouths.

"God, I love that thing," Green said, letting out the breath he was holding. "Damned if I know how it works, but when it does, it gets them every time."

Somehow Professor Kleist had discovered a weapon that got to the creatures' nervous systems and froze them like so many ugly statues in an alien park. The problem was that it couldn't always be counted on and very seldom worked for longer than sixty seconds. The Professor kept promising he was working on making it better, more reliable, but in the meantime Green had lost more than half his platoon. But this time it looked like the Sound Cannon, as they all called it, had saved their lives.

At least all but Boone's.

He pointed to the biggest and closest warrior on the corridor wall. "Web that one and let's get out of here."

Dillon's and McPhillips's two Taser Webs fired at the same moment, pulling the huge, stunned warrior off the wall with a loud, smacking thump. Surrounded in nets that not even the acid blood of the aliens or their super strength could eat through, it lay on the corridor floor, drooling.

Beep! Beep! Beep!

"Shit!" Dillon said as the sound echoed through the rock chamber like the timer of a bomb.

Green knew that sound. It was the sound of their funeral if they didn't move damn fast.

"Sarge," Dillon managed to choke out, his voice trembling more than Green had ever heard it before. "This damn thing is malfunctioning. We've got about thirty seconds before it blows and sends us and this entire station into space."

"Choi," Green shouted at where the Marine stood over his lover's body. "Help with that bug. Now!"

Beep! Beep! Beep! Beep!

The sound echoed off the stone walls and the frozen aliens around them, increasing in tempo and matching Green's racing heart. He knew it was the sound of the clock ticking away their final seconds of life.

Faster and faster with each beep.

With a final look at Boone, Choi did as he was ordered. He turned and was beside McPhillips almost instantly, yanking on the webs around the bug.

Dillon backed slowly toward the airlock holding the Sound Cannon.

Green kept both his Taser Web in his right hand and his Kramer automatic rifle in his left covering the frozen aliens as Choi and McPhillips dragged the stunned warrior down the corridor as fast as they could go.

Beep! Beep! Beep! Beep! Beep!

"Fifteen seconds," Dillon said. "I got to shut it down or it'll blow."

"Hold on as long as you can," Green said. "Then run!"

Beep! Beep! Beep! Beep! Beep!

"You're telling me," Dillon shouted back. Quickly he was backing toward the entrance and Green was matching him step for step.

Beep! Beep! Beep! Beep! Beep! Beep!

"Shit! Not much longer—"

"Hold it!" Green shouted.

"Eight, seven, six—"

"Hold it!"

The beeps had almost become one long scream echoing off the slime formations and the stone walls. Another few seconds and the explosion would destroy the entire base.

"I'm shutting it down!"

Green, still backing up beside Dillon, glanced around.

Choi and McPhillips had the warrior to the airlock. Another few seconds and they would be through and to safety.

He and Dillon had backed to within twenty meters of the lock, but that might be twenty meters too far if the bugs around and in front of them reacted very fast.

Dillon clicked off the cannon, stuffed the long tube under his arm, turned, and ran.

The silence in the corridor seemed almost as loud as the beeping.

Green waited for just a moment as the bugs started to move, slowly at first, then angry as hell, before he also turned and ran behind Dillon, keeping right with him every step.

Choi and McPhillips had the captured warrior through the airlock and had come back to the lock with Taser Webs aimed over the two running Marines.

Green sucked in lungful after lungful of air and did his best to run as fast as he could, his body armor pounding every joint in his body. These suits just weren't meant for exercise.

Ahead, Choi and McPhillips pointed Tasers at him. He trusted them to be good shots, but he still didn't much like how they were aiming straight at him.

Dillon cleared the airlock as McPhillips fired, barely missing Green and connecting with a bug that was too damn close behind him.

Green figured at that moment he was dead. His heart was pounding so hard that he felt like it might explode—that is if a bug didn't grab him first.

Choi punched the airlock close command and the doors started to grind together.

Green dove headfirst through the closing airlock, tumbling like a white ball of armor as Choi fired another Taser at the closest bug. Green stopped his tumble and lay on the carpeted floor, face-to-face with the captured warrior, trying to catch his breath.

Saliva dripped off the bug's open jaws and Green caught a glimpse of its interior jaw in that black hole of a throat. It was aimed right at his head.

He quickly scrambled to his feet and moved a few meters away, where he did his best to suck as much air as he could get into his lungs.

Too close.

Just too goddamned close.

2

Professor Kleist leaned
back in his chair, his fingers steepled in front of
him, his bright blue eyes focused intently on the
wall of monitors in front of his glass desk. Fifty-
meter-square screens filled the huge wall, all following one activity or another around the base. If
the Professor wanted, he could divide each screen
by four or eight or even sixteen, all showing different scenes. It was the most sophisticated security system available in the corporation and since
the system's installment he had upgraded it con-
siderably. It was one of his most prized tools and
he spent many hours in front of it, just watching
the fifteen hundred people under his command.

With his system, no one on Charon Base

sneezed, whispered, or made love without him knowing about it.

As with many things on Charon Base, the Professor had seen to every detail of the construction of his office. On Earth the almost gymnasium-size room would have been considered excessive. The oak walls and shelves a frivolity, the thick carpet almost too plush.

In one corner was a full kitchen, always stocked with fresh food and drink. Shelves of real books—research, reference, and fiction—filled two walls. Those books were his personal collection and it had taken most of one transport ship's capacity just to get them here. But it had been a small expense in exchange for his needs and what he had accomplished for the corporation so far.

But the central feature of the office was the huge oak desk and high-backed chair facing the wall of monitors—a wall that curved slightly such that there was nothing else in view, like a surround vision movie, only those screens weren't showing a film.

The surface of the desk was larger than most king-size beds, measuring two meters deep by four meters long. From that desk and the control board that occupied the left third of the top, he could access the thousands of miniature video relay systems and microphones hidden throughout the base.

Larson, the chief of security, stood slightly behind the Professor and to his left. From there he could work the monitor control board on the desk when the Professor asked him to.

Unlike Kleist who was built solidly, with broad shoulders and thick arms, Larson was tall, skinny, and deceptively strong. He had short black hair and deep black eyes. It seemed like he never blinked, which unnerved many around him.

Like the Professor, Larson now stared at the center four monitors, all presently showing different scenes from Sergeant Green's recent mission into the alien sector. The monitors above the center four were focused on the Marine's current activities.

Kleist pointed at the bloody picture of Boone, deserted in the alien section. With a few key strokes on the inside right of the control board, he focused the camera in close and sat forward in his chair. Boone lay sprawled on the stone floor, the head and upper chest of the alien warrior slightly across her legs. Her hair hung out of the hole in the back of her helmet and one alien arm and claw still clung to her waist. There were no other bugs in sight and nothing had disturbed the scene since the retreat of the Marines. "Can we save the body?"

Larson stared at the scene for a moment before answering. "I'll have some of my men check, but I doubt it. The idiot who killed the alien managed to cover the woman's body in acid blood. I doubt the armor could hold it all back."

Kleist nodded. "I hope you're not right, but I suspect you might be. Check anyway. If the burns are only superficial we could use it."

Larson turned away from the Professor and softly gave instructions into his personal mike.

The Professor nodded in satisfaction, leaving one screen on the woman's body so he could watch when Larson's men got there.

His hand did a quick dance on the control

board, then he leaned back in his chair and ran both hands through his thinning hair, his gaze again intent on the four Marines as they half carried, half dragged the alien warrior toward the labs. He watched, following their progress through the corridors as the system automatically switched from hidden camera to camera until the four Marines had the warrior delivered to the dissection vat.

Then he leaned forward and punched another key, sending his voice into the lab. "Nice work, Sergeant Green. It looks like a fine specimen."

He paused for a moment until all four Marines were looking up at the one obvious camera in the corner of the lab above them. Then he said, "But I am distressed that you slaughtered the other one, however."

"He's distressed," Private Choi shouted. The Professor could see the private shaking and he smiled. Good. He had gotten to the kid.

The private pulled off his helmet, his red hair falling long over the back of his suit. "Kleist, you son of a bitch! I should—"

Green grabbed the private's arm and yanked him almost off his feet. Green was twice the size of Choi and just one arm was as big around as Choi's waist.

Kleist sat back in his chair watching, smiling. Sergeant Green was not one to be underestimated. Not only was he a big brute of a man, he understood very well the ruling systems here on Charon Base.

"Sir, I can explain," Sergeant Green started, but Choi yanked his arm away and stepped closer to the one obvious camera.

"Kleist," Choi said, "we could have all been killed in that ant farm of yours. Boone is dead. You understand? Dead!"

He yelled the words though the meaning of them started to choke him up. But he went on, "And all you can be distressed about is that we killed one of your bugs. I don't think you're playing with a full deck."

Kleist smiled and turned to Larson, who was also grinning.

"Sir," Sergeant Green started to say, stepping up beside Choi and shoving him roughly aside.

"Sergeant Green," Kleist said softly, but with enough force to make the sergeant stop. "I can appreciate the private's feelings, but I suggest he restrain himself before he says something he will regret. It was a successful mission. That will be all for the day."

Kleist punched the microphone off, then leaned back to observe what happened next. He could hear everything they were saying, even when whispered. This was going to be interesting.

"Kiss his big ass, why don't you?" Choi said, turning square on the sergeant. His face was almost as red as his hair and he was half crouched in an attack posture.

"Private!" Sergeant Green said sharply. "Do yourself a favor and rein it in."

Choi seemed to deflate slightly. His shoulders slumped and his gaze dropped to the floor.

The sergeant took a deep breath and let it out. "Look. I'm sorry about Boone, but there's a time and a place for everything. Here and now is *not* it. Understand?"

"Yeah, right," Choi said. He threw his helmet

across the room and it smashed into a wall, scattering files and making a lab table jump under the force of the impact.

Green put a firm hand on his shoulder and said softly, "The bugs aren't the only things you have to worry about around here. Now clam it up and hit the showers."

He waited until Choi had shrugged off his hand and started toward the door, then he turned to the other two members of the squad. "And that goes for both of you, too."

Professor Kleist laughed and leaned back in his chair. "How right you are, Sergeant. How right you are." He spun to face Larson. "It seems the stock needs some new breeding material, and Private Choi there just volunteered."

"It seems that he did," Larson said, smiling.

The Professor stood and slipped into his white lab coat. "I have work to do. This new warrior just may be the one. I'm close, so very close."

Captain Joyce Palmer pulled the yellow Harley-Davidson cap down firmly on her head and then strapped herself into the pilot's chair, buckling first the lap belt and then both shoulder straps. Deegan was already strapped in beside her, running diagnostic checks and preparing for docking. In front of them was the main control board for the shuttle and two windows looking out into the blackness of space. In the center between the windows was a large monitor, at the moment black and not in use.

Their passenger, Mr. Cray, looked tired and somewhat ruffled. He was strapped into one of two passenger seats along the wall behind Deegan. He wore pressed cloth pants, a dress shirt unbuttoned at the neck, and a brown leather jacket. She had nodded hello as she passed him in the small cockpit area of the shuttle and he had nodded back without a smile.

In the entire trip he hadn't said more than two sentences to her. Deegan had talked his ear off over the one dinner before cold sleep, but she doubted if Cray had even said three words back. Of course, Deegan didn't usually need much more than three words to keep him going for hours.

"Nice shirt," she said to Deegan as she finished her adjustments and slipped the headset over her cap. It was a ritual they always went through right before landing. Deegan always wore his lucky Budweiser T-shirt with a faded picture of an ugly dog on it. He said it had been his dad's. It had been patched more times than she wanted to think about and it still had holes all over it. But it was his lucky T-shirt and he always wore it for landings.

"I'm glad you like it," he said, smiling.

Behind them she heard Cray give a snort of disgust. That was good. At least he had some taste. Her lucky landing clothes were far less obvious. She just had on a white T-shirt, brown cloth slacks, and a brown open vest. In the pocket of the vest she had a picture of Cass and Drake. That picture always rode against her chest and her heart every takeoff or landing. It wasn't as obvious a good-luck charm as Deegan's shirt, but it was her private one.

She adjusted the mike so it was just below her lower lip, then nodded to Deegan and punched up

the transmit code. "Charon Base Flight Control.
This is the transport vessel *Caliban* requesting
landing clearance. Sending identification codes
now." She punched in two more sequences on the
console in front of her, then said, "Over."

Deegan pointed through the viewport at the
bright light growing quickly in front of them.
"There she is. Hell in space, our soon to be home
away from home."

"Roger, *Caliban*." The deep voice of Hank, the
flight controller, filled the control cabin. "Hangar
twelve is clear and ready to receive you. Hope you
had a safe trip, Joyce. Over."

Deegan glanced at Joyce and smiled, the glint
in his eyes letting her know that *he knew* what
had happened between Hank and her on the last
run here. Or at least he thought he knew. Knowing
the lack of privacy on Charon Base, he probably
did. Every damn detail.

She ignored her copilot. "So far so good," she
said. "Over."

"We're in the tube," Deegan said. "Normal to
profile. Cutting thrusters." He was still smiling at
her.

"All right," she said. "Let's tuck her in. And,
Deegan—"

"Yes, boss?"

"Watch those corners this time."

Deegan laughed. "I missed that door by a good
ten meters last time. This is a walk in the park."

She snorted. "When did you last see someone
take eighty thousand tons of ugly metal for a
stroll?"

He again laughed, but didn't take his eyes off
his instruments. She sat back and watched as

Deegan, one of the best solo pilots working, took them in. Within thirty minutes he had the transport sitting snugly in the middle of the docking bay.

"Hangar deck secure. Outer doors closed. Deck pressurized," Hank's voice announced a moment after Deegan cut thrusters. "Crew and passengers please report to decontamination."

"Will do," Joyce said and cut the link. She had to admit she was looking forward to seeing Hank again. It seemed like it had been a long time, even though for her it had only been a little over a month real-time. But for Hank it actually had been a long time, a little over a year and a month. Maybe he was married by now or more likely no longer interested in her. She let the thought drop. No point in worrying about it. She'd find out soon enough.

She let Deegan, now wearing a cloth jacket over his tattered shirt, lead her and Cray out of the ship and down the ramp. They strode across the hangar deck in silence as service technicians swarmed around the transport.

The decontamination chamber was nothing more than a narrow spot in the main passage leading from the deck. As the three of them stepped inside, big metal doors ahead and behind them slid shut with a loud bang. She thought it would be much easier on the nerves to not have such loud doors. But at every base the decontamination doors slammed shut, a very annoying design feature.

A fine mist and bluish light filled the area. Joyce always thought the decontamination chamber smelled like apples, but Deegan said it was more like floor polish. They had argued about it a number of times. Again she smelled apples.

She turned slightly as they stood for the required thirty seconds so that she could see Cray better. He seemed to be used to the process. No trace of emotion crossed that cold face—at least none that she could see.

She, on the other hand, hated the procedure. She always felt naked in these chambers. Not only were they killing the unwanted microscopic bugs that might be hitching rides, but somewhere, behind some monitors, people she didn't know were looking her insides over very carefully for bigger bugs. Alien-type bugs. She was glad they did, but it still made her feel very exposed knowing someone—maybe even Hank—was looking at her every private part.

She again shook off the thought and turned to Cray. "So, what brings you to scenic Charon?"

"Apart from us, that is," Deegan said.

"Excuse me, Deegan, but I'm trying to have a conversation with a real human."

Cray smiled slightly and Joyce immediately liked him better. "Thanks for the interest, but it's classified." He turned and actually looked at her. "Need to know and all that."

"And we don't need to know?"

"Got it in one," Cray said, but his eyes told her it was nothing personal.

"Figures," Deegan said as the chamber doors banged open and they entered the carpeted area of the base. "Kleist has this place sewn up tighter than a frog's butt."

"Mr. Cray," Professor Kleist said as he rounded the corner ten meters in front of them, and Joyce instantly tightened. The Professor gave her the creeps. His cheeks seemed to always be flushed and his eyes felt more like animal eyes than human ones.

Two others followed the Professor and Joyce shuddered again as they came into sight. One was the Professor's main henchman, Larson, a tall, wiry man who was by far the nastiest human she had ever met. The other was the Professor's android secretary, Grace. Grace had short blond hair, a body only science could manufacture, and a smile that could freeze a waterfall. Joyce regarded all three with equal loathing. She'd never had a run-in with any of them, but she had heard enough stories.

"Speak of the devil," Joyce said softly as they continued toward the Professor.

"And he shall appear," Cray said, just as softly. A moment later he was smiling and shaking the Professor's hand as introductions were made.

"I trust you had a comfortable flight?" Kleist asked Cray.

"Yes," Cray said, glancing at Joyce. "It was most enlightening."

"Good, good. Glad to hear it." Kleist patted Cray on the back, then steered him away from the pilots and down the hall. "We must get to our business."

Joyce and Deegan stood and watched the Professor's party walk away. When they were far enough away Joyce said softly, "Hmm . . . he could be interesting."

"Who?" Deegan asked. "Kleist? Or the corporation suit?"

"None of your damn business," she said.

"Ha, you have a heart under all that ice after all."

"Yeah," Joyce said, "I do. It belonged to my last wise-ass copilot."

Deegan laughed as they followed the Professor and his group at a safe and sane distance into the human sections of the station.

In the silent quarters of the Marines, Sergeant Green slowly picked through Boone's locker. Choi was nowhere to be found and the others were at dinner. It was as good a time as any to finish up his most dreaded chore.

He glanced down the row of single, tightly made beds and green lockers. When they had arrived this room had been full. Full of life and energy. Full of his men.

Now only half of them were left. He had cleaned out over half his troop's personal effects and shipped them back to families on Earth. Half dead. How could that be?

And now he was doing another.

This was wrong. This was different than losing good men and women fighting an enemy. Here his soldiers had died at the hands of alien prisoners, solely for the benefits of Professor Kleist and Z.C.T. Corporation's research.

This wasn't war; this wasn't honorable death. This was just profit.

He picked up a photo Boone had of her friends. It was taken on a green lawn on Earth, with the Earth-orbit shuttle in the background, right before their departure on this mission. Boone's arm was around Choi and they were both beaming like the world was the nicest, safest place to be. Green supposed that together it had seemed that way then.

But now Boone was dead, rammed through by an alien and covered in acid blood. And Choi was alone.

Green shook his head. As they always said, the corps took everything you've got to give.

And then more.

Green dropped the photo on top of the few belongings Boone had left and closed the box. He picked it up and tucked it under his arm. Such a small box, so few things for a human to leave behind. He glanced around the room at the freshly made beds, the perfect order of the lockers. Alive or dead, he was proud of his men and of the Marines. It was all he knew.

It was his life and his soul..

Maybe the corps did take everything you had to give, but it was never in vain.

Never.

As long as someone remembered.

3

The Professor escorted Cray to the living quarters and left him to get settled in, taking with him the transmission disk Cray had brought from the Z.C.T. Corporation headquarters. The disk he had said was the only reason for his long trip. A very strange reason, indeed, to eat up fifteen months of a man's life.

Back in his office, behind breach-proof doors, the Professor gave only a slight glance at the screens in front of him, then settled into his chair and keyed the transmission disk with his thumbprint. A red light blinked for a moment, then reset to green on the disk cover.

The Professor nodded and inserted the disk in the play slot of the decoding imager. If nothing else, this was going to be interesting. He knew a great deal about Mr. Cray. A black belt in karate and a spy with no equal. The list went on. Much more information than Cray would want him to know, he was sure. And everything that involved Cray was always interesting.

The Professor leaned back, his fingers steepled in front of his chin as the hologram shimmered into place over the front edge of his desk. The image first relayed the standard corporation gold and black logo, Z.C.T., with the "Z" and the "T" overlaid over the "C." Following the logo after a few seconds were the blocklike words "EYES ONLY: PROFESSOR ERNST KLEIST FROM G. D. SQUAZA, CONTROLLER, RESEARCH AND DEVELOPMENT."

A moment later the words were replaced by the image of the Professor's old friend, Gordy Squaza, the second most powerful man in Z.C.T. Corporation, sitting behind his glass and chrome desk. Behind him a window overlooked the parklike setting of the corporation headquarters. The Professor had looked out that window a number of times while visiting Squaza and planning this base and the Chimera Project. Even though the image was smaller than life, the feeling of being at the headquarters was very real and for just a moment it gave the Professor a sinking feeling of home. He shook the feeling, slightly angry at himself. This was his home; this work was his life. He didn't have time for wondering about Earth, or anyplace else for that matter.

The Professor leaned toward the holographic image of his old friend. "This is going to be fascinating."

"Hello, Ernst," Squaza said, then the image seemed to hold and flicker in repeat mode.

The Professor sat back and watched it, recognizing the standard coding for corporation holographic messages. If the wrong response or the wrong voiceprint was heard next, the disk would destroy itself.

"Hello yourself, Gordy," the Professor said carefully. His voice and words triggered a recognition sequence and the holographic image continued and sharpened. Again the Professor said softly, "I knew this was going to be good."

"Sorry about all the cloak-and-dagger business," Squaza said, his smile not totally hiding the seriousness in his brown eyes. "We have something of a situation here. Actually, 'situation' is a mild way of putting it. We have a mess here, plain and simple. And I thought you should be brought up to speed on the current events, even if this takes six months to reach you."

Actually, the Professor noted that the message had taken two days over seven months to get to him, but he didn't say a word, just listened and waited.

The image of Squaza grew until only his face filled the holographic image hovering over the Professor's desk.

Squaza took a deep breath and went on. "Ernst, your work on the Chimera Project is garnering unhealthy attention from certain quarters, including the Grant Corporation, B.M.I. Affairs, and a new Asian-Chinese consortium that's attempted to infiltrate Z.C.T. on a number of occasions. All have been fruitless efforts. Fruitless, that is, until now."

The image of Squaza pulled away and after a

moment Squaza stood and moved toward the window, obviously contemplating what to say next. The Professor just sat at his desk, his fingers again steepled in front of his chin, his gaze never leaving the image.

Finally Squaza turned and faced into the recorder directly. "Ernst, your last project update had problems. When we received the transmission, it had been intercepted and decoded."

"Really," the Professor said softly, without moving.

"It was a tidy job," Squaza said. "But close investigation showed that the data had not only been intercepted and decoded, but had been altered and infested with viral time bombs. Nasty things to say the least. They've cost us more time and energy than you can imagine. I'm not blaming you at all, so don't take what I am saying that way."

Squaza took a deep breath and then sat back down at his desk. "The point is that we can't be certain that this was the first time they have cracked our transmissions or the hundredth. We're having to deep-clean all our systems, which is a nightmare as you can imagine. And we don't know who or, for that matter, how they managed to crack our codes."

Again the camera focused in close on Squaza's face. "Ernst, we don't know if the problem is on our side or yours, but you must be extra careful. Your project is our corporation's highest priority, and until we discover the leak you are to cease transmissions to Earth until further notice. Security code Alpha C fifty-one."

The Professor smiled and sat back in his chair.

Now he was starting to understand. He watched as Squaza shuffled some papers on his desk, then looked back into the camera. "I know this will be hard on you and your fine staff, but it must be done. You can trust no one. Understand?"

"Oh, I understand all right," the Professor said softly. He didn't say out loud that that had been his belief from the start. He had never trusted anyone and had no plans to start now.

"We can't rely on our existing data because of the changes, so I have sent Cray to collect disk copies of everything you have for personal delivery to our labs."

The holo image suddenly switched from Squaza to a photo of Cray. Squaza's voice continued over the picture. "Ernst, I know what you are thinking, but relax. He's the best operative we've got. You have him to thank for that gel that reduces alien blood to the pH of water. He took that out from under the noses of the Grant Corporation. He also won for us the specs on the Taser Web launchers our troops use. There is no one else I'd trust on this mission, and I'm sure you'll give him the respect he deserves under the security code Alpha C fifty-one."

The Professor laughed softly and then said, "You can bet I will give him the best of everything. Just for you, Gordy."

For a moment longer the picture of Cray remained on the image, then Squaza's face reappeared. "Ernst, everyone around here is walking scared. Security is working on the problem of who broke the codes and how they just walked into our computers like they did. But as far as we can tell it has to be an inside job."

Squaza looked directly into the camera. "It's going to be a bad time, Ernst. As an old friend, I'm warning you to *protect* yourself as best you can and watch your back at all times."

"Always have, old friend," the Professor said softly. "And I hear you this time, too. Loud and clear."

The image panned back to show Squaza sitting at his desk again with the parklike corporation grounds through the window. "I envy you, Ernst, out there on your island in space. We could all do with a little extra security and isolation around here. Good luck."

The words "MESSAGE ENDS" filled the air above the desk and a moment later the disk popped out of the holo player.

Professor Kleist leaned back in his chair and stared at the empty air in front of him.

Then, after a long time, he laughed. Not loudly. Just a soft laugh at something that seemed really, really funny.

Private Choi was giving much more than he was taking in punishment from three of the Professor's elite security force. "Larson's goons" as most people called them. They always wore dark slacks, green shirts, and sneakers. Usually they carried small arms like pistols, but lately they had taken to wearing full shoulder belts full of ammunition and carrying Kramers, the newest in high-speed automatic rifles. Twenty-six shots in a clip and ten clips on a belt. On fully automatic fire setting, twenty-six shots from a Kramer could drill a hole through a half meter of solid concrete in a fraction of a second.

They were nasty weapons.

In the fight with Choi, however, the guards hadn't considered him dangerous enough to bring rifles and it had taken him only a moment to disarm all three of their handguns. Now Choi's white T-shirt was stained red with the blood of the three men who had jumped him. If Choi hadn't already been looking for some way to avenge Boone's death, he might have been caught by surprise.

But he wasn't and now he stood panting, his back to the corridor wall, his fists clenched in readiness. His right eye was quickly swelling shut and blood trickled down from his right ear, almost matching the color of his bright red hair. He could feel that he had broken some bones in his right hand, but he didn't really care. It felt good to be fighting humans again, not stupid bugs. And since it was the Professor who had ordered Boone to her death, he would certainly take it out on the Professor's security force with pleasure.

One blond-headed security man lay on his back in the center of the corridor, his head cracked and bleeding, his brown uniform rumpled and torn in two places. Choi doubted if he was still breathing and didn't care much one way or the other.

The other two remained standing, weaponless, one on each side of the hall from Choi. The one to Choi's right had blood streaming from á crushed nose making the front of his brown uniform appear almost black. The guy was looking pale and would be slow moving.

"Give it up, Choi," the other guy said, but didn't

make a move. Choi laughed to himself. The guy was smarter than he looked.

"Screw you," Choi said, his voice low and mean. "And your asshole Professor, too." With a quick faint toward the one who had spoken, Choi spun and connected with a hard left-footed kick to the already smashed nose of the guy on the right as he started forward.

He caught him with his arms at his sides and a surprised look on his face. Choi could hear the bones in the guy's face crack and splinter as his head snapped back. Blood spattered the walls and ceiling and with a loud scream the guard tumbled backward, ending up facedown against the wall. A pool of dark blood quickly formed under his head. He wasn't moving and Choi doubted he ever would again. No great loss.

Choi spun to face his last attacker. "Your turn."

The guy shook his head and was slowly backing away when two more security guards entered the narrow hall from a side corridor and moved in beside the last remaining goon. Choi recognized Bergren, Larson's second in command. In his hands he carried a Taser Web gun used to take down aliens.

"Now it's a fair fight again," Choi said. He wiped his hands on his pants and moved into the very center of the corridor, preventing any of them from flanking him.

"What's the problem?" Bergren asked, giving a quick glance at his two men on the floor.

"You sci-tech maggots aren't fit to lick Boone's boots," Choi said, his voice hard and calm. "And now she's dead and you're not. That pisses me off."

The guy who remained from the first round turned slightly to Bergren. "Larson said the Professor wanted us to give this insubordinate grunt the treatment, but we couldn't get near him. He fought like a mad dog."

"I am *mad*, you stupid ass." Choi made a fake lunging move at the men, and all three took a step back.

"Cowards," Choi said, shaking his head and laughing. "My Boone died for a scum professor and a bunch of cowards. I just don't think that's right, do you?"

"But she didn't die in vain," Bergren said. "Luckily the suit protected her beautiful skin and body from most of the acid so she could be *used* again."

Choi stood slowly from his fighter's couch, his mind trying to make sense of what Bergren had said. "Used? What—" But before he could say anything more Bergren raised the Taser Web and fired.

The web, with its numbing, stinging needles, covered Choi before he had a chance to react. He dropped to one knee, the needles working instantly, making the web feel as if it weighed a ton.

He managed to get his hands under the web, but before he could pull it off his legs gave out and he fell over on his back to the floor.

His mind shouted that he should struggle, but his muscles betrayed him and he lay there, bound by webs designed to hold and control aliens twenty times stronger.

Bergren turned to the man Choi left standing and pointed to the two on the floor. "See what you can do for Pavin and Thomas, there, if you can manage to get that right." Then Bergren motioned for the other man to help him as he leaned over Choi.

"I'll kill you," Choi somehow managed to spit out at Bergren as the room spun and he began to lose consciousness.

Bergren laughed. "Dream on, dog boy. I'm the least of your problems. When you see what comes next you'll be begging me to save your stupid hide."

And the last thing Choi heard as the blackness overwhelmed him was Bergren's laughter.

Joyce sat up straight and took a deep breath, doing the best she could to pull oxygen into her lungs. Sweat ran off her forehead and into her eyes and an intense heat seemed to radiate from every pore of her body. She could heat half the base from what was pouring off her.

"I can die happy now," she said, her voice no more than a whisper. She let her upper body sag onto Hank's chest and then she rolled to the right and off of his panting, sweaty body. She lay on the rumpled and damp sheets staring up at the tiled ceiling of Hank's bedroom, just letting the warmth of the moment flow into her memory for the next time she woke from cold sleep.

"You all right?" he asked. His hand eased over and touched her arm.

She laughed. "A lot better than I ever expected to be this far from Earth." She took a deep shuddering breath and forced herself onto her side, her head propped in one hand.

Then she looked at him. Really looked at him.

His face was flushed, which gave him a healthy look seldom seen on the pale deep-space workers. He had a full head of dark brown hair that at the moment was slicked back off his forehead with sweat. His chest was well muscled and it was clear he worked out with weights regularly. She had always liked the feel and the look of his white skin against her black. It was as if there were a line drawn between them that left her feeling just a little safer. A line that wouldn't allow him, or anyone else, all the way inside her defenses.

Yet at times like these she was glad he was with her and she didn't want to exclude him in any way.

She ran her hand over his mostly hairless chest. "How about you?"

"Very, very glad you came back."

"Thought I was gone for good, huh?" She let her finger trace a line in the sweat on his arm.

"I figured after that last time you'd stay on Earth, or get runs closer in, and I'd never see you again."

"Can't say as I didn't think about it. But the money out here for this one last trip will let me finish raising the kids the way they need to be raised."

He nodded and took a deep breath. Not looking at her he said, "You just be careful while you're here." Suddenly his voice had a sad and very serious edge to it.

"Why?" she asked. "Are things getting worse?"

He turned and looked at her for a moment and she could tell that she might have gone too far with that question. His eyes were almost shouting "No!"

With just a slight hesitation he laughed. "Nope, just about the same as always around here, from what I can tell. Of course, I don't pay that much attention." He patted her slick thigh and let his hand drift upward into her damp crotch for a moment. Then smiling, he said, "How about taking a long hot shower with me?"

She gave his hand a quick squeeze with her legs and beat him off the bed. "Only if we can start the water off cool for a few minutes."

"Deal."

They made small talk for the few minutes it took them to get into the shower and then after they both were standing naked together under the spray, Hank whispered in her ear, "You've got to be really, really careful. The Professor and his goon, Larson, have cameras and bugs everywhere. Not only the ones you can see, but many more you can't."

Joyce recoiled slightly at the thought of Larson and the Professor watching as she and Hank made love. Could he have listened to their every word, their every sound of passion?

Hank spun her around slowly, grabbed the soap, and started working slowly up and down her back. It felt wonderful, easing the sudden tension the thoughts of the Professor had brought to her shoulders.

"It's the truth," he said softly in her ear. "You have a great ass," he said more loudly as he ran the soap over her cheeks and then down the backs of her legs.

On the one hand it felt wonderful, and on the other she couldn't shake the possibility that someone was watching. Even with the soap and the hot water, the very thought made her feel dirty.

She turned around and pulled Hank into a hug, as if they were slow-dancing. In a whisper she asked, "What's been happening around here?"

Hank soaped her back as he answered. "Two years ago there were over fifteen hundred people—civilians, scientists, and just simple hired hands—on this station, including forty Marines. I bet if we were to do a total now it wouldn't break fourteen hundred. And there's only twenty Marines left. People just keep disappearing. Some are accidents. Some without reason or explanation. And the Marines keep getting killed on missions into the hive area."

"You're kidding," she whispered and he shook his head no. He wasn't kidding, but she didn't want to let herself believe what he was saying. That many people disappearing on a closed station like this wasn't possible.

"I wish I were kidding," Hank whispered, turning her slowly around so that her back was under the warm spray. "The Professor has become like an evil god around here and his security force is much more powerful than the Marines, numbering over a hundred men the last time I heard."

"A hundred men out of fourteen hundred." That seemed like overkill to her. Why would the Professor need that many security men on a closed, isolated station in deep space? It simply made no sense.

"That's right," Hank said. "Anyone who stands up against the Professor or Larson, or even Bergren, disappears very shortly. And anyone who even questions what happened does the same."

Joyce shook her head. "There's got to be some-one to investigate this, stop it."

Hank didn't say anything for a moment, just letting the water run down her back and shoulders. Finally he asked, "Did anyone back on Earth or at Z.C.T. headquarters mention the name of the project being worked on here?"

Joyce again shook her head. "Nothing. I wasn't even allowed to mention that I was leaving Earth's system until we were in deep space and ready for cold sleep. I didn't even know exactly that I was coming back here until we were well away from Earth. I just knew it was a deep-space mission. Then it turned out I was just to bring one man here and wait for his return. Very, very secret."

"That's the problem," Hank said. "We're so damn far from Earth that there just isn't anything we can do about the missing people. What few ships do come and go with supplies are monitored so tightly for security reasons that nothing leaves here without Larson and the Professor knowing."

"And Z.C.T. is behind him?" Joyce asked, knowing the answer to her obvious question.

"Totally."

They stood under the water, letting it pound their bodies without breaking into their thoughts.

"So how do we stop him?"

Hank shook his head. "*We* don't. *We* get out of this shower before we turn into prunes, go back to those sweat-stained sheets, and get some sleep. Then in the morning you make love to me or I make love to you, depending on who wakes up first."

"And we just let the Professor go on being God?"

Hank turned off the water and grabbed towels for both of them. "You got it." He hesitated for a moment, then said in a normal voice, "I think they're still delivering pizza from the west kitchen. Should I call for one?"

Joyce nodded and then studied the soft golden towel in her hands for a moment before moving to dry her hair. Hank was right. She had no stake in this. Better to just get back to Earth and then report it.

Larson watched Joyce towel off and move into Hank's bedroom before he turned and faced the Professor. "You think she's going to be a problem?"

Kleist watched on the center monitor as she climbed into bed and huddled next to the flight controller. "I'm sure she is. No telling what Cray told her on the way out here, and since we're going to keep her passenger for a time, she might find out things on her own."

"You want me to take care of her?" Larson asked. "I'd be glad to do it."

"I know you would," the Professor said, then shook his head. "No. We may need her and her ship. Let's just keep a close watch on her until that time comes."

Larson nodded, and with one last glance at the naked couple on one of the many screens that filled the wall, he moved toward the door. It would be his pleasure to watch her closely.

Very closely indeed.

4

Choi slowly fought his way back to consciousness, his first thought of Boone. He had always loved the way she looked after working out, her face covered in a fine sheen of sweat, her thin, soaked T-shirt stretched almost invisible by her muscles and chest. Her small brown nipples always poked through her shirt like they were calling for attention, and he tried to give them as much as she would let him.

But most of all he loved the way she smelled after exercising. An earthy, wet-clay sort of smell that turned him on like nothing else ever could. He would run his face across her sweaty arms or back or shoulders burying himself against her, never wanting to let go. Choi had been lucky that

Boone liked his love of her smell. They had made love after almost every workout. Boone called it her reward.

But Choi knew secretly it was much more his reward.

In his mind he could see her face—her small nose, her bright eyes—as if they were in front of him now. She smiled at him, called to him, and then the alien jaws cut through her face, smashing her smile, cutting off her call. The alien's jaws drooled her blood, leering at him, laughing at his inability to help her. He fought to go to her, but something held him back.

The alien's jaws sliced through her face and her blood was everywhere.

She was dead.

Overwhelming sadness caught him like a hard blow to the stomach. Boone was dead. He had watched her die, unable to move fast enough to save her. He wanted to die, too. Join her wherever she was now.

He moaned and tried to roll over, but something held him like a heavy, wet blanket. He could barely feel his legs and arms and his head felt thick, like he had a bad hangover. He struggled to remember where he was, what he had been doing that would cause this, but the nightmare of her face exploding in front of him kept filling his vision and he couldn't shake it.

"End of the line, dog boy," a voice said from above. Choi's mind cleared a little and the smell of rotten eggs filled his senses like a hammer pounding his thick skull. Oh, Jesus Christ Almighty! He was in the alien sector. What the hell was going on? He fought to open his eyes to blurry, faint light. Was Boone really dead? Had that all been a bad dream? Had he gotten hurt on the last mission instead?

"Nice nap?" the voice said and a rough hand pulled Choi into a sitting position with his back to the wall.

Choi shook his head carefully and took a few deep breaths of the humid, rancid air. He knew that voice. "Bergren?"

"Nice to have you back with us," Bergren said. He was standing over Choi with a pistol in one hand. "That was quite a job you did on my men."

Choi's hands quickly fought to pull some of the remaining Taser Webs from his legs and body. He blinked and his gaze finally focused on Bergren, then he glanced around. They were in the alien section all right, just inside the west airlock. Slime formations covered some of the walls and the smell was so thick the air seemed to have texture to it.

It looked as if they were alone. None of the Professor's other men were in sight at least.

"Bergren," Choi said, pulling off more webs and flexing his legs, "you're gonna die."

Bergren laughed, but his pistol never wavered. "I don't think so. You Marines have just pushed the Professor a little too far. Someone's gotta slap you down."

"Yeah, and you're elected, right?" Choi almost had the webs off his legs and was struggling to stand. He would show this two-bit jerk that no one got away with shooting him with a Taser like he was some damn bug.

Bergren laughed again. "Yeah, lucky me. I get to help you Marines know your place in the Professor's larger plan. Only, I'm afraid, it's just a little too late for you to learn much from the lesson."

Bergren's gun moved slightly lower and the sound of a shot echoed through the stone tunnels and caverns.

For just a moment Choi thought Bergren had missed him. He started to move, but then, as if in slow motion, his own blood splattered his face and the pain from his leg almost blacked him out.

He twisted around and grabbed his leg, focusing on releasing the pain like he and Boone had learned in basic. Don't think about the pain. Just react.

Don't think about the pain.

Just react.

He could almost hear Boone's voice repeating that with him, over and over.

Don't think.

React.

"You—you bastard!" Choi pulled his good leg underneath him and pushed off, lunging for Bergren.

Bergren quickly stepped back a few steps and the lunge fell short, leaving Choi to fall twisting on the hard floor, in even more pain than before as his wounded leg banged the hard surface.

"You were a dead mother the minute you smeared that damn bug," Bergren said, standing just out of Choi's reach. "The Professor doesn't like his pets being hurt."

Choi fought the blackness back. Don't think about the pain. Just react.

Don't think about the pain. Just react.

Quickly he dragged himself back over to the stone wall and forced himself to stand. For a moment the dizziness and the pain held him down, but he fought through it and finally gained his feet.

Bergren was walking quickly toward the airlock to the human quarters.

"Wait!" Choi shouted, glancing around the damp, smelly corridor. For the first time it dawned on him what Bergren was doing. Choi started to jump one-legged for the airlock, but the drugs from the Taser and the shock of his wound made him too weak. He fell face-first on the floor, his right hand searching for the small knife in the boot holster on his injured leg. It was slick, cov-ered in his own blood. He palmed it and again shouted for Bergren to wait.

Bergren opened the airlock and stood just in-side the alien section framed by the light from the corridor beyond.

Choi got a burst of fresh air, but it was smoth-ered by the stench and humid thickness of the alien caverns and that hated smell of rotten eggs.

With his hand still on the airlock button, Bergren glanced back at Choi. "I'd love to make this clean for you, but it's not worth my life. Crossing the Professor is never a wise move, but I suppose you understand that now. Right?"

Choi pulled himself hand over hand toward the airlock, dragging his useless leg behind him, ignor-ing the pain and the weakness.

Just react.

Just react, he repeated, over and over. Don't think. Just react.

Panic blurred his thoughts, but his training won out and he kept moving, pushing to escape.

Pushing to get closer to that door.

Bergren watched for a moment, then shrugged like it didn't make any difference. "I've got to hand it to you, Choi, you are one tough mother. Maybe you'll be lucky." He started to step through the door. "Maybe you'll bleed to death before implantation."

Without thinking or even aiming Choi swung up into a sitting position and sent the knife in a practiced underhand flick toward Bergren.

The thick sound of the blade burying itself in Bergren's chest filled Choi's ears with pleasure.

Bergren, one hand on the knife, a look of total shock and dismay on his face, staggered against the door frame.

Choi crawled toward the open door as fast as he could.

Bergren looked down at the knife, then back at Choi as his eyes glazed over and he toppled into the alien sector. Behind him the airlock slid closed with a resounding clang that reverberated down the dark corridors.

"No!" Choi shouted.

But his words only echoed through the hot, dark corridors. He was alone where no man dared to be alone. Behind him he heard a rustling noise that quickly grew to fill the small stone cavern.

Don't think. Ignore the pain. Just react.

He pushed Bergren's body aside and stretched up for the button on the airlock, pounding it hard over and over again.

Nothing. It was closed and it wasn't going to open. He could tell.

He turned, pushed himself up with his arms, got his good leg underneath his butt, and stood. Insistently he punched the open button, but the door wasn't moving. He tried to yank it open with brute strength, but it didn't even budge. He was trapped.

He almost toppled over as he reached down and pulled his knife out of Bergren's chest, wiping the blood on Bergren's shirt. "At least you went with me," he said.

He stood and leaned lightly against the airlock door. "Boone," he said intently to the air around him. "I ain't going down without a fight. You're going to be proud of me." He pulled another knife out of his other boot and stood facing the darkness.

There was a rustling in the shadows and the smell grew stronger.

Choi shouted into the dark caverns, "Come and get me, you Bitch!"

And almost before he had time to blink, she did.

The Professor nodded and turned from the wall of monitors to face Larson. "Too bad about your man Bergren, but this only proves he was careless and soft. Have your men retrieve his body. I can use it."

Larson nodded, still staring at the screen and the body of his second in command.

"Also," Kleist said, "you can expect trouble from Sergeant Green."

Larson forced himself to look at the Professor. "Not if he doesn't find out."

"Oh, he'll know," the Professor said. "And please make sure that he does. Do you understand?"

Larson just nodded, glancing back to the picture of Bergren's body. The alien had killed the struggling Choi by breaking his back like a dry stick. Blood rolled out of Choi's mouth as the alien pulled him out of the range of the camera and toward the center of the hive.

"Any movement from our shuttle pilot and her boyfriend?"

"She was asleep, last time I checked," Larson said. "I have someone monitoring her round-the-clock. Hank's on duty. They have a date for dinner after he gets off."

The Professor turned back to face the screen and sat unmoving, thinking. Every detail seemed to be in place. It would be another thirty hours before he knew if his latest experiment was going to succeed. So many failures, so many close calls. But he had a feeling this would be the one and thirty hours from now he would know.

"It seems," the Professor said, "that I have a little time to kill. Where is our Mr. Cray?"

Larson leaned over the edge of the desk and punched up a view in the center screen, then nodded toward it. "In his quarters, just sitting on his bed. From what I can tell he hasn't moved in two hours. That guy's a strange bird."

The Professor studied the solid frame of his guest. For being one of the best spies, he certainly didn't look much like one, whatever a spy was supposed to look like. Maybe it would be interesting to bait the guy a little, give him just a little rope. See how good he really was.

"Have Grace bring our guest to the labs. I might as well show him around." The Professor stood and took his lab coat off its hook beside the door.

He put the coat on and was about to leave when a soft bell chimed. Larson punched a key on the control board on the Professor's desk and listened for a moment, then clicked it off and looked up at the Professor. "Just our shuttle pilot. She's awake and headed for the lounge."

The Professor nodded. "I'm not sure exactly why I don't like that woman, but I just don't. I can sense the trouble she's going to bring."

"I'll watch her," Larson said.

"Of that I have no doubt," the Professor said.

As the door clicked closed behind Kleist, Larson dropped into the Professor's big padded chair. With a quick series of keystrokes he cleared the images of Bergren from the center screens.

Then, on three screens and from three different angles, he followed Joyce Palmer into the main lounge.

He loved to watch her.

In just the last day he knew most of her habits, where the scar on her right leg was, and what she did in the bathroom when she brushed her teeth. Someday he might even catch her alone and if the Professor gave him permission she'd find out she had a really true admirer.

The cool, clear taste of Mountain Crystal cut the fog from Joyce's mind and she nodded to the bartender, indicating her drink. "Nice, Jonathan. Real nice."

He smiled back at her, patted the bar lightly twice, and moved off to help the waitress at the end of the counter. Joyce took another sip, letting the cold, clear liquid fill her mouth as she settled

into the high-backed bar stool. Being with Hank
had been wonderful, almost better than it should
have been, but she couldn't—or maybe it was
"shouldn't"—let herself care too much for him.
She would be leaving within the week, maybe
within the day, to go back to Earth and her children, never to see him again. Getting too attached
would be just plain stupid.

Good sex. That was all it could be.

Ever.

Of course, she didn't want to believe that deep
down. There was just something between her and
Hank that she hadn't felt in years, and it felt good.
Really good.

She took another sip of the Mountain Crystal
and tried to force her thoughts from Hank. She
glanced around the bar, noting that there were
only a dozen people in the room, most sitting together in one corner laughing and talking. This
place was officially called the East Lounge, but
many called it the "Jungle" because of all the
plants. Vines ran along dividers between the cloth
booths and the wooden tables in the middle of the
room were separated by small trees in pots and
large fernlike bushes. The carpet was a deep
brown, the walls oak and the ceiling low. The
lighting was spotlights, mostly aimed at the plants.
The place always felt warm, almost cozy, and it
was one of her favorite places on the base.

She studied the large group, wondering if there
was anyone there she knew. And that thought reminded her that besides Hank she had other
friends here on the base who would be mad at her
if she didn't say hello real soon. She'd already left
a message for Jerry, her and her husband's best

friend. She hadn't heard back from him yet, which wasn't like him. Maybe she would give him a quick call while waiting for Hank to get off duty and have him join her and Hank for dinner. She was sure Hank wouldn't mind. He could have her alone later in the evening all he wanted.

"Jonathan," she said, waving her drink at the tall, slim bartender who stood talking with three men in white lab coats near the end of the bar. He wore tight black slacks and an open-necked shirt and was without a doubt the best-looking bartender she had ever seen.

He smiled and motioned that he would be right there. She took a long, slow drink and almost before she had the glass back on the bar Jonathan had another in front of her.

"That was fast," she said.

He laughed softly, his voice deep and rich. "That's what they pay me for."

"Jonathan," she said, "have you seen Jerry around lately? I left him a message right after I arrived, but haven't heard from him yet. That's not like him at all."

The bright, happy look on Jonathan's face slipped into a frown and his gaze dropped to something under the bar near his feet. He half choked on something, then said, "Guess you didn't hear?"

"Hear what?" It felt like the bottom of her stomach had dropped out.

Jonathan hesitated, not looking at her. Then he glanced up and blurted, "Jerry was killed in an airlock accident two months ago."

Hank's words about people disappearing, people getting killed for no reason, filled her mind like an echo chamber.

But not Jerry. Jonathan had it wrong.

She glanced up at the sad look on Jonathan's face.

He reached out but didn't touch her. "I'm sorry, Joyce."

Her mind wouldn't let Jonathan's words in. That couldn't happen to Jerry. He'd never die in an airlock accident. Never. He was too damn good a spacer for that. She started to get angry and was about to yell at Jonathan for pulling such a nasty trick, when she looked into his eyes and saw it was the truth.

Jerry was dead.

The realization overwhelmed her and she fought to keep control. She felt dizzy and the room blurred.

She must have been staring at her drink, not moving, because the next thing she knew Jonathan had a hand on hers and was squeezing it.

"I thought you would have heard."

She shook her head slowly, fighting to keep the tears from her eyes. God damn it all to hell, not Jerry.

Jerry was always there. Always. For the kids' birthday parties, sometimes to just baby-sit for them.

"Just a second," Jonathan said. "I'll get you a napkin."

She remained motionless, the cold glass of Crystal gripped tightly in her hand, fighting back any sign of tears and remembering Jerry. Remembering his bright, smiling face, his quick sense of humor, his stupid dirty jokes that still made her laugh.

She remembered all the nights she, Danny, and Jerry had drunk and laughed together, most of them ending with Jerry passed out on the couch. She remembered all the missions they had been on together during the invasion. Jerry had been there for her when Danny was killed, had helped with his funeral, had hugged her and let her cry.

And she had tried to be there for him at the same time. Danny, after all, had been his best friend. Together they had mourned for Danny and Jerry had become almost a second father for the kids before he was shipped out here. He had been due back on Earth in two years to retire and just fish and work in his bike shop.

Now he'd never get the chance.

Jonathan came up from digging under the bar and quickly moved back in front of her. He slipped a wadded-up napkin into her free hand. "Here. Use this."

She nodded her thanks and dabbed her eyes with the napkin. As she did so she noticed there was something hard in the napkin. She was about to stop and unwrap it when Jonathan put his hand over hers.

She looked up into his dark, worried eyes. She could see concern in them for her, but also fear. Fear in his eyes and in the way he gripped her hand, forcing her to hold tightly whatever was inside.

"I'm really sorry about Jerry," he said. "He was a good guy. He didn't deserve to die."

She only nodded again, not trusting herself to say anything.

"As a bartender, I'm pretty good at giving advice," he said, holding her gaze solid in his. "You might want to go someplace private, like your *ship*, and really just let go. Cry all you want. Might do you some good."

As he said the word "ship" he squeezed her hand and the message was clear. Again Hank's words about the Professor being able to see anything came flowing back to her, cutting through the anger and the grief, making her think cold hard thoughts.

"Thanks," she said, her voice sounding odd to her. "That's a good idea. I think I will."

She fumbled around in her pockets for a moment with one hand, not sure what she was looking for. Finally it dawned on her and she said, "What do I owe you for the drinks?"

Jonathan let go of her hand and waved. "Don't worry about it. Just take care of yourself."

She caught the double meaning in that last sentence, too. "Thanks," she said. She slid off the bar stool and headed slowly for the door, wiping away the tears and anger. She was real good at taking care of herself. If somehow the Professor was responsible for Jerry's death, she would take care of that, too.

But first she would see what Jonathan had given her. She couldn't imagine what it might be. But whatever it was, one thing had come through her anger and grief very clearly. He had been risking a great deal doing so.

Could things on this station really be that bad?

Twenty minutes later while sitting in the pilot's chair of her ship, she suddenly realized just how bad things on Charon Base really were.

* * *

The Professor stood just inside the lab door admiring the bustle of activity going on in the huge white room. Twenty or so lab techs in white coats sat or stood at monitors or moved quickly and with reason from one place to another, doing their jobs. He had some of the best scientists in all humanity working with him, right here in this room.

The room itself was almost a pure white and always scrubbed perfectly clean, yet to him it felt warm and friendly. Of all the places on the station, this was the area he was proudest of. He could spend days and nights in here, without the problems of the station and the outside world—or corporation politics—bothering him. His duty in this room was to the greater good of humanity and he knew that without a doubt.

The door behind him slid silently open and Grace escorted his visitor in. Cray was wearing tan slacks and a tan dress shirt with the sleeves casually rolled up. The colors stood out in sharp contrast to the bright white lab coats of everyone else.

The Professor noted that Cray's gaze took in the room quickly yet carefully, in a left-to-right scan. The Professor had no doubt that if Cray was to turn around and leave immediately, he would still be able to tell someone exactly what the room looked like and probably identify most of the machines in use. He was rumored to be good enough to even give descriptions of the twenty white-coated techs. Too bad there wasn't a way to test that theory.

"Welcome, Mr. Cray," the Professor said while

nodding to Grace that she was excused. "I thought you might like a little tour of my world."

Cray smiled and nodded. "I'd enjoy it a great deal."

The Professor laughed softly. "Wonderful. Follow me."

He led the way across the large, high-ceilinged white room. Today the Professor noted a slight smell of alien blood mixed with the cleaning solution smell. Not unusual, considering the work they did here.

As they moved through the room the Professor nodded to different workers at computer consoles. There was never a time that the main stations in this room were left untended.

The Professor led Cray over to a glass wall and stopped.

"The main dissection tank," the Professor said, indicating the clear, liquid-filled tank, itself the size of a good room. Three human figures in what appeared to be deep-space gear were carefully working over the remains of a large alien floating in the center.

"How do they avoid the acid blood?" Cray asked, taking a step closer to the glass and intently watching the work.

"I adapted the gel that I understand you acquired for the company into an effective dissection medium. This has enabled me to extensively analyze and catalogue the alien's morphology."

"Ingenious," Cray said.

"I agree," the Professor said, and then laughed at his own half joke. "Although I discovered more about function and alien physiology than anyone ever has before, it was at the molecular level that

I made the most startling find. The one the corporation gave me a blank check to pursue."

"The DNA Reflex?"

The Professor nodded, not exactly happy that Cray had that level of knowledge before he arrived. Now he was starting to understand exactly why Cray was here.

To Cray, with a nod of approval, the Professor said, "You've done your research, I see. Yes, tests show that an adult alien exhibits certain physical characteristics inherited from its host. We call it the DNA Reflex."

"So to change future generations of aliens, you give them different hosts."

Kleist nodded, again impressed. "That's exactly what we're doing here. Let me show you."

The Professor led the way down the hall and into a second large white room, two sides of which were walled with glass tanks. Behind the thick glass floated what looked to be human bodies. The Professor noted that his guest stopped suddenly, almost in shock. Good. Cray hadn't known about this aspect of the work.

The hairless, white bodies seemed to hand upright, naked, suspended in a clear fluid, bubbles drifting around them to the surface. Hoses ran from the backs of their necks, their heart areas, and their groins into the wall below and in front of their feet. A control panel monitored each body's functions and a white-coated technician was in charge of the monitoring stations, moving from one to the next, slowly and systematically, never stopping.

Every one of the naked forms hanging in suspension had a face-hugger alien on his face.

"You like my dummies?" the Professor asked after a moment.

"Dummies?" Cray asked, not taking his eyes off the human forms floating beyond the two glass walls.

"Dummies," the Professor said, closely watching Cray's expression as he studied the bodies. "That's what I call them. I cloned body tissue designed to mimic living matter to trick the alien implantation process. Yes, the aliens have inspired many new commodities."

"Amazing," Cray said as he turned and looked at the Professor. "I had no idea cloning had gone so far."

"It is amazing, isn't it?" He gave Cray a large smile, then indicated a door to the right. "Let me show you something else."

He led Mr. Cray out of the lab and into an area labeled "RESTRICTED" in bright red letters. As they walked their footsteps echoed off the smooth concrete walls.

"Imagine, Mr. Cray," the Professor said, "what might be the results if these creatures, these killing machines, could be bioengineered to become man's tool instead of his adversary?"

"Consumer biologicals?"

"Exactly," Kleist said, stopping in front of an airlock. A huge warning sign over it read: ALIEN SECTOR. DO NOT ENTER.

As he fumbled in his pocket, he went on, "I have removed the alien's innate hostility by splicing their DNA with that of more passive, less predatory creatures. I got the best results with sheep, lamas, and even some cattle. Of course, there were a few setbacks. There always are."

"The old adage about omelets and breaking eggs?" Cray said.

"Exactly," the Professor said. "All progress has its price. A necessary attitude, I think you'll agree. Logic and truth leave little room for moral posturing."

"I suppose," Cray said. "So from the way you sound I can assume you have had some success?"

The Professor smiled, pleased. He pulled a small instrument from his pocket, then turned to the wall in front of the airlock and started keying a command sequence into the control panel. "I'll show you some of my progress. It is quite extraordinary, if I do say so myself."

He finished keying his commands into the door panel, then turned to face Cray. "However, I admit I have yet to produce the equivalent of a queen. Royal jelly alone doesn't prove to be enough."

The airlock slid open with a clang.

Hot, stinking air hit them both and the Professor took a deep breath, relishing the odor as if his mother were baking his favorite pie.

Cray, on the other hand, choked and seemed on the verge of throwing up. Most humans hated the smell of aliens, but the Professor loved it. That wonderful smell signified his work.

He was making history.

"We're going in there?" Cray said, looking into the dark, slime-covered corridor ahead, obviously not happy with the thought.

The Professor laughed softly. "It's good to respect your fears, but don't let them rule you. Any good soldier should know that. And that's what we are, isn't it? Soldiers in the war against the aliens?"

"I suppose you might call us that," Cray said as he took a shallow, shuddering breath and hesitantly followed the Professor into the dimly lit corridor.

"Stay close to me," Kleist said. "No matter what happens, make no sudden noises or movement."

"Don't worry," Cray said.

The Professor raised the small device he had fished out of the pocket of his lab coat. It looked like a toilet paper tube, only with a few buttons on top.

"Interesting device, this." He held it up for a moment, but Cray seemed more intent on watching the shadows and the slime-covered walls where aliens had formed stringy, slick shapes and dark round pockets.

"I stumbled on its potential quite by accident," the Professor went on. "It somehow disrupts the impulses of what passes for the alien central nervous system. I've devised a larger version for securing wild specimens for study called a Sound Cannon by the Marines. This small one works more like a dog whistle."

He pointed it down the hall and pulled the trigger. It seemed that nothing happened, but he could feel the device in his hand humming.

A slight rustling started in the dark shadows down the corridor, like a den of snakes being disturbed on a hot summer day.

"Down there," Cray said, his voice a loud, insistent whisper.

"Keep calm," the Professor said. "They're coming." He continued to hold the trigger down until the black shadows at the end of the hall separated and became clear alien forms. Then he clicked it off and put the tube in his pocket.

The overpowering stench grew stronger and Cray took a step back toward the open airlock.

The Professor moved forward.

"Come on," the Professor said, talking to the forms in front of him, forgetting Cray and the open door behind him. "Don't be scared. It's only me."

Cray had backed step by step to the open door and stood watching, his mouth open in shock.

Two small aliens separated from the shadows and moved toward the Professor.

"Come to Daddy," the Professor said.

Both aliens crawled on the floor in front of Kleist like slaves in front of a master until the Professor finally reached down and stroked the hard shells on the back of their heads.

"There my good children," the Professor said softly, over and over. "There my good children."

5

Grace, the Professor's android secretary, walked silently up to where the Professor sat in the large white lab, intently studying his latest experiment on the computer monitor. Shoulders hunched, his gaze intent on the image of the alien on the screen, he seemed to be oblivious to all the other work going on around him. Grace stood silently behind him, waiting for him to acknowledge her. Everyone knew not to disturb the Professor until he wanted to be disturbed. And he had the uncanny ability to know who was behind him at any given moment.

After a full two minutes he finally said, without looking up, "Only ten more hours, Grace. Did you know that?"

"Yes, sir, I did."

"Ten more hours until I finally succeed. Ten more lousy hours until the course of human history is changed forever."

"Yes, sir," Grace said. "Ten more hours."

The Professor sighed and pushed his chair back from the computer monitor. "Now why should I hope to get a reaction from an android, especially when it comes to helping humanity? I must be losing touch with reality." He shook his head, half laughing at himself. "What did you need to report, Grace?"

"You told me you wanted to know when the possible subject is on the move. He is on the move now."

"Wonderful timing," the Professor said, clapping his hands and standing quickly. "Inform Larson that I would like him to meet me in the lower storage area. We might as well give our guest a personal welcome, wouldn't you say?"

"If that is what you want," Grace said.

The Professor looked at Grace, then sighed. "Yes. That's what I want. Get Larson."

He walked away shaking his head.

Grace smiled at his back. She loved doing that to him.

It took over two thousand convicts fifty years to hack the thousands of kilometers of tunnels known as Charon Base out of the cold hard rock. Over two thousand men who dug their own graves as they went along. All but a very few of those convicts still remained in the tunnels and caverns,

their mummified remains filling the sleeping
bunks carved into the ice-cold stone walls.

Andy Carrier had learned that the bodies were
still there two months earlier over a poker game.
The guy who told him had claimed to have helped
in the original conversion of the base from a
prison camp to a research facility and had seen
dozens of convicts' bodies.

Two days later Andy had started searching,
mostly on his days off from the kitchens, explor-
ing the tunnels with a stolen oxygen mask. He
would sneak through an old air vent into the unoccupied sections of the station, the areas not
converted to the luxury needed by the Professor
and his workers, or the walled-off and sealed sections of the alien hive. Thousands of kilometers of
tunnels and caverns, carved out of solid rock simply for the purpose of keeping convicts busy and
shortening their lives in the process.

And Andy wanted to explore it all.

In the black, cold tunnels Andy Carrier looked
for the bodies of the dead.

Andy Carrier was a grave robber, a sideline that
could turn the strongest stomach, but Andy was a
practical man. Working the kitchen had given him
a healthy disregard for dead meat. Besides, he figured the convicts didn't need the rings and gold
teeth they took to their graves. They were dead.
He wasn't.

And his "hobby," as he liked to call it, had
turned out to be fairly simple and very, very prof-
itable. Most of the lower tunnels had been carved
in a clear pattern that made searching easy. Unlike the larger caverns in the upper areas, two levels below the human section the tunnels were in

mostly square patterns in the horizontal directions
with vertical shafts cutting up one side wall of
each tunnel intersection.

These intersections were usually no bigger than
a large living room, with four black doors—one
on each wall—and a large hole in both the floor
and ceiling near one wall. If you left an intersection and then kept turning left every time you
came to a new tunnel, you would find yourself
back where you started. The distance between the
tunnel intersections sometimes varied from as little as fifty meters to as much as two hundred meters.

The tunnels never seemed to be exactly
straight, but yet seemed to go in a fairly uniform
direction. And the tunnels varied from normally
wide enough for two people to walk side by side
on the flat floor without ducking to large caverns
with stone tables and bunks carved into the walls.

It was those larger caverns that Andy searched
for.

Today, the shift in the kitchen had been shorter
than usual, so he had a little more energy. Twenty
minutes after hanging up his apron he had the oxygen mask draped around his neck, was bundled
in his heaviest coat, and was working his way
down the stone ladder one level lower into the
caverns than he had ever been before. Seven levels down total. He had no idea how deep this
place went, but he'd have time to find out eventually. He had three more years on his shift before
heading back to Earth.

Down here it was colder than the higher levels
and he could see his breath. The air smelled dry
and stale, as if nothing had moved it in years.

Andy was used to that smell, and to the dusty, almost paperlike smell of the mummified corpses. But today, as he reached the seventh level, there was a new smell, faint yet distinct. The smell of antiseptic fought with the stale smell. It brought back memories of his mom taking him to the doctor when he was a kid back on Earth.

Andy flicked the beam of his light around on the floor, looking for any sign of disturbance. Nothing. It was clear that his boot prints were the only ones in the light dust. No one had been down here in longer than he wanted to think about.

He shook off the smell and memories of his childhood doctor and shone his light first down the dark tunnel to the right, then to the left. To the right, if he went far enough, he would approach the sealed-off sections of the alien hive. Andy, when given the choice, always went in the opposite direction, away from the alien hive. Robbing dead human bodies was one thing. Meeting an alien in a cold, dark tunnel was quite another.

Andy turned left and moved along, taking his time, not pushing himself too fast in order to conserve oxygen. Usually there was enough in the tunnels, but he had learned quickly the first time down here that taking an oxygen bottle along never hurt, especially on the long climb back up. And on the first trip down he'd learned about how cold it really was down here. Now he wore his thickest coat and gloves and the cold still got through.

Two corners and a short hike down a tunnel with an unusually low ceiling, he finally found a wide area with sleeping bunks carved into the stone wall on the left.

As the convicts had dug deeper and deeper into the rock, they carved new bunks closer to where they were working. As convicts fell ill, or died in accidents, or were shot by the guards, they were placed in the abandoned bunks and left to mummify in the extreme cold, dry air. This room had three bodies, one seemed fine, one had a missing arm, and a third had its head severed and placed on its chest. The head had a massive amount of damage to the bones where his nose and eyes used to be and the neck bones were crushed, not sawed or cut.

The day Andy found the first bodies he hadn't touched them and he hadn't slept a wink that night. But intrigued by a large gold ring on one of the bodies, after a week he had gone back, rationalizing that the convict sure didn't need that ring anymore. Now, after months of finding bodies, Andy had seen so many that this scene didn't even bother him.

He first checked the hands of all three bodies, finding only one silver wedding ring. Then he dug into the pockets and found only empty wallets and worn and faded family pictures. Then he checked the teeth, finding two silver caps in one and in the head that had been severed three gold fillings among the shattered teeth.

A fairly decent find. Whistling, he continued on down the tunnel, noticing now that the odor of antiseptic was getting stronger and stronger, even blocking out the intense cold. Chances are it was coming down a ventilation shaft from one of the Professor's labs.

Ahead, the tunnel turned sharply to the right, then back to the left, and Andy found himself facing an open heavy metal door, much newer than the original tunnel construction. Beyond the door the tunnel turned again sharply to the left and Andy could see a faint light.

"What the hell?" he said to himself, snapping off his own light. Slowly he moved through the door and onto the now smooth concrete floor of the tunnel. The floor in this area had been swept clean of dust and he was leaving gray footprints.

The smell of antiseptic now completely filled the air. Carefully, Andy stuck his head around the corner and looked into the bright lights of what appeared to be a lab of some sort just beyond another open airlock-style door. He could see white-tiled floors, shelves, and some lab equipment on a far wall, but not much else.

He waited a few breaths but no one moved, and no sound came from the lab, so he crept silently forward.

He'd heard a lot of strange rumors about the Professor and what went on behind the closed doors of this station, but he had made it a point not to pay attention. He figured it just wasn't his business.

But something open like this down here seemed just plain wrong, and he moved forward until he could see the contents on the shelves ahead of him.

Now, in robbing graves, he had seen a lot of human bodies, but it still took him a moment to register what he was seeing.

Shelf after shelf of human heads, all with wires and tubes leading from them into instrument panels, filled the room. The skin on most of the parts was a deep blue or black, and some had large patches of flaking. But yet they seemed full of fluid and somehow alive.

Andy moved slowly forward until he stood between five shelves of human heads on the right and three shelves of human heads on the left.

He stopped in front of one head with brown hair and looked at it closely. The hair was long and matted and the skin tone on this one seemed to be a pasty white. What looked to be an oxygen mask covered the nose and mouth and wires ran from about twenty different places on the side and forehead. The head was secured by a rubber ring around the neck that seemed to surge every few seconds. Obviously a liquid of some sort was being circulated through the head and brains.

"What the hell . . . ?" he said out loud.

His hand shaking, Andy slowly reached out and pulled the head up slightly by the hair.

The eyes opened.

Blue eyes.

The blue eyes of his old poker-playing buddy Charlie. Charlie, who had supposedly left for Earth unexpectedly, six months earlier.

Andy screamed and jumped backward square into the waiting arms of Larson. The man's grip on his shoulders felt like steel clamps and he fought in panicked kicks and twists to get free, to run away from those heads and those chilling blue eyes.

With one quick arm twist Larson took Andy to his knees in sharp pain.

Andy quit struggling. He just kept staring at the now sad blue eyes of his old friend, as if the head could understand what was happening, could recognize him, was somehow still thinking.

"Well," the Professor said, moving forward out of the shadows of the shelf of heads, most of whose eyes were now open and watching.

Green eyes. Blue eyes. Brown eyes. They all watched.

"It seems we have another volunteer for our program," the Professor said.

"Seems that way to me," Larson said, yanking Andy's hair back and making him look up at the Professor.

"What—what are you doing here?"

Kleist glanced around and then laughed. "I need these alive to keep the bodies in my labs alive. For some reason I can't fool the face-huggers without having the real head still hooked up." He gave Andy a good looking over. "He seems to be in good physical condition. Get him ready. His body just may be the one to carry our new queen. Now wouldn't that be a privilege, Andy?"

Andy screamed like a wildman and struggled to free himself, to force his way to his feet.

To run to the safety of the dark, cold tunnels and the dead convicts.

But he was no match for the cold, brute strength of Larson. With a quick blow to the back of the neck, Larson sent Andy into blackness.

Most of the heads on the shelves closed their eyes as if they had witnessed this sad sight before and didn't want to watch it again.

As indeed, many of them had.

The next time Andy opened his eyes, he looked down from the second shelf, the closest position to the door into the tunnels on the left.

He could still feel his body alive, somewhere

else. He could feel his heart pumping blood, his
arms floating, and something growing inside him.

The blackness of space and the faint light of a
thousand stars filled the bubble ceiling of the observation lounge. The room had been designed
and built by the Professor, stuck five hundred meters down a long stairway out on a rock outcropping so that it could be above the base. It had cost
a great deal extra, but the Professor and the designers from the corporation thought it worth the
cost.

From almost every square foot of the lounge
the view of the rocky surface of Charon Base and
the stars was spectacular. The emptiness of the
rough surface of asteroid bathed in the faint light
from the sun and the even fainter light from the
sky full of stars.

But the lounge was very seldom used after the
first few months. It seemed that no one wanted a
reminder that they were living like rats in tunnels
under hundreds of meters of rock. And they didn't
want to think about how far they were from Earth
and the black sky full of stars reminded them of
that. Many felt that if they didn't think about it, it
didn't bother them.

Going to the observation lounge made them
think about it, made them realize they were
trapped.

So after six months of very little use Kleist
closed the bar that had filled one corner and just
left the lounge open to the few stragglers or the
occasional lovebirds. At one point the place had
been filled with plants, but even those were gone,

moved out or allowed to die off. Now only the
empty containers remained, making the furniture
and booths seem naked under the faint light. The
overall feel was of a deserted living room or a forgotten old house.

Cray was the only occupant of the lounge as
Joyce walked in and glanced around. She had
guessed she would find him here. He seemed like
the type to love the openness of the stars and she
felt glad about being right. It pushed her forward
with her plan.

He stood against the rail in front of the main
window, staring off into the blackness.

"Is this a private moment of moody introspec-
tion," Joyce said as she moved up beside him, "or
can anyone join?"

"By all means," Cray said. "Be my guest. Intro-
spect all you want."

She smiled and glanced around at the empty
room. "Seems we're the only ones who enjoy the
view."

"That it does," Cray said without turning from
the window. "Sort of reminds me of the old lover's
leaps back home. See how the rocks slope off
there." He pointed to where the edge of the cliff
rounded off and disappeared into blackness below. "You have a place like that where you grew
up?"

The memories of her and Danny parked in his
old Ford at the top of Thunder Mountain flashed
back through her mind. It would always take them
an hour to get up there, but it was worth it. They
used to sit in the dark, holding hands and staring
at the stars. They used to talk night after night
about how they would go into space when they

got out of school, live in space, bring up a family among the stars.

On Thunder Mountain, on a blanket under the stars, she had lost her virginity.

She turned to Cray. "I sure did. How about you?"

He laughed. "Of course. And call me John."

"I'm Joyce."

He nodded, then turned back to face the stars. "We called our little hideaway Roman Way. It was a wide spot on the top of a small hill just outside of town. The hill looked out over the Kansas farmlands and was damn near the highest place in twenty miles."

"Roman Way? Like in roaming hands?"

Cray laughed and glanced at her. "Cute, but no. Actually a farmer named Barry Roman owned the land."

Joyce grinned. "Ours was called Thunder Mountain, named after a bad storm, I think."

He laughed softly and they both went back to watching the stars. After a moment Cray stirred and turned to her. "Tell me," he said. "What brings you out this far from the main Earth systems? Isn't that where most pilots ply their trade?"

Joyce reached into her back pocket and pulled out a small folding wallet. With a gentle flip she opened it and held it up in the faint light for Cray to see. "These are my reasons. Drake and Cass."

Cray studied the picture of her two kids, both dark-skinned like their mother. She watched him gaze at the picture, wishing she knew what he was thinking. Finally he said, "Good-looking kids."

"You got that right," she said. "At least as far as

I'm concerned. Of course, I'm their mother so I would think that."

Cray smiled. "Justified, in this case."

Joyce flipped the wallet closed and went back to looking at the stars. After a moment she decided to go on and tell him more, trust him a little more. "Their father was killed during the war and we barely made it. The kids live in Geneva now with my mother. I get fifty times the pay out here than I do in the central systems. That's why I took this haul one last time. After I'm back I can spend a few years with my kids. I sure do miss them."

"Sorry," Cray said softly. "I didn't mean to pry."

"No problem. It's just the way things are. You learn to live with it."

Joyce glanced around quickly, studying the ceiling and the walls around them. She needed his help, but she wasn't sure if she could trust him. Damn, this had been a dumb idea.

"Something wrong?" Cray asked after a moment.

"You seem like a straightforward-type guy."

"Thanks. I guess," he said, looking intently at her.

She took a deep breath. "You know, there are just some things in this world I don't think I *can* live with?"

Cray nodded, waiting.

Joyce flipped open her wallet again and pulled a slip of paper out from behind the picture of her children. She pulled it out just far enough for Cray to see. On it she had written, "Don't say anything. Please meet me on my ship in one hour."

Out loud she said, "This is a picture of my husband. Bugs killed him in the last days of the war.

For some reason I have problems living with that, and being this close to an entire hive of the things."

She slid the paper back behind the picture and put the wallet away.

"I can understand that," Cray said. "Some things really are hard to live with."

"Yeah," she said. "I'll be damn glad when I get headed for home."

They both turned to face the cold, black night and the thousand points of light so far away.

Joyce tried to keep her hands from shaking. She had just put her life into the hands of a total stranger. She didn't know why, but when it came right down to it she felt she could trust him. Besides, she had no one else to turn to and she needed his help.

Above her, just past her left shoulder, was Earth and her two children.

She kept her gaze away from that area of the black sky.

T-shirted Sergeant Green stormed through the main lab, his fists clenched in tight balls, his gray-eyed gaze focused intently ahead. His thick muscles rippled with power under the shirt and men and women in white coats scrambled out of his way like they would jump away from the path of a moving train. His movements just dared anyone to try to stop him, and no one did.

No one was stupid enough to even try.

He reached the Professor's outer private office on the far side of the lab and yanked the door open, almost pulling it off the hinges in the process.

Behind a large oak desk across what seemed like ten meters of thick white carpet sat Grace, the Professor's secretary. She glanced up as he wrenched the door open. She wore a tight maroon skirt and a white blouse open one button too far showing a little too much very real-looking skin.

The same basic thing she wore every day.

"Can I help you, Sergeant?" she said calmly, standing and moving into his path as he stormed toward her desk and started around it toward the Professor's inner office.

"I want to see Kleist right now!" He didn't even slow and started to brush right past her.

With what seemed to be a slight push, with very little force behind it, she knocked him into the oak wall sending an oil painting tumbling behind a couch.

The sergeant bounced off the wall, twisted off the couch, and instantly went into combat posture, crouched and facing her.

She stood upright, looking almost bored as she studied one of her nails. "I'm afraid he's in a meeting. He left strict instructions that he was not to be disturbed."

"Outta my way, bitch, or I swear I'll—"

"He was most insistent," she said, smiling at the sergeant. "Why don't I just make you an appointment and you can come back. I'm sure he has some time open tomorrow."

The sergeant's face turned bright red and he growled low in his throat. "I'll show you and that ass of a boss an *appointment*."

He again started for the door that led into the private back office.

Grace stepped lightly to the left and directly into his path, stopping him cold with one hand to his chest.

The sergeant raised his left hand to shove her aside, but she merely added, "Now, Sergeant, you wouldn't strike a woman, would you?"

"Yes," the sergeant said, but he had hesitated just long enough for Grace to get a firm hold on his forearm with her right hand and his T-shirt with her left. With a quick twisting motion she turned and flipped him over her shoulder and away from the Professor's door, into the middle of the huge white carpet.

"That's good, because I'm no woman," she said, laughing.

He landed square on his back with a loud thud and the sound of air forced from his chest. He twisted sideways and scrambled to his feet. Without a moment's hesitation he charged back at her like a bull at a red cape.

She hiked her skirt up slightly with one hand and caught him square across the side of the face with a high side kick.

This time the sergeant tumbled head over heels along the empty top of her desk and came up rolling, his hands on the desk chair Grace had been using.

"Really, Sergeant. Why can't you just make an appointment like everyone else? It would be so much simpler."

He again growled like an angry wolf. With a quick motion to the right, he faked her into a defensive stance, then hit her from the left with the chair. She staggered sideways, but didn't fall. Her fake skin wasn't even slightly cut where the chair had sliced across her face.

She ducked to the left to avoid his right hook, then kicked him again squarely in the face, her high heel digging a long, wide gash in his cheek.

The sergeant tumbled back onto the carpet and before he had time to move Grace kicked him twice more, once in the ribs, once more in the face.

He rolled hard over to get away from her, but she was inhumanly fast and was on him again with two more kicks to the head. "That'll teach you to stain the carpet." She kicked him again. "And that's for not making an appointment like a good little boy."

Through the haze of almost blackness he heard the Professor say, "That's enough, Grace. I'm sure the sergeant has learned his lesson."

Grace grabbed Green by the back of his shirt and like picking up a young child hauled him to his feet, turning him to face the Professor.

Kleist stepped closer and smiled. "I think I know what he's upset about."

The sergeant spit a mouthful of blood on the white carpet at the Professor's feet and then looked him directly in the eye. "You murdered one of my men, you bastard."

"As you witnessed, Sergeant, Private Choi deliberately destroyed an expensive specimen."

Green couldn't believe what he was hearing. "You killed him for that?"

"See my side of this, Sergeant," the Professor said. "Choi could easily have subdued the alien with a Taser, and yet chose not to. I call that a conscious act of sabotage."

"What? I should take you apart one ugly limb at a time."

Grace's grip on the back of the sergeant's shirt tightened and she lifted him slightly off the floor, holding one arm in a tight and very painful grip behind his back.

The Professor nodded to her that it was all right and she let him back down so his feet at least touched the floor. But she didn't ease the painful grip and he did his best to focus on the Professor and ignore the pain.

"As director of this facility, I felt obliged to authorize the maximum penalty."

"Choi was right," Green said, spitting another glob of blood on the white carpet. "You are insane."

The Professor laughed. "This is a scientific research establishment, not a military outpost. You're under my jurisdiction and will follow my orders."

The sergeant tried to make an unexpected lunge at the Professor but Grace held him firm, one hand on the back of his shirt, the other on his left arm in a lock grip.

The Professor only shook his head, then turned his back on the sergeant for a moment, seeming to think. When he turned back around he was frowning. "I'm tired of your men's insubordination and locker-room mentality. As of now Mr. Larson will relieve you of all duties. Grace will arrange for your and your men's immediate return to Earth. You and your grunts are an irritation I'm no longer prepared to endure."

The sergeant relaxed slightly in Grace's grip, not totally accepting what Kleist had said. He had come here expecting to die trying to kill the Professor, but somehow it had turned into freedom for him and his remaining men. That made no sense.

The Professor nodded to Grace. "Now, if you'll excuse me, I have business to attend to."

As Kleist's door closed with a soft click, Grace turned and shoved the sergeant forward through the office door into the lab. He stumbled forward, then fell, blood flowing down his face and the front of his shirt. He lay sprawled on the hard white tile of the main lab, staring up at Grace's unruffled short skirt, red hair, and slightly open white blouse.

"Get your men packing. I'll have a transport ready in two hours."

The sergeant struggled to his feet and stood weaving slightly, as if there were a slight breeze blowing him around. His mind was having trouble accepting what had just happened. Finally he nodded and turned to leave as everyone in the main lab silently watched.

"Oh, and, Sergeant," Grace said as she moved back into the office and to the desk.

He stopped and looked back at her. She picked up the desk chair and bent the metal leg back into shape with one hand before placing it on the carpet.

Then she looked up and smiled. "Next time make an appointment."

6

Captain Joyce Palmer stood behind the pilot's chair of her ship *Caliban* and let her hands glide over its cloth back. The familiar feel somehow gave her comfort and slowed her breathing. She loved the slightly stale smell of the ship's air mixed with the light odor of oil from the control area. She felt in control when she was in here.

She glanced around, automatically checking the different boards, looking for warning lights like she had done a hundred times in space. Now, here in the hangar, most of the lights were showing systems off or on standby. Nothing looked out of the ordinary at all and that settled her jumping nerves a little more. She always felt better when the machinery worked.

Would Danny have been mad at her for talking to Cray? Would Jerry? Would they both have said that she should keep to her own business and just leave this place. She knew that was exactly what they both would have said, yet she just couldn't let Jerry's death go. And she knew if Danny were still alive, he wouldn't let it go either.

She moved around and sat in her chair, letting her hands glide over the silent control panel, letting the feel of the familiar cushions hold her. She wouldn't be able to live with herself if she didn't try to stop this madman. There was a plague running wild on this station and it was killing people. It had killed one of her oldest friends. It was a virus of terror and sudden death, one man's madness killing hundreds.

Maybe she could stop it, or maybe she would die trying. Either way, she couldn't go on living without doing something.

Behind her she heard the sound of someone entering, walking up the long ramp from the deck. She tensed and waited, half expecting the Professor or Larson and some of his goons, but after a moment Cray stuck his head in. She let out a silent breath and motioned for him to come forward and take the chair beside her.

"I'm not sure this is wise," he said as he slid into Deegan's usual seat.

"Neither am I," she said. "There's a problem here and it has become very personal for me. You're about my only choice to turn to for help."

Cray shrugged.

Here goes, Joyce said to herself. No turning

back now. She reached under her seat and pulled out a miniature video disk. She held it up for Cray to see. "This was slipped to me yesterday."

Again Cray said nothing, so Joyce went on. "Professor Kleist is Z.C.T. Corporation's golden boy, right? Intense, but he gets results."

She slipped the disk into a small slot in her control panel and pointed to the large monitor. "This is how he does it. I hope you have a strong stomach."

The monitor flickered slightly before the picture focused on the tanks that filled the walls in the Professor's lab. Row after row of bodies floated in liquid, tubes running into panels in front of each. White-coated technicians worked in front of the wall at control panels and computer monitors. It was obvious from how the picture was being taken that it was from a hidden camera, most likely tucked into the pocket of a lab coat with only the lens peeking out.

Joyce noticed that Cray wasn't that startled by what he saw, but he did push himself back away from the monitor deeper into his chair.

The picture focused on one body, zooming in until only the head and chest area were visible. The skull was hairless and the face totally covered by a face-hugger, or what looked to be one. The chest of the body seemed to be moving, pulsing like it had a heart ten times too big that was pounding out of control.

Cray watched the screen while Joyce watched him.

The movement inside the chest went on for only a few more seconds, then suddenly the skin ripped in a quick spider pattern, like a rock hitting a large glass window. A small alien exploded from the chest in a spurt of black blood and frantic squirming, swimming off into the liquid and disappearing along the bottom of the tank.

The force of the eruption sent the body twisting in the tank, yanked back and forth by the lifelines connecting it to the machines.

Then the monitor flickered and went blank.

Cray took a deep breath, then slowly turned to Joyce. "All right, what's the problem? An experimental alien birth from a cloned body. Not pleasant to watch, but not a crime that I know of."

Joyce snorted. So that was the Professor's line. Cloned bodies? No wonder so many people were letting him get away with this. Most of them just didn't know, or didn't have enough courage to question his explanation.

She reached forward and punched a few keys on her board, and the monitor lit up again at the start of the disk. She jumped it quickly to the point where the alien was ripping a hole in the chest of its host, then froze the picture.

"See that?" She pointed to a small mark on one arm of the body, the arm that had been turned away from the glass wall and the room and only twisted into camera view because of the force of the alien birth.

Cray leaned forward. "What is it?"

"Just a second and I'll show you."

Joyce's fingers flew over the keys in front of her, and the still picture on the monitor zoomed in closer and closer on the mark until it became clear exactly what it was.

"A tattoo?" Cray said, leaning forward and

studying the mark. "A tattoo of a black raven? On a clone? That would make no sense at all."

"That's because that body isn't a clone. I doubt if any of them in that tank are." Joyce pulled a cigarette out of her vest pocket and lit it, half surprised that her hands weren't shaking much more than they were. "The Professor has come up with some pretty amazing stuff, but I doubt this level of human cloning is one of them."

She lit her cigarette and let the smoke soothe her as Cray stared at the monitor. Finally she said, "The person you see there was named Jerry. My husband Danny and I were with him when he got that tattoo done in Melbourne twelve years ago."

Joyce pushed the sleeve of her vest up until it rode over her shoulder and then turned for Cray to see the small black raven there. "We were such close friends we thought it would be great to have the same tattoo. The Black Raven was the name of a bar we used to meet at while in college."

Cray glanced at her tattoo, then back at the screen. Then he seemed to sink into the copilot's chair like a heavy weight was pushing him down.

Joyce rolled down her sleeve and took a long pull on her cigarette. "Jerry supposedly died last month. Faulty airlock is what they said. Explosive decompression is what the official report and what his death certificate says. I know. I checked."

She pointed at the monitor with the frozen close-up of Jerry's black raven. "They should've had to scrape him off the walls of that airlock but, surprise, there he is. Or at least what's left of him."

Joyce dropped back into her pilot's chair and

tapped the control panel. The picture on the monitor disappeared and in another moment the miniature video disk popped out. She took it, glanced at Cray, and then returned the disk to the hiding place under her seat.

Then she swung around to face him. "Well, there's not much doubt the Professor has lost it. The question is what are you going to do about it. No, what are *we* going to do about it?"

Cray shook his head without turning to face Joyce. "You don't know what you're asking."

"I know this," Joyce said. "Kleist's a psycho who's killing people for his own gain. He's got to be stopped. You have to let Z.C.T. know what's going on out here. Someone back there must have an ounce of sanity left."

Cray shook his head slowly from side to side. "It's not that easy."

Joyce grabbed the arm of Cray's chair and swung it around until he was facing her. She leaned forward and grabbed him by the shirt collar, pulling him toward her sharply. "I want to live to see my kids again, you chicken-shit piece of a man. I'm risking everything even talking to you."

"I know," Cray said softly. "I understand better than you would imagine. But there's much more that you should know, especially about me."

She let go of his collar and he dropped back into the chair. She took a long pull off her cigarette. "I'm listening."

Cray took a deep breath and sat up. "You trusted me, I suppose I now need to trust you."

Outside the ship the sound of footsteps running up the gangway echoed through the control room. "What the hell?" Joyce shouted and sprang to her feet to meet three of the Professor's men all carrying Kramers, fully cocked and set on automatic.

"Nobody move!" Larson shouted. He was the fourth man through the door. "Keep your mouths shut and your hands where I can see them."

The three guards swarmed around Joyce and Cray.

Joyce turned to Cray. "You bastard! I should have known."

"You deaf, bitch?" one of the guards said, and hit Joyce across the side of the head with the butt of his rifle. The pain took her legs out from under her and she rolled back against her pilot's chair. Through pain-watered eyes she saw Cray move.

Almost without effort he grabbed the guard who had hit her by the neck and twisted. The sound of the guard's neck snapping filled the small control room like a gunshot.

A second guard fired a blast from the rifle, but Cray had twisted the body of the now-dead guard in his arms around to take the force of the blow. Blood splattered against the wall as a few stray rounds ricocheted inside the ship.

Now the smell of charred flesh choked the air as Joyce fought to clear her head.

Almost effortlessly, Cray tossed the dead body at one guard while taking the other down with a quick kick to the head. With what seemed like a lightning-fast movement to Joyce's slowed-down senses, he was on his knees scooping up the dead guard's rifle when Larson said, "Go ahead. Pick it up."

Cray froze, the gun just barely touching his fingers, as Larson smiled at him. Larson held a forty-five pistol pointing directly at Cray's head.

The remaining two live guards quickly regained their feet and yanked Cray into a standing position, quickly binding his arms behind his back.

Joyce fought to get to her feet, to help Cray, but as she did one guard kicked her solidly in the side of the head and the pain took her into blackness. Her last thought was a simple one.

She had been right about Cray after all. Too bad she wasn't going to get a chance to tell him.

Hank ambled into the main lounge, doing his best to look calm and unhurried as he wound his way through the plants and tables to the bar. Actually, he was in more of a panic than he had been in in years. Joyce had stood him up for dinner last night and hadn't returned to her room at all. This morning, while looking for her, he had discovered from Jonathan that she had a copy of the video of Jerry's body in the tank. He was hoping he would have been the one to tell her about Jerry's death, but now he couldn't even find her. And as the day wore on he became more and more worried.

He ambled up to the bar and dropped onto a stool. "Vodka tonic?" Jonathan asked as he slipped a napkin in front of Hank. "Looks like you need it."

Hank nodded and Jonathan moved back to the well. The words "looks like you need it" were a code and meant that Jonathan had news he would be passing with the drink. Hank kept himself relaxed and looked wearily at the other people scattered around the lounge until Jonathan returned with the drink.

The underground movement against the Professor had discovered that the bar was a fairly safe place to pass notes and because of all the constant cleaning the staff did, they had every hidden camera and microphone spotted. They knew the exact dead spots in the room.

Jonathan sat the drink down on the napkin and Hank immediately picked it up, feeling the piece of paper attached to the wet outside of the glass.

He swung the stool around so that his back was turned at about a forty-five-degree angle from the bar and toward the main entrance. Then he pretended to drink, reading the note through the clear liquid and the glass.

"Professor has Joyce and Cray. Both still alive. Meeting at seven at #8 to plan."

Hank's stomach twisted and he glanced at the small note one last time before swinging back more directly to face the bar, keeping the note covered with his hand. His worst fears had been confirmed. Joyce was in the Professor's hands, and if they didn't do something quickly her body would soon be floating in that tank. Or worse, she would be put out in the alien section to serve as breeding stock for the Professor's pets.

He glanced at where Jonathan stood, casually cleaning the bar. He didn't look very happy either. He was probably feeling responsible for her capture and he would be there tonight also. Maybe it was finally time to move against the Professor and his men. Maybe they had waited long enough.

Hank downed the last of the drink and placed the glass on the bar, but he didn't let go of it. Jonathan saw the movement and moved unhurriedly back to him. "Need another?"

"Nope, thanks. One's enough. I've got a long night ahead of me."

Jonathan nodded and picked up the glass with the note still stuck to it a fraction of a second after Hank had released it. "I hear you there," he said. In a few seconds the note, along with the ice and lime in the drink, would be ground up in the garbage disposal.

"See ya," Hank said and slipped off the stool.

From the exchange Hank knew that Jonathan was thinking the same thing he was. Maybe it was time they finally quit sulking around and started moving. Maybe if they were all lucky the Professor and Larson would both be dead before the night was out. And Joyce would be back in his arms.

That would make it a great night.

But that assumed that Joyce would live. The Professor's victims didn't have a habit of living very long at all.

He forced that thought out of his mind and went in search of his Marine contact, a young private named Choi.

At that moment Hank had no idea just how late he really was.

Sergeant Green glanced down at his men as they buckled into their flight harnesses in the "cattle" compartment of the transport. It was a bullet-shaped room with two benches on either side. Vertical bar handles were attached to the walls between the seats, and seat belts and shoulder harnesses hung off the walls. Green glanced down the line at his men, all joking and happy.

Still, what seemed like an enormous number of empty seats near the tail haunted Green. Nineteen men were going home out of his original forty. Those were huge, unacceptable losses, especially on an assignment as stupid as this one. There would be an investigation when they reached Earth of the Professor and his little operation. Sergeant Green would make sure of that.

"Man, can you believe this?" Private Young said from down the row. "We're actually going to see the back end of this damn place."

"Yeah, imagine that," Private Richerson said. "What's the plan, Sarge?"

Green took a deep breath and tried to shake the feeling that something was wrong. They were going home. What could be wrong with that? "We're to rendezvous with the battle cruiser *Saundakaur*, then deep-freeze it from there."

Young shivered. "I hate those ice boxes."

"Price you pay," Richerson said, "for working out in the butt end of the universe."

Grace's voice echoed over the intercom system. "Buckle in tight, boys. We're on our way."

Green glanced up at the speaker, startled that she was on board. He'd love another shot at her, only this time on his terms and under his conditions. Then he'd see how well that pile of bolts and tubes in a skirt would do. Maybe before this trip was over he'd get that chance.

"Wow, the voice of God," Richerson said.

"More like his secretary," Green muttered as the roar of the engines started and the acceleration pushed them all into their harnesses.

But instead of the steady, six-minute burn needed to clear Charon's gravity well, the engines

quickly throttled back and Green could feel the
ship banking in a hard, tight turn.

"Whoa!" Young said and others cursed the
change.

"What gives, Sarge?" someone shouted.

"Damned if I know," Green said, "but I got a
bad feeling about this." He cussed himself for being so stupid. No way was the Professor going to
let them go. He couldn't afford to let him—or anyone else for that matter—make it back to Earth
alive. He was going to crash the ship back into the
planet and call them dead by accident. Case
closed.

Sergeant Green unsnapped his harness,
grabbed his pistol, and started toward the front,
shouting orders to the man at the very head of the
line. "Lynch, get that door to the cockpit open.
The rest of you stay belted in and brace yourselves. This might get bumpy."

Lynch had his harness undone and was at the
door as Green joined him. "It's locked!" he
shouted over the roar of the thrusters.

"Override it!" Green shouted back and together
they fought to open the door.

What seemed like hours went by, but Green
knew it was only seconds as Lynch worked ex-
pertly on the lock, his fingers flying over and
around it. Finally, with a hard yank, he shoved the
door open and Green was through into the cockpit of the shuttle with his gun cocked and ready.

Two empty pilot seats greeted him.

"Shit! We're on remote." Green stood braced
against the back of the pilot's seat, watching as
the shuttle turned and braked into an old shuttle
docking area. From the look of the instruments

and where they were headed, it seemed Kleist didn't plan on killing them by crashing the shuttle. That way he could save the ship and maybe reuse it down the road. But if not a crash, what the hell was he doing?

Sergeant Green scanned the docking area ahead looking for any sign of life. But there was nothing. The place looked as if it had been unused for years.

"Sir," Lynch said from where he was braced on the other side of the cockpit. "Isn't that the . . ."

"Shit!" Green said, the sudden realization of where they were heading hitting him. He turned to his men. "Get suited up, full armor. Fast. That son of a bitch is dropping us right into the middle of the alien sector."

Eighteen harnesses unsnapped simultaneously and nineteen men and their sergeant went quickly to work, struggling against the forces of the landing shuttle to don full battle armor and get weapons out of storage in the crowded "cattle" area of the small transport.

By the time the landing thrusters finally cut off thirty seconds later and the shuttle moved automatically toward the airlock door, Sergeant Green and his men were ready.

Green looked back at his men and made a decision. They were now in a war. It was them against the Professor, with an alien hive in the middle. He had underestimated the Professor before. He wouldn't do it again. It was now his job to take the son of a bitch down. And take him down hard.

"Check your ammunition!" Green shouted as everyone shouldered arms.

"Shit!" Lynch said from beside him. A few other

curses came from down the line. "Blanks, sir. Everything's been switched. Nothing but blanks. We're screwed."

"Hold it down!" Green shouted, and his men immediately quieted. Outside the airlock clanked into place and the opening and sealing process began. That side door was going to open and stay open into the alien sector in just a few seconds. If they were lucky none of the bugs would be waiting outside. But it wouldn't take them long to arrive.

"Unload the useless stuff from the guns and shoulder your weapons. Keep your ammunition belts on and full of the blanks. I want a tight formation following me the moment that door cracks open. Stragglers get left behind. Understood?"

Everyone nodded and the useless ammunition clattered on the deck of the shuttle like a hailstorm on a tin roof.

"Full armor. Helmets down and locked, but no talking on the intercom system. Hand signals only, no exceptions. Understood?"

Again as a unit everyone nodded and helmets clicked into place and were locked. He didn't have time to explain to them that the Professor was probably watching them at this very moment and that he probably had their helmet intercoms wired. If he could get to all their ammunition, he could easily do that, too. But Green doubted if Kleist had cameras and speakers on all areas of the alien sector. That was a fact Green was going to count on to save his men's lives.

"Get ready," Green said as he moved to the closest spot near the airlock and stood waiting for whatever would be on the other side. "And keep the noise down. We go silent."

Nineteen men crowded in behind him, moving almost as a unit.

The airlock door slid open.

The smell of rotten eggs hit first, followed by a blast of hot, humid air.

Nothing moved in the slime-filled shadows.

Green took a quick look to the left, then ducked out of the ship and in a crouch moved silently but quickly down the corridor to the right away from the ship and the docking area.

Like a silent snake, his men followed in close formation.

Followed him unarmed into the heart of an alien hive.

There was silence in Professor Kleist's office as the last of Green's men disappeared off the only monitor near that entrance to the alien sector. Finally the Professor swung around in his chair and addressed Larson, who stood behind him.

"Any chance we can see what they're doing in there?"

Larson shook his head. "Not until they get near this side of the alien sector, and they'll never make it that far."

"Don't be so sure," the Professor said.

Larson smiled and reached over Kleist's desk and punched up the center screen. On it was a map of the alien sector. Twenty points of light grouped tightly together near the farthest entrance moved slowly down one passageway. "I did manage to put tracers in their com links. We'll see right where each of them dies."

"Good," the Professor said, his head nodding, his hands steepled in front of him. "Nice work? Now if you could just guarantee that none of them make it back here."

Larson nervously glanced at the monitor and then back at the Professor. "I think I can, sir. They're unarmed, twenty klicks deep in an alien hive. No one, not even the Marines, could live through that."

Kleist nodded. "I tend to agree with you, but just to be sure, let's post double guards on all airlocks between the human and alien sectors. If one or two of them do manage to sneak through, I want them turned back."

He laughed. "Besides, we couldn't let the queen be deprived of such good breeding material, now could we?"

7

The nightmare continued.

The blackness of the moonless night covered the old green Ford like a smothering blanket that nothing could crawl out from under. John Cray had been given the used car by his father for a wedding present just six months earlier. He'd had it repainted and some much-needed body work done first. But now, as the starter ground on and on, he wished he'd worked on the engine first. A stalled motor, probably nothing more than a loose switch or wire, had them four short kilometers from the spaceport, sitting in the most dangerous of dark nights.

Four impossible miles with the aliens swarming closer to this area every hour.

"Damn it!" He pounded on the wheel. "Start, damn you." He fought the ignition one more time, but it was clear from the grinding sound that there would be no more distance from this car tonight, or maybe ever. He knew that much about cars.

And about aliens.

"John," Linda said softly and touched his arm.

Her soft touch calmed him somewhat and he stopped. Angrily he twisted the key to off and turned to face his beautiful bride in the faint light from the dashboard.

He could see the worry on her face. Her long blond hair was pulled back tight making her face like a small, white moon in the faint light. Her clean soap smell filled the car like a fine perfume. All he wanted to do was hold her, curl up in a warm bed, tell her they would be fine.

But they wouldn't be fine until somehow they reached the spaceport and joined the evacuation off Earth. In this area of the planet that was their only hope and they both knew it.

He reached out and patted the soft skin of her leg, doing his best to fight down his panic and reassure her, as well as himself. "If we stay here and keep quiet we should be all right until someone comes along."

She nodded. She had trusted him since the first night they had met at the Christmas party. She worked as an account executive for the Grant Corporation, the same corporation he did troubleshooting work for on computers. The same company he spied for after this night.

"If there's no traffic tonight, we'll walk at first light. We should be able to make it to the port in

a few hours. The corporation will have enough
ships to get us to Earth orbit."

She was about to say something when, as he
watched in shocked terror, an alien appeared out
of the dark shadows directly behind her.

It was a huge creature with a black bony shell
and thousands of teeth in saliva-filled jaws.

Before he even had time to scream a warning it
smashed the window behind Linda and with a
four-fingered hand around her chest yanked her
back against the door.

"No!" He frantically reached for her, straining
against the seat belt he still wore.

"John!" she screamed. Her eyes were wide with
terror and disbelief. "John!" She fought at the
hand on her chest fighting to pull the slick black
fingers off her.

Behind her the alien hissed deep and long.

Another alien hand snaked in the window on
the other side of her, and the awful smell of sulfur
and rotten eggs filled the car like a choking gas.

He grabbed for her, but the seat belt still held
him and all he could touch across the car was her
leg. He grabbed it and tried to pull her away from
the bug as she fought madly to pry the hands
away from her.

Then, with a sudden hard yank from the alien,
she was bent over double, her skin pulled roughly
from his grasp. Her seat belt snapped, and with
her head between her legs, she was pulled roughly
through the window. Her legs and back left
bloody strips of skin and cloth on the broken
glass.

"No!" he screamed again, fighting to free himself from the safety belt. But it seemed snagged

on something, or he wasn't pushing the right area
of the clasp or something. It wouldn't release. He
fought at it, ripping at it, struggling to free himself
so he could save his wife.

But the nightmare continued.

The belt wouldn't let him go.

Linda's screams were cut off in the dark night
beyond the car as he fought with that buckle,
twisting at the straps, struggling to be free.

The nightmare continued.

"He's coming around," a voice said through the
thick blackness and the terror.

The horror retreated slightly, only to be replaced by the memory of Charon Base and another nightmare. A nightmare of a mission gone
bad.

"Good," another voice said from his other side.
"Did you get anything?"

"Nothing of any worth."

John Cray struggled back to the reality, the
sounds of Linda's screams still echoing in his
mind.

He was totally nude with large straps holding
his arms and his legs like firm, rough hands. Another strap held his forehead tight against the
back of a huge padded chair. Tubes ran from both
his arms, the area above his heart, and the sides
of both legs to nearby machines. His penis and
balls were encased in what looked to be a large
suction hose that extended under his ass. Three
needle inserts had been stuck into his brain and a
mass of wires ran from them to something he
couldn't see behind him.

"He still denies everything," Larson said, "and
he is somehow blocking the mind probes."

Cray opened his eyes, letting the image of Linda go for the moment.

In front of him stood Professor Kleist in a white smock. He looked huge, like a white judge standing at the pearly gates as Linda's screams faded totally away in the back of his mind.

The Professor smiled when he noticed that Cray's eyes were open. He knelt down so he could look at his captive directly. "Why are you doing this?"

Cray just blinked, not responding. He tried to think of the good times with Linda, but they just wouldn't come. Only being trapped by that seat belt in the middle of that awful night. It was the only thought of her that he had at the moment.

"We know you're *not* really working for Z.C.T., but for Grant Corporation, so you can stop pretending. Just tell us what you know and you'll die painlessly. I can promise you that."

Cray thought of how he had finally freed himself from the seat belt during that awful night. It had been too dark to follow Linda and the alien's tracks, but he had still tried, over and over, scrambling through the brush and trees, calling her name, begging for her to be all right. But he never saw her again, and her body was never found.

He had been sitting in the middle of the road shouting and crying when the Marine transport had picked him up.

The Professor glanced up over Cray's shoulder at Larson, then, disgusted, he turned back to Cray. "Continue to try my patience and you'll suffer beyond all imagining."

Cray focused on the Professor. "I ... I don't know ... don't know what you want."

The Professor leaned back and half smiled. "Then I will tell you exactly what we know and what we want." He again glanced over Cray's shoulder and then back at Cray. "I will grant you," he said, "that your plan was an audacious one. I admire that, to be honest with you, especially the holo of my old friend at headquarters. I'm amazed that he could keep a straight face when he was doing that for you. I even bet you were sitting in his office watching him record it, weren't you?"

Kleist smiled as Clay fought to keep the memory of that day in the Z.C.T. headquarters from his mind. But from the look on the Professor's face, he hadn't succeeded.

"You were hoping," the Professor said, after glancing again over Cray's shoulder, "to make me so paranoid about infiltration that I'd hand you the Chimera Project data without a second thought."

The Professor laughed hard and sharp and then moved closer to Cray so he was looking him directly in the eye. Cray noticed the Professor's breath smelled dirty and sour, as if his insides were rotting out. He could only wish.

"You made one fatal mistake a long time ago," the Professor said, grinning right in Cray's face, gloating with brown teeth just inches from Cray's face. "Z.C.T. agents above grade nine have a security code surface-coated on their right kidney. You, a supposed grade twelve, did not. That was clear when we checked you in decontamination when you first walked onto the station."

Cray struggled to think of his wife, of the night she died, anything but the implications of what the Professor had said.

Kleist leaned back and laughed for what seemed to be much too long. Finally he caught his breath and faced Cray straight on again. "That's right. We've known you worked for the Grant Corporation all along. For years now. We let you feed us the Taser and gel data to get our trust. Wasn't that nice of us?"

Again he laughed, but this time he cut it off quickly. "We wanted to know what you were after, who your contacts were. We've netted quite a haul thanks to you. Including Captain Palmer."

Cray fought against the belts to sit upright. "No, no. She's not . . ."

The Professor laughed. "I may be as mad as they all say I am, but I'm not stupid." He nodded to Larson who moved around into Cray's line of sight. He was carrying a square box with instruments attached to one side.

"We even came up with a plan to get you out here, away from any support you might have in the corporation. We even made it seem as if it was your idea. We needed you here so you'd tell us everything you know. And trust me, you will tell us."

The Professor glanced at Larson and nodded. Then he stared directly into Cray's eyes. "Otherwise, you'll soon discover there is such a thing as a fate worse than death."

Larson turned the box and held it inches from Cray's face so that Cray could look directly into the small window. Then he turned the box so Cray could look directly into the slime-covered underside of an alien face-hugger.

He turned the box so that Cray could see his own living death.

"No!" Cray screamed as the box got closer.

He fought against the belts on the chair, fought against the seat belt as Linda was hauled through the window of the car.

Fought against the thought of that thing on his face.

He lost all three fights.

And the nightmare continued.

8

At the second corridor after leaving the airlock, Green had his men pull the metal grate off a large ventilation duct, then led them inside, shutting the grate behind them. The ducts in this area were carved out of solid stone like separate tunnels. Shoulder width and just barely tall enough for them to run in slightly stooped over, Green figured the ventilation tunnels were their best hope for the moment. They would have no chance at all in the main tunnels.

In this area of the hive there were very few signs of alien habitation, and in this ventilation tunnel there wasn't even any of the alien slime. That was a good sign, at least for the time being.

He had no doubt that the aliens had penetrated

the ventilation system, but there would be fewer of them. Plus he hoped the men could move more quietly through the ventilation system, staying away from any of the main chambers and as far away as possible from the queen. And if there was a fight, he would lose fewer men in a close quarter drill than in an open and high-ceilinged corridor.

After three hundred meters the shaft suddenly widened into a small room with a grate leading back into the main halls, another shaft leading off in the direction they were going, and a shaft crossing vertically, dropping into blackness.

Robinsen went into the room first, his light checking the corners and both up and down, then he signaled to the sergeant all-clear.

Green entered the area and went to the vertical shaft. It dropped farther than the beam from his light would shine. Handholds were cut into the side of the rock going both up and down and Green studied them for a moment before nodding. They would work. Not as good as the ladders in the main corridors, but these would serve.

Green pointed down and motioned for O'Keefe behind him to join Robinsen on the point.

Green knew their only hope was down. He'd studied all the plans for the base, as well as the rough tunnel layouts left behind after the last of the prisoners were taken off. He knew there were vast levels of tunnels under both the human base and the alien sector, all sealed off. If somehow he could get his men into them they might be able to work their way back to the human section and pay the Professor a surprise visit.

While they waited for Robinsen and O'Keefe to

signal the all-clear for the next level, Green had Lynch take apart one of their com units. It would be nice if they could use them, but until they were checked out he wasn't going to chance letting the Professor know where they were or what they were planning.

And that, for the moment, they were still alive.

Lynch made fast work of the helmet and within a few seconds was pointing to a tiny black dot attached to the underside of the mouth guard. "Tracer bug," he whispered. "There may be more."

Green nodded just as Robinsen signaled the all-clear.

He pointed to four of his men and indicated they should take off their headsets and all body armor and leave them. All nodded and did what they were told, letting the armor lay like the discarded white skins of dead humans.

Three levels down he had seven more men take off their helmets, com links, and body armor and put them in a cross corridor outside a ventilation grate. He'd let Kleist think they were putting up a running fight, losing a few men at a time.

The next level six more of the men did the same.

At the lowest level of the alien hive he had the last com links and helmets left beside a grate going into a main hall, including his own. Now all twenty of them were only wearing their brown pants and combat boots, brown T-shirts, and ammunition belts strapped over their shoulders.

Green had everyone stop and look for any more tracer bugs on any of the equipment and on their clothes. Like monkeys picking lice, they split up into pairs and inspected each other carefully, but quickly. Green checked Lynch while Lynch checked him.

Everyone came up negative. It seemed all the bugs were on the armor. Good. Now if the Professor just bought his decoys.

They had been running very silent and so far had been lucky not to be found by an alien. But if his memory served him correctly, on the next level down they were going to have to make some noise to get through a blockage. Enough noise to attract every damn alien in the place.

Robinsen signaled the all-clear to the next level and one by one nineteen Marines went down the narrow shaft.

In this small intersection the ventilation tunnel going on down had been sealed shut with what looked to be part of the wall carved to fit the hole exactly and then cemented into place. The plug on the hole could only be a meter thick, or it might be as wide as five meters.

A thin layer of dust covered everything and the air smelled stale in the small intersection. They had been so long in the rotten egg smell of the alien hive that it wasn't until one of the men coughed softly from the dust that Green even noticed the alien smell's absence. They must be a long ways from the main dens and the queen. Maybe they'd get lucky, but he discounted that thought quickly.

Green posted guards above and down both side tunnels, and told the men to conserve on the lights. Then he had Lynch and Robinsen gather around him.

"Seems we're a distance from the hive here," he whispered. "But we need to keep going down." He pointed at the sealed-off area. "Since we have no ammunition or explosives that I know of, anyone have any ideas how we can get down there quietly. Or if not quietly, quickly? And then seal it behind us?"

"My ex-wife's cooking would eat through that in a second," Lynch whispered and shrugged. Robinsen punched him lightly and Green smiled.

"Since, unfortunately, she's not with us," he whispered, "you two check with the others to see if they have any ideas."

Both nodded and silently moved away. With his men scattered around him Green went to the center of the small room and sat on the rock plug. He knew the longer they stayed in one place the more likely an alien would track them.

But ten meters down through a solid rock plug was their best hope at long-term survival. It was worth a little time to find a way.

While faint whispering from his men went on around him he closed his eyes and did his best to bring back up the vision of the rough prisoner maps he had looked at two years earlier. If they did get through, they were going to need his memory to keep them from getting lost in the maze of rock tunnels below.

"The Marines are gone," Hank said to the five men gathered around him in the circle of bright lamplight. The glow outlined the old tunnel carved out of rock six levels below the human section. The tunnel at this point was as high as his dad's old barn roof and about as wide. The air was dry, thin, and biting cold. Hank could see his breath in the lamplight and a fog seemed to form in the center of their group as they talked.

Bunk beds were carved in the rock wall opposite of where they gathered and one mummified prisoner's body lay curled on a top one, his back to the meeting. From where Hank stood the body looked peaceful and he envied it for that.

Their footsteps in the dust were the only sign anyone had been down in this tunnel for years and years. The six of them had had three meetings before like this one, all in different sections of the old tunnels.

"Gone?" Jonathan, the bartender, asked. "How? When?"

"I went to find Private Choi, my contact, and their bunk room was cleaned out. The guy cleaning the floors there said they had been shipped home."

"They're not totally gone," Ray said softly. Ray was a quiet guy with dark hair and more doctorate degrees than the rest of them combined. He had been the one who had gotten the secret film on Jerry's body. He worked with and around the Professor a great deal, as well as having access to the computers at times.

Ray glanced around at the group in the lamplight and then went on. "The Professor promised them a flight home, then dumped them on the far side of the alien sector. They were alive when they landed, that much I do know. But I doubt if they'll make it back here."

"Shit," Jonathan said. "You got any proof of that on tape?"

"Wish I did," Ray said, shaking his head sadly. The silence in the tunnel seemed to grow louder, pressing in against the thin wall the light had put up around them, making the circle of safety seem ever smaller. Six men stood inside that circle, lost in what the news of the Marines being gone meant.

Hank stared at the body of the prisoner in the shadows on the far wall. Gray coveralls hung over the body with a layer of white dust making his upper side look almost sun-bleached. It seemed so peaceful, yet Hank knew he hadn't died in peace. Hank doubted the Marines would die easy either. If he knew them, and Sergeant Green, they wouldn't go down without a fight.

Hank kept staring at the mummified body, thinking about what it meant to wipe out an entire company of Marines. The Professor had done it almost without a fight in less than three years, and would probably get away with it. How could the six of them and a few other loyal friends now stop such a madman? It didn't seem possible.

And maybe it wasn't, but the least they could do was try to save Joyce. Hank turned to Ray. "You know where they're keeping Captain Palmer?"

Ray nodded. "Cell Block Sixteen. I don't have a clue how she is, though."

"Is there a ventilation duct near there?"

Kent, who worked in maintenance, knelt and unrolled a bunch of large maps on the dusty floor. He thumbed through about ten before pulling one to the top and holding it flat. "Here and here," he said after a moment of study, pointing to marks on the maps. "In the halls outside the cells. They're not secured as far as I know."

"And we can get there from here?"

Kent nodded. "Sure can. Hell, you can get damn near anywhere in this base from these old tunnels and ventilation shafts that run through the base walls. What do you have in mind?"

Hank knelt and indicated that the others join him closer to the maps. "I think it's time we started a revolution," he said, studying the floor plan where Kent had pointed and at the square labeled CELL BLOCK SIXTEEN. "And since we're outnumbered, I think Captain Joyce Palmer would be a great addition to this side of the fight."

Hank looked around at his five friends. All were nodding. It seemed the loss of the Marines had got to them all. This time there was no arguing about waiting, no thought of just sitting and hoping the Professor would screw up somehow. Now they were ready to act.

And since he seemed to have a plan, they were ready to follow him.

"Here's my idea," Hank said.

Five men leaned in closer as Hank's frosty breath misted the air above the maps.

The Professor stood in front of a huge, reinforced window staring into the blackness of a very special cage. Somewhere in that blackness was his success, an alien like no other alien.

His baby.

A human body with its arms, legs, and head cut off and a gaping hole in its chest where a young alien had once emerged had been tossed in on the floor as food for his creation. He knew the creature was in there, back in the shadows, waiting. The Professor knew without a doubt how huge it was. He knew it was as big as any queen, because he had watched it grow.

But now, finally, it had reached maturity. Now he would finally know just how much his success meant.

The sound of the door opening behind him broke his thoughts and he turned to nod to Larson before returning his attention to the blackness beyond the glass.

When Larson halted behind him, the Professor spoke without turning. "Did our guest have anything further of interest to offer?"

"No. I'm pretty sure we've got everything. The prospect of a kiss from that face-hugger loosened his tongue real well, you might say."

The Professor gave Larson a sharp glance. "Spare me your pathetic attempts at humor."

There was a moment of silence as the Professor continued to stare into the blackness.

Finally Larson spoke again. "The pilot, Captain Palmer? She's clean. Cray's mission was apparently solo. Palmer just got in the way because of the death of her friend, Jerry."

"Jerry?"

"A tech guy we used up about two months ago. No one special."

Kleist nodded. "And the copy of the film she had?"

"Still working on where that came from. Might have been one of the techs or maybe a doctor. I'll find him."

"Or her," the Professor said. "Don't overlook the women. As for Captain Palmer, she's more trouble now than she's worth. Give her to the aliens. The livestock could use some boosting. That will be all."

After a moment Kleist heard the door close behind him and he was once again alone with his creation.

"Come to Papa," he said into the blackness as he pressed against the glass. "I've got some nice meat for you. Aren't you hungry?"

But for the moment nothing moved in the blackness beyond the glass.

9

The memory of the first day her kids went snow skiing had been keeping Joyce contented for the past few hours. The biting cold of the dark stone cell had brought on the memory and she had gone with it, lying on the small bunk bed in the cell focusing on how the kids had looked in their brightly colored suits, how they had laughed with every fall, and the feelings she enjoyed when she had been with them. Her memory was strong enough that she could even pull up the smells of the fresh air and the pine trees. If she ever made it out of here alive she would take the kids back to that same resort for a vacation.

She was about to start the day over, replaying it

one more time in her mind like a favorite movie, when the door to the cell snapped open with a bang.

"Don't you ever knock?" Joyce said, swinging her feet off her bunk so she could face whoever was coming in.

"Let's go," a rough voice said as light flooded the small room forcing Joyce to cover her eyes for a moment. Before her vision could completely adjust rough hands pulled her from the bunk and half shoved her toward the door. She couldn't see the guy, but he smelled like he needed a shower and had been eating too much garlic, a stiff combination.

"I can walk," she said, twisting from his grip and stepping away from him.

She moved toward the open door, keeping her pace slow ahead of the guard to give her eyes enough time to adjust.

There looked to be only two of them: the smelly one who had come into the cell and another who stood just outside in the corridor, automatic rifle cocked and aimed right at her stomach. Both men were slightly taller than she was and dressed in the standard green uniform of Larson's goons.

When she reached the corridor she got a better look at both of them. The one in the hall had slicked-back black hair and blue eyes, enhanced, it appeared, by contact lenses. The one who smelled bad had greasy brown hair, a scar on his right cheek, and a potbelly. He looked downright mean through and through.

"Where we heading?" she asked as she stepped

into the corridor and the black-haired guard indicated with his gun that she turn left.

"Nowhere without these tied," the other guard said. He grabbed her hands and yanked them behind her back, pulling a cord around them and yanking it tight.

"Take it easy," she said as the cord cut into her wrists and her shoulders strained backward. "I'm not a piece of meat."

"You are to us," Garlic-breath said and laughed. He let his hands run over her ass, then up her sides toward her breasts.

"Shit, Carl. Cut it out. You don't want Larson pissed, do you?"

"Just having a little fun is all," Garlic-breath said and pushed her roughly to the left. They flanked her, forcing her to move between them toward a cross corridor to the left of her cell. It took her just a moment to realize that the only thing in that direction was the alien sector. She had no doubt she was going to be meeting bugs in very short order and that thought scared the hell out of her.

"You don't have to do this," she said, trying to slow down, give herself some time to think.

"Keep moving," the black-haired guard said and, with a firm grip on her arm, pushed her slightly ahead.

"Kleist's insane," she said, focusing her attention on the guard on the left. He seemed to be the most likely to listen to reason. "You know that. If we work together we can stop him. No more killing."

"Shut up," Garlic-breath said and squeezed her

arm even harder. "Just shut up before I shut you up."

"Wow, that's original," Joyce said.

The intersection of two corridors was coming up and no one else was in sight, at least as far as she could see. There was no doubt she was running out of time. She had to act now.

"You're sure," she asked, again slowing down her pace, "that you want to kill me? I'm a nice person, honest."

With no answer from either of them except to push her forward again, it was time. Move now or she'd be facing bugs and even facing Garlic-breath here was a giant step above that option.

"You know," she said, turning slightly to face Garlic-breath, "didn't anyone ever tell you that you needed a bath?"

With a sudden twist she broke the grip of Garlic-breath and knocked him hard into the stone wall. His gun clattered to the floor. With a quick movement she landed a direct kick on the black-haired guard's chest pounding him back into the opposite wall.

She spun on Garlic-breath. Before he could even climb to his feet she kicked him as hard as she could directly in the crotch. She could feel her foot sink in deep.

He screamed and fell to the floor. She doubted if he'd be walking anytime soon. Couldn't have happened to a nicer guy.

With five quick running strides, her hands tied and flopping behind her back, she was down the hall and around the corner, but she knew this wasn't going to work. She could already hear the black-haired guard climbing to his feet and starting after her. With her hands tied she couldn't even quickly open a goddamned door.

"Joyce!"

The voice sounded familiar, but she didn't know from where and she didn't want to stop at the moment to chat.

"Joyce, damn it! Duck!"

Now she knew the voice. It was Hank's. She flung herself sideways and down as shots cut the air where she had been a moment before. She tumbled head over heels and ended up on her stomach, facing back in the direction she had just come.

Behind her both guards twisted in the air as red holes appeared on their green uniforms. Blood splattered the walls around them as they tumbled to the floor.

Joyce lay on her stomach on the cold stone, breathing hard, watching the life drain out of the two men who had been taking her to her death only a moment before. Her only thought was that she must not have kicked Garlic-breath as hard as she thought she had. Either that or he had nuts of stone.

Then someone was kneeling beside her, working quickly to untie her hands.

"You all right?" Hank said as he finished with the bonds and helped her to her feet.

"I am now," she said. She gave him a hard hug, then nodded to the other red-haired man who stood beside them.

"Kent," Hank said, smiling, "this is Joyce. Joyce. Kent."

"My pleasure, Kent," Joyce said, grabbing the red-haired man's hand and shaking it. "And thanks."

"No, *my* pleasure," he said, laughing at the craziness of the situation. "Anytime."

"Let's hope it's not too often," Joyce said.

"Well," Hank said, glancing quickly around the hall and then pointing to the obvious camera near the ceiling. "It seems we have started the revolution and won the first battle. Shall we retreat?"

"With pleasure," Joyce said. "But first I need a little firepower." She moved quickly to the two dead guards, took both ammunition belts and then picked up both automatic rifles. She slung one over her shoulder and the other she cradled in her arm after quickly checking to make sure it was loaded and ready.

Then she kicked the very dead body of Garlicbreath as hard as she could in the crotch. "That'll teach you to stay down when I kick you the first time."

Hank laughed. "See what I mean, Kent?"

Kent's laugh was hard and long as he ducked through an open ventilation grate in the corridor wall. Hank was right behind him, still laughing.

"Hang on there a minute," Joyce said as she followed them into the dark, narrow ventilation tunnel. "Just what did you mean by that? And what's so funny?"

In the dark in front of her both men laughed even harder.

The Professor watched the huge alien finish devouring the human torso he had just supplied and felt like a proud parent watching his child take its first steps. But this was no normal child. This alien seemed to fill the entire area behind the re-

inforced window. One clawed hand was bigger
than the Professor's entire body, and the jet-black
head and huge carapace were larger than some
cars. Saliva ran from its huge jaws. With two bites
the man's torso was devoured, leaving only a few
bloody specks in the pools of alien saliva on the
floor. The Professor could hear the faint cracks as
the human bones were broken and swallowed.

Kleist clapped his hands together like he was
applauding a great stage play. He had done it. He
had created the greatest creature in the galaxy. A
male alien the size of a queen, maybe even bigger.

And, he hoped, totally tame.

His experiments should have removed all desire to breed or mate from the huge creature. With
all matriarchal ties removed and the overwhelming desire to breed removed, the innate ferocity
becomes redundant and therefore should also be
gone. That was the theory, his theory. He had been
right about its size, but was it truly tame?

"Time for the first test," the Professor said. He
turned to a control board in front of the window
and punched a key. "Is our guest ready?"

Larson's voice came back through the speaker.
"Yes, sir."

"Then stand clear," the Professor said, then
waited for a moment before punching up a quick
sequence of key strokes.

Bright lights filled the area around the huge
alien while huge doors clamped down blocking
the alien's retreat into the back areas of the alien's
pen. The alien reared, startled, its tail swishing
back and forth on the floor as it glanced around.
It was clearly agitated. Good. That would make
this an even better test.

Almost simultaneously with the large doors closing a small, human-sized door slid open on the far wall. A large chair with a human form strapped to it slid on smooth tracks into the very center of the room, jerking to a stop almost quicker than the alien could react.

The Professor noted that the alien hovered over the chair but didn't attack it. Good.

He keyed the microphone for the pen and spoke into it. "Greetings, Mr. Cray. I'd like you to meet my pride and joy."

The alien leaned its huge head down directly in front of Cray's eyes.

All Cray could do was stare in terror as, behind the protective glass, the Professor applauded.

"Sarge," Lynch whispered as he knelt down beside where Green was sitting on the stone plug. The ventilation tunnels flickered in the faint light from Marine lanterns, and distant whispers of men talking filled the air.

Green took a moment to finish planning their next moves after they made it through the blocked passage. Their first chore was to get live ammunition, then slowly but surely start taking out the Professor's guards in a guerrilla action, hitting and pulling back and then hitting again. With Larson having over a hundred men and there only being twenty of them, it would be the only type of fight they could win. Eventually they would reach the Professor. Green didn't know exactly how they would manage that, but he had a few ideas. He sighed and then glanced at Lynch with a nod that he should go ahead.

"Robinsen has an idea that I think might work, if we're lucky." Lynch held his ammunition belt away from his chest. "We dumped the blanks from the rifles, but our belts are still full. These blanks have a good supply of power in them. We should be able to fashion a few quick bombs, at least one that would be big enough to knock the cork out of this." Lynch tapped the huge stone plug that Green was sitting on.

"And how do we slow the bugs down," Green asked, pointing below, "when they follow us right on down there?"

"That's the tricky part," Lynch said, sitting back on his heels and taking a deep breath. "After we've blown open this hole and we're through it, we should be able to cram stuff in the open hole behind us, at least enough to make the blockage solid enough to hold some falling rock from above." Lynch pointed overhead. "We set off two more explosives that will cave in that roof up there and the debris will fill the hole we make with the first blast. No hole, no aliens."

Green glanced up at the ceiling where Lynch had pointed. That might work if they set the bombs right. He could see some structural cracks in the rocks that, with enough explosive, would cave in this entire area.

"The trick," Lynch said, "will be after the first explosion opens the hole. We've got to get down there fast, get the hole blocked with some sort of support, then set off the other two explosions to cave in the roof before the bugs swarm the place."

"How long will it take to pull off?" Green asked.

"Fifteen minutes to fashion and place the bombs. We'll use canteens for the bombs, but the time comes in opening enough of these blank shells for the powder. Then three minutes between explosions, tops."

Green looked around at the men and then down at the sealed passage. He nodded. "Make an extra explosive charge in case the first one doesn't punch through. If we don't use it, we can always toss it at some bugs or maybe some of the Professor's men."

"Will do." Lynch started to move, but Green touched his arm.

"Quietly," Green said. "And fast. We may not have fifteen minutes."

10

The choking smell of the huge alien almost blacked Cray out, but the sheer terror of having something that big, that ugly, that nightmarish, within a few feet of him kept his eyes riveted open and his muscles frozen.

He was still tied to the chair and could barely remember the grilling Larson had given him after threatening him with the face-hugger. The stupid politics of the corporations seemed to carry little weight when faced with wearing one of those. He'd seen pictures of alien births and had prayed many nights that it hadn't happened to Linda, that she had died before implantation.

The huge alien leaned in closer to Cray, as if studying him. The alien's head was far bigger than

Cray's entire body. It extended its interior jaw slowly toward him, like a giant tongue wanting to taste him. The sharp, glistening teeth on the end were all Cray could see. The razor teeth of the small jaw and the huge arm-length teeth of the main jaw became his total world as that huge mouth loomed over him.

Saliva dripped on Cray's left arm, burning the skin. Cray could smell his own sizzling flesh mixed with the overwhelming stink of the alien.

But total paralyzing fear kept Cray perfectly still.

All of his training was gone. He couldn't even bring Linda's face into his memory. All he could do was stare into the huge black throat.

And those razor-sharp teeth.

A small voice in the back of his head fought for his control training, fought for the picture of Linda, of her beautiful face. Anything to leave this reality. But this was too much.

The alien retracted its inner jaws and closed its mouth, the sound of teeth and shell clicking echoing in the room.

Finally the creature backed away slightly and Clay let out the air he'd been holding very slowly. The pain from the acid that had dropped on his arms and leg and the sweat off his forehead were blurring his vision. In the background Cray could hear the Professor talking, but his words meant little to him.

"Isn't he a wonderful creature, Mr. Cray? One of the greatest of all creation, don't you think?"

Cray didn't move as the alien lumbered around him, staring at him, choking him with a thick stench so bad that Cray felt like retching. But he didn't dare.

Once the huge tail brushed the edge of the chair, rocking it almost off its track. Again Cray didn't make the slightest move in the straps that held him. He was nothing more than part of the chair.

The alien again leaned in close, the jaws coming down within a meter of Cray's face, then backing away.

Slowly what was left of the sane part of Cray's brain began to question.

Why was he still alive? Maybe his lack of movement was the reason. Was this how his wife had felt? Did she have time to feel this numbing terror?

"Actually, Mr. Cray," the Professor went on over the speaker. "He is part your son, you might say, sharing your DNA from a scraping of tissue taken when you first arrived. Remember when Grace shook your hand? She's very good at getting needed samples like that."

Cray held totally still, not even daring to let his eyes follow the creature as it moved around him.

Kleist went on. "The rest of this wonderful creature's makeup is a cocktail of alien DNA, concentrated human male hormone, and a rather complex biochemical soup that your employers at the Grant Corporation would have killed to get their hands on.'"

A huge alien hand snaked out and one razor-edged claw touched Cray on his bare chest leaving a red cut from his right nipple to his navel. Then the alien withdrew and studied Cray again.

Cray had no choice but to look into those evil

jaws and not acknowledge the intense pain from the cut and from the acid the alien had left in it like salt in an open wound.

Over the speaker the Professor laughed. "It seems, Mr. Cray, that your son is interested in getting his hands on you. But I don't think he will. You see, I think I have succeeded in finally breeding the first tame alien male. Wonderful, isn't he?"

Cray didn't move, didn't say a word, but in his mind he was shouting: *Tame? Tame? This creature looming over him was far from tame. This creature was pure evil.* But Cray didn't even blink and said nothing out loud and the huge alien continued to hover over him.

After a moment the Professor said, "It seems that this experiment is a total success. Congratulations, Mr. Cray. It seems your son likes you enough to let you live."

The Professor laughed just loud enough for it to come over the speaker, then said, "I, on the other hand, am not nearly so beneficent, as you will soon discover."

The chair jerked hard, tossing Cray against the straps. Accelerating, it slid backward out of the room, again before the huge alien could react.

The last sight Cray had of the creature was its first tentative step toward him as the door closed. It looked angry and very hungry, and not at all happy that it had been tricked.

He prayed to every god he knew as the chair came to a halt that it would be the last time he would ever see that thing.

* * *

Sergeant Green had his men spread out in two groups on both sides of the coming explosion. Half were around the corner of the tunnel intersection to the left and half around the corner to the right. The concussion from the explosion in these close quarters was going to be rough. But with a little distance, a little luck, and a few intersections of tunnels to take off the pressure, they would survive.

Now it was just he and Lynch standing over the plugged hole.

He checked the jury-rigged bomb one more time. The explosives were rigged and in place with a ten-second delay on the trigger. When he clicked the trigger, he was to go to the right and Lynch to the left. If the explosion collapsed the entire tunnel they were to each take the men they had with them and run in opposite directions, trying again as soon as possible to break out of the alien sector and into the abandoned tunnels below. Each of them carried two more jury-rigged bombs.

"Ready?" the sergeant asked Lynch. He looked over at the dust-stained and sweating face of his friend and second in command.

Lynch glanced down the tunnel in the direction he would be running, then back at Green. "As I'll ever be. Let's do it."

"Let's hope this works," Green said as he leaned over the bomb. "Be ready to get your ass back here and plant the new charges if it does."

"No sweat," Lynch said.

"Go," Green said. He triggered the ten-second timer, and took off at a full run. He had barely made the corner and tumbled out of the direct line of the blast when the bomb went off.

It felt as if someone had put his head inside a small metal bucket, then smashed it from all sides at once. His ears rang in a high-pitched wail, and his head instantly ached as the pressure changed.

A sudden hurricane of dust from every nook and crack filled the air of the intersection, reducing visibility to nothing in an instant. He held his breath, letting some of the dust settle before trying to breathe again.

The shock wave buzzed against his palms on the stone floor, and then the rumble of falling rocks could be heard from down the tunnel. God he hoped that wasn't rock from above blocking the entire area. That was one of the risks they were taking, but if it happened he knew they wouldn't stand a chance in two separate groups.

Hell, they didn't stand much of a chance now seeing as they had called every alien in the sector to come down for dinner.

He rolled to his feet and moved his neck and jaw in an attempt to clear the pressure in his ears. Through the dust he could see a few of his men scrambling to their feet. "Be careful as you move around," he shouted, his voice sounding hollow in his ringing ears. "I don't want anyone falling down a damn shaft."

He glanced around at the few men he could see. "Let's move." He started at a slow run back in the direction he had just come.

It was like running into a blinding snowstorm. The gray dust filled the air and ate the beam of his light within a foot of his head. The dust instantly coated his face and nose and he had to keep swallowing just to keep his throat clear enough to breathe.

He felt his way along the wall with one hand on the cold stone, moving as quickly as he could. Behind him he could hear his men doing the same.

He reached the intersection and suddenly the air seemed slightly clearer. A draft was pulling the dust down through the new hole they had punched where the sealed shaft had been a minute before. The hole was rough, but not so large that they couldn't plug it with supports that would hold the falling rock from a second explosion.

Lynch appeared out of the dust on the other side of the intersection, a rope in one hand and a light in the other.

"Let's go!" Green shouted. "Set the new charges and make sure that plug is the right size." Two men instantly went up the stone ladder above the shaft to plant the charges. Two others pulled the equipment they had tied together to make a plug closer to the hole and started some quick measuring. The plug was made up of rifles for support tied with rope and supported with other standard equipment such as shovels and climbing gear from their packs.

Green grabbed the rope off his belt and dropped it through the hole, swinging it over his shoulder and under his arm. He spread his legs and braced himself. Lynch quickly followed on the other side of the hole. Then, with Green and Lynch holding the upper ends, the men were quickly through and down to the lower levels, including the two who had set the explosives in the passageway and ceiling above them.

"All set?" Green asked Lynch, glancing through

the dust at where the explosives were placed above.

"Enough to bring the whole section down," Lynch said. "One-minute timer rigged out of my watch and secured on the wall."

Green took the rope from Lynch's hand and dropped both through the hole to the men waiting on the level below. Then he quickly stepped over to the trigger dangling from a wire down one stone wall.

"Plug ready?" They were going to need something blocking the hole that was strong enough to hold the falling rock from above. Otherwise there was a chance that the rock they were going to blast from the ceiling would just go right on down the shaft, leaving it open for the bugs to follow.

Lynch pulled the mass of tied equipment a few inches closer to the hole. He pulled and twisted at it, then glanced up at Green. "It'll work," he said. "Open enough to let the blast through, but strong enough to hold all the first rocks that hit it. I just hate leaving the rifles." He patted one that was tied into the plug.

"No choice. Let's do it before we get unwanted company."

He clicked the timer. One minute and counting.

With two quick steps he was at the hole and on his stomach working his way over the edge of the rough blast crater. Lynch snapped off his light and tucked it in his belt. Green left his light on the edge shining down into the hole. Below them one of the men had left a light shining upward so that they had at least dim light to work in.

On the opposite side of the hole Lynch was

lowering himself over the edge at exactly the same time until his back touched Green's.

They paused for a moment, making sure their backs were square, their legs braced against the rough stone, and the pressure as even as they could get it between them. There were handholds in the side of the stone down about ten feet, carved there by the prisoners, but the blast had blown the others above it away. They had to get to the stone ladder, as well as seal the hole as they went. Back to back down the hole was the quickest and safest way and something they had practiced at times over the years.

Green scraped his knees and hands on the sharp rock as he went, and after a few seconds he could feel blood start to run down his right leg.

But quickly they had their heads below the top of the hole.

"Pull it over," Green said.

Lynch quickly and smoothly scraped the mass of equipment that would serve as a new plug over the edge and down on top of them. Using one hand each to work the plug down and the other hand and both legs to hold themselves in place, they continued down the hole until the equipment snuggled into place about three feet from the top.

"Got it," Lynch said.

"Make sure," Green said. Both he and Lynch pulled and tugged on it, almost hanging their total weight on it to make sure it was secure.

"Twenty-six seconds," Green said as they finished securing the plug and started down again. He reached the cut handholds on his side and with one arm swung Lynch around so that he too had a firm grasp. Lynch started down, then suddenly paused and sniffed.

But Green had already caught the familiar odor of rotten eggs that filled the dusty, dry air of the dark tunnels.

"Aliens," Green said. "Go! Go! Go!"

Like two monkeys the men scrambled ten more feet down the wall and then dropped the rest of the way to the stone floor, both barely missing the vertical shaft that disappeared off into the dark below the ladder.

"Run for it!" Green said as both men turned to the right and headed down the tunnel through the dust at a full run. The tracks of the other men covered the floor. They had been ordered to get three or four intersections away from the blast in the direction of the human sector and then wait. If he and Lynch didn't make it, the men's orders were to search for and destroy the Professor at all costs.

All the men were secure behind solid rock a hundred meters distant.

A lone flashlight sat in the middle of the corridor ahead, marking the intersection they were trying to reach.

They'd be lucky to make it to that first corner.

The sounds of aliens filling the area above the plug filtered after them as a reminder to run even faster.

Green could feel his heart pumping as he sprinted right behind Lynch toward the promising light.

And for a moment he thought they might make it.

Then the concussion from the huge blast sent

Green flying forward like a giant hand had caught him squarely in the back and just shoved.

He tucked in midair and rolled as best he could. The impact against the stone floor jarred him and snapped his head around as he tumbled, letting his forward motion take up as much of the impact as it could.

After what seemed like a nightmare of pounding noise and spinning rock he finally came to a smashing stop against the wall on the far side of the intersection.

A shooting pain cut through his head, and as the blackness took him his last thought was a silent hope that the hole was sealed, not only by tons of rock, but by a few bug bodies as well.

Joyce sat on the cold stone of the passageway, the comforting feel of the automatic rifle in her hand beside her. She couldn't remember being so cold before, but there was no hope of getting warm soon so she was ignoring it as best she could. But seeing her breath crystallize in front of her every time she breathed didn't help. It also didn't help that all she wore were cloth slacks, a sweat-stained T-shirt, and a cloth vest. A good ski parka right now was what she really needed. And maybe some mittens and a knit hat.

Hank and Kent were talking with four other men over plotting the best way to take out the Professor and his goons. Joyce didn't really care what plan they came up with, as long as it had her pulling the trigger.

The men stood in a circle, their breath misting in the lamplight between them, giving the scene a surreal quality straight out of a black and white movie.

She watched Hank, how he moved his hands when he talked, how he brushed his hair off his face. She was really glad to see him again, to see him alive. Somehow it gave her a warm feeling inside. Not enough to cut the cold of the stone tunnels, but at least it was something.

She heard the name of her ship mentioned a few times and was about to stand and join the discussion when a low rumbling filled the corridor and dust drifted from the walls, giving the lights around them even more of a ghostly look.

She picked up the rifle and studied the shadows in the tunnels around them.

"What the hell was that?" Hank asked as everyone stopped and looked around.

"Maybe," Joyce said, standing and moving over to join the group, "there are more than just us fighting the Professor. Could that be possible?"

"Might be," Hank said, "but more likely it was one of the Professor's experiments gone bad. Could we be so lucky as to have it take him out?"

"I hope not," Joyce said as she calmly adjusted the strap of the rifle over her shoulder with cold fingers. "I don't think the man deserves such an easy death. Something like a face-hugger would be more along the lines I'm thinking."

All the men stopped and looked at her through the dusty light. It was clear to Joyce that they were all thinking their private thoughts of how they would like to see the Professor leave this world. From the slight nods and the looks on their faces, Joyce doubted if any of them seriously disagreed with her.

Finally Hank rested a hand on her shoulder and then broke the uneasy silence. "We have to assume the explosion, or whatever it was, doesn't change a thing."

"Agreed," Kent said and the others, including Joyce, nodded.

"But what we're not agreed on," Hank said, "is what we do next."

Joyce glanced around at the six men, noting that she was by far the best armed of the group. Seven people against Larson and his goons. Larson must have a good hundred men, all armed and ready to die. They didn't stand a chance.

She cleared her throat and stepped forward slightly, forcing Hank's hand to drop off her shoulder. "I'd say the first course of action would be to get more firepower and more help."

She glanced around the dim, dust-filtered light at the others. They all seemed to be agreeing, listening intently to her, willing almost to let her lead. So what the hell. She would.

"I've got a copilot somewhere who's a damn good shot. And the guy Cray, who they caught me with, killed at least two of Larson's men with his bare hands before they got him. He'd be a good addition to our little force if he's still alive."

"I agree," Kent said. "And he's still alive. Or at least he was an hour ago. He's in what serves almost as a holding pen next to the Professor's private labs."

A tall, thin guy dressed in a white shirt and black, dust-covered pants said, "Your copilot left the bar with a blonde about three hours ago. I'll bet he's in his room."

"All right," Joyce said. "Someone give me a

shove in the right direction and a rough map of these tunnels and I'll get those two. Who else can we draft?"

For the next twenty minutes they outlined whom each of them were going after and where they would meet when they finished. Then one at a time the group broke up, scattering in different directions in the dark tunnels until only Joyce and Hank were left.

"You sure you want to go this alone?" Hank asked, his hand a faint touch on her arm, his breath ice crystals in the remaining lamplight.

"Yeah," she said, giving his hand a quick squeeze. "We need all the help we can get. You're going after three recruits. I can manage my two."

He nodded, but Joyce could tell he didn't much like the idea of splitting up with her again. She reached up and grabbed his forearm as tight as her cold fingers would allow. "What'd you tell Kent about me before you two came to my rescue?"

Hank looked puzzled for a moment, then smiled.

"Come on," she said, smiling back at him. "I can take it."

Hank looked down at the ground for a moment, then back into her eyes. "I told him you were a woman who could take care of herself."

She smiled at him, holding his gaze. "Then let me do it," she said.

He smiled back, then nodded. "Two hours?"

"Two hours," she replied. "And you take care of yourself."

"I will," he said.

"Promise?"

"Promise."

She smiled and without another look turned and headed off down the dark tunnel, her small-beamed light cutting a weak line through the blackness.

Cray first, if he was still alive, then Deegan. That was her plan. Cray first because he might not live much longer, then Deegan if she could find him.

It felt good to be doing something.

Real good.

She checked her rifle for the tenth time to make sure it was fully loaded, then slung it over her shoulder. Holding the flashlight in her mouth, she started up the ladder cut into the wall.

Her fingers were numb on the cold rock as she climbed slowly toward the Professor's labs, but she didn't notice. She was hoping to find the Professor alone and get off a shot.

Just one shot. That was all she was asking for.

One shot for Jerry.

Sergeant Green awoke to the feeling of a bandage being applied to his right arm. He was leaning against something hard, with sharp edges.

"He's coming around," a voice said. "Back off. Give him some room."

Shadows beyond his closed eyes retreated and suddenly he was bathed in bright light. He blinked against the dust caked on his face and the glare of two lamps shining directly at him.

"Give me a break," he said, using his good arm to shade his face. His head felt like a jet engine was taking off behind his eyes and there was a high-pitched whine in his right ear. He was afraid

to move, unwilling to find out how many bones he
had broken.

"Sorry, Sarge."

The lights were quickly shifted out of his eyes
enough for him to see the dirt-covered faces
around him. Private Young stood over him, looking concerned, while Robinsen, kneeling beside
him, finished on his arm. Both of their breaths
showed in the lamplight as frozen crystals sparkling like a light Christmas snow. Getting out of
the alien section of the base had cooled things
down in more ways than one.

He started to move, but an intense pain shot
through his head. He moaned and slouched back
against the wall, wishing someone would just kill
him and get it over with.

"You got a good egg there above your right ear,"
Robinsen said. "Has to hurt like hell."

"Wow," Green said, using his good hand to
slowly touch the lump. It was soft, swollen, and
felt hot and sticky to his touch. "What a headache."

"You're lucky that's all it is," Robinsen said.
"I've given you some Black-Ace for the pain. It
should be easing in a few seconds. I don't think
you have any broken bones beyond a few cracked
ribs and the lump on the head. We'll have to
watch you in case that lump is a bad concussion,
but I don't think it is."

Green sighed and leaned back against the wall.
No broken bones. That, at least, was good news.
The last thing he wanted was his men carrying
him. He took some deep breaths, feeling the
cracked ribs that Robinsen had mentioned. He
could feel the wave of Black-Ace cleaning out

the aches like a hot shower after a good workout. That was some good shit. The soothing felt so good he just wanted to sleep. He couldn't do that, but he wanted to. Maybe just until Robinsen finished working on his arm.

He closed his eyes to the bright lamps, then immediately opened them again. No sleeping. He could live on these drugs for a while if he needed to. And judging from the pain in his head it looked like he was going to have to. It wouldn't be the first time he'd been hooked on Black-Ace. Damn near every Marine was at one time or another. It was standard issue and they used it, but coming down off the drug was going to be a bitch. He just hoped he lived long enough to worry about it.

He took another two deep breaths of the cold, dust-filled air to help his head clear, then he sat up slowly and glanced around. Only three men were near him at this intersection of corridors. Robinsen working on his cut arm, Young holding the lamps, and McPhillips standing guard before the right-hand tunnel. But he could hear others talking a short distance off.

"That'll do it," Robinsen said, patting the bandage on Green's arm and then standing. Robinsen reached out and offered Green a hand up. Green took it and was gratefully helped to his feet.

He felt dizzy for a moment and leaned against the cold stone wall, but it quickly cleared. The drug was kicking in. Now his head only felt like it had been hit with a bat, not crushed by a truck. It was an improvement. He'd be even better when his ears stopped ringing.

He glanced around at the intersection, then back the way he had come. "I assume," he said, "since we're all just sitting here, that the hole we made is plugged?"

"Totally," Young said. "That was one wail of a blast."

Green nodded. "It took a few bugs with it, too." He clapped his hands together to try to warm them. "Looks like it shut off the heat, as well." Green glanced around, looking at the scattered rock and for the first time really remembering the blast. "Where's Lynch? How's his head?"

The three men around him were silent and none of them looked him directly in the eyes.

He got the message.

"What happened?"

Robinsen pointed at the vertical shaft leading down to the lower levels. "Looks like when the explosion went off you were tossed against the wall and Lynch was unlucky enough to tumble into the shaft. He went down three levels before hanging up on the edge of the hole. His neck was broken, as were about half the bones in his body."

"Damn," was all Green could say. What a stupid thing to happen.

Robinsen and the other men said nothing.

Green walked to the edge of the shaft and glanced down the stone handholds cut in the wall. The hole went into the dark as far as he could see, with faint lights showing three levels below.

He stepped back and took a few deep breaths letting the painkiller work its magic. Everyone in the outfit knew he had been closer to Lynch than any of the other men. He depended on Lynch, had confided in Lynch. Lynch was his second in command.

"Damn it," he said softly, staring at the black

mouth of the shaft. He knew better than to think they were going to get out of this without losing some more.

That was the nature of their business.

That was the nature of war.

But why Lynch after all this time? After surviving all the stupid missions the Professor had sent them on, why die like this? It was just plain stupid.

The Professor was going to suffer for this. And for Choi and Boone and all the others.

He was going to suffer very long and very hard.

Green glanced back at where Robinsen stood quietly. "You're now my number two. Young, you're three. Understood?"

Both nodded.

"We're in a war here and we have a mission," Green said. "If I go down I need you to carry it out. The mission in plain terms is to take out the Professor and Larson and as many of his goons as we can. And do it in as slow and as painful a way as possible. Is that understood?"

"On the money," Robinsen said.

"With pleasure," Young said.

Green nodded, pleased at their responses, but not showing it. "Round up the men and meet three levels down in five minutes."

Young nodded and quickly disappeared down the tunnel. Robinsen followed Green to the edge of the shaft and Green let him go down first.

Professor Kleist was soon going to get a big surprise. He now had nineteen very angry Marines after him. Green knew it wasn't going to be pretty when they finally caught up with him.

And that thought helped him through the pain going down the cold stone ladder.

And through the pain of seeing one of his best men, and his best friend, laid out dead on the cold stone floor three levels below.

Joyce finally had her hands almost warm and was beginning to get some feeling in her feet again when they brought Cray out of the lab across the ten-meter-wide corridor from her. She had been sitting out of sight in a side ventilation shaft, watching the wide, carpeted corridor along the Professor's private labs, waiting to get any indication of where Cray might be. Now, suddenly, he was being pushed along in front of her.

He had on the same brown slacks and tan shirt he had worn earlier, but they were now torn and looked to be bloodstained across his chest and down his right leg.

She watched, staying out of sight behind the ventilation grate in the stone wall as Cray was tossed by Larson and one of his goons into a small room beside one of the Professor's labs. She could tell Cray wasn't doing that well, and from the way they were handling him, it didn't look like he was going to get better much quicker.

Larson checked to make sure the lock was secure, then left a single guard standing in front of Cray's cell while he went back into the main lab toward the Professor's office.

She wished Larson had been alone. She'd have taken him out without a second thought. And if it had been the Professor she would have, even with a dozen men around him. But right now her first

job was to get Cray out of there and to see if he
was going to be of any help to her.

The one guard stood with his back to the door
in parade-rest position. His gun hung on a strap
over his shoulder and he didn't seem to be paying
a great deal of attention. Joyce studied him, thinking of the best ways to get past him. He looked to
be not much older than twenty, with blond hair
and very white skin. He had, what might be called
under the right circumstances, a nice face. In the
bored rest position it seemed almost friendly. And
he looked much cleaner than the two she had
fought with earlier.

Joyce studied him for a minute, giving Larson
plenty of time to get a distance away. She was going to make some noise and she wanted as few
people close as possible. For the last half hour the
corridor had gotten very little traffic. And what
traffic there was seemed to be techs in white lab
coats.

Silently she took the second rifle off her shoulder, checked to make sure it was ready, and then
put it silently back over her shoulder. Her plan
was to take out the guard with one shot from hiding, break open the grate, shoot open the lock on
the door, and then she and Cray would disappear
back into the dark ventilation system before anyone was the wiser. But just in case someone was
too close she wanted the extra gun in Cray's
hands when he came out of that door.

She quickly checked the corridor to make sure
no one was coming, then pushed herself away
from the grate, bracing her back against the stone.
She checked to make sure the rifle was set on single shot, then carefully aimed at the center of the

guard's chest, not looking at his face as she did so. The shot was going to be damn near deafening in this tight place, but firing in the ventilation system would also be an advantage because it would be hell to pinpoint quickly.

She just hoped her ears survived.

She took two slow breaths, and then, keeping the rifle leveled dead center on the guard's chest, moved the barrel of the gun up and through the grate just enough to prevent the bullet deflecting off the metal.

Then she squeezed the trigger.

The concussion bumped her head backward with a sharp knock into the stone. The sound hammered her like her head was in a sleep tank and twenty people were pounding it with steel pipes. The smell made her cough and she did once, hard, before kicking the grate off with her foot. It landed on the carpeted corridor floor with a loud thump that seemed very distant in her ringing ears.

In a smooth motion she clicked her Kramer to fully automatic and did a quick scan of the hall. The guard, a round hole in his chest and a startled look on his face, was slumped over next to the door. A red smear covered the expensive wood paneling behind him.

Before the guard's head hit the floor she was out of the grate and across the corridor. "Cray," she shouted, "stand away from the door!"

She gave him only a second and then sent three shots in a downward angle into the lock. With a hard kick, the door crashed inward.

Cray appeared out of the dark interior like a ghost. He was barefoot and she had been right about the spots on his clothes being blood. He looked to be bleeding from four or five different places, but he seemed to be alert and Joyce was very glad he was moving so quickly. She wouldn't have taken the time to carry him.

With a quick shake of the head, "No" to Joyce as she started to swing the second gun off her shoulder, he bent over and yanked the Kramer off the dead guard, grabbing the extra clips of ammunition and the full combat belt with another quick motion.

Joyce watched for a second, then turned and in four running steps was back at the grate opening.

She was through it in a fraction of a second, with Cray right behind her.

Two hundred meters of ventilation shafts and three levels down, she stopped to catch her breath.

Cray slumped to the floor across the tunnel from her and smiled. "Thanks," he said, his voice raspy.

"Don't thank me yet," she said, working to catch her breath. Now she was hot and sweating, which felt wonderful compared to freezing. "We're outnumbered about thirty to one and the fight looks impossible."

He laughed, almost a high, insane laugh. "If you'd seen what I have in the last few hours, you'd be glad you even have the chance to fight. So thanks."

She looked at him, at the blood splattered over his shirt, at the red and purple areas of his face. He had obviously been through hell. Maybe, like her, he'd want a little payback.

"You're welcome," she said.

He smiled and closed his eyes. She'd give him ten minutes of rest and then they had another person to draft.

Kleist glanced away from the window looking over his creation when Grace entered his private lab. He was angrier than he had been in years. He hated incompetence and it seemed to be all around him. Moreover, he hated being wrong and his creature had just proved him very, very wrong.

He kept his voice as calm as he could and asked, "Have they found him yet?"

"No, sir," Grace said. "There would seem to be at least ten and maybe as many as twenty people involved so far, all seemingly heavily armed. Besides Cray's release, there have been six incidents on the station in the last hour. We have four men dead at this point and two wounded."

"Find Cray and Palmer and bring them to me," the Professor said and turned back to the carnage beyond the reinforced window. He stared at his beautiful creation as it tore a normal-sized alien male apart with a ferocity he found hard to imagine. The body of the adult male smashed against the wall, acid blood splattering everywhere.

"I've been a fool, Grace. A complete fool."

"You're being too hard on yourself," Grace said.

The Professor gestured at the mess beyond the window. "No, I'm not. In my conceit, I overlooked the obvious. I ignored the primary fundamentals of nature. I imagined they wouldn't apply to this unique strain. But, as is now clearly obvious, I was wrong. Wrong, Grace. Wrong. Do you understand?"

She said nothing and they both continued to watch the destruction.

Of the ten mature adult aliens he had let into the contained area with his new creation, only two remained. And as he and Grace watched, one was picked up like it was a light snack, its head bitten completely through. Then the body was tossed in an acid smear against the window in front of them. Before the last survivor had a chance to even run, the huge alien was on it, tearing its arms off first, then its legs, and finally its head, adding its body to the pile of others.

The Professor turned his back on the window and walked a few steps away. "Don't you see, Grace? The alien king refrained from attacking Cray not because its natural savagery had been bred out, as I thought, but because Cray was strapped down, incapacitated, not moving."

Kleist glanced up into Grace's beautiful android face. "Don't you see?" He so wanted someone to understand. "Cray was spared because he wasn't perceived as a threat."

He turned back to the window beyond which the huge alien was smashing the remains of its ten smaller cousins. Cousins who could kill ten men without a problem were now tossed aside like a child's broken toys.

He stood there for a moment, staring at the destruction. Then slowly he smiled. "Maybe it's just a matter of perspective."

"Perspective, Professor?" Grace asked, moving to stand beside him in front of the bloody scene.

"What we have here"—the Professor indicated the huge alien beyond the wall—"is in essence a rogue male. He's a living engine of destruction, the exact opposite of what I had planned for. He considers all others to be his rivals."

"That would seem to be obvious, now," Grace said as the rogue picked up a large piece of another alien and savagely smashed it against the wall.

"Don't you see, Grace?" The Professor was now beaming.

On the other side of the glass the huge alien rose on its hind legs and opened its mouth like it was screaming in celebration of its victory.

"Don't you see? This is the perfect prototype for Z.C.T. Corporation's bio-weapons arsenal. From the ashes of defeat come success."

Grace was about to say something when suddenly she put her hand to the side of her head and looked off into the distance.

"Is something wrong?" the Professor asked.

"Professor, I've just picked up two transmission signals on the upper EF band. To my knowledge we have no facilities for broadcasting on that frequency."

The Professor glanced at the rogue as it stood in the center of its victory, its huge mouth open in a silent scream.

"Can you trace their source?"

Grace nodded, her hand still beside her head as if she had a headache. "One is on this level, in the very heart of the alien sector."

"And the other?" the Professor asked, already knowing the answer.

"From there," Grace said, and pointed at the rogue.

"A challenge," the Professor said softly, and then smiled.

His rogue was challenging the queen.

This might turn out much better than he had ever dreamed. Much better, indeed.

12

With a small map in one hand and a penlight in the other, Joyce led Cray up a series of dark, narrow ventilation shafts cut through solid stone. It seemed like it had been an eternity since Hank and Kent had rescued her. She was starting to memorize the maze of ventilation shafts and tunnels that surrounded the main corridors of the human sector. She had a natural sense of direction, and almost instinctively knew which tunnel would take them where. She had a sneaking feeling that sense was going to come in real handy before all this was over.

Cray, on the other hand, still seemed in shock. Whatever the Professor and Larson had done to him had affected him at a very deep level. He wasn't the same man who had arrived here such a short number of days before. Instead of cocky and sure of himself, a man walking tall and confident into any situation, he now moved like he was afraid of every shadow, hunched slightly forward, almost cowering.

And when he glanced at her, his eyes didn't seem to actually see her, but instead some vision he didn't want to witness again but couldn't shake. She had seen that look in people's eyes a number of times during the war and she would never get used to it.

At one intersection she stopped and turned to Cray. "How you doing?" she whispered.

"Besides feeling like a lost gopher?" he said. "Fine."

She patted his leg and motioned for them to keep moving.

Twice in the next few minutes they found themselves crawling on their stomachs, the weight of meters of rock pressing down on their backs, their rifles pushed ahead of them in the dust.

A few minutes later at one intersection of larger ventilation ducts they were almost surprised by two of Larson's guards crouched in the dark. If one of the guards hadn't tapped his gun against the floor as they approached they might have been dead. Instead of getting into a fight in such close quarters, Cray and Joyce had silently worked their way back and around another way, climbing up two levels to avoid that area.

Finally, after almost an hour of silent and steady movement, they were at their destination. Or at least Joyce hoped it was Deegan's room vent. She motioned for Cray to be quiet and guard her back, then she handed him her rifle and got down on her hands and knees. In this area the vents were near the ceilings of the rooms, but on the floors of the tunnels.

The vent itself was small, not more than a meter wide, two thirds of a meter tall and two meters long. And it was far from smooth rock on the four surfaces. She could feel rough edges scrape against her back as she eased forward to the grate and air filter into the room.

Through it she could see some of the room including Deegan's favorite jacket and his hat tossed on the dresser. This was his room all right.

She could also hear some low moaning, like someone was hurt or had been beaten. Her stomach twisted. Maybe Larson had already been here and had tortured Deegan looking for her. She wouldn't put that past Larson or the Professor.

She backed silently out of the tunnel with only a slight scrape on one elbow and stood to face Cray. "He might be hurt in there, or there may be someone with him. Can't tell, but I'm going in."

She didn't wait for Cray to respond She turned and glanced at the small vent again. If she worked it right she could get the surprise on whoever was holding Deegan. But it would have to be a timed and very fast movement. Otherwise she was dead and in that tight a space there would be very little Cray could do to help her.

She turned back and again whispered in his ear, "I'm going in feetfirst. You come in behind me headfirst and cover me from the vent. If I'm captured or killed, make a run for it."

He nodded that he understood what she was planning. She could see him taking deep breaths, fighting to push back whatever demons were plaguing him. She appreciated that. Maybe there was hope for him yet.

She handed her rifle to him again and then laid down on the floor scooting silently into the tunnel feetfirst. She could feel the dust and dirt bunching up under her shirt and vest. The sharp edges of rock scraped lines in her skin. She refused to focus on the rock walls of the small vent. It had already flashed through her mind once too many times how this looked and felt very much like a coffin.

When she was in position Cray handed her back her rifle.

With a quick nod she indicated to him that she was ready.

She took a deep, silent breath, and then with a violent kick sent the screen flying into the room.

The crash of her foot kicking the grate sounded like a bomb going off. But almost before the screen could hit the floor in Deegan's room, she had slid forward and dropped to the ground, crouched, ready to fire. Behind and above her Cray came through the tunnel face-first, rifle also ready.

In the bed a very surprised and very nude Deegan sat up, his eyes round and his hands above his head. An equally nude blond woman sat up beside him, her hands also shooting above her head in the traditional sign of surrender. Her eyes were bigger around than Deegan's, but Deegan looked more like he was going to choke.

Joyce glanced quickly around the small room to make sure no one was hiding anywhere, then went quickly to the door to make sure it was locked.

In the vent above her head Cray chuckled.

Finally Deegan swallowed hard, and with a glance up at Cray sticking out of the vent, he looked back at Joyce. "Jesus, boss. You could at least knock."

Cray snorted and Joyce laughed, some of the tension easing from her shoulders and back. It was good to be back with Deegan. She hadn't realized just how much she had been worrying about him.

"I'll guard the passage," Cray said. "Be quick. They know we're here by now."

"Thirty seconds," Joyce said to Deegan, "and then we leave you to Larson's goons."

"What the . . ." Deegan started to say.

Joyce grabbed Deegan's old shirt off the floor and tossed it his way. "Twenty-nine. And I'm not kidding."

Joyce turned to the blonde who, from the look in her green eyes, was about to go into total shock. "If you know how to fire one of these"— Joyce held up her automatic Kramer—"you can come along. Otherwise you might want to get dressed very quickly. I suspect you will be having some company from Larson and his goons very, very shortly. And from my experience they don't treat women very well."

The woman choked and jumped from her side of the bed at the same time as Deegan was out the other. Without a glance back she bolted for the door. But Joyce beat her to it, holding it closed.

"You forgot your clothes," she pointed out. "Besides, we need to be out of here"—Joyce pointed to the open vent—"before you go out there. Understood?"

The woman nodded, her face so pale she almost looked like a ghost.

"Get dressed," Joyce told her, then turned to see that Deegan was finishing with the buckle on his pants and had already tossed his boots through the vent.

"Give me a boost," he said.

Joyce moved quickly into position, cupped her hands, and then lifted, watching as Deegan forced his overweight body through the narrow vent. It must have really hurt. Next trip she'd force him to lose a little of that weight.

If there was a next trip.

"Nice meeting you," she said to the stunned woman who stood with a gold blouse in one hand not even attempting to cover her chest or thick blond pubic hair. Joyce made a second mental note to talk to Deegan about his choice of women.

As she heard running outside in the hall, she turned and pulled herself up and through the duct.

They were already to the first cross vent and going up a level when she heard Deegan's door crash open.

That poor blond woman was not having a very good day.

With the upcoming fight with the Professor and Larson's men, Sergeant Green could see no other option but to leave Lynch's body near where he died. They had found an area where fifty bunks were dug into the side of the wall of one tunnel. Two bodies of prisoners, mummified by the dry, cold air, rested in two of the upper bunks. Green had the men put Lynch into a middle bunk about chest high off the floor.

Green had arranged him so that he looked peaceful, his gun gripped in his hands in front of his chest along with the picture of his dead wife, Karen, that he had always carried in his wallet. Just like Green's wife, Marybeth, she'd been taken by the aliens in the invasion of Earth. He and Lynch had killed a lot of bugs over the years to make up for those two human deaths.

Green put a light over the bunk and then, without words, all the men filed silently past and moved off down the tunnel toward the human section. Some touched Lynch lightly on the arm to say good-bye.

A few saluted

Young left a small gold pin on his chest.

Green was the last to pass and he stopped for a moment. He patted his old friend's arm. "I'll try to come back for you," he said, "when we finish the mission. You'll be safe here."

He glanced around at the dark tunnel and then back at his friend. "If I don't make it, I suppose we'll both know about it together, upstairs, huh?"

He took a deep, almost shuddering breath. "Going to miss you. Say hi to Karen for me. And to Marybeth, if you see her."

He stood for a moment, not knowing what else to say. Neither he nor Lynch had a religious bone in their bodies so even a short prayer seemed just plain wrong.

He adjusted his rifle on his shoulder, shifting the weight. "See you, old friend."

He picked up the light and moved off quickly down the dark tunnel after his men. They had a fight to fight.

One they were going to damn well win.

The Professor's office was deadly silent as Larson and Grace stood behind Kleist and all three watched the four center screens on the wall play the same event from four different angles.

Finally Larson said, after rerunning the recording of what occurred in Captain Palmer's copilot's quarters, "They're using the damn ventilation system like a highway."

The Professor turned to Larson. He was getting angrier by the minute. Not so much because of the escape of Cray and Palmer and the small insurrection by a few malcontents. That actually didn't bother him beyond annoyance. It was something he had been expecting and now wasn't in the slightest surprised that Captain Palmer had triggered it.

No, what bothered him the most was Larson's apparent inability to handle the situation. The Professor had put up with a lot from his chief of security, but he had thought he had the man fully trained and ready for this. But now the idiot was letting them all down.

And Kleist hated it when people let him down.

"So what have you done about it?" the Professor asked. "At the moment I have much more important matters to attend to. Do you realize that I have just made a breakthrough of unparalleled importance in the lab?" The Professor glanced at Larson's blank face. "No, of course you don't. But I have. For your information, I have just created the ultimate fighting machine. And what is my reward for such an achievement?" He gestured at the screens in front of him in disgust. "I find myself dealing with your petty problems."

He looked Larson directly in the eye. "Do you understand what I'm saying?"

Larson swallowed and nodded. "Yes, sir."

"Fine," the Professor said. He swung back and faced the wall of monitors, his fingers steepled in front of him. "Now show me what you are doing to remedy the situation. And be quick about it."

Larson leaned over the board and punched a few keys. The center four screens of the huge wall displayed a large map of the main level of the human sector. Larson punched another key and blue lines appeared lacing the map through the walls and thick areas around rooms. It was a view the Professor had never seen before and it shocked him.

"This shows the ventilation system that we have mapped from the very poor records left us when they redid this place. There are many more ventilation and service tunnels than this, but at the moment we are working off this layout."

Damn. He should have had those tunnels mapped in the first year. He had no idea there were so many of them. How, with his work with the aliens, was he supposed to think of things like this? He nodded to Larson to continue.

"I've got men stationed at all the major ventila-

tion tunnel intersections on this level, as well as
the ones above and below it. They've heard movement, but so far no contact."

"Double the normal guard on the lab areas."

"Already done," Larson said. "And I have men
on every person we have suspected in the past of
anticorporation activities. At least the ones we
can find. At this point we have about twenty missing."

The Professor nodded. "All right. And you figure all of them have joined Cray and Captain
Palmer?"

"I'm afraid so," Larson said. "If we don't flush
them from the ventilation shafts pretty soon, I'll
take a force down into the lower tunnels with motion and heat sensors. These ventilation shafts all
empty directly into the tunnels below, so they
won't be able to hide for long."

The Professor studied the map of ventilation
tunnels for a moment, then said, "A good plan.
Check with me before you start the operation in
the tunnels."

"Yes, sir."

"Now," the Professor asked. He'd been looking
forward to this next question. "Show me what
happened to our friendly Marines?"

Again Larson's fingers tapped over the control
board beside the Professor and the center four
screens changed to a map of the main level of the
alien sector.

"Looks like the aliens took the first group of
them here." Larson indicated the dots on the map
of the tracers in the helmets and on the armor.
"They haven't moved, so I assume they're dead."

The Professor shuddered. No! This couldn't be

happening. Larson could not really be this stupid. But he didn't say anything. He just waited for Larson to continue, the sinking feeling in his stomach growing by the second. It was a feeling that this was going to take a great deal more of his attention than he had hoped it would.

Larson punched another two keys and the map was replaced by another, two levels down. "They lost a few more here."

He brought up a third and a fourth map of the next levels down. "And the last ones here and here, including Green. Your plan worked, sir. They're all dead and accounted for."

The Professor stared at the map for a moment, then slowly swung around to face Larson. He couldn't believe what he had seen on those screens or the stupidity of his second in command. This total incompetence was going to drive him crazy. As soon as this entire event was calmed down and Cray recovered and killed, he would find a replacement for Larson. The man was just too stupid to let live.

"Nice job, sir," Larson said, still looking up at the screen. Then he looked down at his boss and his eyes widened.

The Professor smiled at the sudden look of fear flashing in Larson's eyes. He enjoyed that look in the people around him. He could trust people who feared him.

"How long has it been since those bodies were supposedly killed?"

Larson glanced nervously up at the screen, still not understanding what the Professor was talking about. That was the problem with Larson. He just hadn't spent enough time with the aliens. The Professor would soon fix that. Very soon.

"About three hours," Larson said.

"And, Mr. Larson, in your limited knowledge of the aliens, what do they do with humans they capture? Why are we always giving them live humans?"

Larson swallowed and kept his gaze locked on the board. "They, uh . . . they implant them and hang them on the wall in the chambers around the queen?"

"Very good," the Professor said in his best schoolteacher voice. "And do they ever just hang them any old place, such as where they find them?"

"No, they usually—" Larson turned suddenly white as he realized his mistake. "The Marines spotted the tracers and dumped them?"

"Now you've got it." The Professor applauded and Larson's face turned even whiter. "But one more question. If you were Sergeant Green, unarmed and stranded on that side of the alien sector, how would you try to escape? Now granted, I'm not saying you're as smart as Green, but just this once try to think like him."

Larson looked at the screens full of maps for a moment, then reached over and punched up a cross section of the alien section. There were at least ten levels of tunnels below the sealed-off alien section. "I'd try to get down into there," Larson said. Then he looked at the Professor, a real look of panic now crossing his face. "The explosions? You think they made it through?"

The Professor nodded, staring back at the cross section of the alien sector. "I'd say, Mr. Larson, that you might want to prepare your men for a Marine invasion."

Then the Professor laughed. "And if I know Sergeant Green, he's going to be as mad as that rogue I have in the other room."

13

It took Joyce, Deegan, and Cray a full hour from leaving Deegan's room to make the arranged meeting place six levels below the human section. They had been forced by Larson's goons to double back twice and at one point had climbed three levels up to go over a guard station.

Now Joyce was leading, light gripped in her teeth as she climbed down a narrow stone shaft. The ladder hadn't been used by anyone in years and the dust on the steps was making it slippery.

She could feel her fingers growing tender from all the climbing and scraping on the stone and she had long since lost the feeling in her feet from the cold. She had thought about stopping in her room to grab some heavier clothes, but then figured the risk just wasn't worth it. She'd go down into the cold again, but it wouldn't be that long until they were back up in the human levels fighting. She figured she could stand the cold for that long.

But now she was beginning to regret that decision.

She reached the seventh level down and stepped aside, waiting for Cray and Deegan to make their way down the shaft and join her. While she waited she flashed her light around the intersection of the vertical shaft and two horizontal shafts. She could go six directions from here into pitch-blackness and for some reason that made her feel safe. At least safe from the Professor's guards.

She glanced around at the dust on the floor, noting that a large number of men wearing boots had come this way at one point from the direction of the alien section. She flashed the light in the direction of where they were supposed to meet the others. No tracks at all in the dust. They would be making the first. That was both good and bad.

She let her light trail along the other tracks as Cray joined her and noticed what she was doing.

"Looks like a type of combat boot," Cray said, kneeling down and looking closely at one clear print.

"Larson's goons?" Joyce said.

Cray shook his head slowly. "I don't think so. They almost always wear a sneaker-type shoe that matches their green pants. Remember?"

Now that he mentioned it, she did. Sometimes they squeaked when they walked. She glanced down at the trail in the gray dust. "Then who?"

Cray shrugged. "Some of the Marines, maybe?"

"That can't be, unless they're old tracks."

"They don't look that old to me," Cray said and stood. "Of course, down here it might be hard to tell. They went down there." He pointed at the continuation of the shaft they had just climbed down. From her rough map it went down at least another four levels, maybe more.

"But the Marines are all dead," Joyce said, "Unless ..."

"Dead?" both Deegan and Cray said almost simultaneously. Deegan jumped off the last step in the rock and joined them. "How can an entire platoon of Marines be dead?"

"I'm afraid it's very possible," Joyce said. "From what I heard the Professor promised to send them home, then landed their shuttle on the far side of the alien section."

"Maybe they fought their way free," Deegan said. "Marines are real good at that sort of thing."

"That they are," Joyce said. "When they have ammunition."

"And they didn't?" Deegan asked.

"That's right. They didn't." Her breath was making a swirling crystal pattern in the lamplight between them. "At least that's what Hank told me."

She glanced down the dark tunnel in the direction the tracks came from, then down the hole. What should they do? If it was the Marines, they would be a great help against the Professor. But if it wasn't, she could be walking into some sort of trap. And they were already late getting to the agreed meeting point.

She turned to Cray and Deegan. "I think we

need to get to the meeting, then maybe come back and follow those tracks."

Cray nodded. "Sounds logical."

"That it does, boss," Deegan said. "Lead the way."

With her rifle cradled in one arm and the light in the other, she headed off through the black tunnel at a quick pace. Her sneakers kicked up a fine spray of dust. This was the right decision. She knew it. But she was in a hurry to get back.

She tried to keep up a good pace to keep herself warm and she could hear Deegan panting behind her.

Three intersections later the tunnel made a sharp turn to the left and suddenly widened. A lantern held back some of the dark in the center of the large area and Joyce could see that three other tunnels came in from the left and two from the right like spokes off a lopsided hub. It was like the long room's walls had been decorated with rock and black holes. A very odd look the way the lantern was sitting in the center.

Crouched with their backs to the walls and rifles ready were Kent and two others, their guns trained on them.

"Hold your fire," Joyce said, quickly raising her hand and pointing her light into her own face so that they could see her. The three guns lowered and ten other men and two women with rifles stepped out of the black holes of nearby tunnels.

Kent smiled. "Glad you could make it."

"Two new recruits," Joyce said, and then quickly did the introductions for Cray and Deegan.

The others introduced themselves around the

circle and then Kent said, "Not all are back yet, I'm afraid."

"Hank? Jonathan?"

Kent shook his head. "I heard some shots up a few levels from where I was earlier, but I don't know who it was or what happened."

"Let's give them all some more time," Joyce said. She swallowed the thought that Hank might have been captured or killed. She wouldn't think about that. "With Larson's goons in some of the ventilation shafts, they might have had to circle a long way around to get here."

Kent nodded and pointed to three of the men who came out of the tunnels. "Might want to go back on guard duty."

They nodded and started to turn when Joyce said, "Hang on just a second. There might be something we need to do and I want everyone involved in the decision."

They all stopped, waiting for her, so she went on. "We saw a large number of tracks in the dust back about three hundred meters. It might be some of the Marines who survived being dumped into the alien sector."

"Really?" Kent asked, his voice clearly excited.

Another man said, "Would that be possible? Amazing."

Joyce glanced around and could tell they were all excited at the thought. There was no doubt the Marines would be on their side in the upcoming fight.

"The tracks looked like Marine boots," Cray said. "No telling how old the footprints are, but it should be pretty easy to track them to find out."

"Which," Joyce said, "if you all agree, is what I propose to do."

"God, yes," Kent said. He glanced around. "Anyone have objections in trying to find the Marines, if there are any of them still alive."

Seeing no objections, he turned back to Joyce. "What's your idea?"

Joyce pointed to Cray and Deegan. "The three of us head back and follow the tracks for an hour or so. If we have no luck we'll come back here within two hours."

"We'll wait," Kent said. He turned and pointed to a large crack in the stone abovehead high on one wall. "If we're not here, I'll leave you a note in that crack."

"Sounds good," Joyce said. "You two want to join me?" She turned to Cray and Deegan and both nodded.

"Anywhere you go, boss, I'm with you."

"There's no need, Captain Palmer." The voice was deep, solid, and seemed to fill in the room with a sound of command.

Everyone in the room dropped instantly to their stomachs on the floor in a wide circle, guns ready, pointing outward at the tunnels around them. Joyce could feel the sweat on her hands suddenly as she clicked the rifle to automatic fire and focused on the black hole in the wall. One leg was slightly draped over Cray's and it felt good there, like he would anchor her.

"We'll come to you," the voice said. "Don't fire."

Out of the shadows of the tunnel directly in front of Joyce stepped Sergeant Green, his hands in the air and a huge smile on his face. He had a bandage on his arm and was so covered with dirt and dust that he seemed gray.

A moment later, from every tunnel leading into the room, a Marine stepped forward into the light.

Joyce didn't know whether to shout for joy or be angry as hell that they had so easily been surrounded.

So instead she put her forehead down on the cold stone floor and said, under her breath, "Thank you. Thank you."

14

The Professor watched as Grace held her hand against the side of her head and seemed to listen into the distance. She kept shaking her head as if she didn't understand, but was close to catching whatever she was listening to. The Professor knew exactly what she was hearing. It was his rogue talking with the queen, probably challenging her. He knew the aliens communicated in some fashion, but he hadn't spent much time working on it. Now the secret had been handed to him, and that alone would make him famous.

"The signals still going on?" he asked without turning around. His feet were up on a computer console and his chair was tipped back, his hands behind his head. He felt as if the world were his for the taking. After so many failures, success had such a sweet taste.

"Yes, sir," Grace said, turning to him without taking her hand away from her ear. The signals seemed to be gaining in intensity and frequency.

The Professor jumped to his feet and strode up to the window. With a few quick key strokes he brought up the lights in the rogue's chamber to their highest intensity.

The room was a total disaster. The dismembered arms and legs, the torn and bitten bodies of the other ten male aliens, littered the room. Alien blood had been sprayed everywhere and now it ate into the walls and doors, leaving brown, smoking stains. The rogue's huge tail was thrashing back and forth, scattering body parts like so many leaves on a windy day. The crashes of the impacts sometimes shook the outer lab.

The Professor turned back to Joyce. "He's very agitated. Far more than I have ever seen him or any other male."

"It's stopped," Grace said suddenly. "It was very intense at the end on both sides, almost like two humans screaming at each other."

The Professor turned back to the window as the rogue moved suddenly. Now it seemed to have a very clear purpose. It toured the room once, quickly, crushing dead aliens' bodies and limbs under its feet.

Then it stopped in front of the window, studying the window and the room beyond for a moment. Then with a quick and very calculated move it twisted around hard, smashing its tail against

the window. A spiderweb of cracks spread out
from the point of impact.

"Grace! Look at that power, will you? A Marine
subsonic cannon at point-blank range couldn't
crack that glass. Amazing."

He turned to face her. "I think what you were
hearing must have been a challenge from the
queen."

She looked at him with a blank look and he realized he wasn't going to be able to share his joy
with her. She just wouldn't understand how important this was. She never could understand because she didn't have feelings. With a wave of his
hand he turned to watch his greatest creation in
its finest moment.

He stood a few meters in front of the glass, applauding, cheering, as the rogue's tail again hit the
window, sending a few splinters scattering around
the lab.

The glass was now a mass of webbed cracks.
The rogue tipped its head slightly, looking at it, then
charged straight forward at the Professor, its head
lowered like a bull.

Grace was android-quick. She caught the Professor in a full dive and they both tumbled out of
the way as the huge alien crashed through what
had been an unbreakable shield a few moments
before.

The Professor could feel Grace's hard, artificial
body twist to protect him as he fell, but he still
banged his elbow and knee hard on the tile, sending waves of pain through him.

With nothing more than a quick look at the Professor and Grace as they scrambled to their feet

behind a computer monitor, the rogue turned and headed for the alien sector.

Pausing only for a second, it ripped a hole in the block and stone wall between the lab and the corridor like it was so much tissue.

It stepped through the dust and rock, smashing blocks to sand under its weight. It stopped, slightly bent over under the lower ceiling of the corridor, then turned to the right and disappeared.

The Professor knew it was going for the queen.

Grace scrambled for the communications panel and hit two quick keys. "Red Alert! We have a bio-hazard breach in—"

"No!" the Professor yelled. "Cancel that order. Now!"

"But, Professor . . ."

Kleist looked at her directly and with his harshest voice said, "I don't want him so much as scratched. If he is, I will hold you responsible. Understand?"

He looked over at the hole in the wall where the rogue had gone. The dust was still settling from the air. His creation was so amazing, so wonderful, no one could harm it. No one would dare.

He turned back to squarely face Grace. "Now cancel that order and relay what I just said. I know where he's going and I want him in one piece when he gets there."

Then very calmly for a man who had almost been killed, he headed for his office. He knew where the rogue was going. He'd be there, in person, to watch the victory and cheer for his baby.

15

For almost two hours Hank had been curled up inside a small side ventilation duct.

He'd been heading for one of the small chemical labs to talk to his friend named Steve when he heard two of Larson's goons coming directly at him in the narrow ventilation tunnel. He'd ducked into the small side shaft that opened out through a screen knee high into one of the main corridors outside the labs.

Larson's two men had decided that this part of the ventilation system would be a good place to set up an ambush, so one had hidden in a side tunnel ten meters down and across the shaft from where Hank lay. The other had gone past Hank, taking up a hidden spot five meters in the other direction.

Hank couldn't come out of the narrow vent he had crawled into fast enough to get a clear shot at the one on the right, and if he even tried coming out of the vent, the one on the left would hear him and have a clear shot at his back. Hank would be lucky to get to his knees before having his body cut in half by a burst from a Kramer. It was a prospect he didn't relish. So at least until the changing of the guard, he was surrounded and trapped.

For two hours he had lain on the cold stone of the duct and waited, doing his best to move his arms and legs slowly, to keep them as loose as possible without making enough noise to attract the guards. He ached in more places than he thought possible, but every time he thought about that he reminded himself he was still alive. That thought always made the aches back off a little.

He had also managed to turn around so that he was facing toward the grate covering the main corridor and over the two hours he had silently managed to take off all but one of the bolts holding the grate in place. If they did spot him he could be through the grate and into the main corridor faster than they could crawl through the small vent. At that point he'd be in the open, but he'd take his chances there rather than a gunfight with two men in a very narrow stone tunnel.

A huge crash from the direction of the lab across the main corridor surprised Hank and he banged his head against the stone ceiling. He cursed under his breath, but didn't take his eyes off the lab door. Three of Larson's guards came running down the corridor to Hank's right.

"What the hell was that?" one of the men said from the ventilation shaft behind Hank.

"It came from the Professor's private lab," the other said.

Hank was straining to see if the two men were coming his direction when right on top of him the world exploded. The entire wall of the lab across the corridor flew outward in a huge cloud of dust and flying rock, instantly crushing the three guards near it.

Hank covered his head just in time to keep from getting a face full of dust through the grate as one big rock bounced off the wall right above the opening of his vent. A few small pieces of rock dropped on him from the ceiling of the shaft, but luckily nothing big enough to pin him down.

Then, through the dust beyond the grate, Hank saw a nightmare appear.

His worst nightmare.

Any human's worst nightmare.

Ducking to fit into the ten-meter-tall corridor, a huge alien emerged from the hole in the wall of the lab and stopped directly in front of Hank's vent. The skeletal bones of its monstrous tail towered above him and Hank could barely make out through the dust the head and upper arms near the ceiling.

Aliens couldn't get that big, it wasn't possible. He'd read that somewhere.

Yet he was looking at one.

The alien swung its head to the right, then back to the left, as if getting its bearing. Then with steps that shook the stone around Hank, the alien went left.

Toward the alien section.

"Red Alert!" Hank heard Grace's voice over the base speaker systems. "We have a bio-hazard breach in . . ."

"Cancel that order!" Hank heard the Professor shout over Grace's voice. "I don't want him so much as scratched."

The public-address system clicked off.

"Holy shit!" one of the men in the ventilation system behind Hank said. "Let's get back."

The sound of their steps running off to the right was covered quickly by the distant sounds of the huge alien tearing at walls and doors as it fought its way through a human base built for beings one-tenth its size.

Down the corridor a few shots rang out and two people screamed.

"Damn good plan, guys," Hank said to the re-treating guards as he quickly scooted away from the grate and the destruction beyond in the main corridor.

Even with his muscles stiff from lying on the cold stone for two hours, he started off at a run. At the first cross shaft he went down, taking the stone ladder as quickly as he could. He was very late for the meeting, but he hoped they had waited. This was news they would want to hear.

He hit the seventh level down and took off at a run toward the agreed meeting spot.

He didn't stop running until a Marine twenty meters from his destination stopped him cold in his tracks.

*   *   *

Joyce couldn't remember a sight making her so happy before. When those nineteen Marines came out of the shadows of the tunnels, she, for the first time since she was captured, let herself think about living through this and maybe getting back to Earth again to see her kids. She knew of Sergeant Green and knew how well trained the Marines were in fighting bugs. And since the Professor was a human bug that needed squashing, who better to do it?

She had climbed to her feet and greeted the Marines like the heroes they were, same as the rest of the rebels. After only a few seconds of cheering, Green had quickly pointed to three of his men and sent them back on guard duty down three of the five separate tunnels.

Then Green had asked for quiet and said, "We have a problem." He pointed after one of the guards. "Those three men are the only ones with live ammunition and that's because we ambushed three of Larson's men two levels down an hour ago. Anyone know where we might get some bullets?"

Joyce had been the first one to break the stunned silence with a hearty laugh. The others joined in and after a moment she moved up beside Sergeant Green and said, "It would be our pleasure to help."

Sergeant Green actually bowed in thanks and for doing that got a rounding cheer and applause from everyone.

She, Kent, Green, Robinsen, and Young all gathered against one wall. Joyce sat with her hands tucked in the bands of her pants hoping against hope to keep them warm as all their breaths froze into crystal cloud.

Other groups formed around the room with so many lanterns working that the high-ceiling stone corridor almost took on a comfortable feel.

They had just started talking about where to attack first and where to get more weapons and ammunition when, from the black mouth of one tunnel, Hank emerged, his hands in the air and a Marine right behind him.

Joyce felt her stomach ease another notch.

"Hank," she said as she rose from where she had been sitting and ran toward him. A few others, including Kent, surrounded him as she gave him a large hug that felt damn good. Then she stepped back and looked at him. His face was red and he seemed out of breath.

Green nodded to the Marine behind Hank who turned and disappeared back into the tunnel.

"You all right?" Joyce asked.

Hank nodded and moved over to the wall where he dropped down on the floor with his back against the stone. He took a few shuddering breaths, then looked up at Joyce and Sergeant Green.

"Just been running. And that Marine gave me a start, let me tell you. A good one, though." He laughed, then tried to take another few deep breaths.

Suddenly he seemed very serious. He looked first at Joyce who knelt beside him, then at Sergeant Green. "Did you hear the Red Alert a few minutes ago?"

"No," Joyce said.

"Red Alert?" Green asked, his voice almost choking.

Joyce glanced up at him. He had suddenly gone pale and he wasn't taking his eyes off of Hank.

"Red Alert, I'm afraid," Hank said. "A huge alien, obviously one of the Professor's experiments, broke down a wall from the lab and disappeared in the direction of the alien sector."

"Broke down a wall?" Green said. "How big was this bug?"

Hank shrugged. "Big. How tall is the corridor outside the main labs? Ten, maybe fifteen meters?"

Green nodded. "About that."

"The damn thing had to duck in there. Trust me, he tore a rock and concrete wall down like it was paper."

"Holy shit!" one of the Marines said behind Green.

Green kept staring directly at Hank. "And you say it was heading toward the alien sector? Did it seem like it knew what it was doing?"

"Now you have to understand, I was looking up at this thing through clouds of dust from a floor vent with two of Larson's goons in the shaft behind me, but I'd say it did."

Joyce turned to Green. "What does this mean? You've fought bugs before? Do they get that big?"

Green nodded. "Yeah, the queens do. But I can't imagine how the Professor had a queen trapped in his lab."

"It's a male," Hank said and again all eyes turned to him.

"Let's hope to God that's not possible," Green said.

"Well, when the Professor countermanded Grace's orders, I heard him say over the speakers that he didn't want *him* hurt. Clear as a bell."

"An alien's loose and he countermanded the orders? I don't—"

"It's a male all right," a voice said from behind the main group around Hank. Everyone turned and Joyce could see Cray, his face a pasty white in the lamplight. He seemed to be breathing fast and shallow and he was sweating even in the intense cold of the stone corridor.

"How do *you* know?" Green asked.

Cray took a deep, shuddering breath. "I was supposed to be its breakfast, but since the Professor had me strapped to a chair, it only looked me over. Real, real close." Clay opened his shirt and pointed to the huge red and scab-covered cut that ran across his chest. "It barely touched me with only one claw. It's as big as Hank was saying. Maybe bigger."

"And Kleist stopped the Red Alert?" Green shook his head. "That son of a bitch has totally lost it."

The silence in the tunnel echoed for a moment before Joyce turned to Green and asked, "Why did you want to know if it looked like it knew where it was heading?"

Green sighed. "Because if it really is that big, chances are the queen has called it. So the big male would head for the queen in the heart of the alien sector and it sure ain't going to use an airlock. Instead it's going to tear a hole all the way from the labs right into and through the side of the alien section. Those bugs are going to be everywhere in the human sector faster than Larson's goons can stop them."

Hank stood. "From the size of the hole in the lab, there won't be any plugging it ever. Actually, considering how long it took me to get down here, it's probably already open."

Green turned to Joyce. "I doubt the supplies we left in our old barracks are still there. We need weapons fast, the heavier the better."

"What about your guns?" Hank asked.

"Empty," Joyce said. "Except for the three on guard duty."

Hank glanced at Green, then unstrapped his rifle and ammunition belt and tossed it to Robinsen.

Green nodded to Robinsen and he took off at a quick pace down another tunnel to stand guard duty.

Joyce glanced at the rifle in her hands, then handed it to Green, who immediately tossed it to a private standing nearby and pointed to the other unguarded tunnel. "No heroics," he said.

"Now," Joyce said, facing Hank and Green. "We need a plan."

"And quick," Cray said, dropping down against the stone wall. "Trust me, you don't ever want to see that thing close-up."

Green laughed. "It's not the big male I'm worried about. It's the three hundred or so little ones that scare me."

Joyce shivered, and not just from the cold.

The screens on the Professor's wall showed the progress of the rogue as it tore its way toward the alien sector. The bodies of a blond-haired mother and her young daughter lay smashed against one wall on one screen, seemingly tossed aside like another small obstacle in the rogue's way.

The Professor watched for a moment, then, smiling and whistling, turned to finish putting on his armor. This was going to be the happiest day of his entire life. He had victory. His name would be listed with the great heroes of all time. He had solved the problems of the aliens.

Grace, already in her armor, scanned the station ahead of the rogue trying to warn people away with the address system. She was only partially successful.

The rogue was mostly through the human section and had now reached the corridor that ran along the extra thick barricade walls between the human and the alien sectors.

With a motion almost faster than the Professor could follow Grace focused every screen in the office on the areas up and down that hall and on the corridors and halls directly on the other side of the wall in the alien sector.

"They're massing, Professor," she said, pointing at the three screens that showed hundreds of alien males filling the corridors and walls and ceilings on the other side of the divide like a living coat of black paint.

"The queen sent them to defend her," he said, adjusting his microphone so it was against his mouth. Then he picked up the big Sound Cannon and cradled it under his arm. It felt good there, and he felt safer with it for some reason.

"I don't think so," Grace said. "They're not lining up in a defensive way. They seem to be mostly staying slightly back from the wall, out of the way, just waiting."

At that moment, on the human side, the rogue stopped, seeming to study a large airlock directly in front of it. Tilting its head from side to side it scanned the airlock. Then, in a mad and lightning-quick run, it darted forward, crashing headfirst into the airlock.

Stone shattered as the airlock was crushed outward, spinning down the corridor into the alien sector.

Thrashing like a wild beast the rogue proceeded to rip a huge hole in the rock and concrete barrier between the human sector and the alien side, sending up a huge storm of dust and rock.

In less than ten seconds the hole was a good twenty meters across and as high as the ceiling. A four-lane freeway could be built through that hole.

The Professor watched in total fascination as the massed aliens hesitated for a few moments, waiting for the rogue to get out of the way, then, as if on signal, they swarmed toward the new opening.

A few got in the way of the rogue and were crushed as it entered the alien section, acid blood splattering everywhere as if the rogue had stepped on a tomato. Without a glance back, it headed off into the depths toward the queen.

Ten of Larson's men were in the human corridor outside the breach as the aliens swarmed through, coming in on the floor, walls, and ceiling, faster than any human could follow. It was like ugly black water pouring from a huge spout. There was no stopping it.

A security-breach alarm screeched throughout

the station as the men fired at the aliens, then broke ranks and tried to retreat. Most didn't make it ten meters. The mass of aliens crushed them, ripping the men's arms and legs off, biting through their heads, smashing them flat like so much red waste.

"Who initiated the security alarm?" the Professor demanded.

Grace just shrugged.

"I won't have my authority countermanded by some gung-ho grunt! Put them all on report in that area."

Grace just looked at him for a moment as he stared at the monitors. Finally she said, "Professor, I must express my concern for your present mental state."

"Excuse me?" he asked without looking at her.

"Your manner seems somewhat irrational, sir. I am programmed to be concerned and to point such matters out to you. Remember?"

Kleist turned to Grace, smiling. "My dear, no matter how thoroughly you are programmed, you will never remotely understand how I feel at this moment."

He laughed and waved his arm at the monitors where the black stream of aliens was still pouring through the hole. "You think this is irrational? This is nothing more than war." He faced her. "What is important is that we shall soon witness the validation of all I believe. In this godless universe there is man and the alien. Only one can be the dominant species."

He turned back to the monitors and continued, "Don't you understand what the rogue means? No, I guess you don't, do you? Well, let me explain. You see, I have taken the brute clay of creation and reshaped it into a superior image. You must understand that point somewhat, being a creation of man yourself."

She said nothing so he went on.

"The rogue is our weapon. The alien empire will be destroyed at the hands of its own kind. The killing stroke? Bio-programming by human cunning and human intellect."

He raised his hands to the screens like they were an altar. "It begins here today."

Grace was silent for a moment, then she said in her normal voice, "We might want to proceed, sir."

He nodded, still staring at the monitors.

"We can go in from above," Grace said. "Considering the circumstances in the main areas, it might be a safer route."

He took his gaze off the monitors and the hundreds of aliens pouring into the human sector. The rogue was heading for the queen and she was sending her males at the same time against the humans who had imprisoned her. He laughed to himself. Never, ever underestimate the enemy, especially an alien queen.

But when his creation got through with her, there would be nothing left of this hive. Man may have a few casualties in this battle, but his creation was destined to win the war for humankind. And on that scale, what did a few meaningless lives matter?

He turned and headed for the door. "You're right, Grace. Quickly. I don't want to miss any of this. History is being made."

He smiled at her as she opened the hidden passageway and went through ahead of him.

16

Joyce glanced around at the group of very cold humans as Sergeant Green pulled the guards in from the tunnels and snapped a few orders. Nineteen Marines and twenty civilians with twenty-four rifles and two pistols among them. Not much of a force against over a hundred of Larson's goons plus the aliens. She was doubting that she would ever make it off this station alive. She just wished she could leave a message for her kids somewhere that it might be found. If she got the chance she would try to do just that.

In the quick meetings after Hank's arrival, they had decided that the best course of action was to get some real firepower, and the best way to do that was to break directly into Larson's armory. It was located on the main human level, so it wasn't going to be easy to get to, but it was possible.

They would have to assume that the alien sector had been opened and Larson's men were going to have their hands full trying to stop the bugs, so very few men would be on guard there. Actually, both Clay and Kent argued that they should be more worried about the aliens, but Green had convinced them first things first.

Hank had insisted that Larson would never expect the Marines to be alive in the first place and thus would think that the civilians would have no reason to attack the armory, so no men at all would be there. But Sergeant Green made a very clear point that when it came to the Professor and, to a lesser degree, Larson, they should never be underestimated. He had done just that and had ended up dumped in the far side of the alien sector.

Hank and Sergeant Green both knew the location of the armory, which turned out, much to Joyce's relief, to be on the opposite side of the human sector from the alien hive. Kent knew how to get them there through the lower-level tunnels and straight up a mostly blocked vertical shaft. He'd gone that way a few hours earlier and stumbled on the shaft by accident when looking for a way around a few of Larson's guards.

In the dust Kent drew them all a map to find what he described as an old elevator shaft that had totally been covered over when they built the human sector and the labs. He said the ladders in the shaft were mostly wood and fairly rotten, but if used carefully, they would hold enough for them to make the climb.

Sergeant Green made sure that Hank, Joyce, Cray, and his second in command, Robinsen, were all clear on the location of the opening of the abandoned elevator shaft, then assigned everyone into one of five groups with equal firepower and sent each off at top speed to meet as quickly as possible at the shaft.

Joyce found herself without a gun but in command of two Marines, Kent, and three other civilians. She was to take her group south for three tunnel intersections, a total of about two hundred meters. She was then to use that intersection's vertical shaft to go down three levels, then cross in a southeast direction under the human section to the elevator shaft.

Green's and the other two groups had just left leaving only hers and Hank's.

She reached out and gave Hank's hand a light squeeze.

"See you," he said, "in a few minutes."

She smiled. "Don't get lost." She wanted to say more, but didn't. She couldn't let worrying about him get in the way. It was like Danny and Jerry used to tell her during the war. If they made it, they made it. Worrying wasn't going to change a damned thing.

With one last quick smile at him, she turned and at a half run, with a light in her hand, led her group into her assigned tunnel. She stationed a blond-headed Marine named Private Rule to stay right near her with his rifle.

Another armed Marine named Warner she assigned to be last and guard their flank. Kent and the others were to stay in the middle and be damn quiet.

She was deep down tired from the day already, but the excitement of moving again with a real plan had the energy flowing through her system. She could barely hold her pace to a steady jog.

Being as silent as they could they made it through the first intersection and were approaching the second when the sound of shots echoed through the tunnels.

Joyce motioned for everyone to stop and they all listened. It seemed the shots had come from down at least a level and to the south. She turned to the Marine named Rule and pointed down at the vertical shaft in the intersection.

He nodded and she led the way to the shaft.

She was about to start down when Rule touched her shoulder and held up the gun. Then he indicated that he should go first and she agreed. With his rifle gripped in one hand, he quietly moved down the cut stone ladder. Joyce followed him closely until they reached the next level. No sign of any movement or even footprints in the dust, so she signaled for the others to join them.

More shots echoed through the tunnels as the last of her group were coming down. The shots seemed loud and very close. Joyce figured they were from one intersection over.

Another shot and a bullet bounced off stone and then scattered dust against a wall in a nearby tunnel.

She had everyone kill their lights and she let her eyes adjust in the pitch-black. Faintly, down the corridor to the right, she could see some sort of light.

She clicked her light on her own face, put her finger to her lips to indicate quiet, then pointed that Private Warner and one of the men should go down the right tunnel and swing around. She and Kent would go down the middle, directly at the light. The other two should circle around the other way led by Private Rule.

"Be careful you don't shoot one of our own," she whispered and they all nodded and silently split up.

Never had she felt so naked. Going into a firefight without a gun. That was stupid. A few steps into the tunnel she saw a rock the size of a grapefruit and picked it up. For some reason that made her feel better. A little stupid, but better.

Then a thought hit her that sent her blood rushing to her head. What would they do if the shots were being fired at aliens? What the hell was she going to do? Toss a rock at an alien? She forced the thought from her mind and focused ahead.

She clicked off her light again and with one hand resting lightly on Kent's arm moved toward the faint light around a shallow corner in the tunnel.

It seemed to take forever, but finally they had silently worked their way around the corner so they could at least see what was going on.

Ahead, crouched down behind a small pile of rocks from a shallow cave-in, were two of Larson's guards. They had their backs to Joyce and Kent and weren't firing at the moment, although both of their guns were poised on the rocks pointing down the tunnel in front of them. Their light had been tossed out in front of them and pointed where they were aiming.

Luckily for Joyce and Kent that at the moment no one was firing at the two. In this small space they were more likely to get hit by a ricochet from friendly fire than by shots from the two in front of them.

Joyce regripped the rock a few times, getting the feel of it in her hand. Then in the faint light she nodded to Kent who silently knelt and raised his rifle.

With as much force as she could she threw the rock overhand, imagining the two guys she aimed at were the two who had killed Jerry. She didn't realize she could throw that hard, or had that much anger inside her.

The rock seemed to take just a fraction of a second to cover the short distance. There wasn't even a slight arch in its trajectory as it flew, striking squarely into the back of the man closest to the wall. The thump was loud in the small tunnel as the rock bounced up and caught the guy a glancing blow in the back of the head. The force of the blow pitched him forward and face-first into the rocks in front of him. His head bounced and he turned blank-eyed to Joyce and Kent, blood streaming from his forehead as he slumped to a sitting position.

The other man, caught by surprise, took a moment to react to his bleeding partner, then he spun to fire.

Kent took him out with a single shot in the chest that sent him sprawling back over his buddy, blood spurting from his back like a pump-

ing fountain, staining the rocks and dusty floor a
dark black.

The single shot sounded huge in the small tunnel and Joyce covered her ears far, far too late.

"Sergeant? Hank?" Joyce shouted, her voice
sounding odd in her ringing ears. "Don't shoot."
She blinked her light twice in the signal they had
set up. "We got two of them here."

"Nice work," Sergeant Green said, a light appearing down the way. "I had my men working to
flank them too."

Joyce watched as the sergeant approached.

The guy she had hit wouldn't be moving for
some time to come. He wasn't dead, but he was
going to have one hell of a headache. She bent
over the guy she had knocked out and pulled his
rifle from his hands. She stripped him of his ammunition belt and slung it over her shoulder, then
emptied his pockets of six concussion grenades
and his flashlight.

The sergeant stood over the two for a moment
nodding. "Nice work. Two with one shot."

"A shot and a good right arm," Kent said. "She
should be pitching for the Yankees."

The sergeant, who was also unarmed, stripped
the other rifle from the bloody hands of the dead
man and checked to make sure it was ready to
fire. Then, without seeming to notice the blood at
all, took the guy's ammunition belt, grenades, and
light. Joyce smiled. Not only was the guy going to
wake up with a headache and a dead partner on
top of him, but in pitch-blackness and with no
light. A true hell. Served the guy right.

As Sergeant Green stood he slapped the stock
of the gun and smiled. "Feels much better."

Joyce had to agree. Having that gun in her hands did feel much better.

Much better indeed.

Sergeant Green's and Joyce's groups were the last to arrive at the old elevator shaft. Hank and Cray already had their groups climbing carefully up the old ladder and Sergeant Green went next, moving quickly and surely up the wooden ladder.

Joyce waited until there were only three Marines left before she strapped the rifle over her shoulder and started up.

The space was about four meters square and looked to have been some sort of freight elevator. Lights from the first people up had been left every ten meters, giving the place a weird glow.

At first she had imagined aliens swarming down the shaft at her, but again she forced the thought out of her mind. If that happened, she and all the others were dead. No point in thinking about it. But the chill remained with her for the next few minutes, even though her hands were already so cold she could barely feel them.

A dozen cables hung down the center of the elevator shaft and the wooden ladder was secured on old wooden beams up one side. Every few meters a horizontal beam gave the climber a larger step and Joyce took advantage of each of those beams. The wood of the ladder felt dry and very old, scraping her hands in the same places that they were already sore from climbing in the tunnels and vents.

At one point she had to stop and clear out a

splinter. But the entire way up, as Green had suggested, she kept her hands and feet away from the centers of the boards and never let her weight rest on only one spot at once.

She seemed to climb forever in the faint light, focusing only on her foot- and handholds, going slow to save what little energy she had left. Finally, when it seemed like the climb would become her lifetime hell, a friendly hand reached in from above and helped her through.

"You all right?" Hank whispered as he pulled her away from the elevator shaft and over against a wall so she'd have something to lean against while she caught her breath.

She took a quick glance around. No sign of Sergeant Green and Robinsen, but the rest seemed to be in a tunnel that had been blocked off when the human section was built.

"Tired, but alive," she said. "You?"

"About the same." His smile was like a shot of energy. She'd been lucky meeting this guy. Danny had been dead for years. Now Jerry was gone, too. If both of them got out of this alive, maybe it was time for her to get on with living and family. Maybe the kids could handle a new dad. Maybe they could get used to a mother around, once in a while, too. The way he looked at her, she had a sneaking hunch she might just be able to talk him into it.

She squeezed Hank's hand. Then nodding at the wall to the human sector, she asked, "What's happening?"

"Sarge and Kent are scouting the armory, seeing what kind of . . ."

Sarge ducked his head through a small open vent. "Let's move. Quick, through here."

Joyce slipped the rifle off her shoulder and followed Hank through the vent and into the well-lit and much warmer corridor. After spending so much time in the dark tunnels and ventilation shafts, standing again in the bright lights and carpeted corridor felt odd, exposed, almost naked. And very, very dirty. She immediately wanted to dust off her pants and vest, but refrained.

Green motioned that they should follow him and at a run they swarmed down the empty corridor to where Robinsen crouched behind a corner.

"Two of Larson's goons," he whispered. "Twenty meters. One standing on each side of the door to the armory. They look nervous, but I don't think they're worrying about us. They keep looking off toward the alien section to their right."

Green nodded and patted Robinsen on the shoulder. "You take the one on the right," he whispered. "I got the left. The rest of you be ready to run for the door when we do. There might be more inside, but we won't know that until we get there."

Robinsen nodded and clicked his rifle to single shot.

Joyce glanced down at hers, making sure it was set on fully automatic and the clip was full. She'd checked it three times already since taking it from the guard, but a fourth time never hurt.

Green and Robinsen were right beside the corner. "On two," Green whispered. "One."

"Two."

They both stepped calmly forward into the

corridor, swung, and took aim as if this were a practiced move and they were only shooting at ducks in a carnival booth.

They shot almost simultaneously, the concussion pounding Joyce's head and starting the ringing in her ears again.

Then both men started at a full run down the corridor toward the door of the armory as if the shots had been a starter's gun at a track meet. Joyce was around the corner two steps behind Green with Hank at her side. Behind her she could hear the pounding steps of the others.

Larson's two guards were clearly dead. One had been slammed against the wall with the force of the shot and had left a red smear down the stone face. The other had twisted sideways and lay in a heap in front of the door, a hole the size of a baseball blown through the back of his bloodstained jacket.

The door to the armory was locked but Robinsen made short work of it with a blast from his Kramer as two Marines scampered down the corridor toward the alien section to stand guard. Two others took up locations at the corner they had just come from. The more Joyce watched Green and his men work as a smoothly running machine, the more impressed she was. And damn glad to be on their side.

The armory was a large gymnasiumlike room with two armored tanks sitting in the very center. "Holy shit!" Green said after checking to make sure no guards were in the room.

Shelves and racks of guns, ammunition, grenades, and other such devices filled the walls and lined the center of the room around the tanks like shelves in a library. Joyce knew what a lot of the weapons were at first glance and had seen pictures of some of the others. But it was clear there was enough firepower in this one room to stage a pretty good-sized war.

"Everyone keep your eyes open for the Sound Cannons," Green ordered. "We might need them more than anything. Robinsen, take five men and get as many ammunition belts as you can carry. Run them back to the elevator shaft area."

Sergeant Green barked one quick order after another.

Joyce stood to his right with Hank, marveling at how organized the sergeant was and how quickly he made decision after decision. Finally he turned to them. "There's more ammunition over there. You also might want to grab a few pistols and stock your pockets with concussion grenades. As many as you can comfortably carry without slowing you down. Speed may turn out to be your most important weapon."

She nodded and as one she and Hank moved to the shelves the sergeant indicated. She took two more ammunition belts, their heavy weight a comfort over her shoulders. She already had six of the small apple-sized grenades in her vest and pants pockets, but she managed four more and a small black pistol with a fifteen-round clip fit perfectly down the back of her pants, held secure by her belt.

Then, at a run and carrying three extra belts each, she and Hank scrambled out of the door and back down the hall toward the abandoned elevator shaft.

It seemed like the entire raid had taken forever,

but in reality from the first shot to ducking through the vent into the dark and cold of the tunnels, less than two minutes had expired.

Now they were armed. What next?

Find the Professor or the aliens?

Or just make a run for the ships.

So many ways to die, so few ways to live.

When the base was first being converted, the Professor had constructed three private tunnels known only to himself, Larson, and Grace. The three tunnels led from a hidden door in his inner office to the hangar deck, the center of the alien section, and the private lab. They were completely sealed and secure tunnels and at the moment the Professor was thanking himself for thinking ahead on this one thing.

He and Grace had ducked into the tunnels and had taken the right branch into the alien sector at a full jog, with Grace in front. Both were in full protective armor and Grace carried a Kramer, three belts of ammunition, and a motion detector. He put his trust in the Sound Cannon in his hand. Why kill an alien when you can just stop it in its tracks?

They reached the edge of the tunnel and Grace quickly scanned the area beyond the door with the motion detector. "Nothing," she said.

The Professor nodded and unsealed it, moving out onto a balcony that overlooked a huge room near the center of the alien sector.

"Still nothing," Grace said as they peered over the railing. The alien smell was intense, filling the Professor's nose and making it hard to breathe.

Under his boots he could feel the slime of the hive that had dripped off the ceiling and walls and ran across the floor.

"Nothing moving at all down here," Grace said. "No traces."

The Professor scanned the large room, then pointed at a large arch on the far wall. "Through there is the queen." He led the way to a stone ladder and they made their way down and across the room, moving as slowly and silently as they possibly could.

When they reached the archway he turned and glanced around again. "Fascinating. I at least expected there to be an inner cadre left behind to protect the queen."

"There was," Grace said. "This looks like what's left of them." She pointed through the arch toward the queen's inner chamber.

Thirty meters down the corridor were two bodies of large male aliens. The Professor moved quickly toward them. It looked as if they had been simply torn limb from limb. Their acid blood was dripping off the walls and pooling on the floor and he stepped carefully around it.

"I think you're right." He moved to study one body at close range. "See the different cranial configuration, the oversize mandibles? This was the queen's elite, her praetorian guard."

"Professor, over here. I have a trace."

Kleist spun away from the body. Grace was holding the sensor and facing down the corridor toward the queen's chamber.

"Is it the rogue?"

Grace shook her head in confusion. "I don't know. It might be. It's a large signal, but the form keeps shifting. I can't seem to get a lock on it. I can't explain it."

The Professor started toward the queen's chamber at a run, with Grace right behind him. He knew exactly what Grace was seeing, but he didn't want to take the time at the moment to explain it to her. Instead he would just show her.

The corridor suddenly widened into a huge chamber full of dripping slime formations and mounds of royal jelly, the new gold of mankind. The Professor halted just inside the queen's chamber, his gun lowered.

"Some things, Grace," he said, pointing, "need no explanation. Isn't this wonderful?"

Alien secretions had completely altered the shape of the room, creating a massive confusion of dripping forms from what had once been human balconies, railings, and ceilings. In clusters around the room were the ball-like egg sacks protected over by the queen and her guards. But now many of those sacks were destroyed, scattered or smashed in brown and gold stains.

Circling each other in the center of the room were the rogue and the queen. Both of an equal size, her maroon-colored skeletal frame and huge carapace contrasted with the metal black of the rogue. Massive amounts of saliva dripped from both their mouths and their second jaws extended and retracted like warning flags.

They circled each other, the queen somehow avoiding the egg sacks while the rogue smashed everything without notice. They weren't quite touching, but their front limbs were doing an intricate dance of position.

Suddenly Grace's hand went to the side of her

head. "They're screaming, Professor. Very intense, both of them."

"History is being made," Kleist said, and as if on cue, the rogue leapt, twisting its huge frame around the knocking the queen from her feet, biting hard on the back of the royal neck.

Grace held her weapon at the ready, but the Professor just watched, smiling.

He had no doubt who was going to win.

No doubt at all.

17

"**G**ather around," Sergeant Green said as the last of the men came through the grate. The narrow rock tunnel seemed almost warm with this many excited and sweating humans in it.

He waited until everyone was still, then said, "I figure we don't have much time until this entire base is overrun by the bugs. We got to round up every person we can, take care of some business, then get the hell out of here."

Joyce had never been so pleased to hear a sentence in her life. She wanted to applaud, and she could tell that many of the others around her felt the same.

"We're going to split up into three groups," the sergeant continued. "All with assignments."

He turned to face Joyce. "Captain, I want you to take all the civilians and make your way to the hangar deck. Get your ship and any other shuttle or transport parked there ready to fly."

He turned to the rest of the civilians. "How many of you can pilot a shuttle?"

Cray, Deegan, and Kent both indicated they could.

Green nodded, satisfied, then turned back to Joyce. "You and your people's job is to secure that hangar area and keep it secure for as long as you can. Understood?"

It was Joyce's turn to nod. She would have rather been going after the Professor and Larson, but she had a sneaking suspicion that special task was coming up for one of the Marine groups. In fact, she would bet just about anything that it would be Sergeant Green who would be taking care of it personally.

"If you can't hold the hangar area," Green continued, "get your asses into that ship and get the hell away from here. Don't wait for us, understand?"

Again she nodded.

"Good," the sergeant said. "The rest of us are going to be rounding up everyone we can and sending them your way. When you get a full ship, lift it. You all clear on that, also? Anyone have any questions?"

No one did, so he turned to Joyce. "Take as much ammunition as you can carry without slowing you down. And go slow."

She was about to start on the pile of ammunition belts when Sergeant Green said, "And one more thing."

He turned and looked at every civilian in the group. "Any of you fought bugs?"

Only Joyce and Cray nodded.

"A few basic words of advice. Aim for the head or knee joints. You hit one in the body and you'll spray acid blood in a ten- to fifteen-meter circle. They will come in above you more often than not and they move like lightning. Don't make a stand against them unless you have to. Hit and pull back, okay?"

He glanced around. "And pay attention to your nose. In an area like this you can smell the rotten bastards if they're nearby before you'll ever see them."

He hesitated, then looked right at Joyce. "One last thing. If a human is taken alive by an alien, they're better off dead than captured. Trust me on that one."

She knew that very clearly already. She'd seen more people, hung up alive in sacks with baby aliens growing inside them, than she ever wanted to remember. A person got like that and they were dead. The best thing another human could do was put them out of their misery real quick.

An uneasy silence filled the corridor. Finally Joyce said, "We'll be waiting for you on the hangar deck."

She hoped her voice sounded more confident than she felt.

Green nodded. "I know you will, Captain. That's why I gave you the job. Now get going. Me and the rest of the men here got some work to do."

Within thirty seconds Joyce had three belts of

ammunition over her shoulder, her Kramer cradled in her arms, and was leading nineteen other
civilians out the vent and to the right, down the
corridor, and away from the armory.

She only had one worry.

The hangar deck was on the other side of the
lab complex, and damn close to the alien section.

Too damn close.

Green watched the last of the civilians go
through the vent and down the corridor. Then he
faced his men, looking at Robinsen in particular.
He wished that Lynch were here, but Robinsen
was a good man. He'd do the job. He'd have to, or
not live to tell about it.

"Dillon. McPhillips. Young. Rule. And Bosewell.
You're with me." He looked at each man as he
called his name and each nodded. All five had
Kramers in their hands, four or five belts of ammunition wrapped around their chests, grenades,
pistols, knives, and God knows what else stuffed
into their pockets and belts.

He smiled slightly. If nothing else, they were going to make a mess of some things around this
good old base.

He turned to face his second in command. "The
rest of you are with Robinsen. Listen up, so he
doesn't have to repeat this."

Everyone took a step closer and Green went
on, talking directly to Robinsen. "I want you to
make a sweep through the living and recreational
areas of the base, rounding up and sending to the
hangar deck as many civilians as you can find."

"Will do, Sarge," Robinsen said.

"Use your best judgment on how to get the people to the ships. You might have to split up and send groups with guards, but I don't want any man striking out on his own. Stay in pairs. Is that understood?"

Again Robinsen, and every Marine behind him, nodded.

Green took a deep breath. "I figure we've got about an hour, maybe two if Captain Palmer and her crew can put up a good fight. So do the job and be back at the hangar deck in one hour. Kill any bug you see and terminate any human you see that's been taken by them."

Robinsen nodded. "Let's go, men. Hansen, take the point."

Green watched, satisfied, as Robinsen quickly had his twelve Marines through the vent and started to the left down the hall. Robinsen was the last through the vent and he hesitated for just a moment, glancing at Green. "See you in an hour," he said. "Then we're really heading home."

Green smiled. "You got it."

Robinsen smiled back. "Good hunting." Then he ducked through the vent and was gone.

Green took a deep breath and turned to face the five heavily armed men he had picked. "I guess you know what our mission is."

All five nodded and Green chuckled, smacking his Kramer to full automatic setting. "Then let's go get us some dog meat. Dillon, take the point and head right. Our first stop is Kleist's private office."

Green watched the men slap each other on the back, big smiles on their faces, and started for the vent opening with Dillon in the lead. The five Marines seemed excited, as if they had just hit the lottery and were going on the greatest trip ever.

Green dropped in behind Dillon. He had to admit, he was excited, too. It was payback time. The Professor and his damn bugs had been dishing it out to him and his men for three years.

Now it was their turn.

They were ready.

18

The corridors of Charon Base now felt very different to Joyce. Just a few days earlier she had walked this very hall with Hank, relaxed, arm-in-arm as they headed for her room. People had passed them, nodding hello, living their lives, going about their own business in what had seemed like a perfectly ordered world.

Now, less than two days later, she was again going down the same hall with Hank, only this time it was with eighteen other heavily armed people that she was in charge of. And they were all moving in single file, crouching, staying close to the walls, watching every grate and shadow carefully.

The hall was no longer a safe, warm place, and she was hoping like hell they could get out of it as fast as possible.

In the five minutes since they had left the Marines, they had heard some distant shooting, but otherwise there were no signs of people at all. The corridors had a deserted feel and she wondered where everyone was hiding.

They were approaching a major intersection, with a wide, carpeted hall leading off to her right and a smaller one branching to the left. If this had just been a regular day and she had been just ambling toward the flight deck to check on her ship, she would have gone right, walked about two hundred meters, then turned back to the right again after passing the long lab complex.

But today was different. She held up her hand for the column to stop and was relieved to see the two men at the end automatically set up to guard in the direction they had just come. They might not be as efficient as the Marines, but she believed they could take care of themselves just fine.

She turned to Hank and Kent and, keeping her voice low yet firm, asked, "Know of a good way from here?"

"Through the labs," Kent said. "By far the quickest and we don't spend much time out in the open."

"Didn't think you could get through that way," Hank said.

Kent gave a snort. "The Professor kept the door onto the flight deck shut off except for special deliveries or his own personal use. He made everyone else go around. His official reason was the decontamination chamber, of course."

"Through the labs, then," Joyce said. "Kent, you want to lead the way?"

He tapped his Kramer and smiled. "My pleasure." He quickly moved around her and with a quick look in both directions ducked around the corner and into the main hall.

Hank was right behind him and Joyce followed Hank. Behind her the rest stayed in line, almost matching them step for step.

The quick trip down the main corridor was uneventful as they stayed against the left wall and moved quickly in crouched positions as if they were running under low-hanging branches.

Kent pushed open a door labeled PRIVATE about a hundred paces down the hall. Carefully, gun at the ready, he checked in all directions, including above the door, and then went through indicating that they should follow.

They entered a large, airlock-style chamber, with places to hang clothes and supplies on both walls and a bench against the right. A window on the left opened into a small room where a guard would usually sit, but now was empty, the chair tipped over backward.

White lab coats were all that hung on the wall hooks now, with a few tossed carelessly on the bench like people were in a hurry to leave. Joyce wondered if that was a good sign, but she didn't say anything. If Kent thought this was the best and quickest way, she would let him lead. She had no better choices at the moment.

Kent did the same routine check beyond the inner door of the chamber and was through it just as fast. The white of the lab was almost blinding as she followed him down a white-tiled hall and around a corner into the main room. The shock of what she saw then brought her to a halt, her heart beating out of control in her chest.

This was the lab in the tape, the lab where Jerry's body had hung suspended in some sort of liquid until an alien had burst from his chest.

Twenty bodies still hung behind those huge windows, floating in a thick, clear liquid, tubes and wires holding them centered in place. Unlike in the tape, there were no lab techs watching the computers and monitors in front of the bodies. A few lights blinked, but otherwise the room was deserted except for the naked human bodies floating behind the glass.

"Jesus," Hank said, standing in front of one. "Isn't that Steven?"

The others gathered in front of the two huge walls in silence, as if they were standing in front of the gates of hell and looking in.

Joyce moved over and stood next to Hank, putting a hand gently on his shoulder. "A friend?" she asked.

He nodded. "Another controller, supposedly shipped home last month. He had a slightly deformed right hand which gave him a little trouble at times."

Hank pointed at the hand on the floating body in front of them. It had four natural-looking fingers, with another tiny, baby-looking finger in the position of the thumb. It would be a hard mark to miss. Obviously the Professor was getting to the point lately that he didn't care who knew he was lying about the bodies and how unlikely they were to be clones.

She glanced at the others. They had to get moving, yet they had to do something about this place. She couldn't leave it like this.

And she couldn't let those aliens inside those bodies hatch.

"Kent," she said, "which way out of here?"

He pointed to a white door near the far end of the left tank. "Leads through another bigger lab and then into the supply area. Beyond that is the hangar deck."

"Let's go, people," Joyce said.

One of the men down the line said, "We can't just leave them."

"We're not," Joyce said. She pulled a concussion grenade out of her pocket and tossed it a meter into the air so everyone could see. "About ten or so of these should do the trick, don't you think?"

Everyone cheered, and she motioned for Kent to lead the way into the next lab.

"Get everyone away from this area and save some room for me to come running. And watch your ass."

He nodded and waved for the people to follow him.

She held back Hank with a light touch. "Help me with this," she said. "Think you can throw five in quick succession?"

He had a grenade out of his pocket like a magician with a much-practiced trick. "Without a doubt."

"Sergeant Green told me these things have a

ten-second delay from pulling the pin to explosion. If we're both beside the door, you can toss five at the computers and monitors on the far wall. I'll toss five along the front of the glass and the monitors there. Ten of these babies should take out anything alive in this room."

"Without a doubt," Hank said. "Without a doubt."

They moved quickly over to the door as the last of the others went through.

Joyce stepped inside and quickly checked to make sure everyone was a safe distance away across the other white lab. Kent waved that they were ready.

"Let's do it," Joyce said, stepping back just inside the lab door and holding it open with her foot.

"On three.

"One."

"Two," Hank said.

"Three," they both said.

Joyce yanked the pin from the grenade in her hand and tossed it as hard as she could down the glass wall. She grabbed another grenade from her pocket, pulled the pin, and threw it.

One right after another, she pulled and threw. Paced, but as fast as she could.

Still, she was slightly slower than Hank, who managed a sixth right in front of the tank with his friend Steven in it just as she got her fifth away.

But she was through the door first.

She could feel his hand on her back shoving her forward at a dead run across the lab.

"The desk," Kent shouted. He pointed to an overturned desk he had fixed for a shield for them, then ducked behind a filing cabinet himself.

Joyce and Hank both went over the desk like two track stars and hit the slick tile floor on the other side sliding like two baseball players stealing second.

Then, on all fours they were scrambling back closer behind the desk when the first explosions ripped through the other lab. Dust and glass and splinters of wood exploded from the door they had come through seconds earlier like shot from the mouth of a cannon.

Joyce thought she could hear five, maybe six distinct explosions as the ground under them shook. Everything around them shook, some books and glassware crashed to the floor behind her.

She was about to stand when a very familiar odor hit her.

The smell of alien.

She spun around in time to see the black-shelled alien grab Cray from behind and pick him up like he weighed nothing at all.

Cray had been one of the farthest into the lab and had been taking cover behind a large tank near the far side of the room. The alien had come off the top of the tank from somewhere near the ceiling just as the explosion hit.

The instant Cray realized what had him, he twisted, using his right boot to kick out hard against the alien in a fruitless attempt to break free of its sharp claws. And for a second Joyce thought he might make it. If he'd just been able to drop free for a second the alien would have been blown apart, but with it holding him, they didn't dare fire.

Cray's struggles failed. The bug had him solid with both hands, its claws cutting into Cray's arms and stomach as Cray fought to free himself.

Suddenly it reared up, lifting Cray even farther above the floor.

Before Joyce or anyone had time to react, the bug's interior mandible shot out from its saliva-dripping jaws, hitting Clay directly in the chest.

The back of Cray's shirt literally exploded, showering bright red blood over the white tile like a water balloon breaking on a sidewalk.

Kent, one of the closest to Cray, had his rifle aimed on the bug trying to get a clear shot when another alien dropped from behind him.

Three blasts from Kramers around Kent cut the air, pulping the new bug against the wall behind Kent and sending acid blood splattering in all directions.

Kent dove for cover under a desk and managed to escape most of it, with a few drops burning some holes in his pants and shoes.

It was clear to Joyce, however, that Cray was dead. The alien's jaws had hit his heart and probably destroyed his spine.

"Take it out," she shouted.

Five Kramers spoke at once, sending the alien's head and knees exploding like small bombs had been planted in it.

As the alien's body did a slow twist for the ground, still clutching the now obviously dead

Cray, Joyce shouted, "Watch your backs. Check the ceiling. Hank, cover me."

Everyone did as they were told as she took off toward the body of the alien and Cray. He looked dead, but she was going to make damn sure.

The alien's blood was eating ugly brown holes in the white tile and Cray was still held by the death grip of the claws. She got as close as she could, but there was no reaching him through all the acid.

Still, even from a five-meter distance she could tell he was dead. His blood had almost stopped pumping through the huge hole in his chest and back and his face had a look of terror glued on it. His eyes were wide open, staring off into his own personal hell.

"Joyce!" Hank screamed out. "Behind you!"

But his warning was too late. From the shadows below another tank, the alien rose up, grabbing her around the waist before she could even move. She could feel the cutting pinch of its claws as it lifted her and pulled her upward toward its mouth.

She twisted around, trying to bring the Kramer clutched in her hands to bear on its head, but the claws cut at her skin and she couldn't.

The only thought in her mind was, *I'm going to die.*

And I won't get to see my kids again.

The fight was going a little differently than the Professor had envisioned.

He and Grace had taken cover just inside a small archway leading into the queen's chamber as the rogue and the queen clawed at each other, their tails and feet smashing the bodies of her guards and the egg sacks around the floor. Golden royal jelly mixed with acid blood splashed the saliva-formed walls and twice the Professor and Grace's body armor had saved them from being burned by flying acid.

The rogue had seemed to have the upper hand at first and the Professor was sure his creation would soon defeat the queen. He had created something superior, far more powerful, far beyond the capabilities of anything nature could have created that he thought the fight would be over in seconds.

In the first contact the rogue had knocked the queen from her feet and had bitten through her lower shell, leaving an ugly wound. But instead of slowing her down the bite had enraged her even more and she had managed to push him off and regain her feet.

Now, except for a few swipes with their razor-sharp claws, they slowly circled each other, screaming at each other at a frequency that only Grace and other aliens could hear.

Ten full minutes now, and it still seemed to be a draw. But the Professor knew his creation would win.

Grace stood watching the battle, her feet spread, the Kramer in her hand always ready. The Professor sat on a stone near the tunnel opening into the chamber, never taking his eyes off the fight, the Sound Cannon beside him.

He was confident of the outcome. He had wagered everything he had, his entire life, on this fight. He knew he was right.

It was only a matter of time before the rogue proved it so.

19

The wall of monitors filled the office with pictures of horror beyond anything Sergeant Green had seen in his years of war. He had pushed Kleist's chair back out of the way and was standing behind the huge wooden desk staring at the screens.

McPhillips was working over the control board on the desk, switching pictures on the monitors as he quickly worked to figure the system out.

"Holy Christ," Dillon said as he too watched the monitors. "He could see every damn inch of this place."

"Makes you feel real clean, huh?" McPhillips said as he kept working.

Green was paying very little attention. His fo-

cus was on the screens and the terrible carnage
going on around the station. Bugs had totally
filled the area near the divide and Larson's men
looked like they had put up very little resistance.
A few bug bodies littered the huge hole in the barrier and a dozen bodies of Larson's goons lay scattered in the corridor on the human side, most of
them smashed or torn in half.

Now about thirty of Larson's men seemed to
have retreated into an area near the kitchens and
were holding off the bugs with pure firepower.
But Green knew they weren't going to last that
long in a pitched fight like that. The bugs always
seemed to have more bodies to throw at men than
men had ammunition to cut them down. Eventually the fight would turn to the bugs.

McPhillips glanced up at the screens focused
on the fight with Larson's men that Green was
watching. "Sarge, we aren't going to their rescue,
are we?"

Green glanced over at McPhillips and laughed.
"Are you kidding? See if you can locate Robinsen
and his men."

McPhillips smiled and went back to work on
the control panel. On the huge wall of monitors
scenes changed with only a flickering. One moment a monitor was filled with the terrorized
faces of a man and a woman huddled in a closet
in a small bedroom. The next was a scene of an
alien carrying a passed-out lab tech in a white
coat toward the alien section.

The west lounge kept flashing up from different
cameras as McPhillips worked. A large black male
alien was making a home behind the bar, spread-
ing saliva over the bottles, coating everything

from the bar stools to the plants with the slime he excreted. Draped over the corner booth was a tall black man with his head cut off.

Another monitor flickered, another scene.

A man fired at two aliens, blowing one apart, but missing the second. The guy's blood exploded over the camera as the alien ripped off his leg and bit through his chest.

"Jesus," Dillon said. "They're everywhere."

Green glanced around at Dillon, whose face was as white as he had ever seen it. The kid's eyes were huge and he seemed to be staring at the monitors. He was going to be no good if he didn't move soon.

"Dillon," Green said, his voice sharp enough to get through. "Relieve Bosewell on guard."

With another quick glance at the wall of monitors, Dillon nodded and left the room.

Green glanced back up at the wall and all the pictures that were making him as sick as Dillon looked. It was clear from this that he may have sent Robinsen and the rest of the men into a suicide mission. He just hoped Robinsen had enough sense to know when to retreat.

A scene of a young woman hiding alone with a pistol in her bathtub. Green hoped she had enough sense to use it on herself before any alien found her.

Another monitor flickered and Green found his attention drawn to two women armed with Kramers ducking down a side hall going in the direction of the hangar deck. They looked like they might make it, if they were lucky. Maybe Robinsen had sent them.

Another monitor flickered and Larson appeared, working frantically on a Sound Cannon.

"Hold it!" Green shouted to McPhillips and then pointed to the monitor showing Larson bent over the counter working. "Can you spot where he's at?"

"Just a sec." McPhillips studied the board, then glanced up at the monitor showing Larson. Then he laughed. "The son of a bitch is in a small private lab just behind this office. I doubt he even knows we're here."

"Is he alone in there?"

"We'd see anyone if there was. It's a small place. See what's in those tanks around him?"

Green looked beyond where Larson was working at the glass tanks on the shelves above him. It took him a moment, but then he realized what he was looking at. Tanks full of live face-huggers, stored right beside his office. The Professor was crazier than they thought.

"How do I get there?" Green asked, checking to make sure there was a full clip in his Kramer.

McPhillips studied the board for a moment, then a center screen flashed up a map. Both of them studied it, then McPhillips pointed to a metal door near the small kitchen in the back of the huge office. "Right through there."

Bosewell came through the big doors. "Rule and Dillon on guard." He glanced up and saw the wall of monitors and stopped cold. "Holy shit," he whispered under his breath.

"You want to watch some fun?" Green said. "Keep your eye on that third monitor from the top near the right corner." He pointed at the wall, then strode toward the door near the kitchen. He'd been wanting to do this for years and now it was finally here. His hands were shaking he was so excited.

"Sarge," McPhillips said from behind him as he reached the door. "You need backup?"

Green turned and smiled. "Nope. This guy is all mine. But you can watch the fun."

Green pulled the Kramer back under his arm and drew a small pistol out of his belt. He made sure the ten-shot clip was full. It was his favorite pistol and he was damn accurate with it. Unlike the Kramer, it would slow Larson down, but it wouldn't kill him.

And for what he had in mind for Larson, that was a good thing.

He took a deep breath and then looked back across the room at the monitor. Larson was bent over intently studying the works of the Sound Cannon.

McPhillips gave him a thumbs-up.

Green silently clicked the latch on the door, then yanked it open so hard it splintered some wood off the wall behind it.

With a quick step he was through and into the small storage area facing Larson's back.

Obviously startled, Larson reached for his Kramer lying beside him on the counter.

"Don't even think about it," Green said and Larson stopped, frozen.

"Face me with your hands up," Green said and Larson did as he was told, moving his hands away from the Kramer.

When he saw Green, he smiled. "So the Professor was right. You weren't dead."

"Too bad for you," Green said. He stared into the dark, black eyes of the man he had hated for so long. This man had killed so many of his men he had to be made to suffer. Killing him was just too easy.

"You're going to need the cannon," Larson said, pointing to the one he was working on. "Besides the one the Professor has, it's the only other big one on the base and it's broken from your last mission. Remember?"

Green didn't say a word and didn't change his expression. He would just let Larson talk for a moment.

"I think I can fix it," Larson said. "Just give me a little time and a promise to take me with you when I'm done."

Green smiled. "Trying to make a deal?"

Sweat was pouring off Larson's white forehead and his eyes were starting to glance back and forth, looking for any way out.

"Just trying to not get killed by you or the damn bugs."

"Oh," Green said softly. "I won't kill you."

The look on Larson's face was starting to lighten, as if he actually believed what Green had said.

Green lowered the aim of his pistol from Larson's chest to his right leg and shot.

Larson's scream echoed in the small room as he grabbed the hole in his upper thigh and fell to the ground. Blood flowed quickly into a small pool on the tile floor.

With another carefully aimed shot Green hit Larson in the other leg.

Larson screamed again.

"Hurts a bit?" Green said, smiling at Larson.

The sergeant moved around the man twisting on the floor and grabbed both his Kramer and the broken Sound Cannon. Holding them under one arm and keeping the pistol aimed at Larson, he moved back to the door and checked to make sure it would still latch solid. It would.

"Don't—don't kill me," Larson said, holding his bleeding legs and looking up at Green.

Again Green laughed. "You don't listen real well, do you. I said I wouldn't kill you."

"Then why'd you do this?"

Green shrugged. "I suppose because I've wanted to for years."

Larson looked at him, the hate boiling away the pain in the man's eyes.

Green stood in the open door staring down at the man he had hated only second to the Professor. At this moment, finally seeing Larson get his reward, he felt wonderful, like he was a kid again getting his first kiss. There was a twisting, excited feel in his stomach.

"You can't leave me like this," Larson said. "I won't stand a chance."

Green nodded. "I suppose that's true. All right. I won't leave you like this if you tell me where the Professor is."

Larson shook his head. "I don't know where he's at. He and that damned android of his got all suited up and disappeared. They were following that huge bug of his into the alien sector. I imagine he's dead by now."

"Now, now," Green said, pointing the gun at him again. "You wouldn't lie to me, would you?"

Larson, sweat pouring off his face, shook his head back and forth. "It's God's truth. He followed that damn monster of his. He was as crazy as a loony bird, I swear."

"Now that's the truth," Green said. "Thanks."

"I was just following his orders," Larson said, his eyes begging Green. "He killed all your men. Not me. I'll even help you find him if you want."

"You'd have a tough time walking, I'm afraid," Green said. He made a motion to close the door.

"Wait!" Larson screamed. "I thought we had a deal."

Green sighed. "I guess you're right. I did promise that if you told me where the Professor was, I wouldn't leave you like this."

Larson nodded, his eyes begging.

"And I suppose you did tell me the Professor's location, so you held up your end of the bargain."

"That's right. I did."

Green looked around at the tanks and then smiled. "Then I think it's only fair that I give you the same chance you gave my men."

With three quick shots he broke the glass on three of the face-hugger tanks, sending clear fluid cascading down over counters and onto the floor where it mixed into a pink swirling river with Larson's blood.

Green saw one of the face-huggers slip off the counter and start for Larson as he shut the door tight and locked it.

Beyond the door he heard Larson shout, "Oh, God! Noooooo!"

Green smiled as he turned back to his men who were both applauding like crazy.

He took a deep bow.

Then he looked at them and let the biggest smile he had ever remembered feeling cross his face. "God, that was fun!"

20

The alien's sharp claws were cutting at her chest and arms as it raised her from the floor like a child and held her in front of its ugly face.

This had to be a nightmare. This couldn't be real. She would wake up screaming at any moment. She wasn't about to die after all this time in the same way Danny had died.

This had been her nightmare more nights than she had ever wanted to count and now it was coming true.

God damn it all to hell! She wanted to see her children just one more time.

But that wasn't going to be possible.

She was going to die.

The teeth of the alien seemed only inches from her face. Saliva dripped from them as it slowly opened its mouth. She twisted back and forth, doing everything in her power to pull the Kramer up and aim it anywhere near that ugly mouth and head. But the claws only cut her arms and stomach deeper the more she struggled.

Inside, down in the black hole of its mouth, she could see the second set of teeth gleaming, pulsing like they wanted to come pouring out and ram through her face.

"Hold still!" Hank's voice screamed behind her. Somehow, through her sheer terror, through the silent screams she was afraid to let go of, she heard him. Hold still. Shit, what choice did she have? She could do that. She didn't want to. She wanted to scream and twist and get free and run like hell. But somewhere deep inside she understood Hank's command.

She froze, forcing her body to become as rigid as possible, her eyes focused on the wide-open jaws of the alien.

Her willpower stopped her from throwing up her last energy snack. Her eyes watered from the pain and the thick smell of alien rot as she forced them to stay totally open.

Behind her she heard Hank shout, "The glass behind her! Blow it out!"

Almost instantly the roaring sound of a half-dozen Kramers on fully automatic filled the room, mixing with the sound of glass shattering and water pouring like a river gone wild.

Her mind screamed, *What the hell was he doing?*

But she kept her body frozen like a log.

The alien glanced away from her.

Then suddenly everything went crazy at once.

It felt as if someone had pulled the rug out from under her captor. The bug jerked her up, then sharply down, the claws digging even harder into her flesh as the wall of water from behind the broken glass hit its legs.

And then it let go of her as it went over backward.

She slammed hard into the floor. The impact knocked the wind out of her and the water sent her tumbling across the hard tiles. She felt wrapped in a thick, oily jell. Slime.

She did her best to tuck and roll, but she still banged her head twice, both times hard, before she finally stopped sliding.

Again the sounds of Kramers screaming filled her every sense. Through her spinning head she had just enough thought to hope she was far enough away from that bug they were toasting to keep out of the acid. She covered her head and face and waited for the deadly shower.

It didn't come.

Hank shouted, "Form a circle and watch every shadow and corner." Then after what seemed like a long time but actually was only a moment, he was at her side, rolling her gently over on the wet floor.

She opened her eyes, letting the room spin for a moment around her like she'd had way too much to drink.

"You all right?" Hank asked, and she could see the look of panic and concern on both his and Kent's face spinning over her.

She took a deep breath and exhaled. The room slowed its spinning and almost stayed put.

Almost.

She took another deep breath and it stopped. Thank God.

She reached up and touched Hank's face gently. "Did you get the number of that damn truck that hit me?"

Hank looked at her for a moment, then laughed deep in his throat.

God she loved that laugh of his.

And this one special laugh was one she was going to remember for a long, long time.

Assuming, of course, she lived through the next hour.

"I think I found them," McPhillips said as he punched up one monitor and then another, filling the center of the wall with pictures from different angles of a main corridor in the living quarters.

"Oh, God, no!" Bosewell said.

Green felt his stomach twist with his worst fear. The joy he had felt from killing Larson a minute before was now totally gone, drained by the scene he saw on the wall.

Three of his Marines lay dead in the middle of the wide main corridor. Teppo had his head cut off and one arm was missing. Freeman was soaked in acid, his skin boiled away, his face missing. Bond had been gored through the chest by an alien jaw, his legs ripped from his body. All three still held their Kramers and looked as if they had all gone down fighting to the end.

Seven, maybe eight alien bodies were scattered

down the hall, attesting to the fight the men had put up.

"Scan down the hall farther," Green ordered. God, please, don't let it be all of them.

"Which way?"

"Into the living sector."

McPhillips did as he was told and each new monitor showed more horror. A hundred meters up from the three dead Marines was a group of fifteen civilian bodies. Six dead aliens lay around them, most with their heads shot off, some with their legs gone.

But what had killed the civilians had been acid from the body of an alien beside them.

From the way it looked a bug was bearing down on them and one of the civilians had just opened fire at the alien's body, causing the acid blood to pour over the humans in a flood of death.

All their clothes had melted away and the entire mess was a steaming, ugly pile of red meat, human skeletons, skulls, and brown acid blood.

Behind him Green heard Bosewell throwing up. He didn't blame the man. He felt like doing the same thing.

He took a deep breath. "Keep scanning," he told McPhillips, who after a moment did as he was told.

After what seemed like a long few minutes of finding nothing in either direction, McPhillips turned to Green. "Looks like that was just one firefight."

Green nodded. It looked that way to him, also. Robinsen must have assigned the three men to try to get the group of civilians back to the hangar deck and they'd been ambushed in the corridor.

"Can you find the rest of the men?"

McPhillips shrugged. "I could if I had a few hours and if they haven't ducked into the ventilation tunnels and gone down."

Green nodded. It did look hopeless. He was just going to have to hope Robinsen and the rest of the men could fight their way to the ship. But now it might not be a bad idea to get there themselves. If the Professor was in the center of the alien section, they sure as hell weren't going in after him. He was as good as dead and Green's only wish was that he die slowly, with a face-hugger tight on his face.

"Can you find the hangar deck quickly?"

"Not a problem," McPhillips said and within a few seconds had four different views of the deck on the monitors.

"Nothing but bugs," McPhillips said softly, expressing the obvious.

Two aliens were on top of Captain Palmer's shuttle and a good dozen more were scattered around in plain sight. God only knew how many were in hiding in those shadows and storage bays.

Palmer and the rest of them were walking into a huge nightmare.

"Let's move!" Green shouted and headed for the door at a full run.

"Hang on a minute!" McPhillips shouted. Green turned around. "Sarge, I think there's a better way."

"Make it quick."

McPhillips's fingers danced over the control board and again the map of the surrounding area filled the middle screen. "The Professor's got some private tunnels from here." He pointed at the bookcase behind him. "I spotted them on the map when we were looking for Larson's location. One dumps directly onto the flight deck."

Green nodded. "Good work. Now let's find it."

Thirty seconds later they had the hidden door open and with Green on point and Rule bringing up the rear they were at a full trot for the hangar deck.

Green just hoped they would be in time to help.

21

No more aliens appeared in the ten minutes it took for Kent to get Joyce's wounds bandaged and for her head to stop spinning. She still felt light-headed when she stood and the lump just above her hairline hurt like hell, but otherwise she was going to live.

The room looked like a hurricane had hit it. All the floors were covered with an inch-deep, jelly-thick water that made the footing slippery at best, and the place smelled a combination of alien rot and her son's chemistry set.

She was wet, bruised, and cut, but alive. That just amazed her. Every time she even blinked she saw the razor teeth of that alien inches from her face and the second mandible waiting to cut through her. But when she kept her eyes open, she knew she was alive.

She gave Hank's hand a final squeeze to say thank you one more time and let him know she was all right. He'd stayed with her like a worried mother, hovering over her while Kent had mended the cuts from the alien's claws. He'd saved her life, and now she was even more determined to get them both off this rock and back home safely.

She did a quick check of her Kramer to make sure it was all in working order, then glanced around at the men circled in defensive positions around her. Five, maybe six dead aliens littered the white lab around them and Cray's body had washed against one of them in a grotesque loverlike position. Behind his body, the wall of glass they had broken to knock out the alien holding her had a human body hanging in it by the wires over his face. Another one of the Professor's experiments. Looking at that body there, she really hoped Green was having some luck finding the Professor and Larson. They deserved whatever Green could give them, and much, much more.

"Everyone ready to see if we can make it to the ship?" she called out, her voice echoing through the big lab and over the dead bodies of the aliens and Cray.

Nods and a few "anytimes" answered her question.

She took a deep breath. "Kent, lead the way. Stay close, people. If the bugs were in here, they for damn sure are going to be on the hangar deck."

Kent patted her shoulder as he passed her and headed for a double-sized brown door on the far side of the lab. Three others dropped in beside him and then she and Hank dropped into line behind them.

She didn't even look at Cray's body as they passed. That could have well been her there beside him. She didn't want to think anymore about that than she already was. Instead she looked at every shadow, at every corner as if an alien was going to come around it at any moment.

From the jerky movements of everyone else's heads, they were all doing the same. They were scared to death, and they all had a right to be.

Kent reached the wide double doors that had obviously been designed to move large equipment from the hangar and storage areas into the labs.

"Hang on until we get into position," Joyce said.

Six of them, including her and Hank, knelt or stood in firing positions facing the door. The others backed off, guns up and ready for anything.

She glanced around to make sure everyone was in position, then said, "Go!"

Kent threw open both doors and jumped back out of the way.

Beyond was a fifty-meter-long room with high shelves on both sides and another double door on the far end. It was brightly lit and clean. Assortments of laboratory equipment and supplies filled the shelves and two carts were parked near the center.

She studied the room slowly and carefully. Nothing seemed to be moving and she could see no sign of alien slime on any of the shelves or the clean white floor.

"Four down one side," Joyce said, "and four others down the other. Stay close to the shelves and protect each other's back. Set up a defensive position at the other doors without opening them. The rest guard our rear and cover them from here."

Kent motioned for three men to follow down the left side of the storage room and Hank on the other side did the same. Joyce positioned herself square in the middle of the door with five others around her and they covered the eight men every inch of the way to the other side.

"No signs at all," Kent shouted as he reached the other door.

"Yeah, looks clean in here," Hank shouted.

"Cover us," Joyce shouted back and Hank nodded.

She turned to the men guarding the room behind her. "Fall back inside the storage room and let's get these doors closed. Better than being out here in the open."

They did as they were told and within a few seconds the big double doors were closed behind them. It wouldn't hold an alien out, but if one came crashing through at least they'd have some warning.

"Four of you stay here and keep the rest of us covered." She turned and started right down the middle of the room toward Hank and Kent. After all this, if she couldn't trust their judgment now, who could she trust.

As she strode through the supply room, her gaze scanning the high shelves, she caught sight of a ventilation grate above the top shelf on the right. There was another directly across from it on the left. She stopped and picked out two men. "Keep a gun aimed at those vents," she said, pointing at the grates. "And if your arms get tired, get someone to take your place. They'll come in that way, if at all."

Two men did as she said and she joined Hank and Kent who had come back to the middle of the room to meet her.

"We got a reprieve, but a short one," she said. "Somehow we have to get to the ship. Off this rock is the only safe place."

Deegan, who had been staying near the back of the group in the other lab, moved up beside her. "Boss," he said, "from what I can figure, the ship is about fifty, maybe sixty meters straight off these doors."

"Can you remember anything of what's between here and there?" Kent asked.

"Just open deck," Deegan said. "A lot of it. Normally there'd be another shuttle there, but I heard the Marines took off in that one."

"Yeah," Kent said. "A direct flight to the alien section."

"Suggestions?" she asked. She didn't have any bright ideas at the moment herself. Covering fifty meters of open deck while fighting off aliens was going to be an ugly task at best. And probably fatal.

On top of that it would take a good thirty sec-

onds to cycle the airlock on the ship if it was
closed. If it was open they were going to have to
clean the ship of bugs. She hoped like hell it was
closed and sealed like it was supposed to be when
no one was on board.

"Form a circle and run for it?" Deegan suggested, but both Kent and Hank shook their heads
no.

"Won't work," Hank said. "They'll rush us so
fast that we'll cover ourselves in acid when we
cut them down. I've seen it happen before."

Kent nodded. "I agree. We're better off going in
small groups, enough to cover each other and
fight our way slowly from different directions toward the ship."

Joyce nodded. She had a clear memory of a
group of kids and two adults being covered by
acid back on Earth when one of the adults had
shot an onrushing alien in the body at close range.
The momentum of the bug had carried it and its
acid blood over all the kids. Thank God none of
them had lived.

Joyce glanced around the long storage room at
the eighteen men, most of whom had their weapons at the ready as they continually scanned the
room. Nineteen of them total. That made a good
round number.

She turned back to Hank and Kent and Deegan.
"I agree with Kent," she said. "Three groups of
four and one of seven up the middle. Each group
moves slow and not only covers themselves on all
sides, but tries to cover the others as well."

Hank turned to Kent and Deegan. "Kent, you
got a better memory than I do for these things.

How wide is the room to the left and right of here?"

Kent pointed to his right as he faced the hangar doors. "Main passageway and decontamination area is that way about twenty meters along that wall. Beyond it is maintenance another twenty meters. There's a balcony over the decontamination area. It's a square room in that direction, but I wouldn't suggest we get too close to the main entrance."

"I agree," Joyce said.

"In the other direction," Kent said, "is mostly just blank walls of rock. I suppose they left it unfinished in that direction in case they needed to expand the hangar deck. Not much chance of that now."

"So fewer places for bugs to hide on the left of the doors."

"A lot fewer," Kent said.

"And a better angle at the ship," Deegan said. "Coming at it from the nose will allow us to see both sides and not get surprised by a bug coming over or under the ship."

Joyce patted him hard on the back. "I always knew there were brains in there," she said, smiling.

"Damn, blew my cover," Deegan said.

Joyce turned to Kent. "Take three men and be ready to go first out the door and duck left. We'll cover you from the door. Stop with your backs to the wall after about fifteen meters and cover us."

Next she turned to Deegan. "You pick three men and be ready to go out ten seconds after Kent. Go even farther left along the wall and again set up a defensive position so that you can see the ship and the deck between here and there."

Deegan nodded.

"Someone needs to guard the right," Hank said. "I can take three men and just go a few meters to defend from there."

Joyce nodded. "I'll lead the rest strung out toward the ship across the deck. When you three feel the time is right, start your men toward the ship, too. Don't wait too long because we don't want to get too spread out. Ideally we should all be closing in on the ship about the same time.

"And, Deegan, like you said, get far enough around to the left so you can see the far side of the ship and keep it clear as you come in."

"No problem, boss."

She glanced around, then took a deep breath. "Well, the longer we wait, the more bugs there'll be to kill."

Kent turned and motioned to the three men who were nearest the hangar doors that they were with him. Hank and Deegan did the same and she told the rest in the room to follow her slowly across the deck when she started out.

Then, with six Kramers pointed directly at the wide double doors to the hangar deck, she nodded for Kent to open them quickly. And very wide.

What she saw made her sick. Aliens. Everywhere.

A fraction of a second later six automatic rifles were firing fast and hard, with others around them joining in.

Kent had opened the doors into hell.

So much for careful planning.

The battle was going poorly as far as the Professor was concerned.

The two huge aliens circled each other, saliva dripping off their teeth like open faucets, their arms waving and slashing, usually missing. Both tails swished back and forth, sometimes hard and fast, sometimes slow and mean.

The huge queen's chamber was a wreck from their dance of destruction. Alien formations had been cut to the ground, pulling the human constructions like balconies and ladders under them down with them. Golden royal jelly, masses of it, a multiple fortune on the black market back on Earth, had been splattered and mixed with acid blood and saliva.

In thirty minutes of circling and fighting, the queen was slowly gaining the upper hand over the rogue.

At first it looked as if he would win easily and the Professor had been so excited. But as he and Grace watched, the advantage shifted to the queen.

She was the crafty one.

She was the smart one.

She had avoided the rogue's lunges after the first one and had slashed him again and again with her sharp tail and claws, letting his acid blood flow down his legs. Everywhere he stepped now he left bloody prints.

Compared to her, he was a clumsy oaf, smashing everything, wasting energy as she dodged away from his frantic attacks more quickly with each passing minute.

"This shouldn't be happening," the Professor growled. "He's bigger and stronger than her. He's a killing machine. She should be dead by now."

Grace hadn't answered any of his ramblings for the past twenty minutes. She stood just inside the small side tunnel they had taken refuge in, Kramer in hand, keeping a sharp eye not only on the two huge aliens in front of them, but on the black tunnel behind them. So far no alien had dared get near this area, but she was taking no chances.

The Professor moved forward and now stood just on the edge of the royal chamber, his helmet off, the Sound Cannon clutched almost unnoticed in his right hand.

Grace's hand went to the side of her head suddenly, as if she was almost in pain. "Sir, they're screaming at each other again."

"It's about to end," he said. "Now he will win. You just watch."

But just as he spoke the queen lunged for the first time in the battle.

She caught the rogue in the side and her tail whipped around and cut off the rogue's left arm as they tumbled to the ground and rolled hard enough to shake the stone under the Professor's feet.

"No!" the Professor shouted, taking a few more steps into the chamber. But his scream was lost and small against the sounds of the titan battle going on in front of him.

Grace stayed beside him, protecting him.

But the queen didn't notice them. She had the rogue gripped by the neck now in her giant teeth, and was twisting, doing her best to bite off a huge chunk of the rogue's plates and skeleton.

The rogue was on his side, thrashing, alien blood spurting from the stump of his arm.

The queen's razor-sharp tail again spun in the air, flicking back and forth before slicing into the rogue's side with an ugly, thick smacking sound.

Alien blood sprayed over the nearby wall and a few drops splattered near the Professor, but he didn't notice. His creation was being killed. He didn't believe it, even though he was seeing it.

He had been wrong again.

"The screams have changed," Grace said. "Now it's only one and it sounds more like pain than a challenge."

The queen ripped a huge hole in the side of the rogue's neck with her mouth and then dove back in for more as the rogue tried his best to roll away from her.

But that deadly tail of hers wasn't finished with him yet. This time it whipped out and caught the rogue's carapace, slicing a huge ugly cut through it like it was so much warm butter.

The rogue thrashed even harder, but he was clearly mortally wounded.

"Kill that bitch!" the Professor shouted, stepping even closer to the fight. "Grace, cut her down!"

Grace stepped up beside the Professor and the Kramer opened up, steady as a rock in Grace's hands. With a full clip she sprayed the queen with deadly shots.

The huge queen roared as she ripped another huge hole in the rogue's neck.

Grace finished the first clip and then at an almost invisible speed ejected it and put another in. But as her attention was focused for a second down at the gun, the queen took advantage.

As if she were swatting a pesky fly, the queen whipped her tail around and caught Grace square in the chest with the razor-sharp point, slicing through her body armor and lifting her high into the air, cutting her in half and then smashing her against the stone wall like an egg dropped on a sidewalk.

White fluid splattered everywhere, dripping down the alien saliva columns and pooling around her on the floor.

She ended up in three parts.

Her chest and right arm landed on a crushed alien egg.

Her head, still attached to one shoulder and arm, bounced off a wall and landed near the Professor.

Her lower torso ended two meters away from her head, her legs spread like a ten-dollar prostitute's, armor ripped away showing her perfect pubic hair for the alien world to see. Her knees, in automatic reaction, went up and down, up and down, like she was asking everyone to look.

On the stump of her neck, where the rest of her body used to be, white tubes pumped her last fluid out onto the floor of the queen's chamber.

Quickly the Professor stepped over to her head. "Grace," he shouted. "God damn it. How'd you let this happen?"

She opened her eyes and looked at him. "You're a real ass," she said, "but I suppose you already knew that."

"Grace?" the Professor said, but she closed her eyes and inside her neck the last of the fluid ran out onto the stone floor.

Behind him the queen screamed, then sunk her teeth again into the rogue.

22

Joyce couldn't believe what she was seeing when Kent tossed those two double doors open. She had expected to see a wide-open area with the deck and her shuttle sitting there. Instead what she saw looked like an anthill of bugs, damn near blocking any vision of the shuttle at all. The smell of rot had swept in over them.

In the first few seconds of the fight she and the rest had taken out a good two dozen of the closest and now had cleared every bug out to fifty meters. She'd used six full clips and the Kramer was starting to heat up in her hands.

Kent and his three men had gone out and left, checking the wall above them first. Then Hank

and his three had gone out and gone right along
the wall, doing the same. That spread out their firing angles and gave them a larger killing area.

She was kneeling beside the door on the right,
carefully taking aim and killing any bug that even
pretended to move. The rest of the group had
spread around the door and were doing the same.
It was now starting to feel to her like a target
practice session as they all knocked legs and
heads off of anything out in that open hangar.

She desperately wanted to get across that killing field of alien bodies and acid blood, but for
the moment it felt much safer right where they
were, their backs to the wall killing anything that
moved in front of them.

Then, through the almost deafening bursts of
gunfire around her, she heard her name being
shouted. "Captain Palmer! Captain Palmer!"

She stood and looked both directions down the
line. Hank and a few others had heard the call
also and had stopped firing. He indicated the
voice had come from the right, closer to the main
entrance and above him. She stepped out and
looked up at the balcony that ran along there. It
was dark and she couldn't see a thing.

"Cease fire!" she shouted. "Cease fire, unless
one moves right at you!"

The firing stopped and the last of the roaring
sound echoed over the dead aliens and the hangar
deck.

"Captain Palmer?"

"Right here," she shouted back.

"Sergeant Green up here."

"Glad to hear your voice, Sergeant," Joyce
shouted back. The relief of having the Marines

with them again was almost as much as she had felt when they first showed up in the tunnels.

"You need to get to your ship as soon as you can," Green called back.

To her left a Kramer opened up and across the deck an alien head exploded like a cherry bomb going off. She waited until the echo died off in the huge chamber, then shouted back, "We were headed that way."

"I know," Green said. "But a pitched fight like this will only draw more bugs to this area. There's more of them than you have bullets to kill. Trust me."

"What should we do?" Joyce shouted, feeling relieved she had someone else to make the decisions for a moment.

"Fan out in small groups," Green shouted, "then fight your way to the ship. We'll cover you from here."

"Will do," she said.

"Back to plan A," she shouted at Kent and Deegan to her left. "Let's move. Hank, you ready?"

"Right with you," he said.

She motioned for the men around her to follow her, pointing to three of the men near her. "You watch our asses. Don't let one of those sons of bitches in behind us. Understood?"

All three nodded.

She clicked a fresh clip into her Kramer and took a deep breath. Then started off slowly toward her shuttle, across the field of dead bugs and acid blood.

All around her Kramers screamed and bugs died.

From the balcony behind her Kramers cut the

air, blowing aliens away at incredible distances across the huge hangar. Those Marines were great shots, of that there was little doubt.

She caught a glimpse of one of the downed aliens in front of her twitching and she blew its head apart like a melon hitting a wall.

Another bug crawled up on her ship over the hatch they were headed for and she and two others beside her sent it spinning off the other side in an acid spray. Joyce hoped like hell that acid didn't get into any important mechanisms on the outside of the shuttle. She didn't think it would, but anything was possible.

On her left the sounds of firing were continuous. She glanced over and Deegan's group was in position approaching the nose of the shuttle. They were firing more often than any, keeping the bugs away from the ship and watching their open left side.

Twenty meters closer to her, Kent and his group paralleled her, mostly helping Deegan's group keep the left clear.

Twenty meters to her right Hank and his crew, supported by help from Sergeant Green above and behind them, had very little to do.

She made the ramp and stationed two men at the bottom and two others to watch the top of the ship above her. She scrambled up the ramp and was damn glad to see the door had been sealed. She let out a deep sigh and started the opening cycle. At least inside would be bug free.

She got the door open and then turned back to check on everybody's position.

Deegan and his men were posted around the

nose of the shuttle, watching both sides of the ship.

Hank and his men were doing exactly the same around the tail and thruster section. The rest had taken up positions around the ship, killing any bug that moved anywhere, sometimes two or three men taking it out with long-distance shooting.

"Sergeant!" Joyce shouted. "Join us. We'll cover you."

"On our way," Green's voice echoed over the chamber.

"Hurry, God damn it," she said under her breath. "Hurry."

She had a sinking feeling that everything was about to go very wrong. She didn't know why. Everyone was in place and no bug was getting within fifty meters of the ship. But it still felt wrong, like it had been too easy.

And Green's words echoed in her head about her not having more ammunition than bugs. She still had two belts left.

The five Marines were down the stairs from the balcony and spread out in an arrow formation, with Green in the center, jogging across the floor through the dead bugs when things changed.

And changed quick.

"Bugs through the storage area!" Kent shouted as the door to the labs smashed inward with a huge crash and a wave of black, ugly aliens swarmed through the brightly lit storage room.

Kent, and some of the men around him who had the best shots straight into the room, opened fire, cutting some of the bugs down under the bright lights before they could even get to the hangar doors.

But there were so many more bugs behind them. They just kept coming, climbing right over the bodies of their dead like they weren't even there.

"Green! Behind you!" Hank shouted.

The entrance to the decontamination chamber was suddenly filled with bugs swarming through like a dam had just broken.

Green and his men, still only halfway to the ship, spread out and took up positions, their guns screaming, filling the entrance and the decontamination chamber with dead aliens.

But the flow of bugs continued, through both doors and from the overhead balcony where the sergeant and his men had just been a few moments before.

And from the shadows of the far side of the hangar.

Clip after clip, she cut down bugs, reloaded, cut down more.

Reloaded.

Cut down more.

And they just kept coming.

And coming.

The Kramer felt like a hot pan in her hands, but she held on. She didn't have time to let it cool. Her ears were ringing. The gray smoke from the guns half blinded her.

"Grenades!" Green shouted and almost as one five headed for the main entrance. To her right she saw Kent and three of his men do the same at the entrance from the supply area.

The concussion from the grenades sent alien

limbs, heads, and bodies everywhere and shook rocks from the roof of the hangar deck.

But the bugs just kept coming.

Climbing over hundreds of their own dead, they poured into the room.

"Fall back," Green shouted to his men and they started moving backward, firing as they went.

"Give them cover!" Joyce shouted and she and her crew did the best they could to keep the bugs back.

But it was clear Green and his men weren't going to make it.

Green had been right. There was just too many of them.

But she kept firing anyway.

The queen bit almost completely through the neck of the rogue and the Professor's pride, his creation, his lifetime of work, lay on the floor twitching like so much raw meat.

The queen bent over her victim, grabbed the rogue's remaining arm, and yanked it off, throwing it against the wall as if disgusted.

The Professor was livid. Behind him the remains of Grace were splattered along the wall. He bent and picked up her Kramer, then cocked the Sound Cannon.

"You're dead, you bitch!"

With the Kramer in his left hand, he punched the on button for the Sound Cannon and set it to high. So high it could kill any alien within two hundred meters by itself.

So high she wouldn't know what hit her.

The room seemed to shimmer and the alien

queen reared up, seeming to scream, her hands at her head.

"Don't like that, do you, bitch?" he shouted, firing at her with the Kramer in his left hand, stepping closer and closer.

Her tail smashed the remains of the rogue behind her and she turned away from the sting of the bullets, still screaming her silent scream.

He pumped bullets at her and stepped closer.

As she swung around, away from his painful attack, her razor-sharp tail went up and then down at the Professor.

Her aim was perfect, and lightning fast.

He saw it coming, but didn't have time to move even a fraction of a meter.

The impact knocked him sideways and sent him spinning across the floor to the left. The pain in his side and arm didn't seem real, it was so sharp. He could feel his blood pumping into the air.

His right arm, cut off cleanly at the shoulder with the Sound Cannon still gripped tightly in his right hand, flew through the air and landed near Grace.

It bounced once, but the impact served to jar the finger even more into the trigger.

The Professor screamed and tried to stop the blood flowing from the hole in his shoulder.

The queen screamed and tumbled sideways, her legs and tail smashing what was left of the rogue.

Beside Grace the Sound Cannon with the Professor's arm still attached started beeping.

Slow at first, but then faster and faster.

Through gritted teeth the Professor laughed.

"It's going critical, you bitch. You're going to die for what you did."

Beep! Beep! Beep!

The queen continued thrashing.

Beep-beep-beep-beep.

"Oh, does that hurt, my dear?" the Professor cried. He tried to sit up but couldn't. "I sure hope so."

The beeping of the gun turned into a long, continuous high-pitched wail as the Sound Cannon went critical.

"I'll see you in hell, bitch!"

The intense white flash ended his insanity.

And her pain.

23

The sound of over twenty automatic Kramers firing almost continuously filled the hangar deck around Joyce like the roar of a river crashing over a hundred-meter falls. The echoes combined with the actual sound and intensified it, banging at her from all sides. She had sweat running down her hands and the Kramer was so hot she could hardly hold it.

She stood, her back against the door frame to her shuttle, aiming and firing.

Then loading, aiming, and firing again.

And then again and again and again at the mass of black bugs climbing over the bodies of other smashed black bugs.

But no matter how many bugs they killed, the ugly things just kept coming.

Within seconds they were going to overwhelm Sergeant Green and his men.

"Pull back!" she shouted to Hank.

She turned to Kent. "Pull back! Pass the word to Deegan!"

He nodded that he understood as he inserted another clip into his rifle and emptied it into the moving mass of alien flesh.

Then suddenly, as if on a string pulled by one evil puppeteer, every live alien within sight seemed to twist, as in pain.

Then they all froze.

"What the hell!" Green shouted.

For a few more seconds the Kramers cut down the frozen bugs where they stood, then the firing slowed and stopped.

"Looks like a Sound Cannon got them, Sarge!" one of the Marines near Green shouted. Joyce couldn't tell which one it was and she had no idea what a Sound Cannon was, but if it could stop these bugs, it was a good thing.

"But we don't have a damn Sound Cannon."

"Well, someone does," Green shouted. "And they may or may not know how to use it. Everyone in the shuttle. Fast!"

Joyce was amazed at how fast some of those tired people could move. She was inside first, her Kramer beside her pilot seat, already starting everything up when Deegan drove into the copilot's seat beside her.

She glanced around at where Hank was crouched, watching the scene outside the door as the five Marines poured inside.

Green stepped through the door, a look of panic on his face. "McPhillips! Dillon! Young! Check the ship for any bugs. Double quick."

Then he turned to Joyce.

"They moving out there yet?" she asked.

"Not yet," Green said, "and if they don't soon, whatever Sound Cannon that's doing this is going to go critical and blow every seal in this base right into space. Those things never work for longer than a minute. How fast can you get us out of this dump?"

"Do it, Deegan!" She didn't even wait to give Green an answer. The total look of panic on his face was more than enough to let her know they didn't have enough time as far as he was concerned.

"Seal the hatch!" she shouted, but both Hank and the sergeant were already working to do just that.

"Engines coming up!" Deegan shouted. "Everything green. Bay door opening. Counting it down."

"Screw the countdown!" she shouted. "Just pray I miss the damn doors on the way out."

Her fingers flew over the board in front of her as the rumble under her seat increased.

Part of that was the ship and the normal vibrations from liftoff. She knew that feeling better than anything. But there was something more happening.

Something much more. It was as if the entire base was shaking.

In one quick motion she swung the nose of the shuttle off the ground and around toward the slowly opening bay doors. There might be enough

room to get through if she hit it perfectly. What the
hell choice did she have?

The shaking grew more intense around her and
between the shuttle and the hangar doors rocks
started to fall from the ceiling.

"Everyone hang on!" she yelled.

She hit the acceleration hard.

It shoved her back into her seat and held her
there like a hand on her chest. Behind her she
could hear a few oaths from those not braced
tightly enough. Rocks pounded against the shuttle
as the roof of the hangar started to cave in, but she
paid no attention. Only those half-open hangar
doors were what mattered now.

With the huge shuttle she took aim.

And hoped.

She missed the doors on both sides by meters as
the shuttle cleared the hangar and broke into
space. With a hard yank she sent the shuttle up in
as steep an ascent as she thought the thrusters
could handle. She wanted to put some distance between them and that rock.

Deegan swore beside her as his fingers danced
over the board in front of him as he did his best to
help where she needed him.

"Rearview monitors," she shouted through the
incredible noise of the acceleration.

Somehow Deegan managed to get the screen
above them focused on the hangar doors. She
would never forget what those doors looked like
exploding outward into space.

Another few seconds and they wouldn't have
made it.

That was close. Too damn close.

She eased the acceleration back slightly and

turned to Deegan. "Think you can get us into a low parking orbit without my help."

Deegan, his face white, the Kramer still draped across his lap, looked at her. His eyes were wide and sweat was pouring off his forehead.

He swallowed, glanced around at the board in front of him, and then back at her. Then he let out a deep breath like he had been holding it for the last ten minutes. "Yeah, I can get us there."

"No walk in the park?" she asked, half smiling.

He glanced at her. "Boss, I've decided working with you is never a walk in the park."

She laughed, also exhaling for what seemed like the first time in hours.

She turned to where Hank and Sergeant Green were braced against the acceleration on the bulkhead behind her.

"Now," she said, "would someone please tell me what the hell just happened?"

"We got out alive," Green said.

Hank glanced at Joyce and then at the monitor over his head. "Yeah, but about fourteen hundred didn't."

24

"**T**his is Captain Palmer of the transport vessel *Caliban* giving a final, pre-cold-sleep status report."

Joyce flicked off the recording and looked around her now silent ship. Sleep chambers, lined up in two rows, head to head, filled the center core of the vessel. It seemed so peaceful and quiet after the past week, with everyone sleeping.

She ran her hand over Hank's chamber, looking down at the peaceful expression on his face. Very soon they would start a new life together. Very soon she would see Drake and Cass, see how much they had grown, how much they had matured.

She did a slow check of the instruments above

Hank one last time. All seemed to be in order and all lights were green, so she turned back to her board and flicked on the recording mike again.

"We have left orbit over Charon Base and I have set course to rendezvous with Moreno Station in eight months. Everyone is in cold sleep and all lights are green."

She took a slow, deep breath, shivering slightly in the cold from being so close to so many sleep chambers. She was wearing only a T-shirt and brief bikini bottoms. That was why she was cold. Or maybe it was from the thought of going into cold sleep shortly herself.

She glanced at her open sleep chamber and then she went on.

"As I have logged, we maintained orbit over Charon Base looking and hoping for more survivors, but we found none, with nothing but static on all frequencies from the base. Sergeant Green thinks the explosion that broke the base containment and collapsed many of the tunnels, at least from what we could scan, was caused by a Sound Cannon going critical in the heart of the alien section. Check his report for more."

She stopped recording and slowly walked back through the ship to the control area.

She always hesitated going into cold sleep with every trip, but this time it seemed even worse. She just couldn't fully understand that the nightmare was over. Every night since their escape into orbit she had had nightmares of bugs crawling out of an airlock or out of a sleep chamber.

But Green and his men had thoroughly scanned both the insides and the outside of the ship and no bugs were with them. Green even put all of them, including himself, through a full body scan to make sure none were implanted.

So she had to believe that for now this fight in this small out-of-the-way section of space, this nightmare, was over.

The aliens had won.

She sat for a moment in her captain's chair staring out at the tiny flecks of stars in front of the ship.

She supposed that the failure had been inevitable. Mankind's prized intellect, in this case, had become its greatest conceit. Out here, in the huge emptiness of space, humans dressed themselves in technology and then thought it made them omnipotent.

Out here the aliens' only function was to reproduce and survive.

Humans called them evil, yet placed men like Professor Kleist in power.

What was truly evil? She didn't know. She just knew a lot of people had died.

With one final glance to make sure all lights on the boards were showing green, she ambled back to the sleep chambers and stood over Hank's for a moment.

Fourteen hundred people dead, yet she and Hank had lived. She hoped that meant good things for their future. She was going to do everything in her power to make sure it did.

It was time to get to sleep and dream about the green of the park and the warmth of the bright sunshine and making love to Hank until she was sweating so hard that the sheets were soaked.

Those were good dreams.

And she could dream about their future. It would be a warm dream, too.

When she and Hank got back to Earth the first thing she would do was take the kids to that park again, no matter how big they had grown since she left.

And she would sit in the warm sunshine.

And she would make love to Hank.

"Good dreams," she said, patting his chamber.

Then she reached down and flipped on the report button.

"This is Captain Joyce Palmer of the transport vessel *Caliban* signing off."

ABOUT THE AUTHORS

SANDY SCHOFIELD is the pen name for the award-winning husband and wife writing team of Dean Wesley Smith and Kristine Kathryn Rusch. Under the Schofield name they have written a number of books, including the popular STAR TREK: DEEP SPACE NINE novel called *The Big Game*. Also writing together they just finished the very first original STAR TREK: VOYAGER novel called *The Escape*.

Kristine Kathryn Rusch is a Campbell and Locus award-winning author who has sold fifteen novels. Her solo novels will come out from NAL, Dell, and Bantam over the next few years as well as uncounted numbers of short stories. She is also the editor of *The Magazine of Fantasy and Science Fiction* and has been nominated the past four years for the Hugo for Best Editor. In 1989 she won the World Fantasy Award for her editing and in 1994 she won the Hugo Award for Best Professional Editor in the world.

Dean Wesley Smith has also sold a large number of short stories and eight novels. His first solo novel, while marketed as science fiction, made it to the final ballot of the Stoker Award. He is also the publisher and editor for Pulphouse Publishing and *Pulphouse: A Fiction* magazine. In 1989, along with Kristine Kathryn Rusch, he won the World Fantasy Award for his work on Pulphouse and the Locus Award for his editing. He has also been nominated four times for the Hugo Award for his editing. He has just finished work on a Spider-Man novel for Berkley Books.